# Fallen Land

## Patrick Flanery

W F HOWES LTD

This large print edition published in 2013 by
W F Howes Ltd
Unit 4, Rearsby Business Park, Gaddesby Lane,
Rearsby, Leicester LE7 4YH

1 3 5 7 9 10 8 6 4 2

First published in the United Kingdom in 2013
by Atlantic Books

A CIP catalogue record for this book is available
from the British Library

ISBN 978 1 47123 632 7

Typeset by Palimpsest Book Production Limited,
Falkirk, Stirlingshire
Printed and bound in Great Britain
by MPG Books Ltd, Bodmin, Cornwall

MIX
Paper from
responsible sources
FSC
www.fsc.org    FSC® C018575

For the grandmothers:

*Ethel Marguerite Linville*
*who asked to be remembered as a farmer's daughter*
*1909–2000*

*&*

*Lucille Katherine Fey who lost everything*
*1903–1985*

1919

In what the writer and polymath James Weldon Johnson called the 'Red Summer' of 1919, race riots swept through cities across the country, and here, in this regional city between two rivers with what was then, outside of Los Angeles, the largest urban population of blacks west of the Mississippi, the county courthouse was set ablaze by a mob of five thousand angry whites bent on lynching two black men, Boyd Pinkney and Evans Pratt. Pinkney and Pratt worked in one of the city's meatpacking warehouses and had been arrested for the assault of a twelve-year-old white girl who recanted as an adult, confessing that the men had done nothing more than say hello to her when she called out to them. The two friends were hanged from a tree outside the courthouse, their bodies skinned and burned before being thrown in the river, turned over in the wash of paddleboats and caught up on snags rising like disembodied limbs in the muddy shallows that spread out from the bank-side, festering with mosquitoes amid a weltering stench of decay.

That same day, Morgan Priest Wright, the

1

sixty-year-old mayor and gentleman farmer who had been elected in the previous year on a reformist plank, was lynched for trying to intervene on behalf of the men, whom he and a number of local officials believed to be innocent of any crime. The courthouse was set ablaze and Wright fled in his blue Studebaker, driving out of town and taking refuge on his farm, where he sheltered in the stone storm cellar beneath his house with the tenants who worked his land. History is silent about the exact chain of events that saw Wright and one of the farmers, twenty-five-year-old George Freeman, pulled from the cellar and hanged from a cotton-wood tree next to Wright's house, which was subsequently set alight by parties unknown. Freeman was dressed in women's clothes, and the two men were tied together facing each other, left hanging after the mob retreated. Freeman's brother John and sister-in-law Lottie, who were also Wright's tenants, had been away from the farm at the time of the riots, visiting Lottie's extended family in the next county. Driving home in Wright's Model T, which he had lent them, they could see smoke from some distance and, having heard news of the riots, feared the worst. They could not have guessed that both their landlord and brother would be dead, or that the house where they had been discreetly entertained on several occasions would no longer be standing. By the time John and Lottie arrived home, Wright's house had burned to the ground while their own small bungalow, down a hill and on the edge of the farm, remained standing and untouched, save for a few broken windows. Looking up at the forty-foot cottonwood tree in which George and Mr Wright hung dead, bodies tied together and twisting as the wind blew up into a late summer thunderstorm, John told Lottie to wait in the house with their children while he investigated.

As John walked away from the hanging tree and the ruins of the mayor's place, back down the hill toward the barn, intending to fetch a ladder so he could cut free the two bodies, he heard a thunderous whooshing sound, 'calamitous and catastrophic, an almighty cataract of noise', and felt the earth vibrate under his feet. When he turned around, the forty-foot cottonwood tree on the crest of the hill was gone, and from John's vantage, the earth appeared barren, wiped flat. It had been a traumatic return to the farm, and he thought perhaps he was suffering from some derangement of loss. Approaching the place where the tree should have been, he began to discern a shadow of expansive darkness on the surface of the earth, as if the grass had been scorched in a perfect circle; he suspected a divine and purgative fire had taken up the tree and the two dead men together in an all-consuming blaze, an event of spontaneous combustion brought on by God. John had seen haystacks go up in flame during drought years, knew the smoldering of the compost heaps on the edge of the farm, had even heard tell of great pine trees exploding in sudden and inexplicable conflagration. But as he drew closer, he saw that the earth was not scorched at all: instead, it was gone. Where the tree had been there was a hole, a gaping cavity, and as he peered over the edge of this hole, he could make out the crown of the tree, its entire height and the men bound and hanging from it swallowed up by the earth. Freeman called out to Lottie, who came running, and the two of them stood at the edge of the hole for a long time trying to decide what to do, looking at the submerged branches of the tree and listening to the wretched peace of the farm where even the grackles and red-winged blackbirds had silenced themselves. As the wind picked up and a pocking rain began to shoot holes in the earth, striking the couple's skin so hard it stung, they decided nothing could be done until the following morning.

The next day, as rain curtained the low undulating roll of the farm, soaking the burned-out ruins of Wright's house, John and Lottie Freeman drove back into town with their children in Wright's Model T to report the deaths of brother George and the mayor. The local law enforcement, backed up by the National Guard but nonetheless overwhelmed by the events of the preceding three days in which no fewer than thirty houses in the city and surrounding area burned, were not unsympathetic to John and Lottie's predicament. With the sheriff and several deputies escorting them, they returned to the farm where two of the lawmen, harnessed and lowered on ropes, descended into the sinkhole, climbing through the branches of the cottonwood tree, where they confirmed the presence of the bodies and the identity of the mayor. The sheriff understood that John and Lottie had nothing to do with the deaths, were in no way responsible, and that justice would never be done: it was suggested that disinterring the men from their unusual resting place would raise questions the community could not face, might never be able to answer, and would only create more tension between the races, since the spectacle of a black man and a white, tenant and landlord, bound together in death, could not easily be explained. It was agreed that the best thing for all concerned was to leave the bodies as they were, to fill the sinkhole with the smoking remains of Wright's house and soil from the adjacent fields. The deputies assisted John, and in the process of clearing the ruins of the house, discovered Wright's strongbox, jimmied it open, and found a charred but still legible last will and testament, leaving the estate in its entirety, including the farm and all its buildings, to George Freeman, and in the case of George Freeman's death, to his brother and fellow tenant John. The sheriff himself had been named as executor, and being a man who wanted nothing more than the return of peace to a city that had run away from him, he saw no point in brooking any contestation of the late mayor's stated last wishes, unorthodox as they were. And thus Poplar

Farm passed, with no public announcement, into the hands of John and Lottie Freeman, the children of slaves.

The county courthouse was rebuilt in the following year. No white man stood trial for the events of the previous autumn, while on a farm to the west of the city two small slabs of granite were laid in the ground to mark the place where a tree and two men lie buried in land stark with promise and death.

# PRESENT

*In this republican country, amid the fluctuating waves of our social life, somebody is always at the drowning-point.*

Nathaniel Hawthorne

It is her first time inside the walls of a prison. Or no, that is not quite true, because when she was still teaching she visited a juvenile detention facility where some of her students had spent time. The county called it a 'Youth Center', as if it were nothing more ominous than an after-school club for the city's underprivileged. It was located in a cluster of bland institutional buildings that included the county and Veterans Association hospitals, all faced in tan brick. She does not remember being subjected to any kind of search or having to pass through a metal detector, although in retrospect both seem probable. It no longer matters nor does she remember if she visited anyone specific, or if it was merely an opportunity to view the facility as a kind of public relations exercise for the local corrections department, making itself look good to the educators whose students might end up inside. Louise is certain she was cautioned not to speak with any of the residents she passed in the halls, solitary kids led by uniformed guards, boys avoiding the gaze of everyone around them, girls with long hair

9

worn flopping over their eyes, children with crew cuts and buzz cuts and shaved heads looking at the walls or the floor or the ceiling, and then the other, tougher kids, who turned to stare at her in ways that were challenging and provocative and perplexingly thrilling. They looked knowledgeable in a way she knew she had not been at their age.

So yes, she has been to a detention facility before, but today is the first time she has ever been inside an adult prison, a state penitentiary, although this one is no longer an arm of the state. At some point in the last ten years it was offloaded by the budget-slashing legislature and is now a profit-making enterprise for a private corporation that specializes in corrections facilities.

When it was built, the prison was a sandstone fortress erupting out of cornfields and pastureland and even when Louise was growing up it was on the remote edge of the southwestern suburbs, a part of town she has still never managed to explore despite spending her entire life in the area. Coming upon the prison now, she is surprised to find it surrounded by strip malls and fast food restaurants and a tall white grain elevator from the days when this was still rural land. Across the street stands a ten-million-cubic-foot white cube with COMPLETE COLD STORAGE across the top in tall scarlet letters that remain aglow twenty-four hours a day. Train tracks run past the grain elevator and prison, straight into the refrigerated warehouse.

Drinking iced tea and watching cars drive by she

waits for her scheduled appointment in a Mexican restaurant across the street. The air is distorted and shimmering from the heat rising off the asphalt. Her head twitches from side to side as if cars mean more to her than freedom, but her eyes are fixed beyond the traffic to the prison yard, open for everyone to see, where inmates in khakis and white t-shirts mill around behind chain-link fencing topped with curling-ribbon coils of razor wire under the aim of nine watchtowers that mark the perimeter.

A white woman and her two adult children enter the restaurant, order their food, sit down to eat. All three are overweight, but the son, in his early twenties, struggles to fit into his plastic chair. His hands shake and he fails to look at his mother or sister. 'This must be the most tranquil restaurant ever,' he says, dipping his fried chicken strips into a variety of hot sauces, melted cheese, and sour cream. Listening as they eat and talk, it becomes clear to Louise that the three of them have just come from the prison, where they were visiting the woman's husband, the long-absent father of the son and daughter. Across the room a table fills with penitentiary employees still wearing their badges. This is the collective purpose of the restaurant: to feed the prison staff and the families of the imprisoned. But Louise is not going to visit anyone she loves, or anyone she could ever be moved to think of as family.

Except for the stand of pines between the street

and the penitentiary parking lot there are no trees for a half-mile in any direction, including the area inside the perimeter fence. As she drives into the lot a sign directs her to park only in a designated visitor's space, not to loiter in her car, and to report without delay to the guard at the entrance. A pervasive smell of flame-grilled burgers from one of the several neighboring fast food franchises clogs the air.

There has been a prison in this location since 1866, although most of the original crenellated stone structures were demolished and replaced in the 1980s with a dozen separate brick units – the same tan brick used in the building of the Youth Center and the county hospital on the other side of town. If not for the razor wire and watchtowers, the facility might be mistaken for a suburban school. Indeed, it could be the same school where Louise herself taught for more than four decades, a period that felt at times like an endless term of daily incarceration, subject to the petty whims of sadistic principals, many of whom regarded their students as no better than embryonic criminals and the teachers as overeducated guards.

When Louise phoned yesterday to confirm her appointment, the secretary in the warden's office directed her to wear long pants instead of a skirt, and explained that open-toed shoes and sleeveless shirts were forbidden. The entrance to the penitentiary is at ground level but stairs inside lead in only one direction, down to the basement. At the end of the long subterranean corridor, decorated with vintage photographs of the prison in its early years, there is a desk and a single guard, tall and fat and smirking. He wears a nametag: Kurt D—. Checking that Louise is on the roster of approved guests for the day, Kurt retains her driver's license for the duration of the visit, provides her with a key for one of the lockers where she must abandon her jewelry and other valuables, and then stamps the inside of her left wrist with invisible ink that will show up only under an infrared scanner.

'In case there's a riot and a lockdown,' he explains. 'We'll know to let you out.'

She laughs and then realizes Kurt is not a man who jokes.

'Remove your shoes, please.'

She does as he says, and then, saying nothing further, he jerks his head to indicate the metal detector. Stepping through the gray arch she waits as Kurt runs her shoes through an X-ray machine. Although she does not set off the detector, he pats her down, fingers intruding where only doctors now touch.

'What's the worst you've seen?' she asks, raising her arms, spreading her legs apart, feeling the involuntary rush of sensation when Kurt's hand moves up her inner thigh. His palms are hot through her cotton slacks and she wonders if he is ever tempted to go too far, or if what he is doing at this moment is, in fact, too far.

Straight-faced and unwilling to engage, refusing

13

to smile or make eye contact, he grunts at her question: he has been trained to do his job, to read from a script, not to extemporize. It is possible that questions absent from his script do not register for him as words with meaning, but rather as extraneous noise. 'Turn around, please,' he sings, 'hands remain at shoulder height, arms extended, feet apart.'

'Alcohol? Weapons? Steel files? Do people still think you can escape from a prison with a file?'

Her teeth find the meat of her bottom lip and spasms warp her hands when she notices a sign warning her that *jokes about escape, bombs, or any criminal activities are inappropriate in a prison environment and may be treated as genuine threats.*

'Put one foot up here at a time.' Kurt points to a machine that looks like a scale imprinted with the outline of a man's dress shoe. Louise extends her left foot, which is dwarfed by the printed outline, and watches as the platform lights up and vibrates for a moment. 'Now the next one – not yet – okay now.' She changes feet, feels the pulse again. 'I guess your feet are clear but I'm gonna wand you one more time.' He picks up the metal-detecting baton, passing it around her body while rattling off a list of prohibitions, warning Louise that she may be searched at any point during the visit and that if she does *not abide by any of the rules heretofore explained and any others that might not have been explained but which nonetheless hold forth,* her visit *may be terminated immediately and without warning*, her personal possessions returned, and her person escorted off the premises and banned from re-entry to the facility *until formal security review by the prison administrators, which will take not less than two weeks.*

Kurt returns Louise's shoes and another guard appears down a second set of stairs. Unlike Kurt, he does not wear a nametag, but introduces himself as Dave.

'I'll be taking you up to secure-side, Mrs Washington, and escorting you to the interview room,' Dave says.

Upstairs, they approach two sets of bullet-proof glass doors adjacent to the Master Control Room, where a wall of green and red lights indicates which doors are open and which closed across the entire penitentiary. A guard in the Control Room sees them and opens the first of the glass doors. Louise and Dave step inside, wait for two other prison staff to join them, and the door closes. Several seconds elapse before the second door opens, allowing them into the secure portion of the prison where Dave leads Louise down the hall past a cage holding a dozen men, newly arrived, waiting to be processed, to be issued their ankle bracelets and identification cards with bar codes and photos, to spend time in the Diagnostic Evaluation Center where they will be assessed and assigned to a cell block. Waiting for their diagnosis, the new men all look terrified.

Dave turns a corner and shows Louise into the

room where the interview will take place. The walls are white concrete block, the trim around the doors royal blue, and across one wall are half a dozen blue-curtained bays that would look at home in a hospital emergency room, but which in this context make Louise feel uneasy, as if the space might be used for sudden triage. A dispenser filled with hand sanitizer is mounted on the opposite wall, and in the middle of the room are two molded plastic chairs on either side of a white plastic table.

Louise sits in one of the chairs, waiting for Dave to return with the prisoner. Alone in the room she feels a flash of panic as she realizes where she has brought herself. It is not because of the proximity to all these dangerous men, although perhaps that is an underlying or ancillary fear: of what men like that are capable of doing, the harms and violations they have committed, that they are still able and liable to commit in this facility shut away from public view, where, for all she knows, even the guards are in on the act. Rather, it is because she fears that in bringing herself inside these bland walls she risks being mistaken for a criminal herself, daring the system to conclude that some error has been made in allowing her liberty and now, as she has in effect turned herself over to the authorities, permitting the prison to process her for the span of a few hours, to judge her likelihood to break the laws of the penitentiary itself, they will see in Louise a criminal quality she has not herself recognized, and after identifying this intrinsic, previously unrecognized flaw, they may lock her away from the rest of society, flush her into their own private septic system, return her to earth. Once, not that many years ago, she broke a law, risking her liberty, and escaped only through the intervention of a man who can no longer assist her. Perhaps, she worries, some record remains of her transgression.

Just as she is reaching a peak of panic and thinking of calling the guards to let her out, to cancel the meeting, Dave returns with Paul. Louise reminds herself why she has come: not for herself, but for him, as an act of altruism. It is not an unconsidered position.

His hair, cut shorter than when she last saw him at the trial, is a close thicket of straight dark spikes flashed with gold streaks, the color of a homebrew prison process, glinting even under the deadening effect of the fluorescent lights that hang from the ceiling.

'So here you are,' Paul says, sitting down in the other plastic chair.

'Here I am,' Louise says, speaking over him.

'To be honest, I didn't believe you'd come.' She watches him flex his hands against the table. The guard, Dave, stands at the door, clearing his throat in what sounds like a warning to Paul before glancing at Louise, offering a corresponding gaze of reassurance and, she thinks, warning as well – not to get too comfortable in this room that is as white and windowless and unbreachable as a bank vault. Dave, however, is not going anywhere. It is his job, no less his duty, to protect her from harm, from this man who has committed such a catalog of harms.

Circumstances and environment being what they are, Paul appears for the most part no different than he did in the past. His face, the muscled curvature of his torso, the landscape of his veins make her shiver and push her chair away from the table, closer to the wall with the dispenser of hand sanitizer. She feels certain that if he wanted to Paul could catch her before she even knew she needed to escape, catch her and kill her before Dave could move his own large body across the room. Paul is big enough and strong enough that he could pick her up in both arms and carry her off, an unholy pietà. An old verse runs through her mind: *And the women conceiving brought forth giants.* The hard planar chest stretching his white t-shirt, the arms bulging from their sleeves seem less parts of an animal form than a system of gears and pistons, hard components moving only in one way because of the nature of their design and manufacture, elements built for a single purpose and not readily adapted to any space other than that which they were meant to occupy, a space he has now lost, which he cannot ever regain. Freedom is finished. He will never again be free, never released, not unless the country collapses into chaos. A diamond-cut file will not liberate him. It would take the bombs of revolution or apocalypse itself to free him from this prison, and for that Louise cannot help feeling grateful.

For years his face has appeared in her dreams, screaming and grimacing. As if from a nervous tic or too much time spent in the dark, his eyes, large and round, the color of Arctic seawater, rove and squint. He must have been in solitary confinement. It would not be surprising to discover he is a prisoner prone to fighting with other inmates or assaulting guards, the leader of brigades of men bent on escape or on nothing more elaborate than dominating the space in which they have been confined. But the skin under his eyes, across the cheekbones, although naturally olive, is an unhealthy shade of brown, a tan so deep that much of his face must be precancerous, pores swollen and popping like goose bumps. Inmates spend most of their waking hours outside under the sun, even in winter.

At first they have nothing to say to each other and she struggles to move her tongue.

'I came, Mr Krovik. Here I am, just like you asked in your letter. So—'

His feet drum the floor, two rubber mallets in motion, and then all at once they fall still as the echo of pounding thunders around the room. In other circumstances he could be mistaken for a department store mannequin or an animatronic model in an amusement park diorama of early man. The features are primitive, with a heavy crudeness in the brow and jaw and cheekbones that is just less than human.

Even if he no longer has full control over his appearance, he looks and smells clean. His eyes are clear, so like other eyes she now knows, irises a fine transparent glaze, crackling with iron oxide. When he adjusts his hands, searching for a position closer to comfort, the veins stand out as if he has been flayed alive. This small movement triggers a series of twitches that contort the left side of his face and brow, rolling back over his scalp until they cascade down his spine, making the whole body shake for a moment before once again falling so still that he looks lifeless but for the spasm that pulses down his arm, bringing to life the tattoo on his biceps of a bird struck through the chest with an arrow. *Cock Robin* it says in cursive lettering under the dying bird. He looks down at his arm as though the twitching belongs to someone else, or as if the bird were an illumination that might escape from its vellum.

'I really never imagined you'd come see me,' he says.

'No, I bet you didn't. And to be frank, neither did I.'

His twitching slows, intervals of stillness expanding until the bird is frozen again on the surface of the skin, the arc of its wing matching the curve of muscle, which flutters with sudden purpose as he pulls himself up against the table.

'I guess we used to be neighbors, though, sort of. Didn't we? Friends, even.'

'No. I don't think so,' Louise says. 'We weren't really neighbors, and we certainly weren't friends.'

Although Paul's story made national news, after her appearance at his trial Louise found herself avoiding all the media coverage, refusing requests to be interviewed; every time she saw his face she turned away from the gaze of a man she did not wish to remember. She never could have imagined that he would contact her, an acquaintance only, hardly a neighbor, nothing like a friend. If she knows anything certain about Paul it is that he never liked her.

The letter came to her in pencil on blue-lined white school paper. Paul's handwriting was in block capitals and, like the houses he built, the letters were out of proportion, the strokes too long, the bars and arms too short, the words stretched along the vertical axis. Although his writing was tidy she could not suppress the feeling that there was something sinister about the exclusive use of capitals.

DEAR MRS WASHINGTON,

I KNOW I HAVE NO RIGHT TO EXPECT A REPLY BUT I THOUGHT I WOULD GIVE IT A TRY. I DON'T HAVE MANY VISITORS AND I WONDERED IF I COULD PERSUADE YOU TO COME SEE ME. I DON'T HAVE ANYTHING TO OFFER YOU, AND MAYBE THIS IS A SELFISH REQUEST, BUT GIVEN

21

THE WAY THINGS ARE GOING IT WOULD BE NICE
TO SEE A FAMILIAR FACE, EVEN YOURS.
SINCERELY,
YOUR FORMER NEIGHBOR, PAUL (KROVIK)
P.S. I AM ALSO WRITING BECAUSE I COULD USE
A FRIEND RIGHT NOW.

The letter took Louise so much by surprise that, after reading it the first time, she put it aside, looking at it from time to time where it lay on the desk in the room she now occupies in a house that is not hers. She wondered at first if the letter was genuine or some kind of forgery. The return address was the state penitentiary and the zip code on the postmark corresponded. When she passed the desk in the morning or late at night, the paper seemed to emit an odor that reminded her of gunpowder, dried cornstalks, and manure.

It took her weeks to decide to visit. Reservations aside, she found herself intrigued by the possibility that Paul could think of her as a friend (in fact, against all her instincts, she was moved by the suggestion), while being unsettled and alarmed that he might have ulterior motives, or that any avowal of friendship was only a way to seduce her into helping him. The lighter notes of gunpowder attached to the letter faded, and those of decay mellowed, sweetened, grew as fertile-smelling as good compost.

Louise knows she has nothing to fear from Paul at the moment since the guard remains just inside the door and two cameras monitor the room from opposite corners of the ceiling. When Paul slides to one end of the table, she can hear the camera behind her shift, reframing and focusing on his new position. It is unclear whether sound is also being recorded.

'You know what the hand sanitizer is for?' he asks, nodding at the dispenser. 'It's for when they have to do a body cavity search.' He cocks his head in the direction of the curtained bays and glances over at Dave, who grins. 'They wear gloves but they still clean themselves afterward. Just to see you today, I had to be strip-searched. Every time I get a visitor, I have to take everything off, put my arms out at my side, lean over, cough, spread my ass, let them finger me if they think they have cause. And after this interview is over, they do it all again. I say to them, come on, just let me do the visit naked, it'll save a lot of time.' He raises an eyebrow as if he expects some kind of response: laughter or disgust. Louise looks at Dave, but his face goes blank, hands tucked into his armpits.

'I didn't realize,' she says, wondering if Paul wants her to thank him, if he believes that he is somehow doing her a favor by initiating this meeting.

'You know, I guess you're right.' His eyes jerk up to the camera. 'I guess we weren't even neighbors, not really.'

'I'd be curious to know what it was I did to make

you so angry, Mr Krovik. Why did you hate me?'
She wants to say, *You are the agent of my destruction, Paul Krovik, and you have no right to be so glib. After everything that's passed between us, all the ways you worked to destroy my world, your tone offends me.*

Paul throws back his head and laughs, as though he cannot begin to count the number of ways Louise inspired his hate. '*Whoo.* What *didn't* you do, Mrs Washington?' He sounds cocky and defensive, a kid still testing the boundaries. It is an attitude she remembers from countless boys she taught in the past, a quality that never failed to put her on guard. If he did not look so composed, if it was not clear that any hatred is now long spent, Louise would be out the door and running down the hall. Paul swallows his laughter and makes a strange warbling grunt, as if he knows it would be safer to leave the hills of hate between them unexplored. 'Never mind all that, though. Because, you know, it's really, really nice to see you here now.'

As his eyes blur wet and sultry in an almost feminine way, he fumbles the air across the table, his thin fingers, white nails cut in straight blunt lines, clawing at the empty space between them. She has never seen anyone make a movement like this, as though he is blind and has no sense that the hands he wants to grasp are within easy reach, just below his own. Louise understands that he wants her to take his fingers, to turn this interview into something like a conjugal visit under the eyes of the guard and the fisheye lenses of the prison's security cameras. She leans back in her chair, and then, almost losing control of her body, begins to extend one hand to Paul until, regaining sense at the last moment, she pulls it back. No part of her wants to touch him. She needs to get out of this white room and back into sunlight and open space, where visible distance is measurable in units greater than feet, where she can think with clarity, remember her purpose in the world, put her feet on earth instead of concrete. It was a mistake to visit him. There is nothing he can say that will change what he has done.

Louise leaves the prison feeling sick, her body shaking, eyes flowing. Watching her pass out of their jurisdiction, Dave and Kurt act as though she is the funniest thing they have seen in weeks, this old woman in tears. She drives northwest, skirting the city, until she finds herself in front of a house with a sharp gable and contorted verge boards, the lace border on a starch-stiffened napkin. Despite what she might wish, this house has put down roots in her brain: she wakes to see its gable twisting, the porch fattening, the windows blinking. Under the moon and a clear sky the house stands still, the whole neighborhood frozen in hot vapors. She hears the buzzing that is now always audible, a noise that might only be cicadas, although she knows it is not: there is nothing natural about the drone.

The house is just off the extension of Poplar Road, the main east–west thoroughfare through the city and a forty-minute drive to the old downtown that has been regenerated in phases over the last decade, the warehouses turned into lofts, derelict buildings razed and replaced with parks. Nonetheless, some neighborhoods that were genteel a decade earlier have seen their houses turned into rental properties, the porches sagging and gutters filling up with leaves that are never cleared to make way for the snowmelt in spring and the torrents of rain that come at unpredictable intervals in the warm months. Out here, on the western fringe of the city, everything remains new. Anything that ages is torn down to make way for shiny replacements.

Downstairs the lights are off, curtains closed, the windows dark and reflective. On the second and third floors there is light and movement; the curtains are open, the people who live inside forgetting that someone might be watching. She pulls the car into the driveway, gets out, and shuts the door without making a noise.

It is nearly nine o'clock and the neighboring houses are dark except for the small red pulse of light on each of their alarm boxes. She looks through the window in the front door and sees light seeping down the stairs from the second floor, shadows moving, someone standing still and then in motion again. Feet come down the stairs. Louise ducks behind one of the half-dozen plantation rocking chairs on the porch, listening as the body inside approaches the door. She edges into deeper shadow as the door opens for an instant and then slams shut. Somewhere a window is open.

'It wasn't locked! You said you locked it!'

'I said I couldn't remember.'

'Anyone could have come in. This isn't the 1950s!'

This is the place she has brought herself at last, the place where she now must remain. She sits in one of the rocking chairs, looking out at the other houses, blurring her vision so the structures begin to dissolve, giving way to the black mass of trees in the distance, the dim western glow as the earth spins itself again into darkness.

# PAST

*All felled, felled, are all felled . . . not spared, not one.*

Gerard Manley Hopkins

# PART I
# SHELTER

The helicopter has been hovering overhead for the last twenty minutes. He knows he can hear the rapid thwacking buzz of a flying lawnmower cutting down clouds, and if he can't hear it through the lead lining of the bunker then he is sure he can feel the vibration of rotors churning the air, buffeting the earth above his head, stirring up the atmosphere, designed to stir him up too.

When people asked him what he wanted to do when he grew up, Paul Krovik did not say he was going to be a fireman or soldier or pilot, as some boys will before they know the kind of drudgery and danger such jobs entail. He did not want to be an actor or rock star or astronaut, nor did he harbor secret desires to dance, design clothes, or write poetry – the kinds of dreams most in his world would have regarded as evidence that his parents had failed to raise a true man, whatever that might mean.

He always wanted to build houses.

And now they are trying to take away the only house that belonged to him. He is not about to give up the one thing he ever wanted.

At first when he heard it he thought the helicopter must be circling the general area, filming rush-hour traffic to transmit to one of the local news affiliates, the shellacked Channel 7 anchors in rictus masks reporting snarl-ups and accidents and slow-motion car chases, transmitting live from a breaking story with innocents sobbing in the background or bystanders weighing in with nonsensical sound bites about the shiftiness of a suspected killer or the long-observed weirdness of a family that has taken itself hostage in a broken-down motorhome none of the neighbors have seen move from the driveway in a decade. Paul remembers that story: a mother, father, three sons living in a ramshackle house. The children armed themselves, told their parents enough was enough, that life on the terms they were suffering was not worth living. Following a two-day standoff the parents yelled out the window to say they were no longer hostages, then knelt down in front of their teenage children, accepted the gun to the temple, and rolled backward, descending into death before they could watch the boys turn the guns on themselves. MOTOR HOME MASSACRE was how Channel 7 described it, the blond anchor smiling as if he were reporting the mass surrender of terrorists. How Paul admired that family, the logic of the boys and the courage of their parents.

If not a traffic helicopter overhead then it must be the police tracking a fugitive racing circles through subdivisions, trying to catch her before she can slip down a rabbit hole or into the woodland thickets of undergrowth that enclose the platter-flat river flowing west of the city. Ten minutes pass and the vibration does not change in intensity or frequency as the helicopter lingers over his neighborhood. Unless he is mistaken, unless it is all in his imagination, the machine is just above the house, watching and waiting for him to betray his position, perhaps even using thermal imaging cameras. Holding his limbs rigid he draws shallow breaths and imagines his temperature dropping, making him invisible to whatever equipment they may be using to locate him. The lead lining of the bunker should obscure him but there are always new advances in sensing technology, ways to see what is supposed to remain hidden. He cannot understand how the authorities found him so quickly since no one knows where he is – not Amanda, not his sons, not his parents. Everyone believes he has moved out of the house, found an apartment, is putting his life back together, starting over from the beginning with nothing but his hands and his tools. And yet the *thwacker-thwack* vibration comes in steady waves, moving down the wall, shaking the frame of his bed in the dark vault of the bunker. Let them seek him with their blindfolded eyes. In his retreat underground he is the only one who can see.

As Paul was building this house he discovered the foundations of a nineteenth-century farmhouse the widow Washington told him had burned down long ago. At the edge of the woods he uncovered the original storm cellar, still intact, wooden doors latched, and beyond them stairs leading down to a vaulted stone ceiling, the entrance obscured by shrubs and accumulations of dead leaves. After cleaning out the debris, he repointed the walls and vault of the cellar, knowing there must be a way to use such a space: he would build a fallout shelter, a bunker, a place of safety for his family. It seemed so logical that when Amanda asked him why they needed it, he lost his temper.

'Read the headlines! Watch the news! Look around you, babe! Because of the base this city will be one of the first to go. When I was a kid Dad told me that in a nuclear war we don't have to worry because in the first twelve minutes the whole city is going to be obliterated. That was supposed to make me feel like, I don't know, some kind of reassurance because we wouldn't be suffering in the aftermath. You have to understand, I'm planning ahead. I'm trying to protect you. We're going to survive whatever this thing is that's coming down the pipe.'

'What thing, Paul?'

'The *future*. We'll ride out the apocalypse together, safe underground.'

Amanda looked at Paul then, for the first time in their relationship, as if she did not trust him, perhaps did not even recognize him. He can see the way her brow drew together in a demonic-looking point. Over and over he tried to explain it to her but she had never been convinced. Now, left alone, he could write a book about all the ways his wife failed him, and in retrospect that was the first moment he knew she was turning away from what had always seemed a happy marriage.

*Thwacker, thwacker, thwack.* Keep the body still, think beyond life, think death into life and the stillness of the other side. Calm yourself, Paul, stop being a child. You're on your own, your wife has left you. You have no one but yourself. You must look forward. He remembers the way his father preached an edict of self-reliance to him as a boy. *Remember the teachings of the great man, Paul. Regret is nothing but a false prayer. Trust the gleam of your own mind. Be brave: God does not want cowards to manifest His work. Your hands are trustworthy. Society is nothing but a conspiracy against you. If the country is at war, then the average citizen has to look out for his own even more than in peacetime, government be damned.*

In building the bunker he was only thinking about the safety and welfare of his family. He loved his wife, still loves her, loves the boys as well, only ever wanted to protect them and still does. If he had the money, he would fly across oceans to find them and bring them back, knowing he is the only one who can truly protect them. It is no longer enough to worry about nuclear warheads from China or Russia or Iran or North Korea hitting the Air Force base south of town. It is essential to plan not just for attack by foreign terrorists or governments, but also for the possibility of hostile fellow Americans, for a new civil war, or for an environmental, technological, or biochemical conclusion to the human era on this planet. Those who have planned for the other side of now, the wise and prepared, are the only ones who will survive the plains of uncertainty that must be crossed in the coming decades.

Once he had the idea for the bunker there was just the question of how to connect it to the basement of the house since he had already filed plans with the city; to make a change would cost even more and be a bureaucratic headache and by then Amanda was feeling that she had taken enough chances trying to help him out in ways that were not strictly legal. So as soon as the house was finished, and the city inspectors were satisfied, Paul began excavating the tunnel for the bunker. There was no one to observe him except Mrs Washington, in her old wreck down the hill. Trees blocked the building site on three sides and he raised a six-foot-high fence around the backyard to ensure even greater privacy for the work he was undertaking without permit. What permission does a man need except that granted by his heart and his God? *Society everywhere is in conspiracy against the manhood of every one of its members*, so the great man said. He covered the bunker's walls with lead-lined sheetrock, borrowed a crane and a buddy to help him lower the containment doors into place one night, and encased the whole structure in a layer of concrete, connecting it with the old storm cellar in the woods and knocking through the finished foundation into his new basement at the opposite end. The bunker has electricity and plumbing, just as if it were another part of the house, except it is not, because it appears on none of the plans. With the bunker complete he bricked up the entrance to the basement, leaving a small hole hidden behind a wooden hatch under a shelf at the back of the pantry, just large enough that Paul could pull himself through on his stomach.

On paper the bunker does not exist, but under the earth of the backyard, behind its containment doors, it has two bedrooms, a full bathroom, an open-plan kitchen and living space, a store of canned and dry goods, a supply of water and water purification tablets, hunting and assault rifles, two thousand rounds of ammunition, energy-saving light bulbs, an extra washing machine and dryer, and an air filtration system vented into the woods, its exhaust pipe disguised within the trunk of a tree hollowed out by lightning. This is his refuge, the last part of his home he is able to occupy. Surrender is out of the question. When technology fails, he will spend his days in the woods, hunting and fishing, descending into his burrow at night, living in darkness, eating and sleeping as a creature beyond light, a demon kept safe by the earth.

*If I am the Devil's child, I will live then from the Devil.*

He worries about exits, believes that perhaps he should puncture the walls of the bunker in other places, create new tunnels, extend the parameters of the space beyond the confines of its impregnable structure. One night he painted the outline of half a dozen doors into his kidney-red walls, imagining the places where other tunnels might branch off, burrowing deeper into the earth.

His fingers find their way along the three-and-a-half-foot length of rifle, from the stock to the trigger and scope, sliding across the tapering blued barrel. When the moment comes, he will be ready. He retreated here only a few weeks ago, more than a year since Amanda had taken the boys, most of the furniture, and the whole of their life off to Florida. At first he tried to be rational: he knew he had lost the game; it would be sensible to pack up what remained after the estate sale, file for bankruptcy, and move to Miami. He had lost the lawsuits brought by his neighbors and that was the deathblow, the end of his limited solvency. Spending one night after another underground, often sleeping with all the lights on, Paul began to realize he could never abandon his house, not even after the foreclosure sale. Necessity forced him to conceal himself beneath the earth, in the den of his nightmares, where all he can do is plot his return. There is no reason anyone should ever discover his presence if he is careful. No one but

Amanda knows about the bunker – not even the boys. He will wait in silence, bide his time, do whatever it takes to reclaim his house, and once it is back in his possession, his family will return. They will have to return: he will give them no other choice.

'Do you like it, babe?' he asked Amanda, when the structural work on the house was finished and only decorating remained to be done.

Saying nothing, she smiled as she walked from room to room, climbing up one staircase to the top of the house and down the other to the basement. She went outside and around the back, came inside and put her hands on the banister in the foyer. When he asked again if she liked it, fearing he might have disappointed her, she cried through her nodding smile.

'This is a wonderful house, Paul. You've done a great thing,' she said, stretching up to kiss him. He'd picked her up then, carried her outside onto the front porch and then back inside, to make it official. She laughed and jumped out of his arms. 'You said you'd build me a dream home. I like a man who keeps his promises.'

If only she had always been like that, so susceptible, so easily pleased, not so focused on her own career. After a good beginning between them, it wasn't long before things had changed.

Listening to the rotors of the machine moving in the sky above, littering the land with clippings of clouds or the feathers of birds whose wings got caught up in its blades, Paul tries to lie as still as possible, willing his body temperature to drop, hoping that whatever technology the police possess cannot penetrate the layers of concrete and lead enclosing the bunker – or, if it does, that his attempts at psychological control of the body will be enough to camouflage him, diffusing the outline of his form, turning a panicked, hot-hearted biped into a mass of low-level thermal radiation. His father once tried to teach him how to cool the surface of his skin without ever breaking a sweat. 'War is psychology,' his father explained, voice always calm, patient with him. 'If you win the psychological war you win the physical one as well.' Paul tried to concentrate but when his father measured Paul's heart rate and temperature he shook his head: 'You're a good kid but you're mentally undisciplined, Paul. Game over. You've already lost. God bless your mother but she's been coddling you.' After that they started hunting together on 'father–son weekends', sleeping in a two-man tent in the woods, shitting and pissing outdoors with no privacy but a tree or a bush. Ralph made it clear that these weekends away were not just about bonding. 'I'm teaching you survival, Paul. I need to know that you're prepared for this world, for when you leave the house and have to make your own way. That's my responsibility to you. I'm not gonna baby you, and from now on, neither is your mother. I've been remiss. I've let you down. I want you to be able to look after yourself. That's the best gift I can give you. You have to learn to trust yourself, but first I need to turn you into your own best Trustee, help you develop your animal intuition. You have to learn to stand tall as God made you: do not be timid, do not apologize. Your height as a man is your virtue, as the height of this country is our nation's virtue. It is by nature's law that the great among men shall *overpower and ride all cities, nations, kings, rich men, poets, who are not.* The great man said that, son, and I want you also to be a great man, to take your deserved place in this greatest of nations, to ride atop the lesser who will try to bring you down.' He can hear the incantation of his father's voice, the way the words both inspired and soothed.

Not long after the house was finished his parents came for a barbecue. His father scrutinized the building materials and design while his mother, Dolores, kept shaking her head. Her own family, far away in Arizona, had always danced along the edge of destitution, and Paul could not tell whether she was proud or disbelieving or both.

'You were always gonna build houses, Pablito. Remember how you loved those bricks? I could keep you occupied that way for hours. You would just sit there in your fort talking to yourself, playing with your little action figures and whatnot.' Now, lying alone in the dark, hands pressed against the stock of the rifle, Paul can see the way his mother ravaged a fingernail between her teeth, as if she

43

had already guessed how things would end up, how he was going to lose everything, the way society would turn against him, the way everyone, even she, was going to abandon him. 'You remember that?'

'Yeah, Mama. I remember.'

'"I'm buildin' a house", that's what you'd say.'

'A house not a fort?'

'I guess sometimes it coulda been a fort. But usually it was just a house. "I'm buildin' my house." Whenever you had friends over you wouldn't let anyone play with those bricks. You hated sharing your toys, but the bricks were the worst. No one except me could touch them – you wouldn't even let your dad. You used to say, "anybody who touches my bricks I'll butcher 'em." You were always so angry. You didn't want to do anything I told you.'

'*A man has to be his own star*, Mama. Isn't that right, Dad, isn't that what you always said?'

His father, talking to Amanda on the other side of the back porch, sucked his beer and nodded as he fingered the vinyl siding. 'Plastic,' he muttered. 'Plastic in tornado country. What you want is brick and mortar.'

'You always knew what you wanted to be. You were always going to build houses. I saw that from the beginning, *chiquito*. Not like your father,' his mother whispered.

As a toddler, his favorite toys were a collection of blocks made from corrugated cardboard printed to resemble red bricks. Stacked on top of one another they formed walls that stood straight but were light enough to come tumbling down without causing damage. He built uncommonly straight walls for a child and the only time they ever fell was when he knocked them apart with his fists or his feet, imagining himself as one of the hulking superhuman characters he watched on television. 'You shouldn't watch so many cartoons,' his mother would say, 'they make you too angry. Go play with your bricks.'

In the corner of his bedroom – the many he had over the first twelve years of his life, bedrooms in four American states as well as in England and Germany – he built forts of two walls with no exit or entrance where he would sit for hours, fortifying and refortifying them with successive layers of cardboard brick until he had exhausted the whole collection, leaving himself almost no room to move.

'You've boxed yourself into a corner,' his mother would say. 'Now what you gonna do?'

'Stay here. Put a blanket over it.'

Dolores would drape a sheet over the opening at the top of those cardboard walls, sealing her son inside until some bodily need forced him to punch through the structure, growling and roaring as he emerged into the world of whatever house they were then occupying. 'Too many cartoons. You get *so* angry. It scares me, Pablo. What did I do to make you angry? Why you biting me all the time? Why you hitting me?'

In the years before they settled in this city, they always lived in tiny impersonal houses that his mother struggled to domesticate, in one case gluing lids from aluminum cans over holes in the baseboards to keep out mice, or dyeing burlap bags to make navy blue bedroom curtains for Paul in another, where the houses were so close together they could hear everything happening in their neighbors' lives. There was nowhere to retreat, no place of refuge. Every man should have a bunker to protect himself and his family, but Paul's own family has now fled. Before the foreclosure was final he received the divorce papers and restraining orders, keeping him away not only from his wife and sons, but even from his in-laws, safe in their gated community on the other side of the continent. Now he is not even allowed to speak to his boys.

The noise seems to grow louder, the helicopter getting closer, readying itself to land. The police are coming to drive him from his hiding place, to flush him out so that sharpshooters can mow him down, spraying him with flamethrowers, burning down the woods to drive him from his lair. He has committed no crime. There is no reason the authorities should come after him, but the noise continues to grow louder, pulsing, rhythmic and mechanical. The streets of Dolores Woods were designed to accommodate a helicopter in case of a newsworthy happening in the neighborhood, or in the event of a major civil or natural disaster requiring the immediate evacuation of the development's residents, or even the prosaic emergency of a neighbor needing a lifesaving medevac to one of the city's several private hospitals. At one point, when things seemed to be going well with the business, he even imagined clearing more trees to make room for his own private helipad.

Closing his fingers tighter around the rifle resting against his chest, Paul reassures himself that the gun is where he remembers placing it. The seven-pound weight of the arm seems to have changed so that its numbness has become a part of his own numbness, the failure of feeling that extends up from his hands and along his forearms to his shoulders and chest. He is lucid, clear of mind, knows what he is doing, where he is, what weapons are in his possession. If he has to, he will flee out the back entrance and into the woods, through the shallow river and across this sparsely populated state until he is no longer traceable. At the county line several miles away, the trees of the reserve pile up against the edge of a cliff that drops to the river. Some of the cottonwoods uproot themselves, tumbling into the brown water where they lie submerged and hidden, rising as snags. In earlier days they drew sternwheelers down into the mud and silt that consumed luggage and china and silverware, a hoard that later generations, hearing apocryphal stories of a submerged cargo of mercury, dredged into life, cleaned, and housed under glass in the county museum. Any mercury that was there had dispersed long ago to poison the river and its tributaries.

The house will always be his; no one can take it from him. He has dreamed of this house since he was a small child, after seeing a similar one during the brief time they lived in Maine. On one of the few vacations he remembers taking as a family they drove down from the remote northeastern corner of the state where they were living, less than four miles from the Canadian border, to the southern seacoast. For a week they stayed in a motel on Highway 1, and every morning drove fifteen minutes to a beach where they sat in silence until lunch, trudged to a hotdog stand, ate in silence, and trudged back to the beach for the afternoon. At four they would walk to a different concession stand for ice cream, and then at precisely six-fifteen climb back in the roasting car and drive to a lobster shack for dinner. At the end of the week they went to a barbecue at the summer home of one of his father's superiors. Before then Paul had not believed that ordinary people lived in houses with more than one story. There was a maid, a black woman, who kept bringing around a wooden tray filled with glasses of lemonade and a silver tray with punch that was only offered to adults. Perhaps it was because they had been staying in such a dismal motel room, but having seen the house just that once, the form stuck in his vision, grew distorted, and became something different but related to the original, a house of three stories, composed of gables and wings, symmetry and light. It was a house he had to have for himself.

Some time ago – he can no longer remember how many weeks – his house sold in a foreclosure auction on the steps of the county courthouse. Rain was beginning to fall as Paul hovered near the small crowd gathered to seize what was his. When he heard the final sale price he stumbled to a trashcan and vomited. It was a fraction of what the house had cost to build, not to mention all the money that went into decorating and furnishing it, never mind what the bunker itself had cost. In addition to all that, he still owes his father-in-law hundreds of thousands of dollars in loans that will now never be forgiven. He can no longer count what he owes to the banks. On the steps of the courthouse the crowd stared at him as if he were a vagrant or a drunk.

'Food poisoning,' he mumbled, to himself as much as to anyone else. A woman nodded, and then an older man, as crumpled and mud-footed as Paul, came forward from the bushes to offer him a handkerchief.

'Hey brother, wipe your face,' the man said. 'Stand up straight. Let's go get some soup.'

By that time the house was already empty. When at last it was clear there was no way to stop the foreclosure, Paul had held an estate sale, keeping only those small items that could be pushed through the man-sized hole at the back of the pantry leading into the bunker. In the end there was little to sell since Amanda had taken most of the furniture. 'I'll leave you the appliances,' she said when she moved out, 'I'm not heartless. But I'm taking the antiques and beds. After all, it was my father's money that paid for them. You can get yourself a cot until you figure out what you're going to do. If you have any sense you'll come with me. We can start over, Paul. This isn't really about you, what I'm doing, it's about the choices you've made.'

It was stupid not to protest then, foolish and weak not to fight for his sons, but he was in such a profound state of shock he could only shake his head.

'What I'm saying is, I want you to understand that moving out would definitely not be my first choice, Paul, but I don't feel like you've given me another one. I'm doing this because you refuse to be reasonable. I have to think about the boys. And I'm thinking of my own future too.' As she spoke to him, her shaking hands smoothed down a feathery white-blond cowlick on Carson's head. 'I still love you, Paul.'

'But you're giving up on me.' It seemed impossible that his wife would abandon him just as the lawsuits from the neighbors were coming to a head, as they were falling behind on their mortgage payments, as the credit card debts were mushrooming and the cost of health insurance doubled.

All that debt was in Paul's name alone. Amanda was free to start over.

'I've given you *so* many chances to turn things around, Paul. You could have sold off the rest of the land. You could have changed your mind and done something different when it was obvious that this dream of yours wasn't going to work.'

'It wasn't just *my* dream.'

'No, honey,' she said, jaw rigid as she tried not to cry or scream, he wasn't sure which, 'you're not rational anymore. I don't know if it's the house or the land or your own mind, but you've become someone else in the last couple of years. Do you see the way the neighbors avoid you?'

'They're suing me, Amanda, what do you expect?'

'They're suing because you're being so unreasonable. These houses are a *mess* and you refuse to see it. You built houses that look great in the beginning but start falling apart after six months. Look at this one! Everything creaks, the roof leaks, the whole thing sounds like it's going to be blown into the air when there's a strong breeze. The neighbors are right.'

His sons gazed up at him, Carson pale and staring through reflective sunglasses, Ajax lying on the carpet swimming his arms and legs in the air, rolling over on his stomach and laughing so hard that Amanda shouted at him to stop. She never shouted at the boys. Paul looked from his sons to the antiques he and Amanda had picked out together. He loved every line of that furniture, the

51

way it all seemed made for the house. The boys – Ajax at least – seemed anxious to go. Carson was a puzzle, the kind of child who might throw himself off the roof of a garage in the belief he could fly, a great billowing piece of dark material fluttering behind him as cape and shroud. Paul never understood Carson. His face was unreadable, a shifting maze of intention and desire. He was not the kind of son Paul ever bargained on having, quiet and studious and attached to his mother, nothing like the boys who had been Paul's childhood friends. Ajax made more sense, was less mysterious, more like Paul himself. But it was Carson he was going to miss most, and whom, by law, according to the order his wife had taken out against him, he could no longer contact. If he had money and lawyers, if he were free to pursue them across the country, everything would be different. He would fly to them now, fly and rescue them before the coming cataclysm.

After half an hour of silence Paul moves his hands, shifts the rifle, slides the safety catch into place, sits up, places the gun under his bed. The helicopter might have been monitoring traffic or a fugitive, but not him. He has done nothing wrong. He shakes his hands and arms to call back sensation, wincing as the blood returns to his fingers. Sitting still for several more minutes, he feels his feet begin to throb. The ration regime is too strict. He will need to augment his diet with food he can gather or kill. If necessary he will retreat to the woods, standing still and silent like his father taught him, building a platform in the trees or a blind on the woodland floor, mounting the suppressor on his rifle, hunting regardless of the season. He will do whatever he must to survive.

*Let us enter into the state of war.*

The foreclosure auction took place on the steps of the county courthouse, a palatial domed building in the French Renaissance Revival style completed in 1913, built of brick faced in pale sandstone and occupying a whole city block. A fifteen-foot statue of Justice stands atop the dome, which is constructed from iron and sheet metal distressed to resemble stone. Even at the time of its completion, everyone in town seemed to agree that the result was less than satisfactory, and the building earned a host of unflattering nicknames including 'the Coffee-Pot', 'the Spittoon', and 'the Tin-Pot Town Hall'. Nathaniel Noailles has learned this only now that he and Julia have made all the arrangements to move, signed the papers, bought a house, and sold their apartment. He never imagined living in a regional city – not great like Chicago or New York or even Boston, where he has spent all his life, but somewhere newer and less sure of its claim to history. To his mind, it is the kind of city still uncertain about what it may become and unwilling to accept what it has been. There is possibility in that position, but also a kind of historical denial that makes him uneasy.

Nathaniel himself has a clear sense of where he has come from and, until very recently, where he believed he was going. Originally French, his father's family has been long established in Massachusetts, while his mother's family came over to America on the *Canterbury* in 1699, on the second voyage of William Penn: stories of the three-month voyage have been passed down, the ancestor who was a stowaway surviving on pilfered scraps of food and emerging only when the ship was attacked by pirates, behaving with such valor in the vanquishing of the buccaneers that he was given his own hammock for the remainder of the voyage. Nathaniel has always assumed the story is apocryphal but already finds himself telling it to his seven-year-old son, Copley, in an attempt to give the boy a sense of his heritage.

When Julia was poached to head up one of the leading labs in the country and Nathaniel's company offered to promote him to a more senior position at its national headquarters, which happened to be located only a mile from Julia's new university offices, it seemed churlish to complain about the location. So here they are, packed, about to depart for a new life in a new city, and all Nathaniel can think is that they should stop before it is too late. Now that the move is in progress, he feels its cold hands pulling him forward, dragging him down. 'Julia?' he says, turning to find her as the movers take the last of their belongings out of the apartment and the rooms they have filled for the past decade begin to echo. A sweat breaks out under his arms, his palms are clammy, and sunlight blazes through the windows.

'Yes, Nathaniel?' Boxes fly out the door and Julia ticks corresponding numbers off her packing manifest, double-checking that each parcel of their lives is properly secured.

'Julia?' he says again, his voice rising though they stand only feet from each other. 'I've been thinking. I wonder. I'm just not sure—' He can see that she understands he wants to call it off, to make the movers bring everything back inside, unpack, and restore their lives to the balance that seems, in a matter of hours, to have evaporated around him. They have spent a decade creating a life of equilibrium and beauty, a space that feels secure despite all the encroaching traumas. High in a tower overlooking Back Bay, Nathaniel realizes how little he wants to abandon his world of white walls, white carpeting, white furniture, white blinds and appliances: a domestic haven of minimalist calm. He is not sure he can face the chaos of this move, or the challenge of starting a new life so far from anything familiar, in a city where they have no friends or acquaintances, no family, no networks of support.

'Nathaniel, sweetheart, it's too late. This is what we've decided.' Julia takes his arm, draws him close to her, and kisses him, holding his gaze. 'I promise you, I've taken care of everything. You don't have to worry.'

'Where's Copley?'

'He's saying goodbye to his room. Will you tell him it's almost time to go?'

Nathaniel wants to shout *no*, to rip the manifest and clipboard from her hands and take charge of their lives in a way he never has. The movers return once more, loading the last of the boxes onto their hand truck, and in an instant the apartment is empty. How efficient they've been. Burglars couldn't have done it any faster. Julia runs out the door after the two men, and Nathaniel is alone in his home with his son for the last time.

'Copley? Copley?' he calls, finding his son standing a few feet from the windows of his bedroom, looking out on the square that is his namesake. Friends had seemed puzzled when Nathaniel and Julia announced their son's name, as if it suggested some hipsterish desire to embrace localism and history. They had been too embarrassed to admit to anyone else that he was conceived after a New Year's Eve party at the hotel on the square.

'Are you ready? What are you doing? Everything's loaded. Copley. Look at me.'

His son turns and blinks, makes a low beeping noise, and marches past Nathaniel out of the room. Without furniture the space is only a white box with two portals on a more colorful world.

Nathaniel leans against the glass and has a passing sense of vertigo. He has never wanted to live anywhere else, and yet, troubled as he feels by the decisiveness and magnitude of this change, a part of him recognizes that, more than anything else, moving away from Boston for the first time in his life offers the possibility of escaping from his parents.

It was in front of the County Courthouse, the 'Tin-Pot Town Hall', that a realtor acting on behalf of Nathaniel and Julia bought the house in Dolores Woods, a house they understood to have been the original model home for the unfinished subdivision. Of the two hundred 'luxury, executive homes' planned, each located on a three-quarter-acre plot, only twenty-one were finished before the business fell apart; another ten foundations have been dug, the cement floors poured, the concrete basement walls raised. These are now empty spaces lapsing back into wildness, an assortment of abandoned archeological excavations gaping between the finished houses, scattered widely around half a dozen broad streets, beyond which stretches a low rolling landscape of empty fields that spill down towards the river. The realtor assured them the stalled development would be going ahead now that other contractors had stepped in, buying up the remaining parcels of vacant land and the ten houses left unfinished by the original developer. Part of the appeal of moving to the Midwest was the promise of a house unlike any they had been able to afford in Boston. With this in mind, Nathaniel and Julia had hoped to buy an elegant home in one of the city's historical preservation neighborhoods, a house old and characterful like the large New England homes in which they were both raised – Nathaniel in Cambridge, Julia in New Hampshire – but when the realtor insisted on showing them the recently built house in Dolores Woods Julia had been overwhelmed.

'Old-style charm, but every modern convenience,' said Elizabeth, their realtor. 'It's a house with one eye on the present, and one on the past.'

'It feels like my grandparents' house, only cleaner. Everything's *new*,' Julia said. 'And the yard. Imagine the garden we could have. It feels safe. I want this one.'

'It's awfully dark, isn't it?' Nathaniel said, looking at the patterned wallpaper, the intricately painted crown molding and heavy red drapes.

'I think we have to see past the decoration, honey,' Julia said. 'This house could look just like our apartment, only bigger.'

'But it doesn't look anything like us. It's so dark. And so cold.' In each room Nathaniel heard the sound of air rushing through the vents. It was ninety-three degrees outside and sixty-four in the house. 'Do we need a house with two furnaces and two central air systems?'

'Still a little warm in here,' said Elizabeth. She turned down the thermostat to sixty.

59

Nathaniel also had reservations about buying a foreclosed house, fearing it was not the most ethical thing to do, profiting off the loss of another person, and in this case the former owner had designed and built the house himself. 'The house's *creator*,' Nathaniel said, asking Julia to convince him it was the right decision. 'This is bad karma, isn't it?'

'The man—'

'Paul Krovik,' Nathaniel interrupted.

'He over-reached,' Elizabeth continued, taking Nathaniel's arm as she led him back through the living room, den, and hallway. 'Let me paint you a picture. This Paul Krovik was not a good man. He went into debt – but *serious* debt, Nathaniel. He was sued by some of the people who bought the other houses in Dolores Woods for failing to complete the work as promised. He could have made good on his guarantees but instead he fought them in the courts and he lost. As a result, he lost his business, and then he lost his family. His wife left him. Rumors are she even had to take out a restraining order because after she left he kept phoning her, endless calls at all hours, cursing at her, threatening her. He must have been a monster. He was certainly . . . unhinged. And now he's disappeared completely, leaving unpaid bills all over the city. He was *triple mortgaged*. Debt collectors want his head. If you buy this house you'll be doing a good thing. You'll be helping the neighborhood get back on track. You'll be giving people hope again. You'll be helping them *heal*. This house is the jewel in the crown of Dolores Woods, and it needs good owners, people like you who understand how to take care of a house, how to live in a neighborhood, how to be outgoing and friendly.'

'We're not—'

'Of course you are, Nathaniel. The community needs you. This house needs you. I think your wife sees that already. She needs this house, too, I think, don't you?' Elizabeth whispered, patting his arm. He thought of how happy he and Julia had been in Boston, the way they had become settled in their jobs and apartment, content with the way life was unfolding around them. His work had kept him occupied if not stimulated, he was making good money, Julia's research had gained her increasing prestige, their son was intelligent and well liked by his teachers, and they had nurtured a community of congenial friends.

Walking the winding streets of Dolores Woods, Nathaniel understood the neighborhood's particular aesthetic philosophy, one in which the past was preferable and this country was at its greatest before it tried to tear itself apart in the middle of the nineteenth century, before the rift and emancipation and urbanization. While each house had its own unique design, they were stylistically congruous, pastiches of Victorian architecture just out of scale, the verticals too long, the pitch of the roofs too acute or too shallow, as though the houses had been stretched or subjected to a deforming growth hormone that left one aspect of their shape enlarged – houses with elephantiasis or localized gigantism, houses that belonged in a sideshow of architectural grotesques.

The streetlights were reproductions of black Victorian gas lamps and the street signs were made from hand-lettered wooden shingles. Most of the garages were separate two-story structures designed to look like carriage houses, with dormer windows and fake dovecotes jutting out of steep gabled roofs. It struck him as New England architecture transposed to an inhospitably open landscape. The finished portion of the neighborhood came to an end in an oval at the center of which was a miniature park with a cluster of trees, a white wooden gazebo, three wrought-iron benches, and a few neglected flowerbeds. Immature trees dotted the large expanses of lawn, and past the gazebo the streets cut a gray and illogical labyrinth through weed-filled wasteland, bordered to the east and north by the woodland that merged into the nature reserve.

On the day they viewed the house, a red-tailed hawk sat on one of the streetlights in the territory of vacant lots, scanning the rolling grassland. Apart from the roads, the fields were punctuated only by a regular rhythm of utilities points awaiting houses that might never be built. Someone had made a patriotic attempt to sow chicory and daisies and pale red columbines in the area closest to the last of the finished houses, but it was impossible to deny that what remained was a sign of failure and waste, fertile land lying fallow. Fine silt blew from the places where the ground remained bare. All the finished houses were occupied, but a majority of the residents owned properties worth less than half what they had paid for them. No one was buying. Everyone wanted to sell. The population of the city, after rising for decades, was in sharp decline. Birth rates were dwindling and the whole region was contracting. Nathaniel had read an article that suggested a bill might soon make its way through the state legislature that would propose leasing more than a third of the state to the federal government, either to be run as a nature reserve, or to build a vast prison farm complex of detention centers for illegal immigrants, failed asylum seekers, enemy combatants, and domestic terrorists. We must be crazy, Nathaniel thought, the hot summer wind hurling grit into his face, to imagine we'd want to live here. The truth was that they could not begin to afford the kind of solid historic home they thought they wanted. A simulacrum was the closest they were going to get, and Dolores Woods, however unfinished it might have been, had pretensions to historical awareness that most suburbs lacked.

That evening, when they were eating dinner downtown in what Elizabeth had recommended as the city's best restaurant, located in the storage vaults of a recently redeveloped warehouse,

Nathaniel tried to explain to Julia the nature of his larger reservations. It was not just about this house that she loved, a house even he had to admit was impressive, tempting in its way, but appealing as a kind of trophy rather than somewhere he would ever want to live. It would be an irrational purchase. They had agreed they were not going to have more children, and three people did not need so much space.

'But it's also got me thinking – I wonder if we're making the right decision about this whole thing. We love Boston. Copley loves Boston. He loves the Lab School,' Nathaniel said, lowering his voice and watching as his son struggled with a bowl of noodles.

'I don't want to leave the Lab,' Copley said. 'I'm not ever leaving there.'

'Come on, guys, we're going to have a much better life here,' Julia said. 'We'll have space like we've never had before. We'll have a yard and a vegetable garden. You can have a playroom, Copley. This is what we've always said we wanted. And if the new school isn't up to scratch, Nathaniel, well, we're intelligent people. We can pick up the slack, or hire a tutor.'

Since making the decision to leave Boston, Nathaniel had begun to think of himself as *deferring to Julia*. She, in turn, pleaded with him to trust her, asking him to abandon his otherwise sensible tendency to play devil's advocate and stop second-guessing what was, by all objective measures, professional progress for both of them, as well as the kind of increase in their standard of living that would have been unattainable in Boston.

'You're leaving the best lab in the country. Do you understand what that means? People will think you're crazy.'

'I never would have made director there. This is about power and autonomy, Nathaniel. I can do things here that I never could have done in Boston. I can do other, better, more ethical kinds of work. I'm not interested in defense applications or space exploration or mapping oil wells. I want to create *useful* tools that can improve the lives of people who need help. That's why I got into this field in the first place.'

'And you need that house, don't you?'

'And I *really* need that house.'

Nathaniel understood that having a house like the one in Dolores Woods – a house, he had to admit, that was unlike any they could ever have afforded in Massachusetts – was important to Julia in a way it would never be to him.

After seeing the house with Elizabeth they left instructions for her and returned to their high-rise apartment in Boston to await the results of the foreclosure auction. Nathaniel knew that Julia had decided the house would be theirs by some miracle of fate, although he privately hoped that in the end they would be outbid, and the difficult logistics of finding somewhere to live in a city fifteen hundred miles distant would put a stop to the plans that were already, in every other respect, so far advanced.

When Elizabeth phoned to tell them 'the good news' that not only had they 'won' the auction, but that the final price was well below their 'target', Nathaniel understood, despite his many misgivings, that they were going to be significantly better off financially than they had ever been at any previous point in their lives together. Even with the downturn in the market they sold the apartment in Boston at a substantial profit and the mortgage payments on the new house are less than half what they were paying on the Back Bay apartment. Although still paying off student loans, their taxes would be lower, the cost of living lower, everything about their new life was going to be cheap, while both their salaries were increasing by more than a third. Judged by any objective measures, they were far luckier than most of their friends and contemporaries.

The sun is going down earlier each evening, summer quitting itself, but still I can see the white man at the bus stop from a block away. It's only when he boards that I realize he's in uniform. For a moment I think the vest he wears says KKK and my heart rumbles, but then my eyes come together and I see the first K is an E and all the man is doing is checking tickets. Under those three capital letters is an unfamiliar phrase: Revenue Protection. Maybe it's because I haven't been riding buses much lately, but it used to be enough to pay the driver and get off at your stop. I fish the ticket from my purse and the Revenue Protection man looks at it and then at me as if the little white slip should somehow correspond to the shape and features of my face. He puts it back in my hand without saying anything and goes on to the next person. Everyone has a ticket. I wonder what would happen if someone didn't, if he'd whip out a smart black fine book or slap a pair of silver cuffs around offending wrists. He gets off at the next stop, crosses the street, waiting for a bus headed back into town.

How many times I've driven this road, watched it change over the last decades, but if I were my young self again I would see nothing familiar about any of it, not the phrases or faces or the houses where there used to be fields surrounding our own. Just before the last stop I press the yellow strip of tape running along the window and as I get off I thank the driver. The man doesn't even look at me, as if I were an apparition, as though I might never have existed at all. I trudge along the hot sidewalk where buffalo grass used to grow, past a brick wall where I remember split-rail fences. I come to our land, to that place where the forest reaches all the way to Poplar Road, and the cotton-woods in their thick-trunked waltz bow down and say *here you are, Louise, here you come*. I remember when this stretch of road was still dirt and Donald and I stood at the edge of the property watching the men and cement trucks, knowing it was the end of the way we and our people had lived upon this land my grandparents inherited, land my Freeman forebears tenanted before a stroke of most unlikely luck delivered it into their name; great-grandparents sharecropped before that, arrived on it newly free and looking for a way of living in the quiet of the seasons, hope humming in their ears.

Through the trees I see the white hem of our house, a silver ghost like my dead Donald, belted with an apron of porch, teacup sky overhead, clouds rimmed in gold. I take the woodpath to avoid the eyes of neighbors where there didn't used to be any, follow my feet along tracks I could walk blind from first walking, fifty paces to the north, feel the tug of the pole, then my old sharp turn left and twenty more paces through treecover until I step into the corrugations of the garden, the sky darkening to a purple bronze. Now I stand alone.

Not that I blame anyone. I don't blame my husband for taking out loans to install an irrigation system, to keep the farm alive, building up a debt that forced my hand in the end, debt to the FHA, and debts to banks to pay off the Feds. I don't blame him for dying before his time. I don't blame my daughter for telling me what was obvious. I don't even blame Paul Krovik with his big plans and big money.

But I do blame myself. I blame myself for giving in to Krovik when he asked me to sell the farm, and for giving in to Rebekah when she said I had no choice but to sell: either sell and remain solvent, my daughter told me, or hang on and let the bank take everything when I could no longer make the payments. All those badgering, shouting people, hollering even when they didn't raise their voices. I don't blame them, but in the end I didn't have the strength to resist. I blame myself for that weakness, for not standing with the land, letting my feet sink in, holding the soil with their fleshy roots, finding a way to make farming pay as we always had in the past.

One foot just fits in a furrow between two rows in my garden, the earth warm and soft, lines clear, all of it my labor: the hoeing and weeding and mulching, the mounding and raking and watering. Between stands of asters in September bloom I can see tomatoes and peppers in twilight, leaves yellow and ragged for neglect. I feel bad about that, but my time has been divided. I've been fighting to save you all, my little that remains. Rent of a sigh rips my chest, and a claw comes snagging from nowhere. I cannot name the hand that scrapes me now, but I feel its hook bring up a coughing cry. Stuff it back inside, fist my tongue behind my teeth, a salt-knuckle silencing. God forbid the neighbors should come investigate or call the cops.

I love this life and I love my freedom. I want them both to last, free on this plot that was supposed to be my people's promised land, the new home at the end of their long exodus from the south. My great-grandparents, born in bonds, came here under their new name, following their own star. My grandparents, the first generation born in freedom, the first to own the land them-selves, started off as tenant farmers. If they managed to do it, then *I* might have found someone again willing to assume the burden and possibility of farming land not their own, farm it in the way it's been farmed ever since people came to culti-vate this part of the country. I should let go of the blame, but I still find myself accountable for caving

70

in to all those people in the weeks after Donald died, his life going out all at once, moving upright from bed, putting his feet on the rag rug. A congenital defect, said the doctor, weakened by a lifetime of labor, time catching up after the decades of handpicking and lifting and early rising.

I can't help thinking that if he'd retired and leased the land to tenants when it was clear the work was taking him down by degrees each day and the returns, ever slim, fast diminishing, were no longer worth the effort of his labor, when there were still farmers around looking for land, then he might still be alive. But no, *I'm no overlord*, he said, *and I'll be no overseer*. We worked harder than ever to stay in the same place, struggled to fall behind slower than we might have otherwise, as crop prices dropped and the cost of everything else went up. We'd never have survived without my job, my commute across town every day of the school year, my long hours. Without that, we would have been finished decades ago.

I kick off the shoes and put my feet in the damp ground, run soil through toes, break leaves and stalks of tomatoes to smell the perfume of fine green hairs, scent of my homeplace and heritage. There are two parts to me: earth and sky. Let me think through the land for now, for a while, for the last hours of my life in this house, however many days they may last. Let me find my way to a reckoning of how it came to pass.

After selling the land to Krovik, paying off the

71

ocean of debt to the banks, I still found myself robed in an almighty blanket of money. But it was stamped and stitched together with blame: self-blame, worst kind of blame. Rebekah said it was the only rational choice given the circumstances: 'You have to be reasonable, and look at the thing logically. You sell this land and you don't ever have to think about working again, not ever. You get out of debt for the first time in your life. You say screw the government for not recognizing our claim. You say fuck the bigots and the neighbors who never helped. You leave it all behind, Mom, and you get a more secure retirement. You get yourself free from worry about bills and food. No more crusts, like you're always saying. Instead, you can buy what you really want.'

Rebekah has always thought she knows what I *really want*, but she could never imagine that what I most want now, and even in those weeks after her father's death, was for Donald Washington to climb out of his coffin, scratch through six feet of dirt, come home, sit next to me on the porch, and for the two of us just to rest there, swinging in silence and laughter, for a good year or two. I might be able to stand it if I could have those two years of Donald and me just sitting together, not worrying about land or crops, two years to get used to the idea of him not being here. I told Rebekah there was no way she was putting me out of my house.

'No one is saying you have to move,' she said.

72

'You can keep this old house, stay here long as you can.'

I looked at my daughter, shifty-eyed Rebekah, and knew she couldn't wait to get me in a retirement home. I told her she should put to rest any ideas about powers of attorney and health proxies, because I will go out looking after my own affairs, making my own arrangements, ushering myself to the grave, through grace and in the company of the dead who have preceded me. The mistakes I make are my own.

'Oh Lord, mom. I'm not making you go anywhere,' she said, finger-wagging, swivel-armed. 'Tell Krovik you want to keep the house and half an acre around it, but you can't keep all this land. Krovik's made you a *good* offer. It's honest money. There's nothing wrong with selling something you don't need anymore once it's served its purpose. Let the land turn into something else. He wants to build houses, so let the fool man build houses. If you don't, you're going to lose it all anyway, and have nothing to show for it.'

But this land was made for farming. It's not suitable for houses. It has secret, sliding ways.

'Come on, Mom, get real. This land is just plain old *tired*. It's been *tired* for a long time. There's nothing mystical about it. Let the land rest. Let it do something else for a century. Be pragmatic, like you always said you were. Sell up, sit tight, find something to occupy your time.'

I should have told Rebekah how much I need

this land, the way the rock, soil, and trees are not merely the only home I've ever known, but *are* my bones and blood and limbs. All my dawns I've woken with this land in my nostrils, lived with it every day each day, gone to bed at night thinking about worms and organisms, all that life-seething, life-smelling brownness. My feet have always been here, in this quiet earth. When it freezes I freeze. When it thaws my limbs begin to move again. When it grows hot and dry in summer I feel the heat kindling in my stomach, a flame taking hold, drafts down my throat drawn to feed the blaze. Without land my feet would be fancy from being earthless: I could not think properly away from the soil.

Donald died on a dull morning in late May and in the following weeks and months we endured a drought more severe than any in recorded history. The corn he'd planted dried up, turned brown, and on the Fourth of July some kids set off Roman Candles and Catherine Wheels in one of the fields. Those fireworks were a match to flash paper or gun-cotton. Talk about flame. All but ten of the hundred and sixty acres burned. Walking the fields in the aftermath of that fire was the same as being broken in torture, and the blackened earth went on staring back, pummeling my limbs and breaking my body. There would be no crop to sell, no hope of servicing the debt that was mine alone to bear. It was the *coup de grâce* that made the sale to Krovik my only choice. He lowered his offer from

$1.2 million to an even million, more than three-quarters of which would go directly to the banks, to pay off the farm debts. Rebekah said I was lucky to get what Krovik was offering, given the state of the place. My daughter failed to see that the fire not only forced me to sell but also cleared the land for him, making Krovik's job easier.

But the dispossessor is now the dispossessed, having lost even more than what he took from me.

My feet burrow into wrinkles of ground, fine soil rising to my nostrils, cottonwoods shushing behind me in the east, Krovik's monstrosity up the hill to my right, Poplar Road to the left, the silver ghost that is my own house ahead under the western, plane-hatched sky. Roots cross-stitch the earth and all around I hear the drone of cicadas fighting for dominance over the electric buzz of houses, the killing power strangling the world, flying into homes, drawing children with forks to sockets, seducing with the promise of hidden strength to bring them low, cut them down with its current. I listen to cicadas to blot out the rest, turn up the volume on the natural, stare back into the woods in search of the smokedrift flicker of fireflies, but it's never dark enough anymore. There is altogether too much light.

After the sale, Krovik's dirty stole of money wrapped itself around me, weighing me down: blame money, self-blame money, lucre filthy with blame. Piled up in a bank account it did no good, made me sick, prolonged the pain of Donald's death, and now it's all gone, almost every cent. Like the land, the money is irretrievable, most of it spent on lawyers.

I take a cherry tomato from the vine, rub it against my shirt, place it on my tongue, close my lips and bite to feel it squirt, sweet-sharp and viscous. I return to find the tree where Donald proposed to me. He tried to carve our initials into the bark but I wouldn't let him. Trees can't cut back. There's no violence in trees, no evil. I check on the old girl's health, run fingers over her deep bark ridges, press my ear to her furrowed flank and hear the beating I have always heard, the pulse of tree sap.

Now that I am no longer supposed to be here, living in a house that has been snatched from my possession by the local government of rich men and women who call themselves democratic, I press the screen door closed and wait for the murmuring latch, a noise only birds and dogs and insects can hear. After issuing the condemnation order, the city put a heavy combination lock on the front door, but the idiots forgot a house has more than one entrance. I wasn't even home at the time. Returned from the store only able to enter my house through the back door. The fools left everything inside untouched.

Sliding through darkness now, to the kitchen door at the back of the house, cottonwoods groaning in a low push of west wind, I take the key from my neck, put it in the lock, feel the bolt slip when it turns, push down on the latch and shove. It scrapes across a worn spot where the kitchen floorboards have risen, drawling a fine-milled daysong. I have chosen to remain in this house inherited by my grandparents, passed down to my mother, then to me, the steward of its last days. I live here now as an outlaw, without power or water or heat except that which I can create from matches and candles and the pump out by the barn, drawing clear waters from deep in the earth.

The rooms are dark and dust-quiet but as in the woods I don't have to see to know where to place my hands. Six years after his death, everything still smells of my husband: Donald in the floorboards and drapes, rising up from the coal chute and resting in the accumulations of lint and debris in the corners of every room. I breathe him in, smell arms and feet and sex in those accretions of skin cells and hair. I feel his touch, the rough fingerskin on my back and buttocks, his hands encircling me, drawing me in.

I put the key on its red gold chain back round my neck and look through the kitchen window at Krovik's house: the cottonpuff seed that shot the root that grew the tree that bears the fruit of my dispossession. Its empty windows flash dark, one watcher watching another. *All shall be afraid, and the Watchers be terrified.*

Before the new neighbors began to arrive I never locked the house. They were neighbors in name alone, looking at me standing on their porches as if I were a homeless woman begging door-to-door. When I explained who I was, the woman on whose land they now lived, I could see how they thought they were better than me in numberless ways. They looked with suspicion at the plates of cookies and loaves of zucchini bread I gave to each new family that moved in. None of them ever returned the kindness, turning their fat backs when I finally came asking for help, as if they suspected all along that my old-fashioned niceties were bribes for some future favor. They don't understand neighborliness. Let them have their rickety new houses made of cardboard and plastic parts. They will never stand as long as this one has. Time and terror will see them all come down.

Locks have little use, even now. There is nothing here worth robbing except the jewelry: wedding rings, my own and my mother's – Grandmother Freeman's ring has gone elsewhere, lost, on the hand of some cousin's daughter. There are the photographs, too, but no one would take those, pictures of Grandma in her ankle-length skirt, frock coat, straw hat, and ones of my mother in gingham dresses, holding me up to the camera. Somewhere I have a photo of the benefactor, Mr Wright, the old bachelor with a soft spot for his tenants, and other photos of the grandparents, John and Lottie, the inheritors, higher branches on the Freeman tree. Surely those old albums are worthless to any but the survivors, and who but me can now call herself a survivor? My cousins never cared for this place, and they went elsewhere years ago, leaving me, the youngest, the only true inheritor, to look after the land that raised up so many. I am the last remaining. We were lucky, unusual, inheriting land where others could only acquire through hard labor and tight saving. The photos of my ancestors are better than gold, but even I do not have names for all the black-and-white faces. I asked Mama too late to help fill in the blanks in my knowledge, scribbles of pencil on the creamy backs of heavy-matte paper rectangles with rippling edges. I make up stories about people I cannot identify, imagining the barrel-bosomed woman with marcelled hair is long-lost Great-Aunt Claudette, who started a cosmetics business and became a millionaire in New York, died, left everything to her housekeeper, caused scandal, was never mentioned in the hearing of children.

'Whose house is this, and who's that next to Grandpa?' I might have asked my mother as she leaned back in her chair, in the days not long before her death. The old woman would tilt her head and look through the bottoms of her bifocals, make a murmuring noise, water-thoughts rising, say she couldn't be sure.

'Might have been a creditor. I can't say I recognize him.'

'Whose house is that?'

'That's this house, LouLou. It was younger then. Didn't have so many years on it. Same way you don't recognize me in some of these pictures. No different with houses. You think it might be the same place because there's a kind of family resemblance, but the yard's all wrong, and the windows look different, and the siding is brand-new. See,' she would say, pointing to an edge of the house in a photograph, 'that's the northeast corner, where the burning bush is now. Used to be a lilac there but it died before you were born.'

'But where's the porch?' I asked her. 'It can't be this house. The porch would be there.'

'My mama and daddy didn't extend the porch to the east side until I got married, sweetheart. A house changes with the people in it. If it doesn't, it dies, and we die along with it. This house is yours now, Louise, yours and Donald's. You should be making your own changes. Look after it in the way you got to, in the way that your life, and that the house itself, dictates to you. It'll tell you what it needs and what it wants. It'll show you how it wants to live, and how it wants to help you live.'

I fear I laughed at her, laughed and then failed to do the house justice while it was still mine, and now, in place of these rooms there will be a new turning lane and a boulevard into the development that was once my family's farm and is now just another neighborhood for people pretending to be rich. A surety on this house and the farm I sold sent me to college, gave me a career, my parents risking home and livelihood to see me educated.

'We don't want you trapped here,' they said. Everything I have I owe to this land.

The key kathunks against the smooth taut skin of my sternum, metal matching the heat of its host, thawing as I cool in the dark empty house whose destruction, I have little doubt, Krovik planned from the beginning. There's a word for him but I'm not going to say it. Say a prayer instead. The family Bible is with that same cousin's daughter, the self-appointed matriarch, who likes to think she calls the shots, says who is and is not a Freeman: maiden name, my father's family, they made a stand with that name, a proclamation, self-naming. Call us what we are, what we will be.

So I sold the land in the year Donald died, a few months after he went into the ground and the fire of the Fourth of July. Crazy time, dark time, replacing that short, quiet-too-good-to-last time. A horrible year of noise: loss of Donald, sale of the land, world still going bonkers, a time of sirens and alarms and the gut-wincing thunder of aircraft. I hate that the rest of my life will be spent alone in a world of terror, where terror is all that people talk about, and the language of the Crusades comes thrusting up into the talk of newsmen and politicians, soil-borne disease like *Macrophomina phaseolina* and its charcoal rot, turning language gray, spreading fungus in the drought of our time, through the dryness of speech, conditions inhospitable to growth, to the flourishing of debate: a time in which only the parasite, the fungus, or the weed survives to take over, conquering everything reasonable and rational and good.

Sell the land that nurtures and watch as the world is rent asunder, two halves, unequal in position and condition, dividing my people and me from that which would sustain us. After the sale was final, and the money clanged into my account on a white-hot Tuesday in September, I paid off the bank and the storms of autumn followed, rain and unseasonal hail, thunder and lightning out of time, a late tornado warning and the greening of the humid air, nomadic emerald city of terror and judgment that hovered for an hour, lashed the land, and moved on. I was without debt and, apart from the half-acre patch of ground on which this house still stands, without any land. I should have felt liberated, but instead I felt shackled to a future whose contours I could no longer predict by following the demands of the season.

The year Donald died there were no children at Halloween, and not for the first time. I knew what they called the place, the kids from the surrounding neighborhoods built on other farms ploughed under, some recently, some as long ago as when Rebekah was a child. For years I had heard them riding past on their bicycles in high hot summer, jeering as I kneeled in my vegetable garden, screaming to each other: 'Faster, faster! It's the witch's house! The witch is gonna get you!' Sometimes I was a witch, sometimes a goblin, always a monster, never a human. *Call me Stheno,*

I once shouted, laughing, *I'll show you how terrifying I can be*, and though the name no doubt meant nothing to them, how the children screamed.

When Rebekah was a child I took her all the way round to the city's old northern neighborhoods packed with big frame houses long run-down but full of welcome and friendliness, always cleaner inside than out. Over there Rebekah could go house to house with her cousins in streets where they were not harassed for being themselves. Donald stayed home, said it was no kind of holiday to celebrate: devil's night, hell night, the memory of unholy fires crackling in sacred forms, the way the neighboring farmers in the bad old days did all they could to smoke us out, did nothing to help in the lean years, made sure that if we stood we did so on our own.

But it was not only the silence of Halloween that fall, my first autumn without Donald, it was a deeper, broader silence, an inland sea of quiet, profound and dark as the great aquifer that sleeps below the surface of this land. There were no phone calls for weeks: a month passed and I did not speak to my only child, in her home and her job on the far side of this country. I sat through years of quiet in the long autumn's shortening days, tired through to my tissues and teeth.

Weeds grew up through charred remnants of corn, yellowed in the downshifting light. I tried to see it through, that time before winter, as I had in the past. It was always a season of 'putting': put the vegetable garden to bed, put up jars of green tomatoes and pickled pole beans, put mulch around the kale and Savoy cabbages. The first frost came late, mid-November, woodland rusting ripe at last: everything was out of kilter, the land gone mad from the people upon it. Not just then, but now: *The time is out of joint*, scrabbled, unjust, a country stalked by ghosts.

If it hadn't been for my job we would have starved, gone under, lost the land, would have had no health insurance or benefits if I had not taught English and History and Geography and Social Studies. As a girl I helped in the fields from May to September and as an adult I continued the schedule: driving the tractor, handpicking corn when no one else could be convinced to work for us, picking sometimes in the dark with a headlamp and the sound of cicadas singing themselves to death. It was a life of long hours, blistered hands, calluses embedded with earth: woodskin grain of fingerprint whorls, tree circles on palms, counting the age and the labor, the dry years and wet.

Walking the blackened fields on Thanksgiving morning that year I found the firecracker debris: snatches of glossy red-white-and-blue paper burned along the edges in an undulating smoky brown line. Frost was on the ground but I could still feel the cornfields burning against my face, hot as Donald's finger on my flank, and I'd sat in my house waiting for it to come, doing nothing, feeling in that moment it might be the best way to end:

*while the earth is scorched up with fervid heat ...*
*you become incapable of walking.* And then the rain
arrived, a torrential midnight downpour turning
flame to steam. Even in November I could smell
it, burning corn and the ozone of storm as I looked
down, studied the white rime of crystals edging
black loam. Ink in the milky sky, geese going north.
Cardinals staying, fire in flight, and when the
ground turned white a week later, blood on
the sheets, splattering but leaving no mark.

On the night of the solstice I took out my snow-
shoes and walked the perimeter of land that was
no longer mine. Even under snow I could still
navigate it with my eyes closed, knew the feel of
the land as it rose and fell, the way shadows cut
from the shelter belt on the west side and the line
of woods leading to the reserve on the northern
and eastern sides, the cottonwoods that intruded
into fields where the old streambed crossed the
land in a diagonal arc, where in the wettest years
a river formed, flooded the land, pooled in ponds
that dried only in late summer. It was flawless
land, uncommon in its compact beauty, sheltered
from arctic winds and the worst of western storms.

Rebekah came from California for Christmas
that year, acted like she was indulging me, favor-
making, the condescending so-and-so. The turkey
was wild, my own kill from the edge of the woods.
I had taken aim on a foggy morning, brought it
down while the other birds fled in low flight, then
plucked it in the barn and kept the largest feathers,

85

remembering legends of a Muscogee Creek ancestor in the Freeman line. I imagined fashioning a feather cape, hiding out in the woods, turning myself into a great shimmering black bird.

No sooner had the snow melted the following spring than Krovik arrived with his backhoe or grader, whatever the machine was. The day I took down the storm windows and packed them away between sheets of newsprint in the cellar he began slicing a street off from the main road, intersecting at a perfect perpendicular, making a crossroads, conjuring up the dead. For a week I watched as he drove back and forth, shifting earth still half-frozen, dumping rich dark soil in heaps that would blow away come summer. Eventually he put down gravel, and, once it was warm enough, asphalt over the top, paving the new street and his driveway. I wanted to tell him that asphalt would not hold in this climate, would crack and fracture at the first succession of hard freezes. In the thaw and refreezing, under the pressure of vehicles, potholes would grow. Concrete slabs were the only way, and even they would need annual maintenance. Thinking back on it now, the slipshod approach might have been part of his plan, works needing the intervention of the city.

Some mornings I walked up the new street and offered him a cup of coffee. Not a friendly fellow. Nodded and took the coffee, drank it in front of me, handed back the mug like I was a boss he begrudged. He did not want me there, made that clear from the beginning. When I told him I'd be interested in seeing the plans he said they were still getting worked out, but two hundred houses in all, a nice generous development, large lots, big places, not too many families, the *right kind of people*. Two hundred families on Poplar Farm! My heart fluttered in the chest-cage. I never would have sold if I'd known what he planned.

Krovik sometimes worked alone, often with others: meaty, shirtless men whose skin scorched red, then darkened to cordovan: shoe-leather backs, hides instead of skins, ass cracks rising up pinky-white out of a sheath of dirty blue jeans. The gangly wife came round as the weather turned hot, stood leaning against her car calling out questions, shouting commands, a silent baby in her arms.

Over that summer the house grew up mammoth, a changeling child or goblin birth, haunted mansion from an old horror movie: *Gables of Fear*, *Balcony of Blood*. It was an invasion of the Gothic, colonizing the land. My own house is Greek Revival and I've always been proud of its classical lines. The benefactor Mr Wright's house was of a piece with this one, columns and porticos, perfect proportions, white siding with black shutters. Krovik was building almost on the very site of Wright's burned-down house. I wondered then if I should tell him about the sinkholes, the way the land can open up without warning to swallow whatever rests upon it. Over the years Donald and

I witnessed the sudden dropping of a circle of corn, the disappearance of a tree, and once, a tractor left out in the field overnight was half-submerged in soil the next morning. We learned to ring suspect places with stones, fill them with brush and dead cornstalks, use the soft spots as natural compost heaps that could be filled without ever expanding beyond a gentle sloping mound. There was the big one, too, on property that no longer belongs to me, a soft spot swollen with secrets, marked by two granite stones.

When Krovik's house was finished it emitted a humming sound persistent as an idling car. I woke up in hours that should have been quiet to find a buzz of machinery burrowing into my brain. After the fence went up, almost a foot taller than me, I could only see the top two floors and nothing of his backyard. I have never believed in the edict of good fences making good neighbors and Krovik's stockade fence made me feel I was living in a reproduction fort on a living history farm, wondering when the costumed bandits might come to sack the homestead. At night, even after the house seemed to be finished, I could hear sounds of digging and machinery in motion, see shadows of indistinct shapes monstering the forest.

A moving van came one Thursday late that year, unloaded, left at 2:38 in the afternoon according to my anniversary clock. Except for the distant whirr of the new house, silence settled again, heavy and dense as wool before spinning. I walked my old rooms through a white silence that slowed my steps, swimming upright through a thicket of invisible fibers, sharp with static.

But that was five years ago, and the man is long gone, lost everything: his house, his land, his family. Standing here now, there's a different breed of silence, thinner and less elastic, taut but worn-sounding, liable to snap from the hum of not one but twenty-one houses, all of them machines rather than buildings, idling and running, gearing up and shifting, opening and closing, rotating and hammering, sapping the strength from the world: the life-giving, life-taking spark. I can feel the sound even if there's nothing to hear, the foundation-shaking tremor and purr. In the morning I will go to the woods, find silence again if it still exists there, scan the backyards of those other houses, imagine shouldering my turkey-feather cloak, moving without noise, head ducking, hair pulled back, ears tuned to snapped branches and the squelch of shoes in mud, to the furtive steps of the sneaky coyote or the swift fox stirring in his lair.

The bunker's ceiling is covered with a mosaic of fixtures that flicker and hum, throbbing into a pattern of cold white light so that this space underground is brighter than the most brilliant day, the power draining down from the solar shingles on the roof of the house. Following a new rule, Paul checks the two containment doors, one opening onto the pantry in the basement of the house, the other onto the old stone storm cellar in the woods, both secured with combination locks and treble-bolted. Although he thinks of them as 'containment doors', they are only antiques, salvaged when an old bank downtown was being demolished. Made of concrete encased in stainless steel, one had served as the door to the vault, the other to the bank's safe deposit boxes. At either end of the bunker he pushes and pulls at each door, spins the combination knobs, reassures himself that he is safe and that no one can possibly enter. The noise of the helicopter buzzing overhead has stopped, he will be all right for now, unhunted, undiscovered.

Underground there is only the time he creates

by turning on and off lights, producing the illusion of daytime or night, twilight or dawn. By his watch he knows it is time for dinner in the outside world, but he has already eaten and tries to ignore the hunger carousing in his stomach. As soon as he has checked the containment doors he feels the impulse to return to his house once more: he knows he should resist the desire, but once the thought has surfaced it won't go away until the longing is satisfied.

He enters the combination on the door to the pantry and spins the dial, the movements second nature already, numbers as integral to him as the date of his birth, and as the bolts slide back he feels a euphoric emptying. The door swings open, he crouches on all fours, drops to his stomach, pushes open the wooden panel that opens onto the back of the pantry, and slithers out of the bunker, leaving both hatch and containment door open behind him.

Fumbling along the cool wall, he finds his way out of the pantry and into the single large basement room. The concrete floor that he poured and polished is clammy under his bare feet as he steps across to the carpeted recreation area, working his soles into the pile. He pauses again to listen for the helicopter but everything remains silent. Where there is now only an assortment of half-empty paint cans there was once a small trampoline, a pool table, a fully stocked bar, a large television, collections of toys and leftovers from life above ground. Amanda took the trampoline for the boys, the pool table Paul sold at the estate sale, the booze and glassware he removed to the bunker, though he does not imagine he will ever begin to drink. Amanda was the one with the taste for alcohol. It was the kind of thing her family did, her father pouring glasses of sherry before dinner. Paul has never wanted anything stronger than beer, he has no taste for bourbon or scotch, but the alcohol may have some medicinal purpose in the future, or be useful for barter in the coming war. The greatest worry now is that the new owners, whoever they are, will be on the wrong side. He will not only have to expel them from his house, but do battle against them just to survive. If anything, the whole disaster has taught him that neighbors no longer exist. There is only the individual, alone in the world, with no one to rely on except himself, stamping out the snakes that swarm at his feet. He hears the way his father used to speak to him when he was a boy, Ralph's voice measured, calm, offering lessons to Paul on the long drives back and forth from hunting expeditions: *Today's nation is tomorrow's dead, leaving nothing behind. Society is no more than a wave. You think good days are preparing for you. Do not believe it.*

A car's speakers thud as it drives past on the street above, stops, and disappears into one of the garages Paul designed and that his crew, now working for other men on other jobs, built with their own hands. When he wrote the by-laws for the development he failed to think of car speakers. A rule should have been written stipulating that car stereos must never be audible anywhere in the Dolores Woods development outside of the cars themselves. There are similar requirements about noise from houses. Outdoor music – except music organized by the residents for neighborhood social gatherings at the gazebo – is strictly prohibited. He always meant for it to be a quiet neighborhood, the kind of sanctuary where a man might forget he lives in the twenty-first century and pretend instead it is the nineteenth, where the sound of thudding car speakers and the unwanted noise of neighbors never intrude, where it is possible to live a life of absolute silence and privacy.

While still only in his late twenties, Paul bought the hundred-and-sixty-acre parcel of farmland near the western edge of the existing suburbs, a purchase funded almost entirely by his father-in-law, Robert, a successful divorce lawyer in Miami. After buying the land, Amanda helped facilitate a change in zoning, pushing through the application, greasing the gears and even pressuring a city official who feared that another subdivision of homes could not possibly be sustained by demand. 'I'm risking my reputation for you, Paul,' she warned him at the time.

Paul and Amanda spent the beginning of their life in a condo she bought just after moving here to work in the city planning office, so this was the first property they owned together. Designed to be not only their family home, the house was also the model for the rest of the Dolores Woods development, the keystone in Paul's plan. After building two hundred houses and selling them each for a minimum of $500,000, with the larger ones going for three-quarters of a million or more, he would have become a multimillionaire. It had all made sense on paper. People would want the extraordinary houses he knew he could build. At least, it had all made sense before the crash. History had other plans, but history alone was not to blame. Society, the widow Washington, and his own failings of design and construction, he believes, are the real causes of his decline.

In the beginning, deed in hand, there was nothing around but cornfields, woodland, and the widow in her house at the edge of the property that became his, which he subdivided and plotted, pouring concrete into loam. Despite his determination to do it right, he now recognizes the shortcomings of his plans. Where there should have been two hundred houses there are only twenty-one, but even these, complete as they are, terrify where they were meant to comfort. He wanted to build a neighborhood that evoked the country's pastoral history, but he has, he knows, created something closer to a landscape of nightmare. The lumber warped, the land subsided, houses split: the surveyor was a friend just out of college who, though qualified, did the job fast and on the cheap.

The inspiration for Paul's designs came from an old copy of Andrew Jackson Downing's 1850 pattern book, *The Architecture of Country Houses*. For his own house Paul followed the basic plans laid out by Downing's colleague, architect Alexander Jackson Davis, for a Gothic Revival cottage with, as Davis described it, 'a high, pointed gable' at the center of the front of the house, rising to three stories and containing the front door, an oriel window on the second floor, and a peaked window with a small balcony high on the third. As he revised Davis's plans, Paul's version became larger, the modest lines of the original exaggerated, the ground floor stretching out, and the second and third floors rising to a much greater height so that the balcony outside the third-floor window is not merely ornamental, as it appears to be in Downing's illustration, but accessible through French doors.

Every Sunday at noon Paul turned on the neon OPEN sign hanging in the front window, put out the mat for shoes, and rehearsed his pitch. Some Sundays they had two-dozen prospective buyers, while other weeks no one came. A woman once asked Amanda if she had been hired to pose in the kitchen with Carson. Living in the model was a stupid idea because it meant having to keep everything clean, always looking as though anyone might live there, but he believed that a lived-in house would sell better than the same old model home buyers see everywhere else, houses that look as though no one has ever taken a breath in them. The people who walked into the house and loved it knew exactly what Paul was thinking.

In planning the houses for the whole development, Paul adapted Davis's nineteenth-century designs to modern needs and materials, adding embellishments such as wine cellars and hot tubs, substituting board-and-batten with vinyl siding, putting a brick or stone façade on a frame house, using solar shingles on the rear roofs so they would be invisible from the street. He resisted the open-plan designs favored by most developers, preferring the more traditional arrangement of domestic space into discrete rooms each with a specific purpose. All the houses in Dolores Woods have carved gingerbread verge boards, gabled roofs, garrets and towers and finials and white picket fences or stone walls. For each one he built, Paul used a portion of timber from the cottonwood trees cleared at the edge of the site, thinking it was a respectful way of integrating the properties into the landscape, but none of that salvaged wood was cured properly and all of it warped and cracked in unusual ways. It is not just Paul's house that now looks sinister. The lawyers, bankers, and junior executives who bought those houses understood his ideas, shared in his belief that the past was a better place, that by living in spaces that reminded them of their country's early history they could become different and better people, but when the boards began to twist and the walls split they demanded repairs without charge since the houses were still under warranty, and when Paul resisted, claiming 'natural weathering and settling', all of the owners banded together and sued. That was a major part of his undoing, the whole romantic idea of the poplar wood, but also the land itself, and neighbors who thought themselves nothing more than customers.

The world has now overtaken him. Paul still believes that one day he will finish what he started, plant more trees to replace the ones he cut down, build the rest of the houses, see his vision realized: a whole community, an ideal new town on the fringes of the old, a rational utopia where neighbors look after one another without recourse to the state. In the meantime the woods are unharmed; only a small number of trees have been taken out, just a few compared to all that remain standing. The widow accused him of something terrible, of hating trees, of butchery, but that wasn't true at all.

The trees, not only cottonwoods but ash and maples and linden, are so thick that during the summer the canopy blocks most of the sunlight from the woodland floor while the preserve of mixed forest beyond, blackened with conifers, has the texture of the great old-world forests, rich with folklore and threat, a place both to hide and to lurk, to retreat and lie in wait. The trees are so dense in the preserve that on cloudy days, if you stand in a clearing looking into the depths of the forest, you can see nothing but the first few ranks of trunks, and then total, light-devouring darkness: not just a black hole but a vast undulating mass radiating night even at noon. It is the kind of forest that made early settlers to the area believe they had found a home whose obstacles could be transformed into sanctuary, spaces of utmost threat and uncertainty become their greatest stronghold and protection.

Paul saw the woods for the first time when the land came up for sale. Looking at that surging green darkness it reminded him of forests seen from cars and trains in Germany and Scotland that seemed to beckon with their unknowability, offering an inheritance from his northern European ancestors: forests of wolves and lost children, forests whose folk were good but crafty, compelled by the dangers of the world to be as cunning as the evil forces that always threatened to swallow them. Often he had asked his father to stop the car and let him explore, but they were always in a hurry, 'and besides,' his father would say, 'that's not our land, so it would be trespassing. Plus the only right way to go into a forest is holding a gun.' Paul had wanted to imagine himself out of the present and into the past, running fast through trees, burrowing into a bracken-sheltered bank. Later, after they stopped moving, he went on a school fieldtrip to the nature reserve that Dolores

Woods now abuts, a forest in a region of open plains, where woodland always seems anomalous. Straying to the back of the line as they walked muddy trails, he fell back, out of sight of the teachers who would not quit talking about plants and animals, identifying spoor and scat and warning against wandering from the path. He wanted silence but those women kept chattering in their nasal-keyed voices about poison ivy and oak, ticks and rattlesnakes, and the sheer drop from Demon Point to the river. Where Paul sensed possibility they perceived a world of absolute danger. He stepped behind a bush and held his breath, watching the class disappear over a rise and listening as the voices of the teachers faded. Alone in a way he had never known before, with no adult next to him, he began to run in the opposite direction, past trees and over the leaf-rotting floor, sliding down muddy furrows until he heard his name being called. He ran faster, away from the voices, striking out until he barreled headlong into the arms of his teacher. At the time his father was away on a mission and his mother scolded him, washed his clothes and made him eat tamale pie, kept him from school the next day when he woke with a fever and earache. His hearing must have been affected. If he had heard clearly, he could have been free, alone in the woods for the rest of his life.

Now his hearing has become superhuman: he can hear what is happening in every house in the neighborhood and is astounded at the way his perception of sound seems only to become more acute the longer he spends surrounded by silence. If he holds his breath he can hear what the neighbors are saying, and not just the neighbors, but also his parents in their overstuffed bungalow miles across town. All of them are saying that he is only a dwarf in a large man's body, a little man who imagines he's big just because of his height. They say he was a fool not to see that times were changing, a fool who overstretched and overspent and overpaid, who could not rid himself of the blight that destroyed his business, undermining its foundations and pulling it down into a festering muck. His neighbors and parents do little else but talk about him, denigrating him, making fun of the way he has failed, as if they have no better way to fill their days. When the widow's house finally comes down, the economy recovers, and the buyers return to Dolores Woods, he will get all of it back, everything that was taken from him, and then they will see.

It should have been apparent from the beginning that Amanda would never be committed to her duties as a wife and mother. She was too involved in her work, too intent on having a career, too much an independent woman – a woman, he now understands, who must hate men. As soon as he has the money he will go to court to prove she is unfit, allowing Carson and Ajax to run wild in Florida. He fears his sons will fall into the wrong kind of crowd, become thugs and join gangs and steal cars, sell stolen goods, do drugs, run out of money, lose themselves while Amanda will only be trying to get ahead, ignoring her sons, doing nothing to save them. Paul knows he has to do whatever might be necessary to reclaim the boys and save them from their mother. It is a father's place to shape his sons into good people, carve strength into their limbs, buttress them with manliness. They must not be afraid of truth or fortune or death. They must learn to live fearless lives in a way that only he can teach them. Strength comes from the battles bestowed by fate. *Gods love those whom other men hate.* These are the lessons of the great man that his own father taught him, lessons it is his duty to instill in his sons.

Upstairs the curtains are closed, drawn tight against the neighbors. When everything began to fall apart Paul hoped that perhaps one of the buyers might come forward to offer assistance, to have a word with the bank or extend a line of credit themselves until he got back on his feet. No one did. They were strangers who happened to be neighbors and customers, and though he tried to be friendly he supposes that all of his rule-making might not have been received in the spirit intended, of mutual respect and community cohesion. A community needs a leader, and Dolores Woods was his community, so it always made sense that its creator should be its first leader. Democracy can flourish only in a mature community, and Dolores Woods is still in its infancy. It has to be shown how to live, kept in line, disciplined, and given clear guidelines, just like a group of children. None of those sons-of-bitches so much as came over to say they were sorry to see him lose his house. None of those goddamned neighbors lifted a finger to show they cared about the man who planned this community. Not one of the wives bothered to bake Paul a loaf of bread or bring around a meal when they *knew* that Amanda had left him.

Not a goddamn one of them – except the widow. That old woman was always coming around, asking questions and making trouble. From the beginning he was sure the old bitch had plans, ulterior motives underlying every kindness she showed him in the early days of his ownership. The day Amanda left, Mrs Washington brought him a banana loaf and said she was sorry for him; by then they were no longer on speaking terms, and he did not want her sympathy. Suspecting that the loaf might be laced with rat poison he put it in the trash and did not even read the card she'd written, sure it contained some double-edged sentiment. From the beginning that woman was determined to destroy him. For all he knew, she had cast a spell over the whole neighborhood, was conjuring demons and the forces of darkness to rise up and consume them all. It was not for nothing that the kids in the neighborhood called her a witch.

With the curtains closed Paul moves through his house. The stairs from the basement emerge in the kitchen where wooden cabinetry hides the appliances. He turns on the water at the sink and watches it run down the drain, out of the aquifer and back into the aquifer, a vast internal sea a few hundred feet down. At night, sleeping in his bunker, he dreams that the water is rising up through the sedimentary rocks, lapping at the foundations of the house. Some nights he has woken in panic, covered in sweat. Convinced the bunker is flooding, he has to place his hands on the floor, shine a flashlight into the corners, hold his breath and listen for the gurgling of water until he satisfies himself the bunker is sound and dry.

Across the central hall from the kitchen, the den's walls are lined with empty bookshelves. In the adjoining living room at the front of the house, windows look west and north. Back across the hall, the dining room is a mirror image of the living room, and a vestibular china closet returns Paul to the kitchen. He makes the circuit through the ground floor more than once, pausing each time to run his fingers over the empty bookshelves. When they moved in, the interior decorator filled the den with books. It was only two walls of shelves, but it still astounded him: surely only public libraries, schools, and universities had collections as big; he could not believe that a single person would ever own so many. Amanda wanted none of the books when she left and at the estate sale Paul sold them back to the same interior decorator, who purchased them for another client, another model home, in another part of the city. 'No one reads books anymore,' the decorator said, 'but they're kind of decorative, and they make good noise insulation in condos.'

Passing once again through the open pocket doors connecting the den and the living room, Paul slouches in the bay window seat, looking through a chink in the curtains at the roll of black-green lawn and the low ornamental wall that separates his front yard from the next-door neighbors, that shifty-looking bank manager, who certainly could have done something to help, with his equally suspicious partner, who may be an Arab or an Indian, it's impossible to tell, but who seems to be home all the time with the little girl, pretending to be a normal family. No one is fooled.

Paul paces the axis connecting the living room bay on the north side of the house to the dining room bay on the south, then spends ten minutes circling the central hallway, gazing at the main staircase before he can bring himself to go up to the second floor, where he inspects the four empty bedrooms, each with its own adjoining bath. Without the furniture that once filled these rooms, it is difficult to conjure memories of the ways he and Amanda and the boys inhabited them. He remembers laughter at first, a kind of raucous joy, and then, as months and years passed and the business began to fail, raised voices and tears, the adults always shouting, the boys either pouting or crying.

The top floor of the house, high in the front gable, is a single room, lit by the French window with its pointed arch that opens onto the balcony and has views over the front yard, the whole neighborhood, the woods and fields and suburbs beyond, all the way to the broad flat river west of the city. When the boys were still here, toys packed the room. There was an old-fashioned rocking horse and solid wooden blocks passed down from Amanda's childhood, and, from Paul's mother, bright plastic machines full of electronic noise: action figures and gray space ships, a purple ray gun firing sparks in an enclosed plastic chamber, a laughing white skeleton with sparkling black eyes.

Paul opens the window and steps onto the balcony. At this time of evening no one will be looking. Televisions flash, lights flare on and off, but the blinds and curtains of the neighboring houses are closed. After their house was finished, Amanda stood on the balcony, her hair blowing in a cold late autumn wind, and said she felt like Juliet, or Rapunzel.

'Will we be okay?' she said, turning to him. The crash had already come. Houses were no longer selling.

'Come on, Mandy,' he said, embracing her. 'Don't you believe in me?'

'Of course I do,' she said. 'But I also believe the world is unforgiving. Tell me we'll be alright.'

'You have to trust me. I'm not gonna let you down,' he said, and lifted her up off the balcony, holding her in the air, leaning out over the railing. He felt her grow tense in his hands, her eyes staring into his own. 'You do trust me, don't you, Amanda?' Her lip quivered, she nodded, and Carson started to cry from the floor of the playroom.

Now, alone on the balcony, it takes no effort for Paul to imagine casting his body into the air, being caught by thermals and borne aloft over the land. As a boy he often saw himself rising out of his chair at school and hovering up near the ceiling, looking down on his awestruck teacher and classmates, who would at last recognize and respect him for what he was: born to lead the world. Just as easily, bending over the railing, he can see himself dropping down, bouncing off the porch roof, and how his impact against the flagstone path between the driveway and front door might result in his immediate death. Lifting his feet in the air, he holds on to the railing to see if it will give under his weight: swinging, shifting his center of gravity, he senses the dizzy pull, how it would feel to plummet over the edge, letting the house itself be the agent of his death. The house is not just a part of him: he is the house. The house is the way he sees himself: the peaks and wings, the hard, undulant lines and disproportionate scale. If he must die, the house should kill him. Momentum tilts him forward: he nearly goes too far, at the last moment throwing his torso back and coming to land on the balcony, its beams shuddering under the sudden jolt of his weight. A solid house would not shudder. A house built to last would shake only under tectonic forces.

Having spent so many early years in houses that fell short in one way or another, in neighborhoods so sterile and geometric that they thwarted happiness, Paul dreamed of creating instant communities, which would protect their inhabitants just as they invited a form of neighborly sociability tempered by privacy. He wanted not only to work on the construction of houses, as he had during summers in high school, not just to set up a carpentry and contracting business, but to design homes that aspired to a vision of residential America so distilled it could only improve the lives of the people within them. It had been his adolescent dream to design houses that would be places of safety as well as congregation, set in neighborhoods where the streets and public areas, the parks and sidewalks, would be half-enclosed by trees and low hedges, walls and fences, with pergolas and bandstands and gazebos: an idyllic small-town American space with enough land between houses that neighbors need never hear the secrets of one another's intimate lives.

'An architect?' his father said. 'I've never needed an architect. I don't – you have to understand, Paul – I don't understand the point of being an architect. I'm not saying it's wrong, but I'm saying I think you could choose better. Why don't you join the Air Force?'

'I don't like flying,' Paul remembers protesting. 'I don't even like birds.' He knew from an early age that military discipline wasn't for him. His father had made Paul fold his clothes according to military rules: t-shirts in six-inch squares, underwear in tight white sausages. From the age of twelve Paul got a haircut every Sunday night after dinner. Ralph put down towels in the living room while Dolores used the electric clippers: number three on the sides and four on top. That was a compromise, because Ralph wanted his son's hair shorter, buzzed all over, and Paul wanted it longer. As he sat in the chair, his father watching while his mother managed the clippers, Paul knew he was getting only the smallest taste of what real military life would be like.

His father said that if he wanted to go to college instead of serving his country Paul would have to do it on his own. For Ralph, Paul understood, it was a matter of principle; there was nothing vindictive about the position. The Kroviks had always been military men and Paul was the first to fail in this legacy. His grades were decent but not good enough for a scholarship, so he knew that if he wanted a college education he would have to support himself. Ralph asked him to be out of the house by his nineteenth birthday, which was, thank God, a whole year after the end of high school, so Paul had time to get himself organized, save up money, apply to college. Friends of his were not so lucky, and found themselves, on the day they turned eighteen, shown the door by their parents. At least his mother kept saying to him, 'I believe in you, Pablo. You can do it. You're gonna make it.' She slipped him money, bought groceries on the sly, did whatever she could to help without Ralph finding out.

Paul was accepted into the architectural studies program at State. He took out loans and worked three jobs. He spent two years in college but couldn't keep up with the tuition and fees and left without a degree. Not long after that he met Amanda. She was already working in the city's planning department, well on her way to having a good career. So while Paul got on his feet with the construction business and secured his contractor's license, she supported them. Six months after their first meeting they were married.

Looking at the neighborhood now, Paul understands that he lacked adequate training. In their finished form, there is something obviously wrong with both the design and execution of the houses, in the way he has situated them on their lots, the way the lots were apportioned and the streets laid out, even something amiss in the neighborhood's landscaping: the sidewalks are too narrow, the parkways too broad, the berms designed to deaden the sound of traffic from the main road too angular, too steep, too high. The neighborhood

109

looks expansive and yet insubstantial, the jerrybuilt back lot of a movie studio where houses exist only as façades, the gardens and parkways too immaculate to feel as though any of it grew up organically, one house at a time.

The main stairs lead him back down to the foyer. He built the two sets of stairs believing that one day he and Amanda might have a live-in maid who would be restricted to the steep narrow 'service stairs' while the family used the broad front staircase. It was a selling point for the development and a full half of the houses completed have this added feature, though as far as Paul knows not one of the families in Dolores Woods has any live-in help.

As he opens the door, sniffing the warm air for signs of other people, he catches grass cuttings, pesticides, and the ozone exhaust of air conditioning units, the smell of a late evening barbecue, but no bodies. Leaving the door ajar, he walks down the path to the driveway and mailbox, itself a handcrafted miniature of the house, mounted on a brick pillar. Inside he finds several pieces of mail, all for the new owners, Nathaniel and Julia Noailles. How is the name pronounced? No-ales? No-els? No-ills? It sounds foreign. Taking the envelopes back up the driveway, Paul opens the lid of the shed that holds the garbage cans and throws the mail inside. People have to learn to be more responsible. They must be taught.

Back behind the locked door he slumps to the

floor. Beside him he sees a spot where he tracked in dirt, but when he tries to wipe it away with the cuff of his shirt the stain spreads – tar rather than dirt – and in the light coming in from the street he sees it expand, sharp lines of black breaking against the grain of the wood. He spits and rubs but the stain only gets larger and as he works at the mark tears erupt from deep in his viscera. By the time the stain has spread across the width of the hall he gives up. It is no longer his responsibility; the new owners can deal with the mess.

In the basement Paul turns on all the lights over the recreation area to read the engraved brass plaque mounted in the wall: PAUL KROVIK BUILT THIS HOUSE. He feels the sharp indentations of the letters. Except for a low buzz the house is silent, and then, somewhere more distant, on the other side of the foundation walls, there is an irregular vibration, a scuffling sound he has not noticed in the past.

Turning off the lights and dropping to his knees, crawling back across the floor and into the pantry, under the shelf at the back, through the open hatch, following the pinkish glow that comes from inside the bunker, fluorescent light reflecting off its deep red walls, pulling the hatch shut behind him, Paul throws its flimsy lock, then stands, heaves closed the containment door in a single movement, and engages its own lock. Listening to the bolts slide into place as he spins the combination

111

dial, he rests his head against the cold metal surface. Breath comes in a pant; his hands are shaky, legs calf-wobbly.

When the new family arrives he will have to come and go through the storm cellar at the back of his bunker, entering and exiting his home through the woods. It will take time and determination to turn things around, to rebuild his business and fight for his family. Apart from his truck, everything he now owns is in the bunker's two bedrooms, bathroom, kitchen and living space, all of the rooms opening off the long hallway. The distance from one containment door to the other is nearly two hundred feet, long enough that he can run back and forth to keep in shape. He has mounted a bar in the door of the second bedroom and does chin-ups every morning before going out through the back entrance to look for work. He has a cell phone that costs him little each month and the tools he needs to perform small contracting jobs. He will build shelves and renovate kitchens and undertake structural repairs. He parks his truck on a different street every night. He will plan, prepare, and be ready to win back his sons, to rescue them before the final reckoning, returning them to this place of absolute safety.

In the meantime, he will wait for the inevitable, for the arrival of people with a name he cannot say.

I no longer remember when the first trees came down, but it was around the time Krovik laid out the roads, must have been five years ago, in the late autumn of the year he finished his own house, before the ground froze again and I put up the storm windows for another winter. I watched him cut his twisting snake deeper into the land, zing down stray cottonwoods at the edge of the arable fields. I grew acquainted with the clattering whoosh and thump of trees falling, the growling thunder of wood chippers and two-stroke screaming of saws, the cutting chains slicing into treeflesh. I might as well have been camped on a log run. When I inquired with the city if there was any way to stop Krovik felling more trees – conservation laws, public nuisance laws, zoning laws – a tart young woman in the planning office said, 'The land belongs to Mr Krovik now, he can do what he likes, Ms Washington. It doesn't sound to me like he's breaking any laws.'

'But these are good trees. There's nothing wrong with them except they're a little old.'

'The health of the trees is irrelevant, ma'am. The

property is his. You sold it to him, he can do what he likes, within the zoning laws, and he's had the property zoned for residential development. Just be glad he's improving the value of the land by putting up houses. It's good for the tax base.'

'I don't see how that improves the value of land that had no need for improvement in the first place,' I said, hanging up before the woman could answer.

I searched the city ordinances but could find no laws to curb Krovik's felling. Laws against nature did not count. Laws against vandalizing a canvas of land as balanced in its composition as a fine painting are not on the city's schedule of ordinances. Those trees saw the land through wars and droughts and fires, through crime and benefaction. They were trees of memory and witness.

At last I mustered strength to speak to him, drew my body as tall as it has ever stood, marched up the road to face him and his chainsaw crew, my arms aquiver with rage.

'Are you going to take them *all* down?' I shouted, pointing at the untouched shelterbelt and the body of woods that rides into the reserve. No longer knowing the slope of the land where his machines had flattened it, I stumbled and one of the men caught my arm before I fell to the ground. I could smell his meat breath and the sweat on his arms carving channels through sawdust.

Krovik removed his headphones and baseball cap and raised a hand to tell his men to stop.

'What'd you say?'

'Is it your intention to fla – to take, I mean, to *cut* all of them down?' Words turned to prickly burrs and caught on my gums.

'Take down what, Mrs Washington?'

'The trees! Are you going to take down every one of them? When I sold I said I didn't want you chopping down the trees. You remember that?'

He looked around, confused, a brute pillager. Opening his mouth, lips thin, hard-pink steel blades, he laughed – not a malicious laugh, but one of power and disregard.

'Don't you worry,' he said, cackling. 'I'm just taking down a few to make room for the roads and houses. I'll plant others if it looks bare. Don't you worry. I'm a good guy, Mrs Washington. I like trees too.'

'But I *insisted* when I sold you this land that I wanted the trees left. I understood you were going to build houses but there's no reason to be cutting down the trees. Lord, you *promised* you wouldn't cut them down, not a one of them. You said you wouldn't so much as *touch* them, that you'd build around them!'

He laughed again, right in my face, crowing at a woman who gives a damn about trees.

'I didn't make no promise. Did I sign anything saying I wouldn't cut them down?'

'You gave me your word, Mr Krovik. You swore up and down in front of me and my daughter and my lawyer that you would not fell a single tree.'

'Mrs Washington, that's a conversation I can honestly say I don't recall. Now you better get on your way or else you might just find yourself under a tree.'

'Don't you threaten me, Mr Krovik.'

'It's not a threat. I'm just sayin', we have to get back to work. And the work we're doing is cutting down trees. Now if you want to stay, then go ahead, but this is my land, and technically you're trespassing on it. So if something happens to you while you're on my land, even after I've told you to go, well then, I can't be held responsible so far as I see it.'

At night, when the chainsaws were put away, I went out with a flashlight, counted the stumps, bore witness to the demise of the witnesses, heard their fall and observed their deaths. A hundred and sixty trees in all were brought down, one for each acre. I leaned over every stump, laid a cheek against the wound, felt the rings with my fingers, saw the events of centuries inscribed in undulating crescents, blood etching the grain.

Over the course of the next couple of years, more houses went up. His wife had another child, and Krovik's roads cut into the land, preparing for two hundred houses where only twenty-one have come: blackjack, dealer's hand. Not that the construction of those he completed was anything but a nightmare. I learned to stay away during working hours. At first I did nothing but drive around town, shocked at the way the city's infection was spreading, consuming the land that created it in the first place. Later, I started going to a bookstore, until it closed, just like the public libraries. Where do people find books in this town? I thought of teaching myself a new language, but I couldn't see the point since I have no intention of travelling. I thought for a while of researching a subject that interests me, like the life cycle of spiders, or wine-making, or mythology, but again I was unsure what the knowledge would do apart from fill the hours. A month later I started spending weekend after-noons watching two or three movies in a row at the multiplex, whether I wanted to see them or not. After the movies I would drive downtown and eat a plate of spaghetti at a restaurant in the Old Town, surrounded by families and groups of teen-agers, the only woman eating alone. Sometimes I would run into former students who would greet me as 'Mother Washington', throw their arms around me and ask how I was doing, expressing what always seemed like genuine sadness when they heard of Donald's death, although most had never met him.

Without Donald everything seemed pointless. It was not about having a man. I never felt myself determined by Donald. Living alone, I became convinced, was not good for my sanity. A grand-child would make things better, if not easier. A grandchild might rekindle my rapport with Rebekah. There is no reason my daughter, only child of an only child, should have wished to become a farmer herself and I never begrudged her the choice. Nursing is just as good a job as farming, caring for the world instead of feeding it, and not dissimilar in spirit. If we'd had another child (we certainly tried), someone who could have sat on Donald's lap learning the land and its idiosyncrasies, the way the climate cannot be trusted to provide from year to year, how you might make a small killing in one harvest and have almost nothing by the end of the next, the way most people round these parts did not want to take orders from a man like Donald, well then it would have made being alone much easier. Seeing that child grown up, taking over the house, expanding, buying up land to turn one hundred and sixty acres into three hundred and twenty or a thousand, what a dream it would have been. But that kind of hope is over. Instead I hope for a grandchild who might become a good person and have children of her own. Hope is not a bird. Feathers are too fragile for hope. Hope is an aging tree that might still drop its seed in a barren world.

It was then, in the weekends at the multiplex, in the dinners at the spaghetti place, that I started to think about going back to work. Teaching takes all one's time, eats up the free hours with grading and lesson plans and reading. I always tried to stay current, expanding my knowledge widely and hungrily. Teaching – the care and nurture of children – would give me purpose again, if only I could find my way back to it, if my former colleagues do not think I am too long out of practice, too far behind, too old to manage the demands of an ever-changing classroom. But the weight of the days drags at my arms; my feet are tired old dogs, and I am past the age of retirement. It might be too much after all. Perhaps I no longer have that kind of energy, the patience and stamina required to lead and illuminate a whole class of children.

Standing here at the kitchen sink, looking up at Krovik's house, I straighten my back, think I see movement upstairs, a presence, a ghost, but the house is vacant. It must have been the reflection of a passing aircraft. There is no stillness on this earth. Everywhere is the movement of machines: if not on land, then underground, overhead, or slicing through seas. I want to scream for it all to stop, for the human world to silence itself and sit still, turn off the lights and put down its collective head on the table of our self-concocted ruin and let the earth recover.

Not that I am without purpose, for I know, however else I may have failed the land, I am still the keeper of its tale. I have never told it to Rebekah in the way I should have. A grandchild might still come, be receptive, listen to the story of Great-Uncle George and Mr Wright, benefactor of the Freeman family, patron in so many ways, giver who also took, beneficiary of free bodies and cheap labor. Fair terms, the family story always went, Mr Wright offered fair terms from the

119

beginning, never tried to take more than his due, took less than others might. He was a peculiar man, Morgan Priest Wright, an unlikely politician who knew he was strange and hid only what could get him killed, then failed in that hiding and got himself killed. A reformist from a family of reformers, he was descended from generations of abolitionists and freethinkers. I have kept his story, written it more than once, as other versions flower from memory: the way my mother told it, hard facts my father left out, details gathered from aunts and uncles and grandparents, the hearsay of family friends and social historians. I've recorded all I can remember and discover. I keep recording and collating, hoping someday to nail down what I know in a version I can leave behind. Speech passes like wind, its effects ephemeral, unless the speech is a tornado stripping bare the land, revealing new surfaces for new growth. What seeds will I sow?

In the years after Krovik's coming, sleep became nightmare: trees burning blood, Donald burning, Krovik with a match and a chainsaw, a monster from a horror movie like ones I saw years ago, like new ones, too, the worse ones I watched on those long weekend afternoons at the multiplex, people spliced with animals, bodies cut apart and re-assembled, folks more mechanical than human. I knew about such men, warping weapons out of tools, slinking through my mind and then suddenly, without warning, flourishing weedstrong in an inhospitable environment. I tried to kill him off in my dreams, or make him something better, but my idea of Krovik grew rank and ugly, spreading on runners that colonized every quarter of my thoughts. Once established, he could only be eliminated by poisoning every acre he occupied, killing off the innocent as well, burning it all to the ground. He was too strong for me, too relentless, spawning his colony of horror houses across land I can no longer call Poplar Farm. That place is dead, a name meaningless to anyone else but Rebekah, who never liked her home in the first place, never caught the farming spirit.

Some days, to escape the horror of Krovik's construction, I drove to the cemetery, sat in a camp chair next to Donald's grave, writing and rewriting what I know about Mr Wright, and not just about him, but all the stories of my family. I worked through a stack of spiral-bound class record books left over from my teaching years. In those shaded grids where I once would have recorded attendance and progress, I found a form for my purpose. Appropriate, it seemed, to record the attendance of my family on this land, their own progress, the successes and failures, the leave-takings and murders, years bumper and lean, in books designed to measure the submission and resistance of pupils to an educational regime. Like students, the Freeman and Washington families were subjects of the nation, submitting at times

121

and resisting at others, too often paying an arbitrary price, as if they'd had the bad luck of being assigned to the classroom of a petty tyrant. I knew teachers like that, shriekers and ruler-snappers, bulging-eyed gorgons beaten by their husbands as women and by their fathers as girls, or male autocrats who thrashed their wives and daughters, all of them people who had no place in a classroom. I prided myself on being firm but kind, a mother to children too often motherless.

I cannot conquer my hate for that man. His vehicles moved the earth until it was no longer land, but something harder and smoother. Even the grass he planted looks artificial, synthetic turf that could be vacuumed and scrubbed with detergent to get rid of the dirt, flowers that never seem to die, an unnatural theme park of a neighborhood full of pointy-headed, bulging-stomached houses that growl and bluster and buzz.

Until this year, every night in summer I walked the street from my home to the last of Krovik's finished houses, swinging a flashlight at my side so the people indoors could tell I wasn't trying to pass unnoticed. I did not want the police called with reports of a prowler, knowing what my neighbors would see, a shadow grown huge by the light of the moon, a *spook* – and I knew when they spoke it they would mean more than just a *ghost*, would hiss that ugly word with the dark bellows of history in their lungs. People like that, they see darkness everywhere and try to create a world without night, believing that light is the only source of good. They do not know the beauty of blackness, the glory of the dark earth. Their lights are everywhere, flooding gardens and houses, blocking out stars. For the first time, I knew summer evenings with no fireflies, as though the creatures saw the light of those blazing houses and realized they were outmatched.

Now, I light my candle in this house I am no longer meant to occupy, condemned for committing the crime of surviving the development of the city around it. I clutch curtains tight where they meet and hope I will be allowed to sleep undisturbed for another eight-hour stretch. I am not leaving my house. I will not leave it until the city comes to tear it down, and even then only in a body bag, suffering under its collapse, repenting for the sale that brought all this to pass, for my lack of faith in the land and what it might still bring forth. I walk the planks, slip off my shoes and peel out of my socks to let my feet feel the boards worn smooth by the passage of lives, boards warm in this late summer night, as if the wood has its own life force, interrupted by the felling and planing but still pulsing a latent rhythm, waiting to be reawakened by purpose: wood put to use with function and utility, practicality and reason, instead of the willful clearing of trees to improve the view or increase the property value, to make room for swimming pools and decking made from lumber shipped across thousands of miles. No chopping down and using the odd trunk to make gingerbread boards for dishonest houses. That was never the spirit of this land. The photos from Grandma Lottie and Grandpa John's days record the trees I have known all my life. They are more intact, with fewer limbs missing from the high winds and tornado days that have intervened, but they are recognizably the same. Most of them are now gone to the Krovik chainsaw, the cottonwoods of history brought down. Only the great body of woods remains, and for that I must be grateful: that Krovik did not penetrate the heart, satisfying himself with dismemberment and decapitation. The woods can no longer think or move, and yet they will go on beating in their hard-diminished way, dull-witted but living.

In the middle of their three-day drive from the East Coast, buffeted by semi-trucks and four-wheel-drive sport utility vehicles through rain so dense and blinding they eventually cannot see the cars in front of them, they are forced to break for the second night sooner than planned in a tiny town ten miles off the interstate where the only motel is all but full of truckers. Although he has allowed himself to be persuaded by Julia this is the right decision, that their futures lie somewhere beyond – far beyond – the city where they have built their lives together so far, Nathaniel can't escape the feeling that the move is not just idiotic but potentially catastrophic. The feeling, he thinks, handing over his credit card to one of the two fat girls behind the desk at reception (the other one watches the local weather report, which forecasts more of the same, 'Biblical rain,' the meteorologist shouts into the camera, eyes goggling), is rooted not only in a negative reaction to moving away from his hometown, or the panic he feels at transferring to a more senior position in his company, but in the new house itself and in the prospect of living out a span of his life on the margins of a provincial city. He is un-prepared for suburban life. He does not speak the language of lawns and yard mainten-ance, of barbecues and block parties and Independence Day picnics, soccer and Little League and all the social pressures he imagines will accom-pany their days in Dolores Woods. His parents never taught him that language. They did their best, he knows, to be sure he had no chance to learn it.

With the keys in their possession, and the time until their arrival at the new house measurable in hours rather than days or weeks, the three of them sharing a motel room last redecorated twenty years ago, the curtains and bedspreads reeking of cigarette smoke even though it is supposed to be a non-smoking room, the crunch of the ice dispenser outside their door pulling him out of sleep every half hour as the party of truckers down the hall stumbles along to fill up their buckets for another round of beers, Nathaniel feels feverish with doubt and regret, holding his breath as three men laugh outside in the hall, cigarette smoke filtering under the door, ice cubes rattling into cheap plastic, stories of sexual conquests stage-whispered among the men and audible in the room. He wants to tell them to shut up and go back to bed, to warn them they are disturbing the sleep of his wife and child, but he fears what they might do to a man as small and obviously weak as he is. He picks up the phone to complain to the front desk but it rings and rings and no one answers.

*    *    *

The house has been empty for some time, and their realtor, Elizabeth, warned them it would need to be cleaned before their arrival. Remembering the many rooms, they decided to hire professionals. Julia, who, after her mother's suicide, grew up under the distracted care of her father in a subsiding eighteenth-century house outside of Portsmouth, has always been fanatical about cleanliness in a way that Nathaniel is not. This morning she showers twice – once before breakfast at the diner across the street from the motel, once after. 'It was filthy,' she says as they pull back onto the interstate, 'it made my skin crawl. Didn't you want to shower again?' There are times when Nathaniel wonders, noticing his wife's occasional tendency towards compulsive behavior, whether Julia might have inherited some aspect of her mother's mental illness.

Approaching the city from the east, they cross a bridge over a river that makes its way through several states in its course from the Rocky Mountains all the way to the Gulf of Mexico. The river is high, out of its banks around the airport, flooding the parking lot of a waterfront restaurant and swamping the marina. Despite this, the city does not look as bleak as Nathaniel remembers: the new baseball stadium gleams and a handful of skyscrapers suggest larger ambitions. In the last fifteen years the city limits have expanded five miles to the west, from 144th to 204th Street, with countless residential subdivisions enveloping outlying small towns. The city is now wider than Manhattan is long by more than three miles, occupying almost four times the total land area, but has only half a million residents – twice that if the even larger 'metropolitan area' of farming communities is included, homesteads laid out in this stretch of country between two rivers, a territory so resolutely unmetropolitan the designation as such would be laughable, Nathaniel thinks, if it were not at once both so desperate and so patronizing.

As the highway turns into Poplar Road, shooting east to west in a straight line, the polish of the riverfront fades. Most of the downtown area is a patchwork of the new and the recently abandoned: buildings only twenty or thirty years old, which must have glistened in their day, are now vacant, the windows boarded up or smashed, OFFICE SPACE and FOR RENT signs covered in graffiti of floating genitalia and cartoons of sexual couplings, captioned with language that makes Nathaniel want to cover his son's eyes. For a mile or more Poplar cuts through urban wastelands at the fringe of the downtown before crossing the major six-lane highway running north and south, then climbs a hill past the glass and steel conglomeration of buildings that makes up the national headquarters of Nathaniel's company.

'There it is,' he says, trying to sound proud, hoping Copley will look at the place where his father is going to work and feel some sense of significance. But the neighborhood quickly diminishes once again, sidewalks cracked and overgrown, pavement buckling, houses with flaking paint, broken windows, and rotting woodwork, a stretch of stores and mid-twentieth-century developments largely vacant, and then a sudden flourishing of wealth: mansions from the 1920s and '30s built on small lots along curving streets thick with trees that surround the university and the largest of the city's parks. Nathaniel and Julia looked at houses in this neighborhood but could find nothing in their price range. After that brief stretch of residential prosperity, Poplar rolls into a corridor of commercial development, of strip malls and fast food restaurants, big box stores and medical centers, corporate offices, a shopping mall, banks, another labyrinth of highways racing beneath it in all directions, and then the beginnings of the most recent suburban developments, one after another, until the road narrows from six lanes to four to two, and seems about to peter out into gravel and dirt, to bisect farmland, easing them down to the abrupt right turn into Dolores Woods, which feels in the hot misty late summer like nothing so much as a mosquito-ridden swamp, waiting for the next torrent of rain in the system that is sweeping across the continent. They will not stay here tonight; the movers come tomorrow, but they wanted to be sure everything is in order, the floors polished, shelves dusted, the basement and garage mopped.

At their direction, a landscaping company has cut the grass and pruned the shrubs on either side of the flagstone path that leads from the driveway to the front porch, leaving the cuttings in an existing compost heap behind the garage. For a moment Nathaniel wonders if he should carry Julia over the threshold, but his back would never manage it and Julia would protest even if he tried. They have never been that old-fashioned kind of couple, nothing like Nathaniel's parents, who did not allow Julia to stay in their house until she and Nathaniel were married. In any case, there is no longer time for gallant silliness: once again rain is slashing and bucketing and blanketing down, and although they are dry in the shelter of the front porch, the three of them rush indoors.

Paul is in the kitchen when the new people arrive. The cleaners nearly caught him yesterday, clattering their equipment against his floors. He was in Carson's old room as the brigade of six women in red and white uniforms surged shouting through the front door. When he heard them, he crept down the back stairs, angling through the kitchen and into the basement before anyone knew he was there.

Car doors slam. He ducks below the height of the windows but not before catching a glimpse of brown hair under a green hood. Keys in the front door, the rush of sound when it opens, rain on the pavement and roof. Crouching in the kitchen, he listens as the man and woman talk in loud voices, and then hears a third set of footsteps.

No-ales. No-els. No-ills.

Three of them: two vocal, a silent third.

Trying to decide what to do, he waits while they stand just feet away from him in the hall. If he coughed they would hear him. If he squeaked his heels they would know they were not alone.

'God, it's so dark in here,' he hears the woman say. 'I'm going to check the kitchen.'

Holding his breath, he hears her weight against the boards. She's coming down the hall rather than through the dining room. He can smell her perfume – roses, like his mother – as he slips out of the kitchen and down the stairs to the basement. At the bottom of the stairs he hides behind the banister, looks up, glimpses shoes and slacks, and ducks away before he can be seen, dashing into the pantry, wriggling through the hatch, easing it closed as all three of them stomp around his kitchen. Without closing the containment door he stretches out the length of his body along the floor, his ear grating against the wooden hatch, listening to the intruders.

Marching ahead of his parents through the house, Copley is making his odd noises, the whirring, whistling, churning sounds that unnerve Nathaniel, seeming, as they do, to suggest that his son may be not merely an eccentric child but a disturbed one. The noises only started in the last few weeks,

after boxes began to appear, clothes and ornaments packed, trifles given away. The noise-making
began with chirps in place of 'yes' or 'no', birdlike
trills that evolved into more guttural mechanical
sounds, which in turn replaced other words and
phrases: 'maybe', 'uh-oh', 'not now', 'good
morning', 'goodnight', 'please stop', 'leave me
alone', 'I'm hungry'. Julia kept what she called a
'lexical and syntactical score', writing musical
notation keyed to the meanings of the sounds so
far as she understood them.

'This is just acting out,' Nathaniel told her as
the pace of the noise production increased in the
days leading up to the move. 'It's attention-seeking
behavior.'

'It may be, but it's not random. He's consistent.
It's all very considered,' Julia said.

Since leaving Boston it has been noises instead
of speech most of the time, but in place of the
intricate sonic vocabulary of recent weeks, there
has been a marked regression: beeps and shrill
ascending notes in affirmative answer to questions;
descending ones if Copley means 'no'; a flat, staccato *zzzhhh* if he feels noncommittal or unwilling
to express more complex meaning. There are times
when Nathaniel wants to throw something at his
son – a glass of water, an apple, a vase – and tell
him to knock it off and act like a human being.
Nathaniel's own father had done this very thing,
once throwing a cup of coffee in his face over
breakfast when he judged Nathaniel's responses

to questions were somehow inadequate: too mono-syllabic, too churlish. 'Speak when you're spoken to,' Arthur Noailles had snapped. 'Don't be a goddamn savage.' The coffee had been sitting in the cup for ten minutes and was no longer hot but it was warm enough to hurt for a moment, and the act so violent that Nathaniel had fled from the dining room and locked himself in his bedroom for the rest of the day. It was not the only time Arthur had done such a thing.

When Nathaniel now feels himself moved to throw something at Copley, he retrieves that memory of coffee splashing in his face, how he chucked out the clothes he'd been wearing, putting them in a neighbor's trashcan the next morning on his way to school with the note from his mother pressed into his hand while his father was glowering in the other direction, a note explaining he had been sick the previous day. If he happens to smell the mass-produced brand of coffee his father drank, he invariably feels a passing surge of nausea.

Until the last few months, Nathaniel and Copley have had a happy if sometimes challenging relationship – challenging because Copley is so intelligent and, at the same time, even before the mechanical noise-making began, not the most natural, the most human, communicator: a boy late to speak and willing to converse only ever on his own terms. The joy of having a child, Nathaniel always imagined, would be in reaching the point when said child could reason and have intelligent

133

conversations. Copley learned to read at three and should, at the age of seven, finally be at that stage. To Nathaniel's growing frustration and distress, however, when he now asks Copley a question, his son often looks as though the terms of the query are so illogical that he does not know how to respond and out will come the mechanical *zzzhhh*, the sound of an older computer processing itself to the point of smoking exhaustion. In a particularly good mood, Copley might shrug in silence, but most of the time the boy acts like his father has said nothing at all, paternal speech a thing his neural circuits cannot interpret. Even though she is opposed to the idea, Julia has agreed it might be worth taking the boy to see a psychiatrist: 'The books say it's the move. He needs to adjust. He *will* adjust. But yes, I agree,' she says, 'it's getting a little out of hand.'

Nathaniel watches his son march out of the hall and into the kitchen. Cupboard doors open, accompanied by new sounds, as if the little machine were curious or surprised or disappointed by what he finds. Whatever else Nathaniel may feel about this behavior, Copley undoubtedly has a sense of humor, and that in itself must suggest he is something other than a psychopath, sociopath, or any of the other psychiatric diagnoses Nathaniel fears might be applicable given what he knows about the history of mental illness on Julia's side of the family.

'Does it still feel the same to you?' he asks his

wife as they stand in the dining room looking at the walls and wooden floors. The rain outside strengthens, pinging against the panes, and a gust of wind sideswipes the house, rattling the windows along the north and west sides, howling drafts through the chimney, while the top of the building groans as if gearing up to twist off its axis. The air conditioning has been left on and the house is frigid and dry. The word *sepulchral* comes to mind, but this doesn't seem quite right. Surely a house can't be *sepulchral*.

Although it might have seemed spacious and characterful on first glimpse, back in the middle of summer, it now feels exactly like what it is: vast, empty, and dark, the corners thin and sharp, as if the whole structure were caught in an enervated spasm. There is a quality to the space, the arrangement of rooms, the proportion of wall-to-window, the heaviness of the crown molding and baseboards, that makes Nathaniel feel claustrophobic. A shiver ripples round his shoulders and down his back. Despite the rain, he tries to open the windows in every room he enters, but they are all locked. He loosens his collar, unbuttons his shirt another notch, ruffles his hair to get the sense of a breeze moving through it. I'm having a panic attack, it's just a panic attack. There's nothing wrong with the place. Calm yourself. Breathe in and out, there's plenty of oxygen. Catching his reflection in one of the windows, he thinks for an instant that someone else is in the room.

'Do we have keys to the windows?'

Julia is taking notes, squinting into dark corners. 'It must be one of these,' she says, pressing a ring of keys from the realtor into his palm. None of the keys is small enough to fit into the window locks.

'We'll have to get a locksmith. We have to be able to open the windows. We can't spend our lives in a house with windows that don't open. It has to be some kind of fire risk or health violation.'

'There are lots of things to do. Calm down,' Julia says, making a note on her clipboard. He can see the word, LOCKSMITH, but it doesn't help. Staring at the empty patterned walls in the dining room he is unable to move, catching his own reflection every time he turns to look out a window onto the dark gray world. All this space! Endless, suffocating, all-consuming space! Maybe it isn't too late to pull out. Of course it's too late. Everything is signed, transferred, transacted. The keys and the house are theirs, the mortgage their burden, the structure and the land it sits upon their new responsibility. God, what a mistake!

As Copley returns from the kitchen, marching across the room, Nathaniel recognizes the steps from the dance recital: the woman taught his son to march like a tin soldier in *The Nutcracker*. The dance class was another mistake. Soccer would have been better – or more swimming lessons. His son had excelled at swimming and there was no expectation that the parent should be involved

136

except as a spectator, no pressure to run and pass balls, to attempt footwork impossible for a body that knows nothing about sports. It is not as if there is anything suspect about a boy with an aptitude for swimming in the way there is with a boy inclined to dance. Nathaniel saw the way friends raised their eyebrows when they heard about the dance class, when Julia invited some of them to the embarrassing recital – embarrassing because Copley was such a *natural*, convincing and fluid and not remotely self-conscious in his movements, so incredibly fey and graceful. That was the real horror. If only the physical intelligence could be channeled into a more masculine discipline, not that Nathaniel cares what kind of person Copley becomes. If he happens to fall in love with men later in life, Nathaniel will of course accept it, but he does not want a son who prances.

The three of them walk circles around the ground floor in the way they did with Elizabeth the realtor, who was so persuasive even as her spiel set Nathaniel's mind racing along a fast-branching trajectory of horrific complications and hidden flaws in the structure. He agrees with Julia that the reproduction Morris wallpapers and painted moldings have to go; the place will look better, more like them, when the walls and ceilings are uniformly white.

'You still love it, though?' he asks her. She jerks back her head, looking surprised.

'Of course I do. It's about the house, Nathaniel,

not the way it's been decorated. You'll see. This house really *has* something.'

After living for so many years in only a few rooms, Nathaniel has to admit feeling relief in finding himself at last with the kind of space he knew as a child – in fact with a larger house than the one in which he and his brother Matthew were raised. He has always worried about Copley growing up in an apartment, fearing that high-density living and separation from nature might be having a kind of distorting effect on the boy's mind. The behavior of recent months has seemed *to bear out this hypothesis*, as Julia is fond of saying. Here, in this new town and this new house, the boy can run free in the fenced backyard, lie down under trees and find a way of relating to the world as Nathaniel did in his own childhood. He will teach Copley to climb, perhaps even hire a carpenter to build a tree house. On weekends, the three of them can unlock the back gate and step right into the woods, a portion of which now belongs to them, and from there hike straight into the nature reserve and all the way to the great broad river, sit on the bank, fish for hours, pack a picnic, pretend they are wayfarers rafting from one side of the country to the other, and at the end of the day they will walk home tired but relaxed and ready again to face the challenges of the week. Nathaniel knows it is going to be a much healthier kind of life than they had back east. There will be time and space and freedom to be noisy in ways apartment living prevented. Too many years have been spent lowering the volume of their stereos and televisions, too many years cautioning Copley to use his 'indoor voice', too many years not vacuuming or doing laundry after six in the evenings. Now they no longer have to worry about neighbors: they can make as much noise as they want and no one can complain.

After completing their survey of the first floor, they all go upstairs, Copley whirring and churning as he tries to climb the steps with his knees locked, legs girder straight. Nathaniel fights the urge to say something, knowing that if he makes an issue of it Copley is bound to burst into tears and hide in a closet, hammering his fists on the floor as he has on several other occasions when Nathaniel's frustrations got the better of his desire for familial peace and he shouted at his son to knock it off.

'Cop—'

'It's the adjustment,' Julia whispers, taking Nathaniel's arm. 'Give him time to auto-correct. He needs to do it his way. The soldier thing is a point of continuity between here and Boston. If it goes on too long, then we'll say something.'

'We have to find a therapist – a psychiatrist. He should be evaluated.'

'Please, Nathaniel, don't rush into it. Let's see if it works itself out.'

'But you *agreed*,' Nathaniel says, words spurting through clenched teeth; his own sudden rage surprises him. Julia drops his arm and looks almost afraid.

'I agreed to consider it, Nathaniel. I think we *should* consider it, but I'm not prepared to make a decision at this very moment, when so many other things are happening.'

A thumping sound comes from the hallway. Nathaniel looks out to find Copley, as though an insect confused by glass, marching headlong into the oriel window.

'Copley. Enough. You're going to hurt yourself. You could go straight through that.' Nathaniel puts his hands on his son's shoulders and swivels him around, although the windows are triple-glazed and there is almost no risk. In their Boston apartment Copley would go nowhere near the sealed windows, terrified of the dizzying twenty-story drop to the street.

The boy walks across the hall and into one of the other empty bedrooms, churning and stomping until he meets another immovable obstacle. *Thumpa thumpa thump*. Nathaniel fears that whatever is going on will require more than just therapy to correct.

'What are we going to do with him?' Nathaniel says as Julia raises a finger to her mouth.

'What do you mean?' she whispers.

'After school. Who's going to take care of him? And what about during vacations?'

'Day care?'

He shakes his head. 'Too many horror stories.'

Copley gives up, turns around, and walks naturally from the bedroom down the hall into the room Nathaniel has chosen as his study.

'Well, we're not getting a nanny, if that's what you're thinking. It seems elitist,' Julia says.

'An au pair, then.'

'As if that's any better than day care. Just as random.'

'At least he'd be at home. At least we'd have some control over the kind of environment he's in, the kind of values—'

'God, Nathaniel, you sound like a fundamentalist.'

'All I mean is you don't know what you're going to get in a day-care environment, who's going to be looking after your kid, what they'll be saying and doing that's going to plant ideas in his brain that maybe we don't want there. And anyway, you said—'

'Lower your voice.'

'You said the university day-care center doesn't take school-age kids, and my company doesn't think kids exist outside of the regular school day. So it means finding something else, some private center, and how do you know it's any good? We don't know *anyone* in this city. We don't know whose recommendations to trust. I just – it seems like it would be safer to have him at home. It won't be forever. Four or five years, and then he can be home on his own.'

'A latchkey child. Remember the moral panic about latchkey children when we were kids?'

'I was a latchkey child.'

'Your mother worked at home, Nathaniel. Not the same.'

'But she didn't supervise. I might as well have been home alone. It did me no harm.'

Julia studies him with her problem-solving face, benign and curious and measuring, weighing all the factors.

'We have to do this the *right* way, Nathaniel.'

'Stop saying my name. You always pepper your speech with my name when you're trying to get your way.'

'What's wrong with you today?'

'Nothing's wrong. Moving is stressful. Aren't you stressed?'

'No, Nathaniel, just—'

'You see?'

'No, I'm not stressed, and I'm not trying to get my way.'

A toilet flushes and a moment later Copley returns to the hall, having run wet fingers through his hair to plaster it against his head, the rough surfaces of nature smoothed down, making him look manufactured, poured into a mold and enameled. Marching back into one of the empty bedrooms he turns to face his parents. 'Hear this. I will have this room,' he says. He blinks twice and rolls his eyes back in his head, rolling them so far that only the whites show and it seems as though he has no eyes at all.

*   *   *

They lock the house and drive back to the hotel where they are staying. For a few hours, over dinner and before bed, Copley acts like a normal child, speaking distinct words and answering in full sentences. He orders his own food at the restaurant and is polite to the waiter. Back in the room he asks if he can watch television before bed instead of reading a book, and when Nathaniel and Julia agree that on this one occasion, because they are staying in a hotel overnight, he will be allowed an activity usually forbidden except for half an hour on weekends, he thanks them in such a genuine way that Nathaniel feels his throat constrict. That it can be so easy to produce such happiness seems, for a moment, amazing. And when they tell Copley it is time to sleep he turns off the television, folds his clothes back inside his small suitcase, and goes to brush his teeth without having to be told. Nathaniel looks at Julia, they both raise their eyebrows, smile, and kiss their son goodnight when he climbs under the covers of his double bed. This is how it once was, how easy relations used to be among the three of them. In retrospect it would have been wiser, no doubt, to give him less time to worry about what the move would mean, the friends he would no longer see, and the school in Boston where he was always so happy.

Unlike the motel of the previous night, tonight's hotel, one of a large chain located on the park downtown, is quiet. Rolling close to Julia, tucking himself into her body, Nathaniel falls asleep without difficulty and dreams that the three of them are taking a trip with a larger sightseeing group. At first, he and Copley are sitting at the front of the bus, but after they stop to visit a tourist trap gift shop, Copley goes to sit with Julia at the back and Nathaniel is left alone at the front behind a bald man. In the back of the man's seat is a plastic sleeve holding a number of brochures. Nathaniel removes one of them, skims it, loses interest, and tries to put it back in the plastic sleeve only to find it no longer fits. The man begins to lose his temper, telling Nathaniel to knock it off and stop hitting his seat. 'You're disturbing me, asshole.' Nathaniel takes exception to the man's language, reminding him there are children on board. The bald man stands, raising his fists, and Nathaniel sees for the first time that he has only one eye, in the center of his face, glaring down the bridge of his fat nose. Nathaniel wakes panting and sees, in the darkness, Copley staring at him, the light from the street outside catching the glassy white globe of his son's exposed eye.

The next morning they meet the movers at the house. As soon as Nathaniel catches sight of the two men rolling out of the truck, he thinks of carnies – barkers and butchers calling out business at their joints, running rides and targeting marks. The older of the two men has nape-length white hair receding in an even line past the apex of his head, and his royal blue coveralls cling to his body, revealing a broad hemisphere of gut arcing from his groin to his sternum: an evil clown, beady-eyed and heavy-jowled, cheeks throbbing for white greasepaint and a nose so red and round it looks ready for the center ring. The other man, younger, ferret-like, and wary of eye contact, does most of the heavy lifting, moving fast and dodging round corners, running back and forth from the truck to the house whistling through the gap between his two front teeth, the tune a melody Nathaniel recognizes but cannot place: carnival music, or some big band song that his parents played. The ferret might be anywhere from his late teens to late thirties, with a creased babyish face that is either a sign of delayed adolescence or years of alcoholism. When it comes to lifting the beds and couches and larger pieces of furniture, the two men work together, the evil clown turning a liverish purple, wheezing and panting with every step.

It stopped raining just after dawn and Copley is playing by himself in the backyard. Julia told him to stay outside, but Nathaniel feels compelled to keep checking that his son has not strayed beyond the high back fence or tried to shimmy up one of the tall cottonwood trees. High-rise apartment living presented few opportunities for major physical harm: with no trees to climb there was no risk of catastrophic falls.

'Cop? You okay?' Nathaniel stands under the

canopy of the back porch watching as Copley walks what appears to be a grid pattern, his knees locked as he negotiates a slight rise that runs down the center of the backyard, from the porch to the fence at the edge of the woods. 'Copley?'

The boy pauses, bows at a forty-five-degree angle from the waist, turns his head to face his father, and lowers his arm at a fixed angle. Nathaniel's hands twitch for something to throw at the boy, and he finds himself reaching for an absent object. He picks up a stick, a broom, beats his son's body until the boy agrees to speak and behave like a normal person. Such scenes flame in front of him from time to time, the two of them igniting, going up in smoke, skin bubbling and charring.

They look at each other for a moment, and then Copley blinks twice, turns his head, stands up straight, and returns to his campaign across the lawn.

'Do you want to climb a tree?'

Copley does not respond, but persists in his marching.

'If you do, just call me and I'll help you. But don't try it on your own, okay? I don't want you to fall, kiddo.'

Even with two long cigarette breaks it takes the movers less than three hours to carry everything into the house. It has always seemed to Nathaniel that they own far too many things, but here he discovers entire rooms remain vacant. Rather than looking as though Nathaniel and Julia have just moved in, the house seems to suggest by its substantial emptiness that, quite to the contrary, other people are still in the process of moving out.

While yesterday he felt claustrophobic, today the rooms feel immense and intimidating, looking so unfillable that Nathaniel wants to tell the movers to pack up everything and take them straight back to Boston. They bought this house without giving adequate thought to the kind of furniture they own and the way it would look in the new space. It is only with everything now in the house that Nathaniel realizes, with a surging, acidic burst of anger and confusion, that the spare lines of their couches, chairs, sideboard and dining set are like dolls' furniture in the vast territories of this new house. Everywhere Nathaniel looks he has the sense that a substantial quantity of the bulk and mass of their old life in Boston must be missing. Since Julia organized the move, Julia must have an explanation. He calls out to her and after ten minutes of searching finds her alone in the basement.

'Things are missing. They're about to leave and this can't be everything. Where's all our stuff?'

'Be calm, Nathaniel,' she says. Her mind is on her work. She ticks numbers off her packing manifest, opens cases, runs her fingers over metal and plastic surfaces.

'But where are our things, Julia?'

'Calm down. Stop acting like a child. Everything

is under control.' She holds up the manifest for him to examine. 'Everything is here, delivered intact. I've checked off all the boxes and furniture and I can't find a scratch on anything.'

Nathaniel knows he should trust her but at the last moment he rushes back outside, catching the movers just as they close up the truck.

'Would you mind if I have one last look?' he shouts, flailing his arms. 'I have a hunch you might have forgotten something.'

The evil clown looks from Nathaniel down to the clipboard that holds the form Julia has already signed to confirm receipt of their belongings. In the clown's other hand is a wad of damp-looking bills, the tip Julia has just given the men. Nathaniel understands that by deferring to Julia's superior organizational skills he has ceded any respect the movers might otherwise have paid him. The coordination of moves and the paying of tips are activities in the course of life that most men – men like these movers – will expect other men to handle. Nathaniel has no idea how much it would even be appropriate to tip, nor did he realize, until this moment, that Julia thought far enough ahead to have cash on hand. Like so many others, it is a detail they never discussed.

'Your *wife*,' the clown says in a tar-clogged voice, 'she had that *list*.'

'I know, the checklist, the inventory. The manifest.'

'She checked *everything* off that list, boss. It's all

inside. There ain't nothin' in the truck.' He chuckles and stubs out a cigarette on the slate roof of the mailbox. Nathaniel reaches out to brush away the ash, rubbing the mark left by the cigarette.

'I'd still like to look inside – I have this feeling that something might have been forgotten. I'm not saying it's anyone's fault, you know, but it would put my mind at ease. Come on, just a quick look. It won't take a minute.'

The clown glances at the ferret, who is wiping his hands on an oil-streaked blue rag, and jerks his head at the back of the truck. Nathaniel follows the wiry younger man, watching as he fumbles with the latch mechanism. More congenial men packed the apartment in Boston, loading Nathaniel and Julia's belongings into a much larger truck than this. At some point the boxes and furniture must have been transferred to this smaller delivery vehicle, which means that anyone could have interfered with their possessions: it certainly seems possible that various items might have gone missing, or perhaps were even stolen en route. Nathaniel trusted the original movers, two men from Roxbury who were both ten years or more his seniors, who made small talk and jokes and teased Nathaniel in an amiable way, wondering why anyone would want to move away from Boston.

When the doors open again Nathaniel sees it: at the back of the truck, closest to the cab, a small gray cardboard box. He pulls his body into the cargo container, worrying for a moment that the men will close the door on him and drive away, sell him into white slavery and traffic him abroad where he would never be found or recovered, spending the rest of his life assembling phones or computers or processing technological waste in a developing nation, or kept alive just long enough for his organs to be harvested and flown out on the black market, transplanted into the bodies of warlords and oligarchs and the children of dictators. He sees all these possibilities in the eyes of the men, waiting, preparing for the moment when he reveals his critical vulnerability.

There is a stink of underarm and the floor of the truck is rough with grit. Long streaks of rust look enough like dried blood for Nathaniel to wonder if the truck might have been used for some macabre butchery. Canvas straps hang from the sides of the space, straps used to hold boxes and furniture in place, but which might just as easily be used to tie up a body until the unscrupulous doctor who must be in league with these men could subdue him, anesthetize him, and flay the skin from his back.

In handwriting Nathaniel does not recognize as either his or his wife's, the box has been labeled CHILD–BEDROOM, but unlike all the other boxes from the move this one lacks an identifying number; it has no place on Julia's orderly manifest of possessions. Without a number, the box does not exist. How many other things, now long dispersed, may also have been overlooked, unnumbered, sold on to a different kind of black market of stolen goods? He picks up the box, tucks it under his arm, and hurries out of the truck. The panic reminds him of a day in his childhood when he was locked alone inside his house while the babysitter and Matthew were outside and he could find no way to open the door. He must have been no more than three or four years old at the time – too small to understand the automatic workings of a Yale lock, or to know that the baroque toy plastic key he retrieved from his bedroom would be useless. He had felt not only trapped, but also cut off from anyone who might render assistance, and unable to understand the mechanisms that could liberate him.

When Nathaniel holds the box up for the men to examine they say nothing. To make a fuss about this oversight might lead somewhere unpleasant and dangerous, to a street brawl in sight of the new neighbors, to a shiv sinking into his gut, the fat man finding reserves of hideous strength and pummeling him without mercy so he would have no choice but to submit to their punishments, finding himself hog-tied with nylon cord and bundled into the back of the truck where his throat would be slit even if his organs were never touched. Whatever the precise nature of their intent and underworld connections, Nathaniel has no doubt these two men are capable of evil. Together they have been in and out of his house, discovered all of its secrets, perhaps even found ways of copying the front door keys: those men will be able to creep undiscovered through rooms that will always now feel somehow tainted, insecure.

At the edge of his new lawn Nathaniel watches as the ferret climbs back into the cab. The clown smiles and gives an odd salute. 'Sorry about that. See you, buddy,' he says. Not so bad after all, quite friendly in fact.

Nathaniel watches as they drive up the street to the little Dolores Woods traffic circle and back around to exit the neighborhood. On the turn, the ferret leans out the window and aims his finger at Nathaniel, cocks his thumb, and fires off an invisible shot, grinning and then spitting a brown viscous arc out the window. Laughter. Squeals. An obscenity Nathaniel chooses not to hear.

He has not lived in a house since leaving home to go to college. After two decades of apartment living, he feels a sudden and vertiginous weightlessness, a total vulnerability. The men whoop again out the open windows as the truck passes the old farmhouse at the entrance to Dolores Woods, swerving onto Poplar Road and almost hitting a yellow school bus whose driver, leaning hard on the horn, swerves into Abigail Avenue before crashing through the planks of the subdivision's faux-Victorian sign. Everything is unsteady, the pavement mobile and fluxing under Nathaniel's feet. There is a reason they lived in the city for so many years and avoided the suburbs. The suburbs are a place of isolation and danger and exposure. Without waiting for the police, the school bus starts up again, reverses a few feet, and pulls back onto the road, continuing its route.

He needs air. He puts the box on the driveway and steps out to the street, staring at the finished houses, the abandoned foundations, the empty fields to the north. Turning around to look back at what is now his own house, he sees the light changing, clouds passing, and as shadows slip across the siding the house seems to shift, as a sleeping animal will change its position: the large gable at the front twists, the windows blink, the porch expands into an over-stuffed stomach. The sun comes out for a moment and once again the house stands still, but there is a constant, low-level buzzing, perhaps from air conditioning units or generators, except that the sound has an insistent if modified organic timbre: nanotech cicadas tuned to a new frequency. All of a sudden a blind rolls up in one of the second-story windows and Nathaniel is certain for an instant that a man is there, standing just beyond the glass, looking down at him, fists raised. But then the light shifts, the clouds turn the windows to mirrors, and the man disappears.

'They forgot something,' Nathaniel calls out, putting the cardboard box on the hall floor.

'That's *impossible*,' Julia says, no place for a stray

153

box in her system. 'I checked *everything* off the list, Nathaniel. It can't be one of ours.'

'It is. You missed it,' he says, although they have been making an effort not to score points off each other over trivialities.

Julia leans over to scrutinize the handwriting.

'I didn't write this.'

'It must have been one of the packers in Boston.'

Julia makes a soft noise of disavowal before whipping open the cardboard flaps with her box cutter.

'Shit.' She holds up a pair of stiff fabric butterfly wings her blade has sliced in half. Nathaniel can see her trying to assemble a rationalization for the failure to inventory this box; the hypotheses and proofs map across her forehead and then clear into a smooth blank field. 'This must have been the first box I packed and I forgot to put it on the list and then the movers labeled it. It doesn't have a number. A logical oversight, if an annoying one.'

As well as several photo albums from his infancy, the box contains all of Copley's Halloween costumes: the butterfly rig, a foam egg suit from his first year, a bumblebee, a bluebird, and an assortment of other benign creatures from the natural world. He has not graduated to the ghoulish costumes favored by older children and Nathaniel hopes he never will. Gore is not a thing he can stomach.

Later, unpacking in the kitchen, Nathaniel catches sight of his son gazing up at the trees, as if unsure how to relate to them. They stuffed him into a windbreaker when he went out earlier, but by lunchtime he had shed the outer layer, leaving it hanging over the railing of the back porch. Singing to himself, he is always looking up, staring in a kind of delirium, his small body further dwarfed by the expanse of backyard, the woods beyond the fence menacing the enclosed space. The unease that gripped Nathaniel as the movers departed begins to expand, opening into an agitation he tries to neutralize by dismissing it as nothing other than ordinary buyer's remorse, his subconscious telling him it would have been more practical to live downtown in one of the converted warehouse lofts on the riverfront, closer to Julia's lab at the university and his own new office. There is street life in the regenerated industrial district, sidewalk cafés and quirky art galleries, independent grocery stores, and a sense of youth and energy that Dolores Woods, with its jarring silence and antiseptic landscape, utterly lacks. Here there is space, to be sure, and space was the very thing they dreamed of having during all the cramped, happy years in Boston, but space is the only thing that has been missing from their lives. In Boston they always lived with the sound of other people. Several years ago Nathaniel listened to his next-door neighbor confess to his wife that he had been fucking his accountant for the previous fifteen years. At two in the morning, every word and sob and recrimination was audible; the two bedrooms abutted each other and there was nothing to do but try to live through it, to ignore the way every time the neighbors pushed the rolling drawers of their dresser closed Nathaniel could not only hear the noise but feel the vibration. Times like those, Julia would turn to Nathaniel in bed, throw an arm across his body, shake him in a good-natured but exasperated way, and say, *We need more space. We can't live like this forever.*

His childhood home in Cambridge was on a large lot with mature trees. In the backyard there was a crab apple that was his fort and retreat for as long as he was small enough to climb it, disappearing into its thicket of branches, hooking his legs over a smooth limb and hanging upside down, watching the world as blood rushed to his head, then swinging his arms, pulling his body back up when he was still limber with youth. At some point he stopped climbing, lost the strength in his upper body, and his core muscles atrophied. He grew up slack and heavy, often gorging himself out of depression.

Of course he wants Copley to have a childhood of trees and lawns before the possibility of houses and yards like the one they have bought disappears into a future of hot and unpredictable chaos, of high-density living as the only possible way for the species to continue. The world Copley will inhabit as an adult is bound to be a far more difficult place than the one Nathaniel has inherited. If it has not already happened, humanity is about to enter a new era, when security will matter more than anything else: not just of person and property but also of food, water, health, medicine, the environment. Security will become the defining quality and concern of human existence on the planet and beyond; to guarantee the long-term security of the human species (if such a thing is desirable), we are going to have to leave the earth. Hawking has already said it, and others agree. Nathaniel believes this, and believes in the work his company is doing to make the world incrementally more secure – not just for nations and corporations, but also for people like him, his wife, and his child.

Nevertheless, it is clear there is far too much house in this house. It was a bad, backward-looking choice. This is a historically conservative state and he fears the neighbors will be religious fanatics bent on converting nonbelievers, while the house itself will need – will *demand* – to be filled with new furniture, ornaments, and art, and before they know it they'll be spending their lives decorating and filling up this monstrosity, because unlike some of the sleek minimalist houses Nathaniel has admired in the past, and indeed unlike their own apartment in Boston, which benefited from a mind-easing lack of disorder, this house will look vacant unless it is packed to the rafters with a life's accumulation of *stuff*. It will demand that they become different people altogether. Unpacking a box of dinner plates in the kitchen, Nathaniel feels one of them slipping from his fingers, watches it falling in an observable arc, and winces as it hits the floor at just the right angle so the china explodes into three large sections surrounded by a number of waxy, feathery little shards. He finds the dustpan and broom, already in the kitchen's utility closet, and cleans up the mess. The trash compacter is already lined with a new bag. Nathaniel dumps the three large pieces of plate and all the shards on a sheet of heavy brown packing paper, folds it up, and throws it away. Julia is in the basement and if she heard the crash she says nothing about it. It is better to let it pass. He has tried to convince her that objects are not important; if a plate breaks, it should be dealt with at once without melodrama. Sentiment is for people, not for possessions, but she attaches meaning and importance to things in ways that still surprise him after more than a decade of life together.

One of the four bedrooms and the room in the attic remain empty, without so much as a stray box to unpack. Their entire Boston apartment would fit, with room to spare, in the basement alone. They have no furniture to put in the den, though at least their books – the college textbooks and self-help manuals and various design catalogues they have acquired – finally have a proper home. They possess no pool table or other games to fill the basement recreation area, but at least the workshop space is more or less in a condition Julia can use.

They order pizza, eating off their own china at

the dining room table. After dinner, they allow Copley to watch half an hour of television before Julia puts him to bed. Everything has been unpacked, put away in cupboards and closets, even if not in quite the right order. There will be weeks of reorganization: *optimization of storage*, Julia says. Nathaniel will defer to her in this as in so much else, watching in amazement while she creates not just exact, but ideal order throughout the house. Perhaps it is obsessive, but he knows it is also born of a gift for efficiency and classification that Julia can adapt to almost any problem.

With the front door locked, he turns off the lights and goes upstairs where he finds Julia reading Copley a story. At the age of seven, the child should be old enough to read his own books, but Nathaniel says goodnight and Copley, acting fully human for the first time all day, says goodnight as well, reaching out his hands for Nathaniel to embrace him. Nathaniel hugs his son, kisses his forehead, and says goodnight again, leaving Julia to finish the story while he goes to take a shower. Stripping off his clothes, he puts them in the hamper Julia has already placed in the master bathroom, and turns on the shower, standing under the water for a long time until he finds himself crying. As steam fills the room he can no longer see his feet and has the illusion of floating, his toes numb from the heat of the water, and for several moments he is certain of hovering in the shower stall, his lower body dispersing as his head is drawn up to the extractor fan, drawn in and cut to ribbons, sucked out through the ventilation pipe and sprayed across the side of the house.

He dries himself off and gets into the bed he and Julia reassembled earlier in the day. It was their first major purchase together ten years ago, costing as much as a good used car. For a year he could never turn off the lights without making the sound of brakes squealing. It was the closest they have ever come to divorce: the teasing, he discovered in retrospect, nearly drove Julia to leave him. He listens as she turns off the lights in the hall and takes her own shower, hangs the towel on the hook behind the door, and slides into bed beside him.

As sleep comes, he is troubled for the first time in nearly twenty years by recurring childhood dreams: of two burly men concealed behind the juniper bushes in the backyard in Cambridge; of a creature, black and featureless and covered with mud, under his bed, hidden by the dust ruffle, waiting for night so it can emerge, fingering the bedspread, pulling itself up onto the mattress, crawling on top of Nathaniel, pinning his arms and legs, suffocating him with its hot oily hands, the fingers slipping into his nostrils and mouth, filling his ears and gouging out his eyes, drilling holes through his nipples and into his lungs, hooking his navel and pulling out his guts, fingers finding their way into every opening, rending him apart while leaving him horrifically intact, blinded, voiceless.

Nathaniel wakes minutes or hours later, aware of someone in the hall. Without disturbing Julia, whose breathing is heavy, eyelids twitching, he rolls out of bed and tiptoes across the room to the open door. It was closed when he fell asleep. Julia must have opened it before returning to bed.

In the hall Copley is walking towards the oriel window at the front of the house. The moon is shining with an intensity that registers in Nathaniel's ears as a sustained C# bell tone that makes the floor vibrate.

'Copley,' he whispers, trying to pitch his voice in the direction of his son's dark shape, but the boy does not stop or respond: he keeps walking to the window until he knocks his forehead into the glass, pressing his palms against the neighboring panes, making a clicking noise that may be coming from his mouth or from his fingernails against the window. Nathaniel shivers and closes the bedroom door behind him.

Crouching in the shadows a few steps down the back stairs, Paul watches as the man walks along the hall, picks up the child in his arms and carries him across the hall to what was once Carson's room. The man is out of shape, his outline bunched and rounded, and he moves with the heavy soft tread of someone who never thinks about his body. It is the kind of body Paul could overcome and subdue, the body of a coward, ignorant of the ways a body

161

in peak condition can move: quick and stealthy and silent.

Half an hour passes in the dark staircase and then the man is standing again in the hall, where he stares out the window at the front of the house. Paul watches him looking at the neighborhood and breathing in clogged asthmatic gasps. The man has no clue how to be silent: his whispers could wake the dead; his tiptoeing makes the boards creak and sing. At last the man lumbers back to the master bedroom, closing the door behind him, and for a moment Paul feels as though he is the only living presence in the house, these new people nothing more sinister than ghosts sent to torment him.

As a boy he once saw a ghost in his grandmother's house. The foundations had been constructed around a granite boulder, and in the basement a great mound of the rock protruded up from the concrete floor. His grandmother had no air conditioning and it was a hot summer day, so he was playing in the basement, building forts and staging miniature wars with a motley collection of plastic soldiers and intergalactic warriors when all of a sudden, even though no one had come down the stairs, he knew he was not alone. A man appeared on the other side of the boulder, as though he had been lying down and simply sat up straight, bending from the waist. The man looked at Paul and nodded and then lay himself down again. It had not occurred to Paul to be afraid and when he went over to see what was there it was just the floor and the boulder, except that where the floor met the boulder on that side of the basement there was a kind of crevice. The concrete, added at some point long after the house's original construction, had been poured leaving a gap between the floor and the rock that was wide enough for Paul's hand to fit through, big enough for mice and insects, perhaps even snakes, to come and go. He stuck his fingers into the gap and, reaching deeper into the crevice, could feel the earth and then a larger cavity, the contour of the granite boulder, its seams and wrinkles, a mass of fine roots, a harder root like the branch of a tree, and something round and smooth and cold to the touch. He'd broken away some of the surrounding concrete and had his arm stuck in almost up to the shoulder, feeling around in the void, when that smooth cold round thing moved, escaping his touch, then sliding against his hand, a muscle of ice stirred to life.

Paul does not know what he is doing sitting here now in this house that is no longer his, watching an empty dark hallway where a man and a boy, father and son, have just staged their strange nocturnal dance. He does not know what brought him out of the bunker in the first place. He has no clear intention or purpose, no design he is conscious of trying to enact. He simply found his body moving, followed it, and is waiting to see what it will do.

Snores at two different registers begin to come

from the master bedroom, resonating through the hall and down the stairs. Paul has created a house that echoes, a chamber of noises. The heavy vibrations of the truck woke him at dawn and throughout the day he listened at the hatch, monitoring the sounds of the house as the movers moved and the new people unpacked, banging boxes on floors, shifting furniture into place, and then, late in the day, arranging tools in the basement workshop, reclaiming and repurposing the space he had designed to meet his own requirements. Expecting to find the man busy with saws and power tools, he edged his body out through the hatch, scurrying to the door of the pantry from where he could see straight into the workshop area. The woman was unpacking a collection of plastic crates, stacking the empty ones in a far corner of the basement next to an existing pile of metal suitcases. While she worked the woman spoke to herself, or perhaps, Paul began to think, to the things she was unpacking. From the distance of the pantry he could not see what kinds of tools she might be arranging, but the way she moved and spoke to herself raised a shudder on Paul's spine and made him retreat to the hatch, pulling it closed and throwing the lock. All the sounds of the house coalesced, pouring into the bunker where they were amplified and clarified – clearer and louder than if he had been in the same room as the people talking. He could hear every word, the whispers and significant silences that passed between the adults, the curious sounds made by the child, the words the child spoke only to himself when his parents left him alone and he tried to narrate the change that was taking place: *I don't know, no. Boston. Yes, we're from Boston. Where are you from? Are you from here? I said I don't know. Corrections. Rehabilitation. No. A scientist. She works in a lab.* In this way, Paul has come to know where these new people are from, the outlines of personalities and behaviors, all in the course of a day. The movers called them *Mr and Mrs No-ales,* but the man, Nathaniel, corrected them: *No-eye.* The *s,* like so much else in the name, remains unspoken, coming out as nothing but breath. Paul tries to form the name on his tongue in the way he hears Mr Noailles do it, but he cannot make the right sounds.

At last when he believed the family was in bed he emerged again from the bunker, examining the basement with a flashlight, ready to recede into some dark corner if he heard approaching footsteps. On the worktables were three computers and a tool collection, unlike any he had ever seen, composed of circuitry, colorful wires, cutters, screwdrivers, pliers, hammers, vises, strippers, wrenches, ratchets, tweezers, vacuums, heat sinks, inserters, extractors, pullers, retrievers, knives, mirrors, soldering tools, meters, and other instruments that looked like medical or dental equipment. All the tools, parts, and instruments – including several larger machines he could not

165

name – were arranged on a series of vinyl mats, while alongside the tools and equipment was a collection of what looked like amputated limbs, all of them in order, like with like: arms with arms, hands with hands, a row of feet and ankles, another of legs, a grid of articulated joints, all made from colorless materials both rigid and flexible. He was too afraid to touch any of it, and afraid, in another cold flash, a blade at his nape, of the people who have invaded his house.

In the darkness, time thins and stretches as Paul crouches on the steep back stairs, watching the hallway that connects the four bedrooms his family once occupied. A green-blue glow from the street fills the landing, defining the outline of the boy, who is suddenly standing above Paul. At the top of the stairs the child's small bare toes, pale and luminous in the night, curl over the nosing to touch the riser. The boy looks in Paul's direction but seems not to see him. He can hear the child's breath alongside his own, and the acceleration of his heart in his ears.

The boy looks right through him and then walks down the stairs, sour air streaming from a small open mouth. A cold smooth hand brushes against Paul's own as he leans against the wall to move out of the way and a shudder rises from his tail-bone, breaking loose along his spine as the hairs rise along his neck and arms. The staircase is full of the boy's breath, acrid and decaying. Paul turns to watch the boy's descent, the small hands reaching out to either side of the staircase, one of them gripping the banister when, all of a sudden, he disappears into darkness.

As the child approaches the bottom of the stairs he reappears, caught by the light from the kitchen windows, moonlight gazing in. When he turns the corner Paul follows him, tiptoeing down the steps to the kitchen. The child is either hidden in shadow or has already left the room. Pulling his flashlight from the pocket of his jeans, Paul presses it on, aiming the beam into the corners of the kitchen, but the room is empty.

Sounds come from the front of the house: an unlocking rasp and then the seal on the glass storm door sucking open, the hiss as it closes again. He kills the flashlight and puts it back in his pocket, running into the dining room and out to the hall. Through the storm door he can see the boy walking down the lawn to the road. Without pausing to think, Paul pushes open the door, flies across the grass, and catches the child up in his arms just as the boy reaches the street. As Paul cradles him the boy's expression remains fixed, unresponsive, blind, although the eyes are open, looking past Paul, the whites caught in the light of the moon, the irises and pupils uniformly black. Gazing into those vacant eyes, transfixed by their whiteness, Paul nearly drops the boy.

Sleepwalkers should never be woken. Paul's mother told him that as Carson began to walk. He holds the child tenderly, one arm supporting the boy's back, one his legs, and carries him back into the house. That blank face, those staring, empty eyes. The body weighs almost nothing.

Paul puts the boy down in the hall and watches as he begins to climb the main stairs, disappearing again into darkness. At the second floor landing the child turns, walks down the hall, and begins climbing to the third floor, disappearing once more. He follows the child up endless flights, the boy receding always into gloom, the house expanding past the limits Paul knows, the two flights of stairs, public and private, crisscrossing each other, ever higher, beyond the three stories he built, the boy climbing and climbing without pause or fatigue, a ghastly unending ascent straight out of the house and into the remoteness of space, the world falling away around them.

He finds the boy at the far end of the attic play-room, forehead pressed against the balcony doors and looking out at the front lawn, across the empty street to the gaping foundations of two unfinished houses, cavities, twin eye sockets scraped clean with a spoon. Moonlight falls around the boy until a bank of fast-moving clouds turns the room black. The boy turns and walks past him, creeping down the stairs one step at a time.

At the boy's bedroom Paul watches the child slip back under the covers and turn on his side to face the door. It is too dark to see whether his eyes are open or closed. The face, the triangular shape of chin and cheeks, the hemisphere of skull, the way the parts have put themselves together, remind Paul of his son's face. For a moment Paul wonders if, by some miracle, this boy is Carson. The child sighs and turns over to face the wall. His whole body twitches, arms seizing and shaking as he cries out, a wail that shakes the windows. Eyes open, the boy sits up in bed looking straight at Paul, and screams.

Paul throws himself out of the room and down the back stairs, sliding through the kitchen, into the basement, past the workshop, through the hole at the back of the pantry. The hatch sticks in the sudden shift of air pressure, the storms moving across the state, swollen with humidity, *pull it shut, shut, throw the lock*, then the containment door, the spinning combination, barricading himself behind it and shut tight, tight, safe and enclosed. With his back against the metal door he pants, slumping on the floor of the bunker, the ceiling's puzzle of fluorescent tubes ablaze.

'What's wrong?' Julia turns over to look at Nathaniel as he climbs back into bed. He knows she's a heavy sleeper but the scream should have woken her.

'Copley. Just a bad dream. Nothing to worry about.'

'Does he need me?'

Get out of bed, go see for yourself if our kid needs you. By instinct, as a child, Nathaniel turned to his mother for comfort, although in his own case there was no comfort from any quarter except his brother. His mother always assured him his father had done nothing serious: *Your father doesn't know his own strength, Nathaniel. No, it's not broken. Stop crying. I can't stand it when you put me between the two of you. You'll have to work it out yourselves. Don't involve me. Don't be so soft. You're going to ruin my breakfast, the food already tastes like cinders.* On visits to the hospital emergency room, his mother always concocted a story, and because of the way she spoke and the clothes she wore, her reputation in the community as a respected child psychologist and her capacity to make even the most esteemed professional feel inferior, the doctors and nurses never questioned her accounts of Nathaniel falling from trees or tripping over paving stones in the rose garden or catching a baseball with his upper lip at Little League. Nathaniel never played baseball. *He's such a clumsy boy,* she would say, *nothing at all like his father or me. Who knows where he came from?* And then she would laugh, a screaming hoot that still caroms round in his ears.

'He thought he saw a giant. He's fine.'

'A giant? Where?' She's half-asleep again, her voice drawn and drowsy.

'He said a giant chased him out of the house and he tried to escape but he couldn't. I told him there aren't any giants, at least not in the house. He was covered in sweat.'

'Does he have a fever?'

'No. It's a muggy night. I took the duvet off his

bed and turned down the thermostat. I sat with him until he went back to sleep.'

Nathaniel looks out the window at the neighboring house, dark except for a light over the front porch that casts a yellow circle on the boards and steps. The neighbors have a three-story tower with a turret at one corner of the house, a mansard roof over the main structure, and a widow's walk at the top. He can imagine how atmospheric the neighborhood will feel at Halloween: already haunted, no need for decoration.

The next morning the rain has returned, so furious it sounds like hail pummeling the roof and windows. Nathaniel thinks he hears dripping but assumes it must be outside, a gutter overflowing and spilling onto the terrace that opens off their bedroom, and therefore no reason to worry. The survey found no major structural problems.

'Do you hear a drip?' he asks Julia.

'No. Don't get so worked up, Nathaniel. It's pouring.'

'Don't you hear it?'

'Honestly, Nathaniel, I don't hear anything but the rain.'

'You're doing it again, Julia. Just acknowledge that you hear a drip.'

'I don't hear a drip. Your hearing is more acute than mine.'

When Nathaniel goes to wake Copley, he finds clumps of dirt on the floor in the hall and in his son's bedroom. It must be left over from those movers, but there is more dirt downstairs in the front hall, smears of mud in the shape of shoe prints and footprints and arcs of dirt going up and down both flights of stairs. He doesn't remember there being any dirt when they went to bed, but it was a long day, the movers trekked in and out of the house for hours, it was raining off and on, and it is entirely possible a mess was made that neither he nor Julia noticed. Nonetheless, thinking of the menacing men, the way they came and went, the access they had to every corner of the house throughout the day, he decides to speak with the technicians at work about installing a home security system. Danger is everywhere, especially in the suburbs.

Since Donald died I have taken to sleeping on the floor. I wake with the sun in my face and turn over on the bedroll the way I used to as a girl when relatives came for reunions and holidays and homecomings. Shoulder's out of joint, hip sore, hand asleep: shake sensation back into the digits and crack the bones to limber. All my suppleness is just about gone. As a child I camped on boards to let the adults have my bed. There were aunts and uncles on the couches, cousins in the barn, the hayloft. I never minded being put out of my room for family because Mama and Daddy raised me to believe instinctively in graciousness like that, giving elders respect. Now an elder myself, I wonder if it wasn't a raw deal. No one left to respect me, I'm afforded respect by no one, young or old. *Dissed* is what the kids have been saying for dozens of years: everyone *dissing* me. Imagine how folks would react if I did what so many others did, picked up a gun and demanded respect.

These are ruminations from a partial night, the beast of fractured sleep, crawled out from the floorboards, long-clawed and slavering, green-toothed. Push it back in, fill the chink with wood dough, varnish it over, wait for the next generation to find it again.

I push this body upright and swing my back erect against the papered wall, fingers running up the posy print to feel ferns and rosebuds through layers of dust that stick to the pattern near the floor. My hands come back populated with orphan particles of earth and skin, remnants of hair. I rub them together until the residue disappears, settling in other parts of the bedroom, once my mother's, my grandmother's, great-grandmother's. It's the room where Donald and I slept, loved, eased Rebekah through her first twelve months, standing at the window with that disrespectful baby until she fell back into sleep, looking out at the moon on the corn, milklight shading the green-gold acres into creatures strange and sentient-seeming: cob-people, yellow kernel bodies, silken hair, wrapped up in their go-to-meeting of crisp viridian linen.

I meet them on the march in my dreams, a platoon of protectors filling this room where Donald died, his head in my hands, crouched on these boards, rainbow rug I made as a girl one winter bunched at my feet. I felt his final current pulsing down to dry riverbed silence, put my lips to his, brushed against the soft foam of beard, tasted him for the last time. The fire was out by the time I got to him and he did not say goodbye, not even with his eyes: empty stare, shock and stark terror, life leaving before he was prepared to go. It was not an easeful death and I do not know if I believe in such things, in the possibility that passing from one world to another can ever be done with ease.

Last night I walked out under the moon, through damp grass and down to the street, put my bare soles on cracking asphalt and went up the road, turned right onto Krovik's old property, took myself up the driveway and through the unlocked gate into the backyard. The moon guided me along contours of lawn to the place I have been unable to visit since Krovik built his fence, the spongy earth where no grass has grown since 1919. A hole had opened up in the surface, big as two manhole covers, and through the hole I could make out the top branches of that old cottonwood tree, secreted in the earth. I sat down on the damp ground and swung my feet through the hole, letting them dangle in darkness and find their footing on a solid branch, put my weight on it by degrees, listened for cracking, felt for the giving way, but found I could stand quite easily, and as I stood there, waist-deep in the earth, the branch holding me sighed and curved, lowering me down into its arms until I could grasp other branches and debris from the bene-factor's burned-up house. I descended through limbs, all of them arcing upwards along the sides of the hole, many of the larger ones broken. I passed through a section of chimney and walked down a flight of old stairs, finding my way by touch, hearing unfamiliar sounds, smelling mice and moles. I felt earth rain down upon me, sensed movement in the dark. My hands found the thick braid of rope, manila or hemp. Climbing down alongside the rigid braid I came to a branch where I could sit, turned on the flashlight, and looked at the skeletons in their rotting clothes, a good black suit, a dress that might once have been blue and must have belonged to Grandma Lottie. I pondered the remains of those men, hanging there in stillness, heads inclining towards each other, ear to ear, chin to shoulder.

Passing the men, I dropped down to the next branch and shone my light deeper. Water was seeping in, bubbling, frothing round the base of the tree. I began to climb back to the surface.

When I woke in the house this morning with the flashlight on, its beam fading at my side, my clothes speckled with grass clippings, I had to wonder.

Listening now to the rain, windows a-rattle in their frames, the kitchen door shaking on its hinges, I imagine the tread of feet I know, the sound of shifting weight upon the floor, an advance, a pause, a turn along the hall. Approach, approach, come forth.

Lightning flashes but there's a long delay before the crack: the strike is more than a mile away, a storm from the northwest flown over the Rockies and building as it moves across the plains. I can feel the coming torrent, suspect a deluge, apocalyptic rain driving down upon us. It might be enough to make me a believer again, if I succumb to the fear. I will not succumb. I pray now to myself and myself alone. What would *I* do? What wouldn't I, given the chance. If the waters rise, meet them with fire.

I push my body all the way up now, leaning against the weight of wall, letting this house help me as it always has. I speak to my own ear, murmuring through teeth clenched with effort and exertion, surprised by the strength of this old muscle-and-bone machine.

A strange eastern wind was blowing on the day the first condemnation notice came from the city, a declaration of eminent domain, as if the council were the lord of the land. I learned that is, in fact, the case. They can do what they like, *in the public interest*, for the 'good' of the many over the good of the few. They mean to tear down this house to build a turning lane into Dolores Woods as a *traffic safety measure* and widen Krovik's Abigail Avenue into a boulevard for *community improvement and essential correction of structural flaws in the existing roadway*. Though there are only twenty-one new families on the land that was once Poplar Farm, unnamed experts have determined that the flow of traffic past the neighborhood – I laugh at their description of that tinker's swarm of houses – is *increasing substantially,* owing not solely to the construction of said subdivision, Dolores Woods, but also to the general western expansion of the city. This has meant that, especially at the time of evening rush hour, westbound vehicles slowing down to enter Dolores Woods cause a hazardous backup to the flow of traffic on what remains a two-lane road. While the city's long-term development plan envisions the widening of this stretch of Poplar Road to four lanes, the immediate traffic congestion and safety needs mandate the construction of a turning lane, which, along with the widened reconfiguration of Abigail Avenue, will have to be sited through your property, requiring the demolition of the existing one-story single-family home, two-story barn, silo, outhouse, as well as assorted other sheds, and subsidiary agricultural structures.

As I stood there, reading and rereading the letter, my hands shook, and then my whole body, so I had to sit down, chase my breath, tame the climb-a-hill pulse that ruptured my vision. Someone from the city had surveyed my property, made a census of the buildings without my permission, without me even being aware an intruder was present. I put the letter on the ottoman and walked back into the kitchen, hands still trembling as I turned the faucet, letting water run over my fingers, splashing it in my face. I felt blood pool in my feet, watched the east wind blowing across the garden, blasting dirt and grit and leaves against the kitchen windows. Black Eurus, a blustering roar and *lateral noise*: augury of hot nights and torrential rains, the trickster wind, unpredictable, bringing locusts, dividing waters, breaking ships, drying up springs and fountains, carrying forth desolation and lies. An east wind would wilt my crops at a touch. *Behold every tree, how it appears to wither, and every leaf to fall off.*

The letter laid out the offer on the house and my remaining land, the 'fair market value' of $155,099.99. I wondered what those ninety-nine cents amounted to: a lone shingle, a cubic foot of earth, a branch from one of my trees? The trees. Christ, I knew they'd be taking down more trees. I did not want their money. I did not need their dollars. I resolved I would fight the city with all I had, and now I have lost.

I stomped up Krovik's driveway that day, before he himself had lost everything, forced by other powers to leave his own house. After I pulled the fake antique doorbell, I could hear his approaching steps of thunder, and then the door flew open.

'I guess this is your doing,' I said, holding up the letter so he could read it.

A wet red furrow sliced across his face. He did not even try to keep from smiling.

'I don't know nothin' about it, Mrs Washington.

179

You'll have to take it up with the city,' he said, and slammed the door. I could hear him hoot and holler as he stomped back into the bowels of his ugly white house.

It has been more than two years since the first condemnation notice and I have spent all that time fighting the city, delaying my loss, winning reprieves that were only ever temporary. I was supposed to be out of the house two months ago, when they came to put the bolt on the front door, but here I remain, and now, at the end of the battle, I have spent all I had left from the sale of the land to Krovik in the first place. By the time I ran out of money to fight, enriching a fool lawyer, the city lowered their offer to $75,000.25, owing to 'the decline in the property market, meaning that a house of comparable size and age and condition could be acquired for the price being offered under the constitutional conditions of eminent domain'.

I consulted other, cheaper lawyers but all said there was nothing more to be done: accept defeat, leave the house by the first of July or face jail. Something happened to me then, a diminution but also a strengthening, a new resolve: I would not leave. I would stay until they came to get me, the last free woman to occupy these rooms. I do not know if it is the house, the land, or the combination of the two, but a spell of place hangs over me, keeping me here despite my better sense.

★    ★    ★

Early morning but already a rumbling comes from the road, a truck turning fast, spray from the tires slashing curbs and trees. Fearing it might be the city come to tear the place down, I step from the bedroom, snipping along the hall to the front of the house. In the living room I unlatch a window, heave it open, push my head into the rain, turn to see the truck parking in front of Krovik's place. Out tumbles a fat man and a thin, and then the new owners, I suppose they must be, a dark-headed threesome, pale as a host of reanimated dead, arrive in their car. Rain runs down my neck, curling round my clavicle.

For once I'm glad to be alone, unobserved, unwatchable, a specter in a house filled with nothing but specters, all those dust-tingling dead. In the night I hear them moving moth-footed over floors and furniture, whispering among themselves. I know the histories of wars and battles. I know I've been vanquished, fought well but was outmatched, outgunned, overrun: raped and pillaged. Not my body, no, but that Krovik was nothing if not a rapist – maybe not of the flesh, but most certainly of the land. We speak artillery when there are no other arms upon us.

The city's 'fair market price' is not much compared to what the land was worth, but it will keep me secure enough, along with the Social Security and my pension. I have sold everything I can: the car, all of the farm equipment Donald collected and cherished, the machines that kept him working and slowly drove him mad, machines bought on credit that drove us into debt, and drove me, in the end, to sell what so long sustained us. I will not live as well as I might have, but I will find a little place and, except perhaps a phone and a radio, survive without technology.

Yesterday afternoon, returning from my daily petition to the city planning offices, I stood waiting for my bus in the coffee-hour heat. The city does not know I remain here. They think I have left, that I campaign for the pardon of my house from a place of safety. Coming from downtown there is no direct route and I had to change buses halfway, walk three blocks south and get the other bus on the line that terminates just east of what is now Dolores Woods: the dolorous forest of infinite sorrow. A thirty-minute trip in the car takes more than two hours by public transportation and foot power, with the added pleasure of fat white men empowered to protect revenue, liveried in letters that conjure historical dread. Walking that quarter-mile from the bus stop to the house, trudging along the road where the traffic thins out to a stream of brittle gray cream, I saw this house waiting for me as if it knew I was coming, the early moon striking the windows and making it look as though Donald had come back, was waiting up, had a fire going, warming the house we occupied in speech and in silence. Not *occupied*. Lived. We lived here together in the fullness of the word, and the house, knowing our life, lived as well.

The new owners next door with their sensible car, a hybrid rolling on silent rubber feet when it passed, will expect the old girl to be knocked down. No doubt they bought Krovik's house with just such a promise from the city. They will have been informed of the plans: the turning lane, the boulevard in place of a perfectly serviceable if poorly made street, the promise of higher property values, road safety, community improvement. I will find no support from people like them.

Climbing back up through the branches and debris, when I once again reached the height of the men I stopped, looked at them, could have sworn they had changed positions, the one in the dress no longer looking down, as he had been, but up at me, sunken black sockets staring into my own. 'Don't ghost me, Great-Uncle George,' I said, 'I haven't come to disturb, just to check, be sure you're all right. I can see you are, the both of you, so I'll leave you be.'

All currents stopped two months ago: no power no water no gas. Potatoes are ready to dig in the garden, pumpkins still ripening, apples red in the orchard, things I would have packed into the cellar in previous years, storing up for winter. The memory of sheltering among that subterranean hoard of plenty when the air turned green, the rain stopped, and the sound of a locomotive came driving down from the sky, never hitting us square but often rolling

183

close enough to take out an acre of crops. What reassurance those roots offered, that fruit, the smell of earth and cool walls, Donald holding my hand, heavy wool blankets pulled over our bodies for protection, Rebekah sleeping through it all, deepsleeper daughter, nodding her way through life. She did not spend enough hours playing in the mud, never had any love for the land, no feeling for trees or stones, thinks dirt is something to cover with concrete, always wanted to be clean as a girl. I told her there was nothing cleaner than dirt but somehow failed to impart this belief to my farm child who was ever too eager to leave the farm. 'Why can't we have a house like that?' she used to say, passing the cereal-box neighborhoods filling old cornfields east of our own. I blame myself for that as well, for not making my daughter see the beauty of this place or have pride in the house she inhabited instead of always lusting after a thing better or newer. I don't know where she came from, what midwife intervened to prick her finger and make her sleepwalk through life. She has her suburban California house now, made of drywall and plywood and a fake stone façade, and she's as proud as if it were an unusually bright child: coddles it, shines its floors, scolds when it gets dirty, dresses it in frills and bows, and keeps it scrubbed so hard it looks uncomfortable with itself, barely alive, afraid of its owner's reproof. I knew children like that when I was still teaching, saw them arrive each morning spotless, trembling, avoiding any risk of mark or stain on their clothes and shoes. When I met the mothers at parent–teacher conferences it was clear those tired women often had nothing to give their children but cleanliness: the line between one state and another, the precipitous edge, the vertigo of falling from no height at all to an impossible depth.

I steal out the kitchen door, off the porch, and along the concrete path that leads in a straight line to the barn. The rain slackens, giving less of itself, and I am scarcely wet when I arrive under the pent where hay used to be pulleyed up into the loft on the long beam jutting out from the top of the barn. From under the gas can I unearth the spare key that has always been kept by the door, unlock it, edge it open just wide enough to dart into the warm dark space that still smells of gasoline, old hay, and more faintly of Donald.

The rain strengthens, dropping pools in the dusty floor, drizzling through the loft and running flame-quick along beams. It will all come down. Without the city, time and nature would have done its work: slower, but destined for the same end. This barn and all these buildings have lived longer than their builders intended. The fight may be lost but I am still not ready to say goodbye. The dead are here, waiting, asking for a word.

A galvanized bucket filled with dust hangs from a nail in the corner of the side aisle nearest the road. I flip it over and rap on the bottom, watching the rain of particles catch and cascade in the light. Outside I lift the singing handle and bring it down and up and down and after a dozen of these blows the gouts of groundwater come, spurting into the bucket. Fill it, swirl it, toss it out, making more mud for the mud that's there. Just as the rain stops I take the third filling inside, leaving it on the porch by the kitchen door while I unlock the storm cellar and in the light that comes despite the rain I can see my pile of wood and kindling. Fuel will be a problem in another month or two.

I make a fire in the old kitchen stove that I kept even after the electric one arrived forty years ago. It has been useful for power outages in winter and in the storm season, for making the house hot when the winds drag the chill below zero. Coaxing kindling into flame I layer the larger pieces in the way my mother taught me, and while the fire takes and water boils in the cast iron pot I return to the vegetable patch with the bucket, harvesting tomatoes and peppers, pulling leeks from the ground, digging three potatoes from the sandy mud, pulling carrots, yanking up celery root, washing it all at the hemorrhaging pump.

I peel and cut, making a late summer soup, and stand at the kitchen window for the next hour, the fingers of my right hand tipped against my teeth, elbow resting under the rib cage, the left hand on my hip: pose of preoccupation and worry, of what-next and wherefore.

I taste the carrot-sweet broth and set it aside to

cool until I can eat it. My mother is here, standing at the window looking up at the Krovik doom house. Although the image shifts in my mind, I can see her clearly, Mother in her young-womanhood, middle years, and death throes, the ages flowing over the ghostly presence as the light changes, a furrow of sun cutting down through clouds and bringing Mama out all matronly, in her prime, the age she was when Donald and I got married. She speaks in her soundless voice.

*You can't stay, LouLou.*

And what happens to you, Mama, if I go for good, and when the house comes down?

*You don't worry about us. We'll all head to the woods. And if they chop down the woods we'll go to the river. And if the river runs dry we'll run into the ground, go deep, wait out the rest of this age, down where all is quiet and dark and good.*

Will you eat? I raise my cup of soup to her face. Mama laughs and the laughter breaks her up, an evanescence that sings the clouds apart, clears the sky, dries out the land.

The national headquarters of Nathaniel's company occupy a fifty-acre campus on the edge of the old downtown, divided from the once bustling streets around the county courthouse by a twelve-lane freeway built in the 1970s, which required the eviction of thousands of people who were subsequently relocated into federal housing projects. These have in turn been demolished in the last decade, as Nathaniel's company purchased entire city blocks of surrounding slum neighborhoods, razed them, and built an interlocking complex of apartment buildings with integrated restaurants, grocery stores, dry cleaners, movie theaters, and health clubs. Billed as the CITY WITHIN THE CITY, the centerpiece of the company's headquarters is a reflective glass-sheathed corporate high-rise occupying the traditional place of the town hall, church, or meetinghouse. On some days the tower appears silver, on others almost black, and under the most favorable conditions it seems not to be there at all, disappearing into its own reflective surface. The meetinghouse has become the mall or, as is more recently the case, the shopping strip or plaza. A church remains untouched on the periphery of the new development, while the actual town hall is a mile away in the old downtown, surrounded by empty lots and vacant skyscrapers built in the previous century and adjacent to the county jail and police headquarters. The downtown remains the preserve of the law: of charges, trials, and temporary incarceration before transit to the state penitentiary on the edge of the city. To the east, near the river, there has been successful redevelopment of the warehouse district Nathaniel loves, the riverfront with its privatized parkland, walking paths, marinas, sidewalk cafés, luxury hotels, conference centers, sports stadia, concert arena, and thicket of public art: a plaza is filled with bronze statues depicting nineteenth-century pioneers with ox wagons, the women in bonnets and ankle-length dresses, men in buckskin with rifles taking aim at bison, children frolicking, a family of American Indians looking on stoically from one corner, as if already in reservations.

Nathaniel has no illusions about the nature of his company's corporate campus development, or of the kind of work EKK is doing in the city. It is promoting a vision of how, from the core of self-professed corporate personhood, a new conception of the body politic can radiate across and subsume the previously blighted urban landscape. Companies must, by their nature, attend to the image they project in the world, and by suggesting

189

in its national headquarters, located dead in this country's heartland, that it is not just an inward-looking corporation, but one focusing its gaze outward, seeing the world around it, attending to it, to the people who live within it, to the way its presence might be interpreted by those who look upon it, the company communicates the truth of its mission: involvement in all kinds of business, in potentially *every* kind of business. The creation of this city-within-the-city, in which the corporation provides and manages all aspects of life and leisure, reflects its own corporate ethos. In recent years it has started calling itself 'holistic', because, as current CEO Alexander Reveley likes to put it, 'we're in the business of *being* the planet'. Although it started off as a security company and defense contractor, EKK – which was, at its genesis, a merger of three companies, one British, one American, and one South African – has expanded into so many different sectors it would be incorrect to describe it simply as a security company, or only a maker of advanced defense systems and weaponry, or merely, as its website says, a provider of *solutions for all sectors of society including corporate, domestic, government, and parastatal security architecture – facilities to meet all protection needs*. The heads of the corporation have a vision, Nathaniel understands, in which the next wave of *global* business will be global in all senses of the word: active everywhere, touching all aspects of a person's life, from conception (there is a new fertility and biotech division), to birth (health care provision, medical subcontracting), education (charter school administration and curriculum development, private tertiary institutional expansion through profit-making universities and technical schools), employment (welfare-to-work contracting), employee relations (end-of-contract consultation), financial and asset management (merchant bank division, pension and retirement planning, hedge funds), security and incarceration (the original core of the business), immigration centers and foreign-national detention, entertainment (film production and financing, games, amusement parks, immersive fourth-wave entertainment environments, publishing, television and radio production, theater management), travel (global positioning systems, transportation management and security, hotel and resort administration, urban bicycle rental schemes, traffic signaling and interstate toll concessions), old age (long-term care insurance and nursing home management; the pharmaceutical wing is just getting started), all the way to death and disposal (cremation, organ and tissue recycling, human remains management). There are no limits to what the corporation might do. This, Alexander Reveley is always keen to remind his employees from the company's world headquarters in Switzerland, is going to be the future of business: a small number of holistic, synergistic corporations managing all aspects of life on the planet. They will be managing the planet itself, and who knows what else; the company has recently broken ground on a space port and is already in the advanced stages of developing next-generation craft and 'a transitional low-earth-orbit infrastructural presence' that will one day allow the manufacture of off-planet installations, preparing for what Reveley foresees as the inevitable mining boom on Mars, however far in the future it may prove to be. EKK will be ready. It has two million employees worldwide and expands every day.

The scope of the company's business is as humbling as it is awe-inspiring. Nathaniel knows he is but part of a tiny circuit in a machine whose size and complexity he cannot discern, and whose true nature is perhaps not just unknowable but covert by design, only capable of being understood in its totality by some future society that will look back to assess the position of people like Nathaniel within it. While there are aspects of the company's work he finds troubling – the defense contracting, the neoliberal welfare-to-work division, the asset-stripping finance divisions – he believes the kind of rehabilitative program he oversees has a true social value that makes the world more secure for everyone. Who would not want criminals to be rehabilitated? If the corporation can produce revenue at the same time, monies to fund other worthwhile divisions, then that must be all to the good. All over the world this kind of work is moving from the public to the private sphere, and to continue in the field, as Nathaniel wishes to do, he has no choice but to accept the nature of the machine.

His undergraduate degree was in sociology with a minor in criminology, a strand of study he passed off to his parents as the foundation for advanced degrees in more robustly intellectual subjects. When he decided to pursue an MBA straight out of college, his father gave him the smug smile that even now, years after the confrontation, comes smirking out of the back of his mind in the middle of the night.

'I'm not going to say you don't disappoint me, Nate,' his father said, the smirk tearing open his face, teeth clenched, jaw muscles twitching. Nathaniel had not gone by the abbreviated form of his name since high school, but his father persisted for years, sometimes shortening it even further to 'Nat', which Nathaniel can only ever hear as 'gnat': a tiny irritant, an unwanted domestic invader, flitting around and alighting on overripe fruit. 'You've always disappointed me,' his father continued, 'even more so than your brother, and he's been a monumental disappointment. You've never been strong enough. Just look at you. What do you weigh now, anyway? One-ninety, two-hundred? Don't you exercise at all?'

'Exercise takes time, I study—'

His father laughed, that smile ripping his jaw free from the top of his head. 'You've always lacked the drive to put in the kind of work that would allow you to overcome your intellectual challenges.'

'I have a 4.0 GPA. I scored 760 on my SATs.'

'You are hardly unique in that respect. You've done very little in the way of extracurricular activity, and I would hazard a guess that your intellectually slack choice of major has a great deal to do with the relative success you've enjoyed.'

'Then what do you want me to do?'

'Show a little intellectual spine. God knows I've tried to get you to stand up for yourself, to stop being so goddamn weak and submissive. That's been the driving purpose in everything I've done for you.'

Nathaniel remembered then all that his father had done before: the taunts and teases and visits in the night when his mother was away at conferences, the whispering and heckling, all in the name of making him more assertive, harder and tougher. His father used to nudge the door open, pad into Nathaniel's room, look around at the contents of his shelves, open his closet and rummage through his clothes, then come over to his son's bed, kneel down next to him, put his hand flat on Nathaniel's back, push his son's body down hard into the mattress, and whisper: *You are nothing. You are no one. You do not matter.* Nathaniel would hardly be able to breathe. He would cough, choke, and spend the rest of the night awake. When Nathaniel got home from school each day, he would survey his room, noting small changes to the positions of his belongings, knowing that his father had been there, fingering his books and toys. For years he thought he was imagining it, even the visits in the night, certain it was all a dream. But then one day his father left his coffee mug in Nathaniel's room. It was a mug that only his father was allowed to use: a cheap brown one given away by a chain of pancake houses. No one else ever wanted to use the mug with a chip in its handle but his father would accuse Matthew and Nathaniel of taking it whenever it went astray. Nathaniel put the mug outside the door to his father's study and taped a note to its rim: *Next time you want to snoop don't leave any evidence.*

'You could have been a professor at a minor liberal arts college,' his father said on that day Nathaniel told him about his plans for business school. 'You might even have made a fairly decent family doctor or corporate attorney. You don't have to be a genius to do any of those things.'

'I've been accepted into the top MBA program in the country. Doesn't that mean anything?'

'What kind of business is going to want someone who's never had any practical experience? Business is not just theoretical. As with everything, you're going about it entirely the wrong way.'

His father shook his head and spat into the grass in the backyard; it was the spring break of Nathaniel's senior year in college. In fact, he did have experience. He'd interned every summer at a security company. Security was important to him in ways he would only understand much later in life. When Nathaniel turned thirteen he had installed a lock on his bedroom door and after that Arthur Noailles stopped coming into his youngest son's room at night, opting instead for sudden and violent physical attacks that were only ever inflicted at home, the curtains and blinds closed against the neighbors, a fire more often than not roaring in the living room, Nathaniel's body somersaulting through landscapes of brocaded pillows and magenta *toile de Jouy* drapery, coming to rest on floorboards and crashing into the black bedrock of the marble hearth. Such attacks were most frequent in winter, clustering from November through mid-March, from Thanksgiving to Easter: the academic term, the long annual season of Arthur's rage, when he took out the frustrations of his professorial career on his children. One night, when Nathaniel was around the age of fifteen, his father ripped the shirt from his son's back because, when Arthur asked about his day, Nathaniel reported that nothing ever happened at school. Their mother was away, or perhaps she was still with a patient. His father was short but heavily muscled, his reflexes quick, hands full of such power that ripping a shirt in two seemed to present no challenge. Matthew rose to his feet and although he was by then both taller and even more muscular than his father, Arthur shoved his eldest son back into his chair, giving Nathaniel the opportunity to run from the house and out into the snow, shirtless and barefoot, fat and horrified to find himself half-naked in public, the white melon of his stomach blanching scarlet. Arms outstretched, his father ran after him, silent except for the sound of his shoes breaking through layers of ice over snow. Nathaniel looked down at his legs and found his own ankles lacerated and bleeding. He screamed for help, but when two separate neighbors came to his assistance and he told them what had happened, watching his father stop suddenly a hundred yards back, panting in the middle of a frozen lawn, up to his calves in snow, they suggested he go back inside and talk it over with his parents. Although he never learned if the neighbors said anything to his father or to anyone else, the physical attacks stopped, only to be replaced with a litany of verbal abuse and psychological intimidation that has continued into the present. Matthew and Julia are the only people who know the truth. 'Maybe business is the best place you could possibly end up,' his father spat. '*Business is for the intellectually indolent and the morally adipose.*' It was one of Arthur's favorite maxims, practiced and polished and routinely deployed to dismiss, castigate, and inflame. Nathaniel understood even then that it was a philosophy his father was free to embrace because he had been born into a family where no one ever had to worry about money.

When Nathaniel's mother heard that he was

going to business school, she turned away from him even more than she had in all the years leading up to that decisive moment when he concluded he could be nothing like the person his parents wanted. Matthew had already done that by becoming a painter and moving to Berlin where he lives with his Turkish partner and two adopted children in an apartment in Kreuzberg, which his parents have refused to visit.

'We're not going to pay for an MBA. If you insist on doing it you can fund yourself,' his mother said, flipping through a patient's file. 'I suppose you think you're escaping from us in making such a clean break professionally, but you haven't – neither has Matty. If you wanted to go to law school, that would be another question entirely.' They were standing in the enclosed porch where his mother saw her patients. Nathaniel started to cry. He couldn't stop himself. He remembers his mother looking at him as if she were about to give him a sheet of paper with a squiggle on it and command him to draw what-ever came into his head. 'Now what do you think it means that you're crying?' she asked. He shook his head. He didn't know whether he was crying because of the tone of her voice or the fact that support was being cut off so summarily. He tried to stop himself but the harder he tried the faster the tears seemed to come and the more acute his paralysis became. At last he was sobbing, his body rigid as his mother stood, arms crossed, never touching him but studying his outburst as if observing an arcane purification rite. 'You need to be in therapy,' she said. He choked down sobs, shaking his head. 'I won't have any protest. I'll make an appointment for you to see Gordon.' Gordon was one of his mother's former lovers, a Freudian who lived a few streets away. Fearing what might emerge in therapy, Nathaniel did not wait for the threatened appointment: the following morning he flew to Berlin where he spent the rest of the break trying to convince Matthew they should press charges against their father, hauling the past out into the light for the first time. As boys they never spoke with each other about what happened and even as adults, up until that week, they had failed to compare their experiences. Nathaniel was not even sure whether Matthew's treatment had been better or worse or equivalent to his own. The language sputtered, gave out, had to be jump-started in ways that kept them barely moving forward, and words were not the only barrier: nausea overwhelmed Nathaniel on each outing of the subject – a queasiness hot and gushing and knife-twistingly sharp.

'Nathaniel – it's – don't you see? We have nothing.' Matthew choked as he lifted the hem of his red t-shirt and pulled down the waist of his jeans to expose the faint undulating scar that snaked from the cleft of his buttocks, across his waist and around the left side of his body to just above his navel. Nathaniel had not seen the mark for many years, but he knew its contours as well as his own face. Before that day they had never discussed its origins. 'It's not evidence,' Matthew said. 'I can't do it. I'm done with both of them.'

Apart from their own bodies, which have healed, there has never been any evidence to prove the monstrosity of their childhood.

Because they own only one car, Nathaniel and Julia drive together to the Pinwheel Academy, built as a concrete abstraction of the toy. 'The Hub', in the center of the building, houses the principal's office, while around it radiate six triangular wings filled with classrooms. One of the guidance counselors, Mrs Taylor, registers and fingerprints Copley while Nathaniel and Julia try to look reassuring. He was never fingerprinted at his school in Boston, but here they insist it is a necessary part of the school's security protocols, and fingerprint scanners are the means by which students check out books from the library and pay for their lunch each day.

'The child's fingerprint is linked to his record, and parents pay lunch money into an individualized account that can be debited for supplies, fieldtrip fees, and disciplinary fines,' Mrs Taylor explains.

'Disciplinary fines?' Nathaniel has no recollection of reading about fines in the school brochure provided by his company.

'If a student defaces or destroys school property, the cost of repair or replacement is debited to his or her account. Detentions and tardiness carry set fines: five dollars for each incident of tardiness, twenty-five dollars for every detention. We find that fines have a very positive effect on classroom behavior. Unexcused absences are charged at the rate of forty dollars a day, and excused absences in excess of five per semester at the rate of one hundred dollars per day. All the information about school policies and procedures is online. This is the parent–child–school contract, which you need to sign in order to complete the registration.'

Nathaniel and Julia skim their portion of the contract. It outlines not only what Mrs Taylor has explained, but also a host of other rules, expectations, restrictions, punishments, incentives and disincentives, benchmark goals, and outright threats. Mrs Taylor leaves them for a moment to take a call.

'We can always move him to another school,' Julia whispers. 'If this doesn't work out.'

Nathaniel lacks the energy to tell her it is not a choice they have. This is the school Copley will attend, whether they like it or not, because it would be bad for Nathaniel's career if they sent their son anywhere else. They sign the form, show Copley where to sign, and watch as the guidance counselor signs on her return.

'Are we good?' Mrs Taylor asks. Nathaniel nods

but Julia is rigid, clasping Copley's hand. 'That's all taken care of then. You don't know what a relief it is to have parents who understand what we're trying to accomplish here. You would not *believe* the resistance we get from some people.'

'I can imagine,' Nathaniel says.

'I don't think you can,' the woman laughs. 'I'm not talking about good people like the two of you. Some of the parents we get these days – straight off the plane if you know what I mean. We like all the expectations to be out in the open. It makes for a much better environment. You'll see the longer you're with us that we pride ourselves on students with good, normal behavior.'

To Nathaniel's relief, none of Copley's toy soldier mimicry is on display this morning, nothing to suggest that his son is in any way abnormal. The boy walks a natural straight line, bends his knees, swings his arms like any child. They accompany him to meet his teacher, Mrs Pitt, who says she approves of parents taking the trouble to introduce themselves to their child's custodians. Something about Mrs Pitt makes Nathaniel wonder whether much actual teaching occurs in this new school, and how much of the program is just about managing the child, making sure he or she does not get into any serious physical harm or destroy valuable property. Mrs Pitt has an oval face and, though she is young, certainly younger than Nathaniel and Julia by five or more years, her hair is already graying and she has the figure of a much older woman. She speaks down to Copley in a way that Nathaniel imagines his son's teachers in Boston never did, and he sees in the long wooden pointer she holds in her hand the threat of a different Mrs Pitt once the parents are safely out of school.

In the lobby of the main building on the EKK corporate campus, Nathaniel presents himself to one of the guards. The man pulls up his record, asks him to place the index finger of his right hand on an electronic sensor, and to approach another device that reads his iris; Nathaniel's biometric records are on file from his time in the Boston office. Once the system establishes that he is who he claims to be, the guard directs him up to the twentieth floor. At the barrier between the lobby and the bank of elevators, Nathaniel touches the palm and fingers of his right hand to another sensor, confirming his identity once more, before it opens the glass gate and allows him access to the left bank of elevators, which serves the first thirty floors of the building; the top fifteen floors are accessible from the right bank of elevators, and only to people with higher internal security clearance than Nathaniel is ever likely to possess.

He knows that the new job comes with more perks than his previous position, but no one mentioned that he would be assigned a corner office on a high floor with views to the east and north over the skyline of the old downtown, the enclave of gentrified riverfront, the distant farmland, hills pitching and tumbling in tiles of brilliant green and dark brown, or the white cube of a nuclear power station north of the city just visible on the horizon. At forty-five stories, the EKK building is the tallest in the city, one of a crop of new skyscrapers that shot up in the peak years of the boom, and it has the most expansive views of any building in a radius of two hundred miles. The city is still nothing to compare with Boston, but its solidity, spaciousness, and attention to human scale are reassuring.

There is a secretary named Letitia, and, to his surprise, a company car already at his disposal, with a reserved parking space in the executive garage. All this privilege requires a kind of recalibration of his sense of himself: a man who has in his possession, if not his outright ownership, two cars, a five-thousand-square-foot house with not one but two furnaces, a wife and a child, nearly an acre of land, a good job doing something he believes is valuable to society, a pension plan, investments, a life insurance policy, and an affordable mortgage. He will make new friends in this new place. He will be outgoing and gregarious. He will invite the neighbors for backyard barbecues. He will settle into the life he and Julia have designed for themselves. He will spend every day forgetting about his father. What better reason to leave Boston than to escape a sphere of the world still dominated – at least for him – by the presence of his parents?

'Here's your welcome pack, Mr Noailles,' Letitia says, handing him an embossed leather binder two inches thick. 'Inside you'll find information about building procedures, emergency contingency plans, services available to you on site, etcetera, etcetera. I'm assuming you already have a copy of your new contract, but if you ever need another copy I can put in a request for one to be delivered through confidential internal mail, either hard copy or digitally encrypted. It's no problem.'

She gives the impression of having everything under control, and, unlike so many other people, even knows how to pronounce his name.

'That's impressive,' he says. 'Most people don't get it right the first time.'

'My mother came from Louisiana, so it kinda made sense, a French name, but I also phoned the Boston office to find out. I wanted to be sure we started off on the right foot.'

Letitia introduces him to his colleagues, the men and women who will be working under his supervision, and the other secretaries on the floor: most of them women, all of them Latina or black; Letitia, he understands, is at the top of a particular stratum of the divisional hierarchy, which reflects the seniority of his own position. She takes him on a tour of the EKK campus, pointing out the executive dining room on the thirtieth floor, the staff canteen, on-site gym and swimming pool on the fifteenth. At her encouragement, he makes an appointment with the internal financial consultant for a review of his investments and pension plan. After lunch, he schedules the installation of the home security system and agrees to take the armed response package. 'It's super reassuring,' the man in Domestic Security Products tells him. 'I wouldn't want any of the other ones myself. I mean you could go with the package that just triggers a call to the local police and whatnot, but I'd trust our own EKK guys more than the cops. A lot of ours are ex-military; we even have a retired Navy SEAL. Before I went to work here my wife and I had a really bad break-in. We weren't home, you know, but they stole fucking everything.' Nathaniel knows what Julia will think of armed response, but decides to take it and see if she notices.

Nathaniel has been brought over as the new National Director of Offender Rehabilitation and Letitia has made him an appointment with his new boss, Maureen McCarthy, Vice-President of Corrections Management. The last several years in the Boston office he worked on rehabilitation at the state level and his innovative programs were judged a model of efficiency and cost-effectiveness, while also auguring well for reduced rates of recidivism.

'So you're the *bright young thing*, the *great white hope* who's going to solve the nation's rehabilitation problem and get all those offenders back on track, isn't that right?' Maureen takes his hand in her fists, pumps his arm once before letting it drop, and indicates a black leather couch. Her office is three times the size of his and has a terrace with a table and two chairs.

'I don't know about all that, Maureen.'

'I do. I asked for you. You did great things in Boston. But now I need you to take all that experience and do something really radical with it, turn it on its head. So let me ask you this deceptively simple question: what is the problem with prisons?'

It is unclear whether Maureen means this rhetorically until she raises her eyebrows and nods, indicating, Nathaniel understands, that she expects him to answer.

'I'm not sure about one *single* problem. As I don't have to tell you, Maureen, there are a number of problems: overcrowding, aging infrastructure, inmate violence, poor staff training, guard corruption, drugs and other contraband.'

'Yes, yes, yes, although those aren't so much problems as irritations or impediments. And they certainly aren't *the* problem with prisons. Think, Nathaniel. What do all governments hate about prisons? Why is EKK in the business of prisons?'

'They cost money. They cost a whole lot of money.'

'Exactly. And that's where you come in.' She points at him, smiles for a moment, pauses, stares with her fixed green eyes. He wonders once more if he is supposed to speak, but then she starts up again. 'Rather than making prisons cost, we want to turn them into *engines of pure profit*. In states like this one, we have a permanent contract for corrections management that can only be broken if some jackass introduces a bill that makes it through the legislature and gets signed by the governor. Such a scenario would require gross failure on our part, and that's just not going to happen. The states pay us a fee to look after their criminals: to catch them in some cases, to process them, to house them, maintain them, *rehabilitate them*,' she says, opening her eyes wider and nodding as if to indicate she recognizes this is Nathaniel's part in the process, 'release them, manage their parole, monitor their movements, and start all over again when they reoffend. We know that most of them do, and – I'll let you in on a little secret – in a way, you know, we kind of *like* that. Recidivism is not necessarily a bad thing from our perspective.'

'It isn't?'

She shakes her head, nods it, shakes it again. 'So far, we've managed to make modest profits on the incarceration division of our Corrections unit. We've drastically reduced the number of guards, imposed more restrictions on prisoner movement, equipped all inmates with GPS ankle monitors so their exact location in the prison is always known, and rolled out a seamless blanket of video surveillance in all our facilities. Guards, in some ways, are the problem. Psych profiling and behaviometrics suggest that in a majority of cases guards are on the right side of the law by pure chance; in other words, our data show that guards are, more often than most people would imagine, criminals who have not yet offended. What I'm saying is that they can be bought off and bribed by inmates. Guards are corruptible. Cameras are not, and when the person monitoring the cameras has no direct contact with prisoners, you increase security fivefold. Now, upper management is largely pleased with our progress so far, and they have taken note of your successes, particularly in reducing over-heads in the Northeastern Division. But they also think there's a lost opportunity here. And that's where you come in, Nathaniel. That's why we brought you here, to the heart of the operation. We want you to upgrade our rehabilitation programs, implementing them across the national infrastructure before moving on to global roll-out, and engineer them to generate more revenue.'

'I wasn't aware that rehabilitation programs were revenuegenerating.'

'Some would say it's a gray area. Wed rehabilit-ation to highly skilled vocational training,' Maureen continues, meshing her hands into a single fist, 'introduce core low-security manufacturing across the board. Require minimum forty-hour work-weeks of all able-bodied prisoners regardless of age; our prison doctors are prepared to declare all but terminal cases able-bodied. At the moment inmates only have to work one hour each day, which is ludicrous.'

'And if they refuse to work?'

'You throw them in the hole. Put them in isolation. Describe them as non-cooperative. Prisoners spend too much time lying around with their dicks in their hands. We're on target to have more than a hundred thousand inmates in our protection by the end of the decade, and we can grow that number through continued lobbying across federal, state, and local government for mandatory minimum sentencing, three strikes laws, you name it. Crime is our oyster: it's an amazing workforce just waiting to be "rehabilitated" into positive labor production. Let's not kid ourselves about these people, we know what they're like, and for the most part we know who they are even before they do. Am I right?'

'I guess so,' he says, finding himself both horrified and transfixed by the rhythms of Maureen's speech. She never loses eye contact, holding his gaze with such force that he feels at once violated and excited by the power she projects.

'The idea is that we pay them one per cent of the federal minimum wage while the rest of that notional pay goes to non-profit victim-support organizations, a donation we can write off for tax purposes. Inmates get paid to learn a valuable skill, they make EKK products and components, in states like this they also do agricultural work, and all those things they make are products we can sell or components that contribute to things and processes we already sell. The revenue generated by inmates will support the running of prisons themselves. It's a genius proposition, Nathaniel.'

'Forgive me if I'm being too modest, Maureen, but it sounds like you've already worked it out. Why do you need me?'

'You're not being too modest, not at all. What I've done is sketch the big picture. All I really need you to do is fine-tune the state-by-state details, and that's still a big job. You have to be sure it's all within the law. If the law is in our way, you're empowered to use our lobbying agencies to get the laws changed. More importantly, though, you'll need to oversee the integration of our manufacturing needs with skills training and operations relocation. You have to work out the numbers. I've seen your record. I know you're capable of achieving this. I'll expect progress reports every other Friday by 10 AM, in my little inbox, and by the end of the year I'd like to see the program start to be rolled out as widely as possible, state by state, wherever we can. Research the law. Research areas where manufacturing is costing us much more than it should be. Find us ways to make the prisons pay.'

As Nathaniel heads back to Dolores Woods in the company car at the end of the day, driving home from work for the first time in his life instead of walking or taking some form of public transportation, he experiences a return of that overwhelming urge to flee, to pick up Julia and Copley and drive straight out of the city without looking back, never stopping until they hit the East Coast, as far from the heartland as they can possibly get. He can see how this new job will change him, force him to become a different version of himself. The nature of the job is nothing like what he was expecting, although a part of him knows that, in its way, Maureen McCarthy's plan is nothing that should surprise him. A corporation is in the business of making money, and making as much money as it can in the most efficient way. He has always assumed, however, that his own work is motivated by a greater, an altruistic impulse, one sanctioned by the corporation because low rates of recidivism can only be good for society as a whole. But then, as he waits in traffic, progressing at two miles per hour through lights that tell him when to stop and when to go as the rain begins to fall again, washing the rolling gray sprawl of the city westwards, he begins to wonder how much EKK wants rehabilitation to work at all. If the idea is to tap prisoners as a free labor force that only has to be housed and fed and regulated by an increasingly technological presence, then perhaps the real goal is not rehabilitation, but the training of an entire group, even a class of people, who will go on reoffending throughout their lives, re-entering a corrections system that exploits their labor potential for the profits of a corporation that manages ever more numerous aspects of life inside and outside the walls of the prison. He has to admit, it has the quality of genius: the criminal class transformed by legal means into the largest body of slave labor since the great emancipation.

For the first weeks after the new owners move in, Paul keeps the containment door to the basement locked, pretending he does not hear the sounds filtering down along the plumbing and electrical lines, the way these new people move through his house shouting to each other from room to room, stomping and running and slamming. On most mornings the woman is in the basement workshop before breakfast, again after dinner each night, and during most of the weekend. He does not have to see her to know she is standing at the workbench: the lights in the bunker pulse off and on whenever she is there, her body bent over tools and machines that produce high-pitched whines and reverberations which shake the foundation of the house.

At such times, Paul closes his eyes, turns off the lights, and pushes his fingers into his ears, feeling the attack of the woman's tools on his skin, metal points puncturing, penetrating, boring into his body.

It is important to pretend he still has a normal life. Each morning he weighs out his cereal and eats it with reconstituted powdered milk. He takes long showers that pull water from the main house, ticking up quantities of consumption on the meter of the people who have forced him into hiding. He keeps the lights on all day, whether or not he stays at home. He lets the hot water run in his kitchen and bathroom sinks. Each morning he leaves the bunker through the containment door that opens onto the nineteenth-century storm cellar, locks it behind him, unlocks the old wooden cellar doors, locks those, and climbs the steps into the woods, waiting for a moment to be sure no one is watching before parting the gates of brush that camouflage the entrance. In the evening he follows the profiles of trees he is beginning to know, looking for the hollowed-out trunk in which his ventilation pipe is hidden, any signs of manufacture obscured by a mass of creeper that grows along its length. As autumn descends, the creeper has started turning red so that in the angle of the evening sun the dead trunk appears to be in flames.

Weeks pass and it is getting lighter later in the morning and darker earlier in the evening. Most days it rains: thunderous downpours that split Paul open, storms that pattern the sky in a kaleidoscope of dark blue and magenta shale, as if the polarities of earth and atmosphere have been reversed, the fiery bedrock of the world cocooning a watery, gaseous sphere. Another tree not far from the entrance to the bunker is hit by lightning one night and explodes, embedding blond shards of wood in the surrounding earth and plowing up the forest floor. The smell of the ruined tree is nauseating: rotten meat, ozone, and gunpowder bonded together, dispersed through the woods by an unholy creature of land and sky, a priestly giant swinging her thurible.

After closing the gates of brush that conceal the cellar doors, Paul adds more branches, sticks, and piles of leaves. At times he fears that making the entrance look so much like an animal's home might attract the attention of a hunter expecting to find beavers or muskrats; although the creek running nearby is often almost dry by late summer, in recent days it has started to flow again, shallow but fast.

In the woods he tries to avoid stepping on fallen twigs, keeping to the stretches of sodden leaf matter and skirting the muddy creek bed where he can identify the spoor of deer, foxes, and coyotes, which he has heard at night wailing to one another. Moving through the woods, he keeps his body hunched, bent at the waist, low to the ground to avoid detection, neck straight, eyes alert, head cocked and swinging from side to side, narrow hips drawn tight. People walk these woods even though the land is private, trespassers straying from the neighboring reserve where hunting is allowed. Turkeys and deer are in season. There are poachers, too, who take their chances with traps, intent on killing whatever they can. In many ways he feels less exposed walking through streets than he does darting through trees, picking his way across an obstacle course of noise-making matter liable to betray his presence. But now he too is a trespasser, walking on land that belongs to Nathaniel and Julia Noailles and which, at some unmarked place, becomes public land: land that once belonged to the old widow Washington but which has now been claimed by the city. On streets there is no ambiguity: a street is a place where anyone can stand, a sidewalk free for passage, observed, open to all. In the woods there are no visible borders other than the sign at the entrance to the reserve or the NO TRESPASSING notices nailed to trees threatening violators with prosecution or bullets if they stray onto private land. There are places to hide, and places where others may be hidden.

He misses the way he and his father hunted, the closeness of sitting together in silence with no expectation of speech on either side, where silence was an oasis open to all comers rather than a vacuum demanding presence and fulfillment. In silence he could listen to his father breathe, hear the hand slide along the rifle, aware of the man shifting his weight from one leg to the other if they were standing for a long time, or leaning back against the wall of a wooden hide and exhaling breath that always smelled clean and alpine. When they hunted alone, even after a kill, they hardly spoke. His father communicated directions in two or three words. Ralph was always more comfortable with nouns than with verbs, with the naming of things that required action rather than a description of the action itself. Action was only to be implied. 'Rock,' he'd say under his breath, and Paul knew he was meant to follow his father to a large boulder and crouch down in silence behind it, waiting, balancing together on a cold late autumn morning, at their feet the smell of leaves, a fawn mustiness and fallow decay. Most of the time his father would see the deer first, and the silence was so complete between them the man only had to tilt his head in the direction of the animal for Paul to follow his gaze, for them both to aim, for his father to exhale the word 'Mine' or 'Yours' depending on his assessment of who had the better shot. In those moments the word was more expulsion of inflected air than anything approaching a whisper, let alone speech. It was the best and purest communication that ever passed between them. Even after making a kill, retrieving the deer and undertaking the field dressing, silence persisted. 'Gut,' his father would say, and Paul knew then to use the steel hook, piercing the hide near the stomach, slipping the point up towards the neck, slitting open the cavity of the animal so his father could reach inside, pull out the internal organs and cut them away, leaving the rest of the body intact until they got it home to skin and butcher in the garage.

The rides home in the truck, the kill or kills secured under the canopy in the back, were as silent as the hunting itself had been, although the ease and comfort of the wood-bound quiet coarsened, thickened into tension by the expectation that now, when silence was no longer necessary, speech should occupy the space between them. Paul could never bring himself to speak first, so he waited for the man to speak, to ask him what he had done in school that week, or, if his father was feeling buoyant about what they had managed to kill, to tell Paul stories of his exploits in the air, of the surveillance missions over war zones, the thrill and significance of work that filled the largest portion of Ralph Krovik's life.

Paul's truck is parked in River Ranch, the neighboring subdivision, which was a horse farm before it sold to the area's largest developer. The houses on those streets are more modest than the ones Paul built in Dolores Woods, the owners less prosperous, a neighborhood of blue-collar families with no resident doctors or lawyers or corporate executives: plumbers, electricians, schoolteachers, construction workers – people more like Paul. Either the residents of River Ranch own more cars and trucks than most people, or their garages are smaller, but there are always vehicles parked on the streets and Paul's truck does not attract attention as it might in Dolores Woods. There, in any case, his former neighbors would be bound to recognize it. Nonetheless, to avoid attracting attention, he parks the truck on a different street in

River Ranch each night, always making a note of its location so he can find it the next morning.

There is nothing more suspicious than a lone man walking through suburban streets. The face he finds in the mirror each morning belongs to someone who can only be suspicious. He shaves, keeps his hair tidy with electric clippers, irons his clothes, anything he can do to trick the world into believing he lives above ground in a house instead of a bunker, free from the burden of more debt than he can ever hope to repay.

During the first days after the new people moved into the house Paul drove around to construction sites asking for work. Most of the guys knew him and were aware he had lost everything. They all looked sorry for him, pretended to be sympathetic, but none had any work to spare. No one was building homes anymore, and the few that were still going up had either been sold in advance or were likely to stand empty on completion.

Paul has never worked any job unrelated to construction or carpentry. He lacks the clothes and patience to do retail work, and when he asks about shifts at restaurants the managers say he needs food service experience. Yesterday a waitress in a diner told him a grocery store was opening a new branch and they might need checkers or – she glanced at the breadth of his shoulders and chest – a few strong men to work in the back. 'I bet you could get a job as a bouncer,' she said, but Paul has never liked bars and does not want to stand outside of one looking like a pimp or a prostitute.

Last week he made signs advertising CARPENTRY WORK AT GOOD RATES BY AN HONEST AMERICAN AND A CHRISTIAN with his cell phone number and email address. After taping a dozen of these to streetlight poles at major intersections, he remembered he has no reception in the bunker and neither a computer nor internet access, while his phone is so old all it can do is send and receive calls. He looks for an internet café but these no longer seem to exist. Everywhere has FREE WIFI, or WIFI HOTSPOTS that charge a fee, but no actual computers. The public libraries, where he might have sought refuge, have all been closed by the city in the last three years.

Each day, as soon as he is sitting in his truck, often in the parking lot of a mall or shopping plaza, rain pounding the windshield, his clothes wet and cold, he dials Amanda's cell. He has phoned every day since she left more than a year ago. At first she answered, would speak to him briefly, and even allowed him to speak to Carson and Ajax.

'Where are you?' he would ask in the first few conversations.

'Mom and Dad's,' she would say.

'How's Florida?'

'Hot. The boys like it, though.'

'Are you getting your own place?'

'Soon.'

He knows he is not an intuitive person, but he could tell even when the number still worked that she did not want to speak with him. A month after moving to Florida Amanda stopped answering Paul's calls. He phoned her parents' landline and her mother or father would make excuses: *she's at work, she's gone out, she's asleep, it's late here, try tomorrow*. They were always polite. Some weeks after that they told him she had moved out.

'Can I have her new number?'

'She – I don't know what it is, Paul,' her father said.

'Don't lie to him,' her mother said in the background.

'She asked us not to give you the number, Paul. I'm sorry. Why don't you come out here? We can try to get things straightened out between the two of you.'

'I have to get the house back first, Robert. I have to get back on my feet. Will you tell her that? I'm getting back on my feet. Everything's going to be okay. She should make plans to move back here by the end of the year. Tell her not to get too comfortable, okay? Will you tell her?'

'I'll tell her, Paul.'

A month later, after Paul had been phoning several times each day, having different versions of the same conversation, Amanda's parents changed their own number. Since then Paul has phoned directory assistance every day but there are no listings for Amanda or her parents. To hide from him, to keep him from his sons, knowing he lacks the money to come find them, they have made themselves disappear.

Nonetheless he dials Amanda's cell and hears the notice of disconnection. His wife has disconnected herself from him, separated him from his sons. When the divorce papers arrived, he burned them along with the restraining orders. At some point, he understands that his signature may no longer be needed, that a judge will rule Amanda is free to pursue other men. It may already be too late: there may be another man now taking the place of husband and father, usurping Paul's position in the family he has lost.

Weeks pass. Paul goes out each morning to look for work, comes home in the late afternoon, eats, exercises in the bunker, tries to ignore the noise of the new owners in the evening, and goes to sleep. October arrives. He buys gas for the truck until he has no money left and can no longer make the insurance payments. He sells his watch and wedding band at a store that advertises in tall yellow letters: WE BUY GOLD. There is nothing in his bank account. He has no unemployment payments, no welfare, and has not registered for food stamps. He does not believe in handouts and cannot imagine turning to the government for help, nor does he have any idea where he would go to find such help in the first place. He puts a FOR SALE sign on his truck and parks it in a wealthy suburb across town. An hour later a kid who has just turned seventeen phones him wanting a test drive. Paul goes to meet him at the kid's house, where a wrought-iron fence punctuated by brick and stone piers encircles the property. Copies of Greek statues fill the backyard.

'Why do you want my truck?' Paul asks as the kid speeds through the curling streets of his neighborhood, the houses half as big again as any Paul built.

The boy furrows his brow and squints across at Paul in the late afternoon light. 'What do you mean?'

'Watch the road, kid. You could have any truck you want.'

'But I like your truck. It's solid. And it's cheap. It's badass.' They return to the kid's house where he pulls to a stop in the driveway. He offers Paul half the asking price.

'Do me a thousand better.'

'Sure man, I'm feeling generous.'

'I just don't get it. You don't need this truck.'

'My parents don't want me to take my car when I go skiing,' the kid says, nodding at a black convertible in the five-car garage.

Paul bites down hard on his lower lip, tastes salt, chews off a flap of dry skin, and agrees to the sale. They drive to the DMV and take care of the paperwork. The kid turns over a roll of bills, which Paul stuffs in the pocket of his jeans.

'You think maybe I could have a lift?' Paul asks.

'Sure, I'll give you a lift. See what a nice guy I am?' the kid smirks, patting Paul on the back as if he were a child.

Without the truck, Paul hoists his backpack onto his shoulders, covers himself in a green camouflaged hunting poncho, and spends each day walking in the rain, checking the construction sites and always getting the same answer: No work here. One of the guys he has long considered a friend asks him not to come around again, telling him the answer will not change; he isn't the only one looking for work and there are lots of younger and hungrier guys than Paul who need a hand. 'Illegal ones, is what you mean. Guys who work for nothing,' Paul says.

'Listen, Paul,' his friend says, 'you did it too. I know you did. All us guys do it, and these days it's the only way I can make ends meet. You've played your cards, man. This ain't a world of second chances anymore. I'm sorry, buddy. I feel for you. It could be me next year. Don't think I don't know that. Are you hungry?'

'I eat,' Paul said, and turned away, trudging into a wall of rain.

He has plenty of food in the bunker, enough to last three months, six if he cuts the rations in half and supplements them with what he can hunt, glean, or gather. Foraging can be learned and he already knows how to kill. He has nothing left to sell except his labor and he cannot ask his mother

225

for help; she has little that is hers to give, nothing that is valuable apart from her own labor, and his father, who believes fanatically in self-reliance, will never do anything for him. This is, Paul knows, not a position of cruelty, but one of principle: self-reliance is his father's church and most profound conviction. 'I love you, Paul,' his father would say, 'but a man must stand by the force of his own power. I would be doing you a disservice if I bailed you out.'

Everywhere Paul walks he is careful to look where he is going, afraid of tripping and falling and breaking a bone. Being a pedestrian in a world designed for cars makes him realize how fragile he is. The newer shopping developments have sidewalks only in front of or around the stores, isolated islands in oceans of parking lot. He is conscious of people staring at him, and wonders if he has allowed some betraying signs of desperation or delinquency to surface, or if it is simply because the world expects a man like him not to be walking, his proper place behind the wheel of a truck. The body he inhabits, the body that confines him and determines how the world perceives him, a body he has worked hard to fashion into a titan's, has to learn all over again how to walk in a world that has always been hostile to man, which has become ever more hostile through man's own dominion over the world.

*Humanity*, Paul hears his wife saying, *Humanity instead of Man. You're such a Neanderthal.*

As he walks, thinking about his family, he finds himself looking at women who resemble Amanda or staring at boys and even girls who remind him of Carson and Ajax. One day he catches himself looking at a mother and her two children. The woman notices Paul staring and pulls the girls closer to her, away from this man, tall and muscular, tented in waterproof green nylon, who stares at small children.

He phones the numbers that no longer belong to his wife or her parents. New people answer in each case.

'Amanda, baby?'

'I think you have the wrong number.'

'I know she's there. Let me talk to her. I want to talk to my boys.'

'Sir, you've got the wrong number.'

'Don't hang up the phone, please, I just want to talk to my wife. Tell her it's okay, it's Paul. I just need to talk to her.'

'I'm hanging up now, sir.'

'If you hang up I swear to God I'll come and get you. I'm going to find you.'

The woman on the other end hangs up. Paul looks at his reflection in the windows of a fast food restaurant, the jeans hanging loose on his legs, hood over his head, a hump of backpack growing beneath his poncho, pressing him into a stoop. He will find no one. He has too little money to travel, and even if he spent the last of his cash getting to Florida he would have nothing left to undertake the search that would be necessary to find his family. There is no choice but to stay here in the city he knows, fighting to reclaim the house that he is certain would bring his wife and sons back to him.

Although it rains most days he avoids malls with their private security guards who will not tolerate a man sitting for hours on a bench. Last Thursday, however, it rained so hard he had no other choice and ventured inside a mall where he walked back and forth for eight hours, asking at every shop if they had any work. They all told him no, but gave him application forms to complete, which they promised to keep on file in case any opening arose. Every form asked about previous retail experience. In one case he had to fill out a personality test with questions so baffling he had no idea which of the multiple choice answers could possibly be correct:

*A co-worker who is struggling with debt confides in you about his/her predicament. Later in the week you see the same co-worker taking money out of the cash register and putting it in his/ her pocket. You decide to:*
  *a) tell your manager*
  *b) confront your co-worker*
  *c) offer to lend your co-worker money*
  *d) call the police*
  *e) secretly replace the money your co-worker stole from the cash register*
  *f) ask your co-worker to cut you in on the theft.*

*An obese customer asks you if a dress she tries on makes her look fat. The dress is a size too small for her, and you do think she looks fat in it. You decide to:*
  *a) tell the woman she looks fat*
  *b) suggest she should try a different size*
  *c) tell her she looks great and offer to ring up the dress*
  *d) tell her about an effective weight-loss program*
  *e) suggest she should go on a diet*
  *f) ask a co-worker to handle the customer for you.*

In that case he chose answers at random, assuming he would fail whatever test of character they wanted him to pass. Completing the application forms was not without its pleasures. He pictured himself working in many different kinds of stores, became acquainted with the qualities of various ballpoint pens, developed a fondness for black ink over blue, appreciated forms printed on heavy paper that took the ink with a voluptuous embrace rather than thin paper that seemed to resist the pen only to break apart when he applied too much pressure. After exhausting the business of filling out forms he walked the length of the mall again, upper and lower levels, passing empty windows with TO LET signs, looking at all the products in the remaining stores, and the few people who were buying. Late in the afternoon a security guard approached him.

'Hey, buddy,' the guard said in a loud voice. The man was older, a head shorter than Paul and a hundred pounds lighter, but he had a baton, a taser in his belt, and an embroidered badge on his chest with the letters E-K-K. 'I've noticed you're doing a lot of walking.'

'Is there a rule against walking?'

'I kind of wondered if you might be casing the joint.'

'I'm looking for work.'

'Have you found any?' the guard asked.

'No. I haven't found any.'

'You got any shopping to do?'

'No. I don't have any shopping to do.'

'You see that NO LOITERING sign?' the man said, pointing at a placard outlining the mall's rules and regulations. Paul nodded. 'Then I think it's time for you to go,' the guard said. 'Let me show you out.' The little man walked him to the nearest exit and stood at the doors, watching as Paul took the poncho from his backpack, slipped it over his head, and navigated across the wet parking lot to the street. Once on the city sidewalk he turned to the guard and waved through the torrential rain; for an instant the guard began to raise his hand but then lowered it again, shook his head, and retreated into the darkness of the mall. One of the anchor stores had shut down two years earlier and was still standing abandoned, its exterior walls covered with vines, weeds and small trees growing out of its roof, the windows and doors boarded up, clattering in the wind.

After that encounter Paul has avoided shopping centers. Yesterday he went to a park and spent a dry afternoon sitting on a bench, watching squirrels prepare for winter, losing track of time until night began to fall. A gray sedan drove past, parked nearby, and an older man in a business suit got out and walked towards him. The man circled the park on foot, came back, and sat down on the bench next to Paul.

'So, how much?' the man asked.

'How much of what?' Paul said.

'Come on, kid. Don't be coy.'

'I'm not a kid. How much what?'

'You know how much what. So how much?'

'Listen, man, I don't have any drugs. Buzz off.'

'I'm not looking for drugs, kid,' the man said, putting a hand on Paul's knee. 'You know what I'm looking for.'

Paul was so stunned he began to hyperventilate. He stood and ran away from the man, out of the park, through residential streets, until he reached a busy thoroughfare and slowed down to catch his breath. When he stopped, slumping down in a bus shelter, he found himself wondering how much money he could make selling his body instead of his labor, and what precisely would be involved in such a transaction. Perhaps one day it would come to that.

Another day he walked twenty-two miles round

231

trip to see his mother. She had phoned his cell to ask how he was, where he was, and why she had not heard from him in weeks. His father had gone elk hunting and she invited Paul to come for lunch. He had to leave the bunker at eight in the morning to reach his parents' house just before noon. It had been months since he last saw his mother, before the foreclosure auction, when she had offered to help him move his things into the apartment he claimed to have rented.

'Are you working, Pablito?'

'Don't call me that, Mama. I'm still trying to find a job.'

'But you're doing okay? You look like you need new boots. Where's your truck?'

'In the shop. I took the bus.'

'Where's that apartment you got, Pablo? I don't even know where you live.'

'It's just a small place, out on Central, near the mall. If you want to know the truth, I'm embarrassed for you to see it. I've got leads, though. I'm getting things back together but right now I'm in the trough, Mama. I promise you won't ever see me this low again.'

Looking at his mother was like staring into a funhouse mirror image of himself: shorter, rounder, feminine, much darker skinned, but otherwise the same. He was blond as a boy and then, as a teenager, his hair turned almost as panther-dark as his mother's. People said he looked Italian or Greek and it was a misconception he had rarely felt moved to correct. They sat across from each other in the dining room, Paul's legs extending under the table, his feet coming out the other side, enclosing his mother's chair, almost encircling her. Glancing at himself in the gold-framed mirror behind her, he looked like a man trying to get out, who could not be safely contained, hardly a man at all, a jaguar god, his eyes glinting turquoise shards, each looking in their own direction, a double-headed snake. For an instant he studied his own eyes, too pale and luminous for the olive complexion around them. He saw them at last for what they were: the eyes of his father transposed onto a thinner, harder, more pointed version of his mother's face, with a stronger nose and a ledge of brow. A person could jump from his forehead, jump and plummet to death down the whole length of his improbable body.

'Take a breath,' Dolores said, 'slow down, *chiquito*. Don't you eat?'

'I eat,' he said. 'I'm on a special diet.'

'You're too thin. I'll send home some food with you.'

After lunch they stood drinking cocoa in the living room, gazing out at the office park across the street, where, until only a few years ago, there was a racetrack. Although a line of trees blocked their view of the track when they first moved in, it was always audible, the announcer calling races on the loudspeakers, and out of the racing season rock concerts so loud his mother's collection of cow figurines would rattle in the china cabinet. When developers replaced the racetrack with an office park, they cleared all the trees.

Dolores sighed, turning her back on the bright white haze of concrete and glass. Where there are now acres silvered with asphalt and cars, horses once grazed, right in the middle of the city. They moved to this house when Paul was in junior high and it was not long before he found his way into a group of neighborhood boys who stole the ornamental chrome valve stem caps from car wheels, kids whose fathers took them to gun safety lessons so the boys learned how to shoot before they were old enough to own a weapon, kids who went on hunting trips over long weekends and came back bragging of kills, sharing stories of skinning deer and shooting squirrels for sport, blasting robins and red-winged blackbirds because they could. Paul no longer remembers whether he pressured his dad to join in these activities or vice versa, but he and Ralph soon became part of the group. Trophies still hang in his parents' living room. That day after lunch, Paul reached up to stroke the fur under the chin of the first buck he'd killed.

'When you and your dad started hunting, you were a natural. But you didn't really like it. I know you didn't enjoy it.' His mother unlocked the china cabinet to adjust the position of a porcelain cow.

'What the hell are you talking about, Mama? Of course I enjoyed it. I loved those hunting trips.'

'But it wasn't your best subject. Your *best* subject was art. You take after me that way, not your dad.'

'Hunting isn't a *subject*.'

His mother did not seem to hear what he said. 'You come from a long, long line of artists and builders. You just didn't know it. I never told you enough about all that.' As she picked up one of Paul's carvings, a wooden cow he'd made for her from a piece of the cleared poplar wood, he knew what she was going to say, the way she would lapse into reveries of a great lineage, distant cloud people, ancient places, vast cities and temples, a legacy of building that was his greatest inheritance, *the skill in your fingers*, chiquito. When she put the cow in his hands he was surprised at the intricacy of his own carving, the way the staring glass eyes and wooden flanks looked real. 'What kind of cow you say this is, Pablo?'

'Greek Shorthorn.'

'That's right. Rare breed.'

He used to make all kinds of fine little things for his mother. In the den are his duck decoys: mallard, canvasback, even a Canada goose, each so detailed it looks like it might turn to snap off a finger with its varnished wooden beak.

Dolores returned the cow to the bottom shelf of the cabinet, closing the doors and locking them with the key she has always kept on a silver chain round her neck. 'You shoulda been an artist I think,' she said. 'You have so much talent.'

'Can we stop talking about me?'

She ignored him and from a drawer in her sideboard pulled out a folder of Paul's childhood drawings. Most of the earliest ones were traced from magazines: fighter jets and soldiers in action, fantasy monsters and cyborgs. But as she continued to page through the sheets of paper, Paul noticed a shift in subject matter to precise drawings of houses. All the houses he drew as a boy were larger and more elegant than any of the humble places they ever lived. 'You were always drawing your dream house. You always said you were gonna build me a house all my own, you know, where I could live alone.'

'Yeah, I know, Mama. Maybe some day I will.'

By the end of each day's vagabond walking, always eating the sandwiches he makes for himself and carries in a backpack, buying nothing if he can avoid it with the money he has left from the sale of the truck, he tramps back westward along Poplar Road, pausing at wet intersections, waiting for lights to change, risking his life even when the light is in his favor because drivers ignore signals, as he himself once ignored them, distracted by the radio or a call from his wife or racing in the urge simply to be back home.

Half a block before Dolores Woods he steps into the forest, hidden within the shaw and picking his way through the brake, tensing his body into the coyote crouch that carries him back to his burrow.

At night, in the bunker, he eats bowls of pasta and sits in silence, concentrating on the hum and heat of the lights above him until he switches them off and tries to sleep. In the darkness he is oppressed by the sounds of the house: water running through pipes, plugs pushing into sockets, music and telephone calls and shouting from one room to another, the television and dishwasher and washing machine and dryer, the air conditioners and dehumidifiers and hot water heaters and chest freezer, or the sounds of the woman at her bench in the basement workshop: the piercing screams and queer frequencies that pitch and roll, the juddering drill that shakes the foundations of the house, all those noises condensing, drawn into the pantry, through the hatch, exploding into his cell.

Then, after the house finally goes silent, there are other sounds as well, rising up beneath the bunker, coming from deep below in the earth, scrambling, scuffling noises that flutter and dodge through the dense mixture of silt, sand, and clay, moving closer, drilling towards the bunker, and then turning, scrambling around and alongside the walls of Paul's burrow, a horrible clawing, scuttling, snuffling noise, sharpened nails scratching against the lead lining. The first night it happened he thought he was imagining it, believing the next morning it was a dream, but when it happened again the next night, and has gone on happening every night thereafter, growing

237

louder and louder each time, he knows it is real. Something ancient and angry is there, in the soil that surrounds him, clawing at the walls of his burrow, trying to get in.

On a Tuesday morning in early October Paul pushes his way out of the bunker, through the pantry, and crawls up the stairs into the kitchen, sniffing the air. The house has changed: it no longer smells like his family, or even himself. Instead it smells like those other people, other food, oils, body scents, cleaning products, ways of living. Its aroma is sharp and chemical and his nose is adjusting to this new odor, thinking of ways to eradicate it, when he sees a ghost in the next room. He sidles across the kitchen to the china cupboard and peers through to find the dining room furniture all pushed together, draped with thick white drop cloths while a heavier piece of canvas covers the floor. At first he cannot process what he sees, why the space looks so different, and then he realizes that the walls have been stripped to their plaster, all of his wallpaper removed. He and Amanda chose it together, a pattern of ivy that dated from the mid-nineteenth century, cost a hundred and fifty dollars a roll, and took a full day to hang in the dining room alone. But that is only the beginning of the deface-ment. The intricately painted crown molding has been removed and in its place is curved, concave white coving, which has also been plastered into the room's vertical corners, eliminating any semblance of angles, so the whole space feels like the interior of a hollowed-out marshmallow.

He feels dizzy, bends at the knee, pulls himself upright again as his heart propels him into the hall, a vein in his neck throbbing. The entire space is painted a luminous eggshell white, all the way up to the second floor; the floorboards have been painted white as well, the stairs, even the banister and railings, all of it coated in white. Everything everywhere is glistening, blinding, the crown molding and baseboards stripped away and replaced with the same coving that has been installed in the dining room. They've done it to the living room and den, too: a whiteout that makes the space feel much larger than it is. The walls merge seamlessly into one another, as well as the ceilings and floors. He doubles over, drops to his knees, heaves out a clear viscous fluid onto the whitewashed boards. His head throbs and he has the illusion of being suspended over a void. Only the windows, gazing out over the yard and the neighborhood beyond, give any sense of scale or context, since even the furniture is upholstered in white fabric with white arms and legs; there is a set of white lacquered end tables, a matching coffee table, a white area rug. The couches have white throw pillows. Books lined up on the built-in shelves in the den provide the only color. Paul can't remember what his own books looked like on those shelves – books he never read, whose place in the house was always purely decorative. Unlike the books owned by these new people, with their bright paper covers, his own books were old, some with leather bindings, because the decorator who acquired them on Paul's behalf said that a library *should evoke age*. There were at least two sets of encyclopedias, several bibles, hymnbooks, a dictionary, but whatever else there might have been, he can no longer say. Nor does he care. Books will not make him money, they will not restore his home or feed him; books are unnecessary things.

Upstairs the windows and doors have sharp angles but everything else looks like nowhere he recognizes, the whiteness and softened edges turning the whole house into an operating room or science lab.

What a fool he was to leave! If he had been at home he might have halted the defacement. He would have emerged from the bunker howling, gun loaded, cocked, finger on the trigger, and escorted the workers to the door, marching them off the property.

Not his! Still his! Always his!

They have peeled away and painted over all his careful decisions, whitewashing the history of his wife and sons as they once lived here, the marks on a closet door recording the growth of Carson and Ajax subsumed by whiteness. His shout stretches into a wail, a scream, echoing around this warren of melting white rhomboid bubbles.

He is back in the kitchen when the front door opens and two men enter, whispering to each other. The painters, he supposes, as he slips down the stairs to the basement, listening as the men move through the house. There are two unmistakable clicks. These men are not painters. One of them goes upstairs while the other circles through the living room and den, back to the hall, into the dining room, through to the kitchen. As soon as Paul reaches the basement he takes quick silent steps to the back of the pantry, drops to the floor, slides under the shelf and through the hatch, drawing it closed behind him. Minutes pass and Paul cracks open the hatch, peeking into the basement as the door to the pantry is suddenly filled with the form of the man: he wears a uniform and holds a gun, cocked at shoulder height.

After several minutes of poking around, the man heads back upstairs, calling out, 'All clear.' The other man answers from higher up in the house and then, quick as they came, they are gone, locking and slamming the front door behind them.

'There was a call-out today,' Nathaniel says. The three of them are eating in the kitchen because the dining room is still covered in drop cloths. 'They phoned me at the office.'

'You mean the alarm went off?' Julia says.

'The guys came out but they couldn't find anything. They think it must have been something falling over, from the painters, or the fan blowing the curtains when it came on. They suggested we turn it off when we go out.'

Julia puts down her fork and knife, leaning her elbows on the breakfast bar where they have pulled up three stools. 'You don't think we should be worried, honey?'

'They said everything was locked and there was no sign of anyone trying to force the doors or windows. They didn't find anything suspicious. Nothing.'

'But if there *was* something suspicious they would find it, wouldn't they?' Copley asks. He speaks so little that when he does it comes as a surprise. Nathaniel worries he and Julia forget from time to time that Copley is even present, saying things in the boy's hearing they should not. Copley, though, shows no sign of worry. His brow is smooth, his voice regular. He is so self-contained and equilibrated that Nathaniel wants to shake his son, to tell him it is worth being a little worried because security systems are imperfect and there could be an intruder in the future even if there wasn't one today.

'Of course they would have found it. They're professionals,' Nathaniel says. 'And if someone did get in, they'd come to—' he struggles to locate the word for what he imagines the guards might do '—they'd come to help us.'

'Do THEY-HAVE-GUNS?' The first word in the question comes out in his normal voice but by the second word Copley has distorted his tone, speaking on a frequency from outer space. They have been careful, not to say strict, about limiting his exposure to television, so Nathaniel has no idea where this kind of mimicry may have originated except at the new school. He knows they are not in the mainstream of parenting; friends in Boston regarded their resistance to media as not only old-fashioned but perhaps even unhealthy, and impossible to sustain in the longer term. The other day, however, Nathaniel found his son playing on one of Julia's computers in the basement. When he confronted her about it she acted as though it was no big deal. *I told him he could be on it for half an hour once a day. It's not like television,* she said. *It's not a passive activity. He's*

243

*playing a learning game, he's engaging. It's not just sitting there watching something. I chose the game, Nathaniel. I know what you're thinking, but the game is fine. It's robins and worms and nests. What did we call it? Concentration. No guns, no killing, no violence, no gender stereotypes. Just memory exercises that happen to take place on a screen instead of the paper and cards we had as children.*

'DO-THEY?' Copley asks again. 'DO-THE-GUARDS-HAVE-GUNS?'

Nathaniel looks at Julia and realizes he never told her about choosing the armed response package. She puts down her fork, looks at Nathaniel, and raises her eyebrows: *Do they, Nathaniel? Do they have guns?*

'Yes, they have guns. That's what it means to have a burglar alarm. If the alarm goes off, then the men—'

'Or women,' Julia says.

'Or women,' Nathaniel continues, 'come to make sure everything is okay.'

'And what if we're here but the alarm goes off and the men and women come with guns and they shoot us by accident?' Copley asks, his voice natural once again.

'That's not going to happen, honey. We hire them to protect us. When we're at home at night the alarm is set to go off only if someone breaks in from outside, not if we're moving around inside. The guards know we're the people they're supposed to protect.' Julia pats Copley's hand and Nathaniel notices his son flinch, brow wrinkling, eyebrows flexing in to meet each other.

'But *how* do they know? We haven't *met* them. How do they know when they come to the house that we're the ones they have to protect? Have they seen our pictures?'

'Yes, they've seen our pictures,' Nathaniel lies. 'They know exactly what you look like, and they'll do their best to protect you.'

'And what about you?'

'What about me, Copley?'

'Will you do your BEST-TO-PROTECT-ME?'

What a question to ask, what an impertinent, annoying little voice. Nathaniel has no doubt he would do everything in his power to protect his son in the way his own parents failed to protect him, either from the world, or from each other.

'Of course, Cop. You don't have to worry about that. Your mom and I will always protect you.'

After dinner Copley and Julia retreat to the basement while Nathaniel cleans up the kitchen. For a moment he listens to his wife and son from the top of the stairs. There is nothing private about their conversation. There is no expectation of privacy. If they wanted privacy they would have closed the door. To speak with the door open is to expect one might be overheard – and, in any case, there are no secrets among the three of them except at birthdays and Christmas, and even then the secrets are far from absolute, secrets that do not have the sanctity of true secrecy. He has to believe that Julia did not mean to keep Copley's use of her computer a secret. Secrets drive Nathaniel mad. His parents were always whispering when he and Matthew were not in the room, whispering so obviously and ostentatiously that the brothers knew secrets were being kept, and they understood, too, that secrecy was the mortar holding together their parents' marriage despite all the infidelity and abuse. Arthur and Ruth would announce one morning they were going on vacation, alone, leaving later that day, while the boys would be staying with a neighbor for the week. *We knew you'd just ask to come with us*, his mother would say, *but this is an adult vacation*. It was not only clandestine vacations or difficulties at work or the lives of his mother's patients, which were strictly off limits, but also the internal lives of Dr and Dr Noailles that went undisclosed. His grandparents on both sides had died long before Nathaniel was born and his parents never told him stories about their own childhoods. He had no sense of their worries or the nature of their relationship with each other, how they had met or even how long they had been together, whether they still loved each other as he was growing up, or if they had a different kind of bond altogether, one that allowed for both of them to stray with the knowledge of the other. For years he did not even know their ages, only their birth-*days*. It would not have surprised him to discover that his mother and father had separate sordid pasts, with other spouses and other children, whole other families and genealogies, which would forever elude him. They were never physically demonstrative, never kissed or hugged in front of their sons, and only kissed or hugged their sons on special occasions. They did not talk about their pasts or share their thoughts about the future. If they were discontent with the present, these were feelings they kept to themselves. They never invited curiosity, making it clear from early in Nathaniel's life that their own lives were no concern of their children. Before reaching adulthood, Nathaniel vowed he would never be like that with any children he might have.

'Speak in your normal voice,' he hears Julia say. There is the sound of paper being shuffled and then Copley speaks, his tone high and clear. With a voice like that, it seems perverse that the boy should ever wish to distort it.

'Just these words?' says Copley.

'Just those words, in the order they appear on the page,' Julia says. 'And like the other times, silently count to five between each word. But this time try using your fingers to help you count a little more slowly. One . . . Two . . . Three . . . Four . . . Five. Steady beats.'

'Are you ready?' Copley asks.

'Yes, I'm ready. Are *you* ready?'

'Ready.'

Nathaniel hears a click – a recorded sound meant

to mimic the button of an old-fashioned tape deck being depressed. They have been doing this every night all week.

'Cab. Cabana. Cabbage. Cabbie. Cabin. Cabinet. Cable. Caboose. Catch.' Copley measures out the words five beats at a time. He takes directions well, learns fast, responding to commands without argument or resistance. They have never known him to have problems with discipline but already Mrs Taylor, the guidance counselor at the Pinwheel Academy, has phoned to complain of *irregularities* in Copley's behavior. *Nothing serious*, she said, *but enough to send up a red flag. We need to nip off the bud before it gets out of control.* Nathaniel wanted to tell the woman the expression is to nip it in the bud but he did not, thinking that, in a way, her version was the more accurate if more ominous one. When he asked her what the problem was, she explained that in a science period during which the students were tasked with measuring volumes of liquids, Copley drank the tap water he was supposed to measure rather than pouring it into the graduated beaker. Nathaniel asked the counselor whether Copley was allowed to explain himself. *Yes*, Mrs Taylor said, *and it was not a satisfactory explanation. He said he was thirsty, but there are scheduled water and bathroom breaks at 10 AM and 2 PM, so he couldn't have been thirsty, since the science unit began at 10:10. According to the classroom surveillance feed the incident occurred at 10:17. We regard this as the first indication not only of a failure to follow directions, but also of a tendency to lie.* When Nathaniel proposed that perhaps Copley was actually thirsty, that the water break had not allowed him enough time to drink as much water as his body needed, Mrs Taylor suggested Nathaniel lacked a clear understanding of child health and invited him to speak with the school nurse. The school would be debiting ten dollars from Copley's student account as punishment for failing to follow instructions in class and destruction of school materials. *What materials?* Nathaniel asked. *The water for the lesson,* the woman explained, *which your son drank* – water that would have been poured down a sink at the end of the lesson had it not been consumed by his son. As for the 'lying', Mrs Taylor conceded this could not be proven, since any judgment would have to rely on an objective knowledge of Copley's own internal feeling, and, *for now,* this was beyond the school's capacity; she was prepared to let the supposed infraction pass with a fine and warning and nothing more serious.

Nathaniel hears another electronic click from the basement – a click so like his memory of the sound made by a brick-sized black tape recorder owned by his mother that it makes him shudder. Countless times as a child he was subjected to recording his thoughts and feelings, answering questions his mother posed in the name of research. He wonders if she still has those tapes. Knowing Ruth, they will first have been digitized into a longer lasting, less corruptible format, and then transcribed and analyzed. Although his mother has published several monographs and dozens of articles in the field of child psychology, Nathaniel has never had the courage to read her work, terrified of finding himself quoted, his childhood dismembered; he has little doubt she has done this, perhaps even disguising his identity with a different name, Bartholomew or Philip or John.

'*Cash*, like money,' Julia says, her voice echoing up the stairs. 'I know it looks like it should be *catch* but it isn't. Start from there.' Another click. The shiver on Nathaniel's spine takes hold and he braces himself against the kitchen door.

'Cache,' Copley says, correctly this time. 'Cashette.'

Click. 'Not *cash-ette. Cash-ay*,' Julia says. Click. Why not go through the list before recording it, to save this kind of interruption?

'Cachet,' Copley continues. 'Cackle. Cacophony. Cactus. Cad. Cadaver. What's a cadaver?' Click.

'A dead body,' Julia says. 'Ready to continue?'

'Ready.' Click. 'Caddie. Caddy. Those two sound the same.'

Click. 'Yes, they do. Ready?' Click.

Nathaniel turns on the faucet and the noise drowns out the rest of the session, which may go on for half an hour until Copley calls time and asks to go to bed. Nathaniel has suggested that Julia pay Copley something for his labors, even an hourly minimum wage, which could go into a savings account. Julia demurred, arguing that the work will benefit all of them in the long run, and Copley will profit from the success in which he has played a small but crucial part. It is not as though his voice will be used in the final product, just in the early prototype stages.

Nonetheless, and reservations about compensation aside, there is something about Julia and Copley's nightly retreat to the basement to record the odd lists of words that unnerves Nathaniel. He appreciates the point of what is being done, the importance and value of Julia's work for scientific and industrial progress, but he wonders why it has to be Copley and not some other child giving voice to the machine she is creating – or why a child at all and not an adult. Why not, in fact, Julia herself? *A child's voice is reassuring*, Julia told him when he protested, *a child is non-threatening*.

The recording sessions have become, in a larger symphony of disquiet, a recurring motif, a melodic line echoing through each movement of this work with no fixed parameters, open to constant revision and expansion as the sources of unease proliferate, all of them chanting at Nathaniel, warning him about the danger of the changes he and Julia have made. Here, in this new city, at home in their new neighborhood, there are not nearly enough people. In the weeks since moving into the house, they still have not met their neighbors, managing to leave each morning and return each night without seeing anyone on foot, learning nothing about names, identities, careers, family structures. People drive into garages in cars with tinted windows, move from garages – behind high fences – into houses, close curtains and blinds, turn on lights. They go about their evenings and then turn off the lights, except for a front porch or back door light, and go to bed. In the mornings the solitary outside lights are turned off, cars reverse down driveways, garage doors close automatically, the houses remaining shut up and silent for the next eight to ten hours. Perhaps next spring, when the warm dry weather returns, neighbors will appear in their backyards and it will be possible to meet people, to find some sense of community in this neighborhood that feels as far from home as Nathaniel has ever been.

At least the changes they have made to the interior of the house reassure him, making it feel more like their Boston apartment, with its perfect balance of the transparent, the hidden, and the observable, where it always felt as though darkness and light existed within each other, creating a poised but variable radiance. In this new house, because of the conservatism of its structural design, the only way to impose a sense of light has been to banish darkness entirely. The dining room is almost finished, the kitchen and basement will be next; the white walls, softened lines, and white furniture make him feel cleaner, calmer, able to forget for a moment the burden and allure of his work, the way the task to which he is having to bend his mind seems to be changing his personality in ways he is already beginning to notice: shorter temper with his family, suspicion of strangers, a strict adherence to rule and law. A few days ago he phoned the moving company to report the odd behavior of the men, whom he described as 'definitely criminal types', and when Julia ran a red light last weekend he lectured her for half an hour on civic and personal responsibility, how a ticket on her record would reflect badly on his position in the community and his company. 'We have to be models of propriety,' he explained, reminding her that cameras on the traffic lights catch every infraction. 'We have to assume that everything we do is always under scrutiny.'

'Oh please, Nathaniel, don't be such a puritan,' she laughed.

The redecoration of the house has been undertaken according to Julia's belief that domestic space should be both an extension of their own bodies and a protection against the world. 'A house is like an oversized and highly complex prosthetic limb,' she explained to him, 'allowing us to move in ways we couldn't without it, letting us rise through space by means of stairs, helping us remain clean, our temperatures optimal, assisting us in the preparation and storage of food, while at the same time acting as a shell that protects us from the damage of the outside world.' Nathaniel had only been able to nod when she said this,

asserting that he wanted nothing more complicated than clean white lines and a minimization
of clutter, not that clutter would ever be a problem
in this house where there is more room and more
storage than the three of them can possibly hope
to fill.

After finishing the dishes he sits in the den
listening to the rain that has not stopped for more
than a few hours at a time since their arrival. In
the last several days the sky has been lighter, the
rain's noise on the windows and roof more melodic
and less aggressive: a rhythm section instead of a
shooting range. He cannot remember a time when
he has felt as oppressed by the weather as he does
in this new place: weather is constant and inescap-
able, the rain ever falling, thunder grumbling,
lightning bolts shearing open squat gunmetal days,
wind threatening to pluck up the house, spin it
round in the air and drop it across the river. It
feels like a land of extreme evil tempered only now
and then by idiosyncratic, fallible good. Between
his house and the neighbors', the creek that was
nothing more than a trickle of mud when they
moved in has swollen to a stream more than six
feet across and three feet deep, running into
a drain at the edge of his lawn. Their house is on a
hill, the stream in a depression, but Nathaniel
worries their insurance may be inadequate, or that
the surveys on the property failed to account for
climate change, topography, and proximity to
larger bodies of water. He knows the entire parcel

of land that makes up Dolores Woods flattens and declines from the hill on which their house sits, falling away into the pancake flats spreading out from the flood plain of the great broad river to the west of the city. In recent nights he has dreamed of the river rising, water flowing downstream from states north and west, merging together to build and spread out from the riverbanks, climbing across the flood plain until it inundates Dolores Woods and surrounds his house, making it an island in the midst of the great inland sea that once covered the region and will soon return, engulfing the country, submerging them all. Twice now he has woken covered in perspiration from a dream in which he struggles to escape the water and get back to land, fighting his way through currents, past submerged trees, surrounded by the detritus of his neighbors' lives, by their drowned pets and their own drowned bodies, bloated with floodwater, floating face down, covered with rats and caught up in the snags of trees where their children once climbed. Julia turned to him the second time it happened, placing her hand on his back to make him realize he was awake and not still asleep, asking him if he was ill. *Of course I'm sick*, he wanted to say, *this whole goddamn place is making me sick*. Instead he told her he was fine, he should not have had the blue cheese and wild mushroom risotto, he should eat milder food, blander ingredients to match this bland life. He dreamed of a wild-eyed man, his hair a two-inch afro receding from his scalp, a jet-dark Bozo approaching the house across lawns covered in snow, looking in the windows to stare as they went about their lives. Nathaniel shouted at the man, screaming at him to go away, but the clown kept coming: eyes shining in the dark, he put his fists on the bay window in the living room, pounding his balled-up hands against the lowest panes of glass, his eyes and hair filling the whole space of the window. Nathaniel shouted again at the man, shouted and shouted until he was shouting out loud. Julia shook him, told him it was okay, asked him what he was dreaming. He was too embarrassed to tell her the nature of the dream, to admit the color of his deepest fear, claiming instead he could not remember. Early in life he learned the danger of recalling his dreams, the way his mother would record them, ask him questions, make pronouncements about Nathaniel's dark unconscious. *You should be in therapy*, his mother would have said. *Unresolved traumas. I can't imagine what they are, but clearly they're haunting you.*

The research and implementation of Maureen McCarthy's vision for *revenue-positive rehabilitation* is another thing that makes his nights fitful and preoccupies his days: from waking to falling asleep at night, if he is not thinking about all the problems associated with the scheme then he is researching what legal restrictions may need to be overcome, while monitoring the work of those beneath him assigned to investigate areas where the corporation as a whole is overpaying for products and services that might be 'insourced' (Maureen's favorite buzzword) to the 'corrections populace'. In a follow-up meeting, Maureen elaborated the true scope of her plan.

'See, Nathaniel, prisons can no longer be in the business of providing cheap labor to the state. We're not going to have our corrections populace making license plates or furniture and providing it at cost to the government anymore.'

'And what about the charitable work they've been doing? Don't you think that's important?'

Maureen squinted, bunching up her lips and nose. 'We just can't afford to have them refurbishing church pews or training dogs for the blind or doing anything else that costs us money or fails to exploit the labor potential of the system. The other factor is that we urgently need to down-adjust inmate income.'

'What kind of adjustment do you have in mind? Right now we're only paying them ten per cent of minimum wage.'

She shook her head: 'I think we need to aim for a top-tier pay of one per cent of minimum, with penalties for poor work and failure to meet quotas.'

'Is that legal?'

'That's your job, Nate.'

'Nathaniel.'

'*Nathaniel*, I'm sorry. The thing is, as I see it – would you like a coffee or something?'

'No, I'm—'

'You're good? Fine. See, we pay to house these people, and now it's time for them to start paying back. This is the crunch. Depending on what happens with state and federal politics, the tide could turn against us as an industry if we're not careful. We're not worried about global reach, because there's always going to be a market for the kind of work you and I are committed to doing. We need to imagine a world in which prisoners are doing something truly positive, producing useful things for a useful corporation that is invested in looking after the whole planet and keeping the law-abiding populace safe.'

'Yes, I know,' Nathaniel said, looking up at the portrait of their CEO Alex Reveley hanging on Maureen's wall. In gold embossed letters on the mount surrounding the photo was Alex's motto: *We're in the business of being the planet.*

'That means we have to think about the business potential of every aspect of what we already do, Nate, and what we might do in the future.' She smiled, and lowered her voice, whispering, 'I've got big ideas. And I've got Alex's ear.'

'Oh? Can you give me a hint?'

She closed her office door and crouched next to Nathaniel, both of them looking up at Alex's photograph as she continued to whisper: 'Once we've got this up and running, we're going to be looking at the semi-permanent tagging and employment of parolees so we can mobilize corrections labor for jobs as various as fire-fighting to data entry.'

'Really? That sounds—'

'Revolutionary. I know. Think of it this way: what is the major problem that the ex-con faces? Finding a job. No problem. No brainer. Let *us* employ the parolees. That's true rehabilitation. And when they fall out of line, we'll put them back inside. This is just the tip of it, Nate. I have complete confidence in your ability to dream as big as I do about the future of our corrections infrastructure.' She put a hand on his knee, squeezed, and then ran her fingers halfway up his inner thigh. Nathaniel did not know whether to push her away or see what might happen. He felt no attraction for his boss, and had never thought of being unfaithful to Julia. When he failed to respond, Maureen patted his shoulder as if nothing had just happened. 'You're a good man, Nate, and you're going to do big things. I have a vision for your place in this company. Play my game and you'll go straight to the top.'

He left that meeting reeling, as much from what she had done as what she had said. 'Facility' seemed a strange way to describe the places where the dangerous are sequestered, perverse in its twisting of a word that has long meant and still means 'ability' and 'capability'. It strikes Nathaniel that this may be a peculiarly American usage, in the same way that Americans describe public restrooms as 'facilities'. Perhaps it is only appropriate that the place where we shit and piss and where not a few people fuck illicitly should be saddled with the same euphemism as the place where we warehouse the people we want to forget, where pissing and shitting is no longer private, where plenty of illicit and unwelcome fucking goes on all the time. In an ideal world, the prison would act like a toilet, flushing away the waste of society into a sewer hidden from view, where the filth is either cleaned and rehabilitated into fertilizer and drinking water or contained in some dark and secret place where it need never be seen again, rendered into a festering sludge that will, in time, be reabsorbed into the earth itself.

Even without Maureen's message in front of him her words jangle in Nathaniel's ear, a contrapuntal rhythm working against the rain, which strengthens and rages, biting into the side of the house, gnawing at the windows. 'Straight to the top,' she said, but he is not sure he wants to go straight to the top, wherever that might be, whatever it might mean for himself and his family. The black sky flashes silver for an instant and moments later a spasm grips the house, shaking it so hard it feels as though it may split apart. Made from nothing, it was not built to withstand the weather of the future. Sitting up straighter in his chair, he places his palms on the white leather upholstery, strokes the ostrich hide, tries to remain calm. Provided he works diligently in the evenings and over week-ends he will be able to do the job Maureen has assigned him, although he worries about neglecting Copley and Julia, as well as his own health. He is no longer just out of shape, but verging on fat. The only consolation is the belief that he will not be in this situation forever; he will either be promoted to a less compromising position, or last long enough to get a good reference – a year, at most two – and then move on, transitioning out of the private sector and into the public, if the state has not, at that point, ceded all responsibility for civic life and public wellbeing to private corporations.

Lightning and thunder break together in the dark, dropping a blade that cleaves Nathaniel's head in two as it hits a tree in the neighbors' yard, bringing down a limb as big around as a man and three times as long. By instinct, Nathaniel puts his hands to his forehead, ducking down in the chair, but the sky is black again, rain tapping an irregular dull staccato on the glass. As he closes the curtains, he thinks again of his dream, the clown in brown overalls and a darker brown shirt, pounding his fists on the window, his face full of rage and desperation, eyeballs yellow, crazed with blood. Nathaniel jumps, aware that Copley, unexpected as lightning, is standing in the living room watching him.

'Hey, Cop. Are you finished with Mom? Ready for a story?'

Face drawing to a vicious little point, his neck hyperextended, Copley shouts, 'Go away!'

Nathaniel frowns, looking at the fine white skin of his son's neck, and sees a noose of prickly fibers tighten around it. 'Go *away!*'

'That's enough, Copley. Why would you say such a thing?'

'I'm not *talking* to you.'

'What do you mean?'

'I'm talking to the *man.*'

'What man?'

'The man in the rain!'

Copley's whole body shakes as he points at the window where Nathaniel failed to draw the curtains all the way closed. He looks out into the dark but sees nothing.

'There's no one out there, Copley. That's not a very funny joke.'

'IT'S-NOT-A-JOKE,' his son squawks, turning to march back into the hallway, knees locked in goose-step. Nathaniel knows what his own father would have done if he'd acted like that as a child. It would have been a knock to the head, a palm clapped against his ear, a foot slamming into his perineum and nights of bed-wetting to follow. *Don't talk back to me. Stop walking like a Nazi*, his father would have said. *You'll disgrace us all.*

The structural alterations and expanses of white paint seem to have deadened sound inside the house so that Copley is always now catching him by surprise, lurking in corners and appearing just when Nathaniel thinks he is alone. Perhaps the concerns of the guidance counselor are not

262

misplaced, and there are behavioral issues he and Julia have overlooked in the interest of making the shift from Boston less traumatic for a boy who has always been sensitive. There is nothing wrong with fair punishment, and Nathaniel is certain it would be possible to discipline Copley without ever straying into the kind of abusive treatment he suffered at the hands of his own father. He can feel Arthur's long fingers, the skin always loose, thick veins standing out on the backs of the man's hands, scoring the space between wrist and knuckles. In recent years his father's skin has become prone to injury, hands and fingers bleeding from traumas as minor as brushing against rough surfaces, the engorged ropey blueness of the veins standing out against yellow-gray skin. Looking out the window once more, Nathaniel sees his father's hands reach to grab him, fingers stretched in darkness at the ends of the arms, muscled limbs sheathed in loose skin, extended at shoulder height, attached to the running body, the body of his father chasing him from the house, screaming at him, screaming for his son's body, for the end of his life. As his father leaps out of memory, a hand suddenly comes to rest on the outer glass of the window, the fingers spreading, digits articulated, like something hardly human at all.

When he has dried himself off and cleaned the mud from his boots, Paul makes his way to the other end of the bunker, opening the pantry hatch wide enough to see the woman bent over her workbench. A high voice says, 'Can I help you?' It does not sound like the woman and although Paul cannot see him, he knows it must be the boy. The woman does not respond and the child says it again, faster this time, 'Can I help you? Can I?' There is a pause, silence for several seconds, and then, 'How? How can I help you?' The woman ignores the boy and keeps working. Perhaps she is wearing earplugs and cannot hear her son, or is so focused on her work that nothing else can intrude. She continues in silence for another hour while Paul watches, lying on his stomach in the dark, resting his body against the open containment door, ready to retreat if the woman approaches.

Her body is tense: head, neck, shoulders, arms held still, and there are none of the usual noises Paul has come to associate with the woman's work. Instead he hears the sound of smaller metal instruments being put down on the table and picked up again as she makes fine, precise adjustments. He begins to crawl through the hatch and into the pantry to get a closer look but then stops, realizing he cannot announce himself by clearing his throat, asking her what the hell she imagines she's doing. Making other words on his lips, he pushes air stripped of sound across his tongue: 'Can I help you? How can I help you?' The last thing he wants is to help these people. His hands grip the rifle; he could draw it forward, cock it, pull the trigger, put an end to the woman's life and disappear. Bringing the scope to his face, he finds the back of her head in his sights. If he could get rid of her, he has no doubt the man and boy would leave as well.

Sitting on the high stool at the bench, the woman, although her hair is darker, reminds him of Amanda. She has the same narrow shoulders and strong back, a similar way of tilting her head to one side while concentrating. This woman might in fact be Amanda, come to reclaim Paul's house with a new husband. Perhaps the boy he carried in from the street might actually be Carson. It was dark, the child was the right size, he moved like Carson, he spoke like Carson, and they could have dyed his hair to disguise him.

It is nearly eleven before the woman puts down her tools and goes up to the kitchen, turning off the basement lights from the switch at the top of the stairs. In the darkness Paul squints, waiting for his pupils to dilate and take in the ambient streetlight from the window wells tucked along the length of the basement ceiling. He listens until the house is silent, the last shower taken, and when all movement has stopped he wriggles out through the hatch and across the floor of the pantry whose shelves remain empty. These people need to plan ahead, fill up their house with food and water for the coming crisis, arm themselves and learn how to defend their property. When the emergency comes they will succumb quickly, starve or be killed off in the chaos, and that will be the moment to retake the house, build a high wall around the perimeter, make it impregnable, and live out the last days of this dark tribulation.

There is a light over the workbench but when he turns it on to see what is there everything apart from the tools and computers has been packed up and put away. Drills, tiny screwdrivers, soldering irons, chips and bolts and coils of wire are arranged in neat order, as though the elements speak to one another, defining relationships through the orientation of their parts. On the far end of the workbench is a six-foot metal case secured with padlocks.

The child's arm, white and disembodied in the dark, is the only thing visible above the covers; from underneath the blankets there is a flickering glow, as if a flashlight were being partially covered and uncovered. Paul has the rifle in his hands, the noise suppressor screwed to the barrel. It would be possible to put his hands around the boy's throat and strangle or suffocate him. The boy cannot be Carson, the woman is not Amanda, these people are nothing but intruders. If the boy is gone the parents will go, too, perhaps even take their own lives. He does not want to be caught, and he will not be caught if he does it right, if he can shoot the boy before he makes a sound and then retreat to the bunker, remaining there until the investigations are finished, the case closed. The parents will be in turmoil for weeks or months afterward, but in time they will leave. By then he will have been able to find work again and have enough money to buy the house when it comes back on the market.

He crouches just inside the boy's room. Across the hall, the door to the parents' room is closed.

'Can I help you? How? How can I help you?' the boy says.

Paul shivers and adjusts his grip on the rifle. As he raises the sights to his right eye, his finger starts to close in on the trigger, but stops when the boy continues.

'Can I help you? Me. How. Can you help me? How can you help me? I. Can. How can I help you? Help me.' A pause, silence, the sound of soft tapping. Paul lowers the gun and opens his mouth. 'Help me,' the boy says, sounding more than ever like Carson.

The boy's exposed arm disappears under the blankets before the light dims and then becomes bright again, and the boy speaks once more. 'How can I help you? She. How can she help you? We. How can we help you? How. How. How. How. Cab. Cabbage. Cache. Cachet. How can I cachet you?'

From the parents' bedroom there is the thud of feet hitting floorboards. The light under the boy's blankets goes dark as Paul creeps along the wall and into the corner of the room, folding himself up in shadow. He hears the door of the master bedroom open but for a moment nothing happens: the boy is silent, no one moves, and then the boy's father crosses the hall and stands just inside his son's room.

'Copley?' the man says, tiptoeing to his son's bed; he pulls back the covers to look at the boy, who moans, turns on his side, and throws an arm across his forehead. The man pulls up the blankets, tucking them under his son's chin, and goes to open the curtains. Light unspools across the white floorboards, catching Paul's extended foot. He draws it back into the shadow where he hides, between a dresser and the wall. The man must not look into corners. He must close the curtains, turn in the other direction, walk out of the room. Cloud must cover the moon, the storm must return. He must not be discovered.

For several minutes the man stands at the foot of his son's bed, and as he does the light from outside only grows stronger, the shadows weaker. It seems impossible that the man will not see him but when Paul next looks up the man is gone and he hears the door to the master bedroom swing shut.

'What are you doing?' the boy whispers, his voice different than before, less formal, more present, but warped by fear. Paul shudders and loses his balance, his arms dropping into the light. 'I can hear you breathing.'

As Paul stands up to leave the room he keeps his eyes on the child's bed and tiptoes backwards, rifle raised, fleeing all the way down the rear stairs.

'The man I saw outside was in the house last night,' Copley says at breakfast. 'He came into my room.'

'It was just me, Copley,' Nathaniel says. 'You were having a nightmare. I heard you talking in your sleep. I came to make sure you were okay.'

'No, it wasn't you. He was in my room when you came. I wasn't asleep. I was awake. You were in my room but the other man was also in my room.'

'If there was someone in your room, sweetie, and I'm not saying there was, then why didn't you scream?' Julia asks.

'I *tried*. I couldn't make the noise. I was too afraid. And then the man disappeared.'

Trying to forget the hand he thought he saw

269

plastered against the window last night, Nathaniel remembers what the guidance counselor said, that the boy is inclined to lie. He is certainly lying now, unless he has had some kind of delusion, or remembers a nightmare as if it really happened. It is time to make an appointment for Copley to see a psychiatrist, as much as it pains Nathaniel to think of submitting his son to the kind of analytical intrusions he himself suffered under the attentions of his mother, the shuttering of his psyche into a neatly labeled box, the naming and classification of his neuroses, the tracing of all his problems to early traumas he still does not wholly remember, claims about his father dismissed as Oedipal fantasy. *Yes, of course you think your father is trying to kill you*, his mother would say, *because that liberates you to do violence to him*. He was never his mother's patient in any official sense, but she used him nonetheless, treated her own family as a group of laboratory rats submitted to various stimuli, deprivations, and hostile conditions to see how they might react. It was all so ingenious, the construction of what were effectively research sessions as 'family talking time' once a day every day, when the recorder was switched on and he and his mother would have a conversation, just after his brother had suffered the same treatment. When he asked her why he could not go first for once his mother explained it was because *birth order is important in these matters. It helps me to*

270

*understand your day if I first understand your brother's. So wait your turn in the other room.* He cannot remember ever loving his mother; at best he has memories that are neutral, but in the case of his father all the memories are negative, even and including the most recent ones. If he were able to divorce himself from his parents, to insist on no further communication, perhaps even to take out restraining orders against them, he would, but the promise of inheritance is too substantial to ignore in the interest of happiness and peace and the possibility of forgetting. He knows that as long as he has contact with them, even contact it is possible to police and mediate and dispense in manageable doses, he will never be able to leave the memories behind: new memories will always be made, rolling off the line with every interaction.

There must be better therapists these days, more sensitive, less entrenched in a particular theoretical school. They will find someone for Copley who is caring and intuitive, who knows how to ask questions they have failed to ask and who will give him ways to cope with his new environment. It is up to Nathaniel to undertake the research and planning, to find the doctor who will rescue his son from whatever brink he is approaching, before the plunge into madness.

'I think it was just a complicated dream you were having, honey,' Julia says. 'Nothing you have to be afraid about. No one can get inside

271

the house. Everything is locked up at night. We're safe inside, absolutely safe.'

Copley sighs, putting his head in his hands. 'Why won't you believe me?' he whines. 'Why won't you *help* me?'

5:00 AM: before the alarm goes off he is already awake. His parents do not know he sets the alarm for such an early hour, nor do they know that most nights since leaving Boston he has hardly slept. There are many things they do not know. They know only what is unimportant: that he gets up before them, that he has showered and is dressed with his hair dried and combed by the time they get up. Sometimes his father asks him if he has really had a shower and checks his bathroom to see if the stall is wet and the towel damp. It is a stupid and unnecessary thing to do. Showering is not something he would try to avoid. Showering is essential. He is already awake before five because he has set his body to be awake at that hour, whether or not he has slept through the night, and his body always wakes him up a few minutes before five. If he gets up early he does not have to rush to be ready when his mother says it is time to go. This has started only since the move. He did not get up so early in Boston. Everything about life was simpler there. It is still dark outside and he gets out of bed without

273

disturbing the sheet or blanket. His parents do not know how well he can see in the dark. Except for reading, he could live without light. He walks over to one of the two large windows in the room and looks out at the old white house down the hill. There is a light in one of the windows and he can see the woman moving inside. He has been watching her since the day they arrived, each morning lighting her candle and working in the kitchen. A few weeks ago, while his mother was working in the basement one Saturday and his father was busy in his study, he was alone in the backyard. The rain had stopped for a few hours. Time was slow. He looked at the grass and tried to tell himself stories, then found a hole in the fence where there used to be a knot in one of the wooden planks. He looked through the hole and saw the woman in her garden. When he said hello she dropped her trowel and looked up at the sky. 'I'm here,' he said, and knocked on the fence. She straightened her back and walked over to introduce herself. 'I'm Louise,' she said. 'Copley,' he said. 'You see that soft spot where grass doesn't grow behind your garage,' she said. 'Yes, I can see it. The place with two rocks and all the grass from the yard service.' 'That's the one,' she said. 'You be careful of that place. Don't go walking on top of it. There's a deep hole underneath it. I wouldn't want you to fall in.' Since their meeting through the fence, each morning before dawn he has raised his hand to wave to her from his bedroom window.

This morning he turns on the light in his bedroom and waves again, but he can no longer see the woman or the candle, only his reflection in the glass. Although he keeps hoping he will see her again outside, on the street, or in her backyard, he has not.

5:02 AM: since moving to this new city, each morning he has asked himself the same question: 'Where are you?' The answer has been the same every day: 'I'm in my new house, in a new town, but it does not feel like I am actually here. I feel like I am somewhere else.' 'In Boston?' he asks himself. 'No, not in Boston. I don't know where I feel like I am, but I don't feel like I am where I know I must be.'

5:10 AM: he takes off his pajama shirt and pants and underwear and puts them on the low white wooden chair in his bathroom. He did not have his own bathroom in Boston and having one here is one of the few changes he likes about the new place. He turns on the shower and waits until the water is the right temperature. He remembers the first shower he took, last year, and how proud he was of making the transition from baths. Before taking that first shower he had assumed there was a risk of drowning because the water came down on top of the head and it seemed impossible you could breathe and be under water at the same time. The discovery that it was all much more straightforward, and that he preferred the feeling of showering to taking a bath, was a revelation. He stands under the water, wets his hair, opens the bottle of shampoo and squirts a portion of the honey-colored liquid into his palm, then works it through his hair while the water slams into his back. Once he has worked up a lather he rinses his hair, picks up the bar of soap, passes it between his hands until suds form, puts the bar back in its tray, and smooths the soapsuds over his face, into his ears, behind his ears, washing thoroughly, careful to get rid of all the dirt, and then turns around to face the stream of water and rinse off his face. He leans over to pick up the sponge, squirts a blob of green shower gel into the middle, and kneads it until handfuls of bubbles form and the air is heavy with peppermint. He wipes the sponge down the outside of his left arm, along the underside, into his armpit, scrubs his chest and stomach and sides, and then the other arm, outside first, inside, armpit. He washes his lower abdomen, passes the sponge over his private parts, washes his right leg, right foot, left leg, left foot. He always cleans his body in the same sequence, always takes his shower in the same way, beginning at the top and working down to his toes. He rinses off, stands under the water for another minute, enjoying the intense heat, and then turns it off by pushing the lever all the way to the right. Standing in the steam that lingers in the room, he listens to the thrumming fan hidden in the ceiling. In Boston his father and mother used to sit in the bathroom reading to him while he took his bath each evening. Since starting to take showers, he no longer wants them to be in the bathroom and, more than that, when he is in the bathroom he now always wants to be left alone. Once, his father came in while he was taking a shower in Boston and after that he began locking the bathroom door. When his father asked why he did this, he said that he did not come into the bathroom when his father or mother was taking a shower and it did not seem fair that they would come into the bathroom now when he was showering. Going to the bathroom is private. Showering is private. Being naked is private. These are all private things, to be done alone.

5:20 AM: next to the shower stall is a bar where his towel hangs. Someone, his father or mother, has put out a fresh towel and he enjoys the stiffness of its pile as he dries his head, his face, the back of his neck, his arms, chest, back, stomach, legs, feet: each day he dries his body in the same way, head to toe, top to bottom. He does not know if this is something his parents taught him to do, but he believes it is not. Instead, it is one of many tricks he has learned on his own, although he cannot remember a process of trial and error, only his arrival at the perfect system. He wraps the towel around his waist, turns on the hairdryer and directs the hot stream all over his head until his hair lies in a way he recognizes as his own. After he has dressed he will come back into the bathroom to put gel in his hair and comb it a final time. His father does not like that he uses gel; he says it is something children don't need to do. What his father fails to understand is that it is not a matter of need or desire. It is everything to do with the expectations of the other children at school.

5:25 AM: while he gets dressed he hangs the towel over a hook on the back of his bedroom door. With the door locked he goes to his dresser, where he finds a pair of underpants: dark blue ones that are new and snug. They make him feel good when he pulls them on. From his closet he takes his khaki school slacks and his blue cotton shirt. First he puts on the shirt, buttons it, and leaves the buttons at the wrist for his mother or father to fasten. He puts on the slacks, tucking the shirt in as he pulls them up. This is the uniform all the boys are required to wear. In winter, and on cold days, they will also be allowed to wear a red wool V-neck sweater or a red wool V-neck sweater vest because the combination of colors, his teacher Mrs Pitt tells them, makes them look like little patriots. The girls have the same uniform except they have to wear khaki skirts that come to just below the knee. Pupils are not allowed to wear shorts except during PE and the shorts are kept at school, where they are washed and dried after each use. He finds blue socks in his dresser and sits on a chair next to his bed while he puts them on, right foot first.

278

Just before walking out the door to drive to school he will put on his shoes, which are downstairs in the drop zone between the back door and the kitchen.

5:45 AM: he makes his bed, pulling up the sheet, tucking it in on both sides, and smoothing the blanket over the top. He fluffs his pillow, centers it at the head of the bed, and arranges his stuffed animals in front of it. When all is arranged as he wants it, he takes his towel back to the bathroom, remembers his pajamas and returns them, folded, to their place under the pillow on his bed, and sits in the chair next to the window facing the old white house down the hill, watching in the dark as the woman moves back and forth with her candle. After the sun begins to come through the tops of the trees in the woods to the east, he notices smoke rising out of the woman's chimney. He wonders why they have not met any of the other neighbors and whether there are any children in the neighborhood, as there were children in their building in Boston, or if he is now going to have a different kind of life altogether, one in which his time outside of school is filled only with adults. He has heard children at school talk about 'play dates' and has been able to infer this is the only way children here get together to see each other: they make appointments for designated times and locations, their parents drive and pick them up. In Boston, he sometimes had play dates but often, if he wanted to play with a friend in the building, his parents would phone the other apartment, see if the child was available, and in minutes, after riding up or down the elevators and running along the hallways, the two of them could be playing. Appointments were usually made only for birthday or holiday parties. He watches the tart reddening sky, but within fifteen minutes the rising sun has disappeared, the clouds unpacked, the rain valve opened, the deluge resumed. In Boston, he did not mind school, but minded it even less on rainy days. Here, the rain does nothing to improve his feeling about the kind of day likely to unfold.

6:15 AM: in the kitchen he takes a box of dry, sugarless cereal from the cabinet, milk from the fridge, and a bowl from a cupboard underneath the silverware drawer, where he finds a spoon. He climbs on a stool to sit at the kitchen island, opens the box of cereal, pours some into the bowl, cuts up a banana with a butter knife, and rakes the sliced fruit from the cutting board into the bowl. He pours the milk, screws the lid back on the carton, and turns on the radio in the center of the island to listen to the morning news on public radio. Some mornings he is down in the kitchen in time to hear the opening melody and first head-lines, but he was distracted this morning by watching Louise in her old white house and has missed those first fifteen minutes of reassurance.

It was not uncommon in Boston for his school-mates to have listened to the morning news on the radio as well, but he understands already that in this new place his behavior is unusual. He eats his cereal, listening to reports of a weather pattern in the Pacific, and how it is going to mean a very wet autumn and heavy winter snows for this part of the country. When he finishes his cereal he climbs down from his stool, and puts the bowl and spoon in the dishwasher. The milk he returns to the fridge, the box of cereal to the cabinet. He pushes the stool in under the overhanging ledge that extends out from the island to create what his father calls 'the breakfast bar'. It is not a name he likes since the ledge is clearly just a part of the island, and 'island' has a nicer sound and means nicer things than 'bar', which reminds him of buildings in Boston with men clustered outside smoking: places where the windows were always dark, at most with a dim light or two inside, and a garish red neon sign outside. He cannot under-stand why his father would want to impose that kind of space into the heart of the kitchen, but his father, he knows, does not understand why the word so disturbs him. It is a feeling he has not been able to explain. Because he can hear one of his parents in the shower in their own bathroom and knows that when they come downstairs they will also want to listen to the morning news, he does not turn off the radio.

★　　★　　★

6:35 AM: walking across the hall to the den, where he will spend the next two hours until his mother is ready to drive him to school, he notices a change. The table against the staircase where a bowl of flowers usually sits has been moved to the opposite wall and the bowl is on the floor, while the flowers – large yellow chrysanthemums – lie on the white floor facing the same direction, each bloom and stem occupying the width of a single board. The man must have done it. The man is not his father. At first he was unsure, thinking that the man sitting in his room at night, the man who picked him up outside and carried him back inside on the night they arrived, was his father in some kind of costume. Now he understands that this is not so, but when he has tried to tell his parents there is a man coming into the house they insist he has been dreaming and remind him that the alarm system would alert them if someone did try to get in: it would go off and the guards with guns would come to protect them. He has not yet figured out how the man can be in the house at night without the alarm going off, unless there is a problem with the alarm. This is the first time the man has done anything to try to get his parents' attention, and he is sure this is the reason for the movement of the table and the dispersal of the chrysanthemum blossoms. The man wants them to know they are not alone in the house. Leaving the table in the wrong place and the flowers where they are, he goes into the den where he finds all the furniture pushed away from the center of the room and up against the walls. It is the same in the living room and dining room, where the white table and chairs have been pushed against the white western wall of the house. Now his parents will have to believe him when he says something is happening, that a dark giant man is present who is waiting for them to acknowledge his presence. There is no point in trying to move the furniture back into position: it is too heavy, there is too much of it, and it is better if his parents see it and learn the truth.

7:15 AM: his father has to leave the house earlier than his mother because he is supposed to be in the office by eight if not before that. 'What the hell?' his father says, coming down the stairs, 'Copley?' He gets up from the couch in the den where he has been sitting, reading his book, and goes into the hallway. As he walks his limbs stiffen, his knees lock. He cannot explain why he feels compelled to walk in this way, but when he sees his father's face he knows it is a bad idea, he loosens his limbs, he lingers at the door to the den. 'Did *you* do this?' his father asks. It is difficult to tell how angry his father may be, or if the thing his father is feeling at this moment is in fact anger and not something else. 'No,' he answers, shaking his head, 'the dark giant man did it.' His father scowls. 'There is no man, Copley. You have to stop talking about the man. *There is no man.* It's just the three of us in this house. Why would you do

283

this?' He shakes his head, he cannot believe his father is accusing him of doing something he knows he did not do, could not have done; does his father not know how much he hates mess, how he can't bear to see anything left on the floor, just how agitated it makes him feel? 'I didn't *do it*,' he says. 'Look in the other rooms. You'll *see. I didn't do it*.' His father seems confused and brushes past him into the den. He hears the air damming up in his father's mouth, his father is about to speak, and then he goes into the living room, 'Copley!', and across the hall into the dining room, 'for goodness' sake, Copley, what the hell were you thinking?' his father shouts. 'But I *didn't do it! How could I do it?*'

7:30 AM: he is sitting in the den listening to his parents arguing in the kitchen. They have closed the doors and are talking about him, but he can still hear most of what they say because sound travels in this new house in ways it never did in the Boston apartment. They both conclude he must have moved the furniture and arranged the chrysanthemum blossoms on the floor – that is not the point of their dispute. His mother contends he must have done it in his sleep, and therefore he could not have been aware of what he was doing, whereas his father insists it had to be *intentional*, because there is too much *purpose* and *design* in the rearrangement. The furniture is all on industrial casters with little locks, so it is possible, he now understands, that he might have been able to move everything on his own. He wonders if his parents are right. In sleep things happen that are often difficult to remember on waking. From the events on their first night in the house he has no memory of getting out of bed and going outside. He only remembers the man picking him up on the lawn, and being so terrified of waking up outdoors in the arms of a man he did not know, whom he could only, for that moment, believe was his father in disguise, that he had not dared to move: he could only play dead. It is possible, though, that if he does not remember how he got outside on the first night, then there might be other events during the hours he assumed he was asleep that are also unknown to him.

7:40 AM: while his parents argue, clanging bowls and silverware and turning up the radio to mask their voices, he unlocks the casters on the couch in the den and tries to push it: the thing is heavy but he manages to put it back where it is supposed to live. If he can do this, then he might have been able to move every piece of furniture on the ground floor. Not wanting his parents to have proof that he is capable of rearranging the house, he pushes the couch back up against the wall and locks the casters in place, lies down on the couch, and returns to his book, to the story of a young boy who is a genius and his journey to a distant planet to rescue his father. His own father has said the book is for older children, and is a religious parable, but this is not what makes the book interesting. What intrigues him are the discussions about time: the single point, the straight line, the box, the cube, the first three dimensions, the fourth dimension that is time itself, the possibility of interstellar and intertemporal travel. He has spent hours making careful drawings on graph paper of the fourth dimension, and is thinking about these forms again, his mind wandering as he reads, wandering so far that he loses sense of his body and wonders again where he is since he does not feel as though he is lying on this couch with a book in his hands, when his father opens the kitchen door and calls out to him across the hall, 'Goodbye, Copley, have a good day at school. I'll see you tonight.' He calls back, 'Goodbye,' without looking away from his book.

8:30 AM: as usual, his mother is running late. She is on the phone to one of her graduate assistants, apologizing and explaining that she needs *an army of virtual helpers just to get out the door in the morning.* They have only fifteen minutes before school starts. He watches as the two men next door, in the house north of their own, say goodbye. One of the men is white: he reverses down the driveway in a car and pauses to speak to the other man, who is brown and stands in the driveway holding an umbrella in one hand with a little girl clutched in his other arm; the girl is also brown, but not as brown as the man. It is the first time he has seen the girl. The white man leans out the car window and kisses the little girl, whom the brown man holds down to the white man. After the brown man looks around at the other houses he leans over to kiss the white man. It would be nice to meet the girl and the men and he wonders why they have not met them already.

8:42 AM: his mother taps in the code for the alarm. As he waits for her to do this he thinks he sees movement from the doorway to the basement, as if the basement door has just swung open or shut, but it is too late to say anything. His mother locks the door behind her and they run through the rain to the garage. While his mother is unlocking the door to the garage he looks back at the kitchen window and sees the man inside the house, standing at the alarm console, pushing in the code. 'The man—' he says to his mother, but she pulls him into the garage before he can continue. 'We're going to be late and Mrs Pitt won't be happy,' his mother says. 'But the man was turning off the alarm,' he says. His mother looks at him and sighs and pulls the car out of the garage, reversing down the driveway, past the house that is no longer protected because the man is already inside and knows all their secrets.

8:47 AM: the first bell rang two minutes ago. They are still several blocks from the school, but there has been an accident on the wet gray roads and traffic is at a standstill as hail begins to fall, turning everything white. 'Dammit, the car,' his mother says. He tries to forget about the man. This is not difficult because the thought of the approaching school day preoccupies him, making him feel sick, as though he might vomit. In Boston, he never dreaded going to school because school was where he wanted to be; it was where he saw friends and where he learned new things. In this new school he learns nothing and has only one friend. 'I'll have to pull over until it passes or your father will kill me.' 'Will he really kill you?' he asks. His mother looks alarmed and shakes her head. 'No, honey, it was a figure of speech.' 'A what?' 'A poor choice of words. Your father would never kill anyone.'

8:59 AM: they arrive at school. He pleads with his mother to come inside to explain why he is late, that it was not his fault. She parks the car and runs into the building, shakes water from her jacket, and speaks to Mrs Taylor, the guidance counselor, who says 'a tardy is a tardy, even when it isn't the fault of the child'. He does not think he will be going to this school again after the winter break. He overheard his mother tell someone on the phone that she does not approve of the school, but feels unable to take him out because they have failed to make any other plans and it would be bad for his father's career if they enrolled him somewhere else. 'Why would it be bad for

Dad's career?' he asked his mother. 'Because his company runs the school and all the executives send their children to company schools,' she said, and then, in a whisper, 'or at least that's what he tells me. Don't worry. It won't be forever.'

9:05 AM: he has missed the Pledge of Allegiance and the singing of 'America the Beautiful' and Mrs Pitt is already ten minutes into math, which is the first period of the day. They are still working on adding and subtracting and fractions, and are spending the week on word problems, which most of his classmates find difficult. No one else in class knows how to multiply or divide and when he has asked Mrs Pitt about when they will be doing multiplication and division, she has explained that those topics will only be covered next year – the first half of the year on multiplication tables, the second half on division. The delay makes no sense to him because he is comfortable with numbers, understanding them as if they were people, boys and girls. One is a boy, two is a girl, three is a boy, four a boy, five a boy, six a girl, seven a boy (his own age), eight a girl, nine a girl, ten a boy, eleven a boy, twelve a girl, thirteen a boy, fourteen a boy, and so on. Ask him any number and he can tell you if it is a boy or a girl. 312 is a girl. 1791 is a boy. 1829 is a girl. When Mrs Pitt sees him come in the door she frowns. Like the students, she wears a uniform: khaki skirt, blue shirt, red wool sweater: 'a grown-up patriot for all of you little patriots to emulate,' she tells them. 'Have you been to the office?' she asks. 'Yes, Mrs Pitt,' he says. 'Take your seat, Copley,' she says, and he finds his place in the desk at the very back of the first row. His name is written on a piece of yellow paper that is supposed to look like a ruler, but to his mind it has been poorly drawn and the 'o' has been left out of his last name. When he told Mrs Pitt his name was misspelled, she said a new sign would be made for his desk, but one has never appeared and he knows he will spend the semester labeled with a name not his own. Although the day is dark and rain is pouring outside, the blinds have been lowered over the bank of windows that extends the whole length of the classroom: the slats are open but the effect is deadening. In the adjacent wing, he can see other classrooms with their blinds also lowered, the lights on inside. The room smells damp, and next to him sits a girl called Emily who has blonde hair that looks gray near her scalp. She has pinkish-gray skin and has missed several days of school since he first arrived. He suspects she is slowly dying because she always smells like rotten eggs and her skin and hair are always gray; she is rotting from the inside out and no one is bothering to notice but him. Of the twenty students in his class, he knows all their names, and almost nothing about any one of them except Joslyn, who sits in front of him; not only is she the only black person in the whole school apart from the lunch ladies, she is also his only friend, although he is not even sure if they are actually friends. Every day Mrs Pitt finds an excuse to say to the two of them something like, 'There, Joslyn and Copley, right where I can keep an eye on you two,' as if they have done something wrong. Joslyn is the only person who has ever spoken to him at recess, because, he thinks, no one speaks to her: the two outsiders of the classroom, thrown together by virtue of being ignored by everyone else. He understands that if he is going to have a 'play date', Joslyn is the only possible candidate. They are the two smartest students in class and this, he realizes, is the reason Mrs Pitt fears them. They know better than to speak before lunch. Speaking is never allowed unless Mrs Pitt calls on them when they raise their hands to answer a question. Speaking is not allowed during water and bathroom breaks because they might disturb other classrooms. Speaking is only allowed at lunch and recess. In his Boston school there was group time and free periods when you could speak to each other and work on creative projects. At the Pinwheel Academy there is no group time and no free periods. He looks up at the black glass hemisphere in the center of the ceiling but cannot tell whether there is only one camera monitoring the room or a number of cameras nesting inside. Sometimes he hears a whirring, churning noise and imagines it is the camera turning, focusing, taking a picture of him and his work.

★   ★   ★

10:00 AM: Mrs Pitt ends the math lesson and asks them to put away their pencils before passing their work to the front of each row. When she has collected the worksheets she asks them to stand next to their desks. 'Fingers on lips,' she says, placing her right index finger on her closed mouth with the tip of the finger pointing up to her nose. They all mimic her. 'Row One, please line up in the hall.' The five of them file out of the room and form a line outside. The first person in the row, a boy called Ethan, who is Row Monitor, stops next to the fire extinguisher, which functions as the guide for the row that is called to go first. The next row that comes out, which happens to be Row Three, lines up next to Row One; Row Four lines up behind Row One, and Row Two, punished because Emily passed forward her work before putting away her pencil, lines up behind Row Three. Mrs Pitt takes her place at the head of the two lines, finger still on her lips, as their fingers are still on their lips, and leads them down the hall to the restrooms. Four boys and four girls are allowed in the restrooms at any one time. He and Ethan and two other boys, Austin and Max, are the first boys in. There are four urinals and four stalls, but the stalls do not have doors. He goes to a stall while the other three boys line up at the urinals. He has tried using urinals but finds he cannot urinate with anyone else present. Although they are forbidden to speak, the other boys whisper words about him he does not understand: they are words he does not know and does not recognize. He gets parts of the words, individual sounds, but cannot piece together any meaning except the malicious, teasing sense he gets from the way the words are whispered. He stands in the stall and is only able to urinate once Ethan, Austin, and Max have left and as the next boys are coming in. He washes his hands and sees that the others are Todd and Steven and Joe, who hiss similar words at him as he leaves the restroom, glancing up at the black glass hemisphere above the door. When he comes out of the restroom he pauses at the drinking fountain, tastes the warm chlorinated water on his tongue, and goes to stand at the rear of the line. Mrs Pitt comes to stand next to him. She puts a hand on his shoulder, presses down on his body, and says, '*You* took a long time, didn't you?' In Boston, he once went into a girls' restroom at school by mistake and was astonished to see no urinals, only stalls. It would be easier to be a girl at the Pinwheel Academy. At his school in Boston no one ever said anything about him using the stalls, which had doors as well as locks, instead of the urinals. He does not understand why his parents have sent him to this school, but it seems to be a form of punishment.

10:15 AM: they walk back to Mrs Pitt's classroom, fingers always on lips. 'Why are children like flowers?' she asks them. They know the answer:

'Because our mouths should be tulips.' *Two lips*. He thinks it is a stupid thing to say. Tulips open in the day and close at night, but Mrs Pitt means their mouths should always be closed. They stop outside the classroom door. The Row Monitors are allowed into the room first, and then four students at a time may enter the room. The Row Monitors help Mrs Pitt and Miss Fox, the classroom assistant, keep silent order. Only when one batch of four students is seated is the next batch allowed to enter. If anyone speaks, the Row Monitors make a note and hold it up for Mrs Pitt or Miss Fox to collect once everyone is seated. If you speak, you are fined.

10:18 AM: they begin the language arts lesson. For this, he and Joslyn and four other students go next door to Mrs Abbot's classroom. It is often the best part of the day. While they are still expected only to speak when called upon, Mrs Abbot is nice. She gives them treats, she praises their work, she smiles in a way that looks happy instead of angry. She never raises her voice. There is never any need for her to raise her voice. Although Mrs Abbot's language arts class is for the advanced students, the stories are still stupid and too simple. At the Lab School he took a test that indicated he had a twelfth-grade reading level. Reading has always been easy; he read before he talked. Letters of the alphabet are, like numbers, either boys or girls or in some cases neutral:

A: neutral
B: boy
C: girl
D: boy
E: boy
F: neutral
G: girl
H: boy
I: boy
J: boy
K: girl
L: girl
M: boy
N: boy
O: girl
P: boy
Q: girl
R: girl
S: girl
T: boy
U: boy
V: boy
W: boy
X: girl
Y: boy
Z: neutral

It is all so obvious, and the composition of letters in a particular word means that each word is itself either a boy or a girl or neutral. Apple, key, dog, house, lawn, car are all boys. Orange, kite, giraffe, river, wagon are all girls. Lake, sky, tree, word, music are neutral. Last week when he told Mrs Abbot he was reading the book about the boy trying to rescue his father she looked surprised and warned him it was meant for older children. She asked him if he understood it. He said he did, and showed her some of his drawings of a hypercube in four dimensions. She kept the drawings and then, over the weekend, his parents gave them back to him at home. He wonders if his father and Mrs Abbot have been speaking with each other.

11:30 AM: he and Joslyn and the four other students return to Mrs Pitt's classroom. He thinks of telling Mrs Pitt he is ill and wants to go to the nurse but he knows Mrs Pitt will put her hand on his forehead, as she has done with other students who have complained of not feeling well, and unless his forehead is hot she will not let him go. He takes his seat at the back of Row One, wondering how to make his forehead hot enough to be allowed to go to the nurse. He concentrates on making himself warm. He holds his breath. Mrs Pitt looks at him and tells him to stop making faces and gives him a first warning for the day. A warning carries a fine of one dollar. If he gets three warnings he will be held inside during recess. If he gets four warnings in a day he will be given detention. If he gets five warnings he will have a one-day suspension. He knows the consequences and schedule of fees for every infraction, but does not always know what behavior will be judged punishable. He could not have imagined that holding his breath for a few seconds and trying to make himself feel hot would result in a warning, but then other students – Emily for instance – have been fined for failing to make eye contact with Mrs Pitt when she asks them a question.

11:32 AM: today they have art on the other side of the building. They go through the same process of lining up in the hallway, fingers on lips, before walking to the center of school, circling round the Hub, and turning down to the Green Wing. Each wing has its own color. Mrs Pitt's classroom is in the Red Wing, where all the doors are red and there are red stripes along the floor on either side of the hallway. The Hub is white. Talking is forbidden in art as well, but in the art classroom they do not have assigned seats. He and Joslyn sit next to each other at the point farthest from the door and closest to the windows. The art teacher, Mr Cross, is tall and bearded, always smells like cigarettes, and wears the same uniform as the other teachers although he does not tuck his shirt into his slacks. He does not smile but he does compliment their work if they do something he likes. He is always trying to tell them to look more closely at the world. 'A tree trunk is not brown,' he says, holding up a brown crayon. 'A tree trunk is lots of different colors. Look at all the colors in the tree trunk,' he tells them, pointing outside to the trees that are closest to the school, at the edge of the playground, on the opposite side of the fence. Today, Mr Cross tells them to draw an autumn scene, and shows some examples: *The Harvesters*, *Haystacks (Autumn)*, *Autumn Landscape with a Flock of Turkeys*, *Autumn Series (Number IV)*, *Autumn Forest*, *Autumnal Sacrifice*, and many different Chinese and Japanese scrolls. Mr Cross hands out large sheets of heavy white paper and gives each of them a box of oil pastels. If they had been given graph paper he would have drawn a hypercube in four dimensions but instead he decides to draw the old white house next to his own, and Louise standing inside it with her candle. He begins by sketching the outline of the picture in pencil and once he has the house, trees, the road beyond the house, and the window with Louise inside all outlined, he begins to color in the shapes, starting with the sky and background and gradually working to the top layer, finishing just before the end of the hour with Louise's face and the flame of the candle. Mr Cross walks around looking at the students' work. He pauses and makes a sound of approval over the picture of Louise in her house. 'Very good work, Copley,' Mr Cross says. 'But you need to put in some fall colors, more trees in the background.' 'But there aren't any more trees in that direction. There's just the road,' he says, and then the bell rings and art is over.

★   ★   ★

12:30–12.50 PM: lunch. The classroom assistant, Miss Fox, collects them from art and takes them to the gymnasium, which is also the cafeteria and auditorium. Tables with integrated benches are unfolded and lined up in a grid across the gym floor. At one end of the room is a stage, at the other the doors leading into the kitchen area where the food is dispensed. They walk in line to the kitchen, and one by one they place their right index finger on the sensor, wait for the screen to register their account, and then are allowed by the attendant to pick up a tray and collect their lunch. There is never any choice. Today it is hamburger pizza, salad, and an oatmeal cookie. When he first arrived he told the attendants he does not eat meat and they said he has to have a doctor's note and otherwise he should eat around it. He has not complained to his parents, who also do not eat meat, because he knows they have enough to worry about already. Each classroom sits at its own table, though there are no assigned seats. He and Joslyn always sit together at the end. He picks the cheese and hamburger off the pizza, eats the crust with the remaining tomato sauce, and then eats the salad and the cookie. The other students, and not just those in Mrs Pitt's class, have started referring to Joslyn as Medusa. He has looked up the name at home and discovered that the goddess Medusa had snakes for hair. Joslyn has braids, but these look nothing like snakes. The students play a game, pretending that if they happen to look at Joslyn they will turn to stone: they freeze in place waiting until another classmate puts a hand over their eyes to 'unfreeze' them. Joslyn acts like she does not hear what they say, and the two of them do not discuss the game. She asks him about Boston and he tells her all he can remember about his other school. 'But I don't understand how you go to school in a lab,' she says, 'because a lab is where you do experiments.' 'I don't know. That's just what they called it. The Laboratory School.' 'Did the teachers experiment on you?' she laughs. 'I don't know. I don't think so.' He asks her about growing up in this city, and what she knows about it. They exchange information, they ask and respond, they have become friendly in very little time at all. He would like to ask her if she will come to his house for a play date but he does not know how this is done and worries she might say no. 'I don't want my cookie,' she says. 'I'm on a diet. My mother says I'm getting fat.' 'I don't think you're fat, Joslyn.' She smiles but does not look happy. 'You're skinny, so you eat it,' she says, and hands him the cookie.

12:50 PM: Miss Fox returns to take them outside for recess, which lasts for twenty minutes. There are balls of various kinds, a jungle gym, and monkey bars. The rain has stopped and they stand in the concrete playground overlooked by two security guards in uniforms with the same logo as the company baseball cap his father owns. The first week at the Pinwheel Academy he walked around at recess on his own, studying patterns in the concrete and thinking about his old school. Now, he and Joslyn continue whatever conversation they were having over lunch. After recess, they will not speak again to each other until the final bell of the day, and then only briefly at their lockers, on their way to the school parking lot where their respective parents will be waiting. The entire school, from first through sixth grade, is out at recess together. Several older girls bounce basketballs in time. If one of them gets her bounce out of rhythm she has to drop out and the last one remaining wins. Half a dozen boys play a game of basketball and then, all at once, the game compresses into a coagulation of bodies at the far corner of the playground, catching the attention of the security guards who begin shouting for the students to disperse. Most run away, thinning out to fill the expanse of concrete, but three of the boys remain, their bodies locked together. The guards shout again, 'Disperse!', but the boys go on fighting. 'Final warning!' the guards shout. One of the boys separates from the other two and a guard catches him by the shirt collar while the other removes the taser from his belt and shoots at the two remaining boys, who both fall to the ground, screaming. The guard who fired the taser puts it back in the holster and pulls each of the boys up by an arm before marching them inside the building. One of them does not look like he is awake and his face is bloody. It is not the first time this has happened. Joslyn makes a clicking sound with her tongue. 'They oughta know better by now,' she says. He agrees. He has seen it happen so many times in the last few weeks he cannot understand why anyone would risk breaking even a minor rule, let alone fighting.

1:10 PM: the bell rings and Mrs Pitt appears on the playground. He and Joslyn are the first in line. He always hopes that if he is prompt, if he shows he is well behaved, then Mrs Pitt will like him and stop assuming he is a troublemaker. She frowns as the others line up behind them. By being first in line, he and Joslyn should be the Line Leaders for the march back to class, except that once everyone is present Mrs Pitt calls for them to turn around, making Joslyn and him the last in line, while allowing those who were the slowest to line up (including two of the three Row Monitors in class) the privilege of leading everyone back to Mrs Pitt's room. This has occurred so often he knows he should expect it: just when he thinks he understands what will happen, the situation is reversed.

1:20 PM: there are three hours left in the day and he has no idea how he will last until his mother arrives to pick him up and take him to the appointment she has made for him to see a new kind of doctor. He does not understand why he is being taken to a doctor, since he does not feel unwell, except for the moments of queasiness about school. Before the end of the day there are three long periods: social studies, science, and then, at the end of the day, PE. If only PE were at the beginning of the day and not at the end, always there to be dreaded, scowling over every hour. Today is even worse, because today is swimming. As they are starting the social studies lesson he hears the sound of an ambulance siren, which comes closer and closer until he can see it drive into the school parking lot. The sirens stop but the lights keep flashing and five minutes later the paramedics wheel a gurney out of the school with one of the boys who was shot by the taser strapped down against it. A guard – the guard who shot the boy – walks alongside the gurney and climbs into the back of the ambulance. The social studies lesson is on maps. Mrs Pitt hands out a worksheet that has a map printed on it with directions to follow. They have to color in the map: the river should be blue, the park green, the fire station red, schools brown, etc. Once they have colored in the map they have to answer questions about whether the church or the school is farther east, whether the town hall is north or south of the river, how many blocks it is between the school and the jail. Some of the students do not understand the questions and Miss Fox or Mrs Pitt has to come around to help them. In the first ten minutes of the lesson he finishes the map, puts down his pencil, and pushes the crayons back into their box. Mrs Pitt notices and asks him why he isn't working. 'I'm finished,' he says, and holds up the handout. 'Check your work thoroughly,' she chides. 'Good work is never rushed work.' He reads over the directions, checks he has colored everything as required, makes sure his answers are correct, and is pleased to see he has made not a single error and never strayed outside the lines. He is not sure what teachers are for in this new school. At his school in Boston, they never had handouts like this. The work was interesting and difficult and always took as long to finish as the time allotted for the lesson. Here he spends too much time doing nothing, waiting for Mrs Pitt to move on to something new, for the other students to finish their work. He has asked Joslyn about this at recess. She tells him he has to learn to go slow: 'Stretch it out. Make yourself take longer than you have to.'

2:00 PM: restroom and water break. They line up, walk to the restrooms, he stands in a stall and urinates while three other boys hiss words he does not understand. He washes his hands, looks up at the black glass hemisphere, gets a drink at the fountain in the hall, lines up again and waits until everyone else is lined up, fingers on lips, silent except for occasional squeaks of rubber sole on linoleum, sounds that draw scowls from Mrs Pitt's mouth. When they are all in line, Miss Fox walks them to the science lab in the Blue Wing, where they spend an hour learning about butterflies with Mrs Rothschild, who shows pictures of different butterflies before inviting them to come up two at a time to examine a display of real butterflies, pinned to a board and sealed under glass. He can see their small faces, and is horrified by the pins stabbed right through their bodies and wings. He wonders why it is not enough just to look at pictures since photographs, as big as they are, provide more detail than looking at the butterflies with the naked eye.

3:00 PM: for the last period of the day Miss Fox arrives at the science lab to take them to the sports center in the Green Wing. The boys go into the Boys' Locker Room and the girls into the Girls' Locker Room. Inside the Boys' Locker Room the assistant PE teacher, Mr Bruce, hands out black swimming suits, which itch and are never the right size. Once Mr Bruce gives him a suit he tries to find a corner where no one else is standing. Knowing the shirt will cover his private parts until he puts on the swimming suit he takes off his khaki slacks and underwear first. The other boys laugh and talk and make jokes among themselves. By the end of the day they usually have other things on their minds than him, so he manages to get changed and into the shower room before anyone can notice his discomfort. After showering they have to line up at the door to the pool and wait for Mr Bruce to let them in. He stands shivering, looking at the other pale bodies, the extreme thinness of some, the protuberant belly buttons, the serious fatness of others, the weirdly feminine breasts. He does not have a sense of his own body. Joslyn says he is skinny but no one else says anything about his body, only about the way he behaves, the way he tries to hide, to not be seen by other boys. His teeth chatter, his feet are cold on the tile floor, he longs for the warmth of the pool. As always at swimming, the other boys are horsing around and Mr Bruce has to tell them to stop. Austin and Ethan don't listen and Mr Bruce has to tell them again, then makes them all wait until everyone is standing silent and still. When Mr Bruce passes the students he turns to avoid touching their wet bodies, and then opens the door and leads them onto the pool deck, directing them all to get into the shallow end where the girls, who always manage to be in the pool before the boys, are already splashing. Mr Bruce and Miss Connie teach the swimming classes together and there is an additional lifeguard. A rumor has circulated among the students that someone drowned a year ago, and since then the school has insisted three adults always be present for each swimming class. It is not the swimming itself he minds. He is a strong swimmer and enjoys being in the water. It is the changing and nakedness that undo him, making him feel he is going to collapse. They spend forty minutes learning to tread water, working on their backstroke, and being allowed, in the final ten minutes, to play Marco Polo. Mr Bruce and Miss Connie are both in the water with them; she is plump, but Mr Bruce is tall and thin with a body broken up by distinct valleys and ridges that make him look like a special kind of three-dimensional topographical map. As he stares at Mr Bruce he knows, all at once, that Mr Bruce is aware of being stared at. His teacher swims over and asks him how he is doing, if he is enjoying swimming. 'Yes,' he says, 'I like swimming.' 'Good,' says Mr Bruce. 'I want you to promise me you'll do something really active this winter, Copley. Do you have an indoor pool of your own?' 'No,' he says, 'but we have a big backyard.' 'That's good,' Mr Bruce says, 'that means you can run around. Get outside, even when it's snowing. You look tired all the time, Copley. Exercise will help you sleep better. You'll have more energy. And in the future one cookie is enough for lunch.' He wonders how Mr Bruce knows he ate Joslyn's cookie as well as his own, since Mr Bruce is never in the cafeteria. He wonders if his parents have been talking to Mr Bruce about him. In fact, he wonders if his parents have been talking to all of his teachers about him. At the end of the lesson the boys go back into their locker room. Some of them take off their swimming suits to shower. They stand under the hot water and don't seem to mind being naked in front of other people. He cannot bring himself to do this. He showers with his suit on, takes a towel from Mr Bruce, wraps it around his waist, and removes his swimming suit only once the lower half of his body is covered. He puts the suit in the hamper and gets dressed, not drying the top of his body properly so he can put on his shirt faster. He pulls the underpants on while the towel is still around his waist and is dressed and ready to go when the dismissal bell rings. At his locker outside Mrs Pitt's classroom, he says goodbye to Joslyn. 'See you tomorrow, Policeman,' she says, using the nickname for him she has devised. 'See you tomorrow, Joslyn,' he says. He has tried to think of a nickname for her but since the other students call her Medusa he suspects the best thing he can do is to call her by her own name and nothing else.

3:57 PM: his mother is waiting in the parking lot. From the front door of the school he runs through the rain and into the cool dry air of the car. They have half an hour to get to the doctor's appointment, which his mother tells him is all the way on the other side of town. The rain coarsens, slamming against the windshield, and at one point it becomes so heavy, the wind so strong, that they cannot see the bumper of the car in front of them. His mother pulls off the road into the parking lot of a shopping mall where they wait for ten minutes. 'We have time,' she says. 'It's not that far now. How was your day?' 'Fine,' he says. 'What did you do?' she asks. 'Lots of things,' he says. The drawing he did in art is stowed in a manila folder in his backpack and he takes it out to show his mother. 'Who's this?' she says, looking at the image of the old white house and Louise holding her candle. 'It's the woman who lives in the house next door,' he says. 'What woman?' his mother asks, as if she does not know. 'Louise. I see her every morning. We met through the fence. She lights a candle in her kitchen. Smoke comes out of the chimney. She's one of my only two friends here.' 'But that house is condemned, Copley. I didn't know anyone lived there. You should have told us earlier.' His mother looks concerned and asks to keep the picture. Adults are always keeping his work, taking it away from him, and then, when he least expects it, returning it without explanation.

4:25 PM: the doctor's office is in a brown brick three-story building. Unlike at his ordinary doctor's office, where he had a check-up last week, there is no receptionist. He and his mother sit in the waiting room. There are magazines for adults, books for children, and various toys: plastic cars and trucks and wooden blocks. He has started paging through an issue of *American Scientist* when the door to the doctor's consulting room opens and he asks them both to come in. Dr Phaedrus looks like an older version of his father: shorter, fatter, balder, his blue and white striped shirt tucked into the waist of his gray slacks, held in by a gold-buckled brown leather belt that matches his tasseled brown leather shoes. He explains that he will be 'speaking with Copley and Mom together and then Copley alone' while his mother waits in a different room than the one they started in. At the end he'll 'talk to Mom alone' and when the session is finished they will 'exit through the back of the building', so anyone in the first waiting room will not see them, and they will not see those who may be waiting. He asks why they have to do it this way since he does not understand why it is important that no one knows they are there. 'To preserve privacy,' Dr Phaedrus explains, 'because some people don't like others to know they're coming to see me.' Dr Phaedrus smiles and closes the door, puts some soft music on his stereo, and asks them to sit down on a brown leather couch that matches the doctor's belt and shoes. Dr Phaedrus sits across from the two of them in a matching chair and holds a pad of yellow paper and pen. The doctor stares at him for a moment and he stares back at the doctor and then the doctor begins. 'I feel fine,' he says, when the doctor asks him how he's been feeling, 'I'm not sick.' 'No one is saying you're sick,' says Dr Phaedrus. 'But you're a doctor,' he says. 'Sometimes people go to a doctor so they can try to feel even better. Let's think of it that way if we can,' says Dr Phaedrus, 'that you're here to try to feel even better than you do already.' The doctor smiles, his teeth very white, his skin tanned and shiny, head almost bald except for a crescent of white frost that matches his teeth, so when he smiles it looks like a white ring is angled all the way round his head. 'Tell me what kinds of things you liked to do in Boston,' says Dr Phaedrus, 'and what kinds of things you like to do now that you're living here.' He thinks about the question for a moment and then begins to answer, conscious of trying to find good things to say about his new home, and not just about Boston. He tries to be balanced: not everything about Boston was great, and not everything here is terrible. The doctor listens, takes notes, and watches him in a way that reminds him of how he feels when he has to change for swimming. The doctor smiles and asks what he likes best about his new house and new school. He thinks and answers the questions: 'I like how big my room is. I like having my own bathroom. I like having a backyard even though it's too wet to go outside very much. I like the new kitchen.' 'And school,' the doctor prompts. He thinks; there is nothing he likes about the school itself. 'I like my friend Joslyn,' he says, 'and I like the art teacher Mr Cross and the swimming teacher Mr Bruce and my language arts teacher Mrs Abbot.' The doctor nods and asks him what he likes about each of these teachers, skipping over Joslyn entirely. He tells Dr Phaedrus about how nice Mrs Abbot is, how Mr Cross liked his drawing today, and how Mr Bruce looks like a movie star. The doctor nods, takes notes, smiles to himself, goes on nodding, takes more notes. 'Now, I spoke with your parents last week and they told me that from time to time you pretend to be a toy soldier. Can you tell me why you do that?' It's not about being a toy soldier, although sometimes when he does it he is thinking of the steps he learned in dance class in Boston, and he knows those were for the March of the Toy Soldiers; he often hears the music in his head. More frequently, however, he is not thinking about the dance steps at all; instead, he is becoming someone else, someone more logical, more stable, someone who does not have to act in ways his parents expect him to act, but he does not know how to say any of this to the doctor. 'I don't know why,' he says, shrugging his shoulders. 'Sometimes I just walk like that.' 'And your dad says you put on a different voice, a funny voice,' the doctor says. 'It's not a funny voice. It's a different voice. It's still my voice. It isn't funny, though.' 'And why do you talk with that other voice?' 'I don't know. Because I want to.' The doctor frowns and writes for almost a full minute: while the doctor is writing he looks at the gold second hand creeping round on the watch his parents gave him for his last birthday. 'Okay, I think it's time for Mom to go in the waiting room at the back, and Copley and I will continue our conversation.' Dr Phaedrus winks at his mother and shows her into the other room. When he comes back to sit down, the doctor clears his throat and says, 'Okay, Cop, let's get down to brass tacks, now that it's just us two guys. Your parents said that you've been having some interesting dreams. Can you maybe tell me about that?' Dr Phaedrus turns over a blank sheet of paper and raises his pen. 'Dreams?' he asks, understanding that he has, in fact, been brought to a doctor who helps people with sleeping problems. 'Yes, Copley, dreams. I believe you've been having some unusual kinds of dreams since you moved here from Boston. I'm very interested in dreams, and in the way people remember their dreams. You'll actually be helping *me*, you know, if you can try to remember some of them.' He is unsure what kinds of dreams he should report. He remembers many of his dreams. In the last several weeks he has been dreaming, night-to-night, about working on a particular drawing. He tells Dr Phaedrus he began the drawing on one night and continued it on subsequent nights, improving it, expanding it, making the colors brighter: it has been, literally, a dream with sequels. 'A recurring dream, a dream you keep having, which is always the same?' asks Dr Phaedrus. 'No, it's different every time. It's like chapters in a book.' He thinks this is interesting but Dr Phaedrus looks bored and asks him if there are any other dreams – about his father or mother or about friends at school or friends he left behind in Boston. In fact, he remembers a dream about his mother drowning, and he woke up to find he was crying, and he spent the whole next day so upset he could not even look at his mother; he decides this is too private to share with a doctor he has only just met, who, in any case, clearly thinks his most interesting dreams are boring. 'No,' he says, 'I can't remember any dreams like that.' Dr Phaedrus mumbles to himself, writes something on his pad, sighs, and looks up at him. 'Is there anything that's been bothering you, Copley? Is there anything happening at school that you don't feel like you can tell your parents?' He thinks about Mrs Pitt and the other boys, but says no, nothing at school, except for the fact that there's meat in all the lunches. 'And you don't eat meat?' 'It's not just me. My parents don't eat meat either.' The doctor makes a note. 'And what about at home? Is there anything maybe happening with one of your parents that you don't feel like you can tell the other one? Is there anything bad happening?' Dr Phaedrus asks. 'What about with your grandparents?' He thinks about his mother's father, Grandpa Chilton, who is kind and funny but who they rarely see, and then he thinks about his father's parents, Grandpa Arthur and Grandma Ruth. They don't see them very often either. The last time they saw his father's parents was before Christmas last year. His grandfather came into his bedroom at night after dinner and balanced him on his knee. He looked straight into his eyes, smiled, and then suddenly grimaced, gritted his teeth, and said, 'Copley, I want you to know your opinion doesn't matter *at all*. You are *no one*. You are *nothing*.' As his grandfather was telling him this, his father came into the room and he has not seen his grandparents since then, not even before they left Boston to move here. 'I want you to know this is a safe place,' says Dr Phaedrus, 'a place where you can tell me absolutely anything that comes into your head. You don't have to keep anything from me. You can trust me, Copley.' He looks at Dr Phaedrus and decides he has nothing to lose; he has told his parents about the man in the house and they don't believe him, so perhaps Dr Phaedrus will, and then something can be done, although what exactly he thinks should be done about it he can't say. The earth spins several thousand more feet around on its axis to let a faint patch of sun through the window. It hits his face and he squints; Dr Phaedrus adjusts the blind. 'Is that better?' Dr Phaedrus asks. 'Yes, that's better. There's a man in the house,' he says, his hands beginning to shake. 'What?' 'I said there's a man in our house. I told my parents but they don't believe me. I've seen him more than once. He's really tall, taller than Mr Bruce. Like a giant, except not a giant. I know giants don't exist. I mean, I know there are really, really tall people on earth, but that they're not magical or anything. I know it's a . . .' – he looks for the word – '*genetic* problem they have. This man isn't really, really tall, but he's definitely tall.' 'And you've seen him more than once?' Dr Phaedrus asks. 'A few times. On the night after we moved in, I think I was sleepwalking and I woke up outside. I walked out the front door. I was walking down the lawn, and then this man picked me up. I didn't recognize

315

him. He didn't say anything. He just looked at me. I was really scared. He was so big and he carried me like I didn't weigh anything. He carried me back inside the house and he locked the door and then I walked back upstairs, really slowly, so he would think I was still asleep, but I wasn't. I told my parents but they said it was a dream.' 'And was it a dream?' 'I don't know, maybe, except I saw him again. He was in my room in the middle of the night. He didn't think I could see him but I could and I spoke to him. I told him I could see he was there. He was sitting in the corner next to my dresser. He said my room was his son's room. He asked me if I was his son. He sounded angry.' 'And were you scared?' 'No, I wasn't scared, not that time. I recognized him. I was scared the first time, and that time I screamed, but the second time I'd already seen him.' 'But if he was a stranger, why didn't you scream the second time? Why didn't you call your parents?' asks Dr Phaedrus. 'If a stranger was in my house, I'd scream.' He thinks about this and wonders why he was not afraid the second time. He does not have an answer. In fact, he knows now that he is unsure if the man's presence was or was not a dream. He remembers seeing the man outside the window and is fairly certain he was awake when that happened, but the movement of the furniture this morning, and his parents' belief that he is the one responsible for the rearrangement, has unsettled his sense of what he has experienced and what he has imagined. He is no longer sure what he may have dreamed, and what he may have experienced in real life, nor is he sure that dreams are not, in fact, just a different room in the house of REAL LIFE than the ones we walk around in during the day. 'Do you think maybe it was a dream?' asks Dr Phaedrus. 'No. I don't know. I don't think so. He held me the first time. I felt him holding me. I didn't dream that. And I saw him this morning as we were leaving the house.' The truth is, he isn't sure, but even if he dreamed it, it still might be true. He dreamed they would leave Boston before his parents ever told him they were going to move. He dreamed they would live in a house that looked something like the one they live in now. He has not told his parents this. It's another thing they don't know. He also dreamed they would not be living alone.

5:15 PM: 'now I'm going to ask you a very important question, Copley. Are you ready?' 'I'm ready.' 'Okay. So my question is, can you tell me where you are?' He thinks about the question and looks around the room. 'You're going to answer me truthfully, aren't you, Cop?' He nods and knows what he must say: 'It looks like I'm sitting in your office.' The doctor frowns: 'You say *it looks like*. What does it feel like?' 'I don't know,' he says, 'it doesn't feel like I'm really here. It feels like I'm already somewhere else.' The doctor makes a note and without looking up says, 'And can you tell me where you feel like you are?' He was dreading this question but also knows what he must say. 'It feels like I'm in the air.' 'In the air? Do you mean flying?' the doctor asks. 'No,' he says, 'falling. It feels like I'm falling through the air, like towards the ocean, from an airplane, but never hitting the water. I think that's how it feels.'

5:20 PM: he has finished his conversation with Dr Phaedrus, who asks his mother to come in while he waits in the rear reception room. He listens at the door as the adults talk. The doctor says he is worried about his 'ability to tell reality from fantasy' and worried about his 'flat affect while describing what sounds like a disturbing experience, even if it was a hallucination. It seems like he's experiencing pretty frightening episodes and I think we should treat this with medication, and continue to see Copley on a regular basis to check up on how he's doing.' He hears his mother clear her throat and cough before she speaks, 'But what do you think it is,' she says, 'that's making this happen?' 'I don't want to jump to a diagnosis,' the doctor says, 'but I do think he's quite a sick little boy. This has been a very distressing move for him. He's having difficulty making friends, and from the little he said about his new school I have the sense that he's not particularly happy there. What we need to do right away is help him sleep through the night, to put a stop to the nightmares, help him begin to regain his equilibrium.' 'Will that

318

cure it?' his mother asks. 'I don't think we should be thinking in terms of *cure*, Dr Noailles. This is probably going to be a chronic condition, something that we'll need to continue monitoring. I also think maybe he should see a dietician. He looks undernourished.'

5:40 PM: his mother's face is as wet as the road. They stop at a grocery store and run inside. Because of the rain it just looks like she's wet, like they're both wet, which they are, but in fact they're both crying. She picks up a few things for dinner and then they stop at the pharmacy counter and wait while the pharmacist fills a prescription. He understands these pills are for him but there is nothing about him that feels unwell. He does not understand how he can be sick with a disease that has no cure. 'I'm not sick,' he says to his mother as she takes the white paper bag from the pharmacist. 'I know you're not, honey,' she says, and then he knows she is a liar. They go to the row of checkout counters at the front of the store. He can see two different bottles of pills in the bag. If he needs two different kinds of pills then he must be really, *really* sick, but sick in a way he does not feel, or at least that he does not feel at this time: sick in a way that is only going to get worse, that needs constant monitoring. If his mother is crying, it must be more serious than he can imagine. He wonders if he might be dying. He is not ready to die but the thought of dying does not make him

319

sad. Instead, he imagines it might be a great and strange adventure, yet another room to explore in the house of REAL LIFE. He remembers a dream he had a few nights ago. The dream took place in their old apartment in Boston. He came in the front door and put down his bag on the chair in the hall and hung his jacket in the hall closet. He went looking for his parents, first in the living room and dining room, then in the kitchen, in their bedroom, in the bathroom. He looked in all the closets but couldn't find them. Finally he opened a closet in their bedroom and discovered a room he had never seen before. His parents were sitting in that room with a little boy who looked like him but had blond hair instead of brown. His parents were different, too: they were both thin and blond and looked like Mr Bruce and Mrs Abbot. *This is your brother, Copley*, they said in the dream, and he knew he had to kill the other boy.

6:30 PM: his father is not home for dinner: he phoned to say he's going to be late because he's working on a report for his boss and they should go ahead without him. His mother makes braised tofu with green beans and rice. They sit at the kitchen island eating their dinner, and when they have both finished she opens the bag from the pharmacy and puts two plastic bottles on the table. One bottle has orange pills, the other pale green. To start, he will take two orange pills each day: one with breakfast and one with dinner. He will take three pale green pills each day: breakfast, lunch, and dinner. The doses will gradually increase. To take the pale green pill at lunch he will have to go to the nurse at school. 'Are you going to keep picking me up from school? What's going to happen over winter break?' His mother looks as though she is going to cry again. She pours him a glass of water and puts the two pills on the counter, pushing them in his direction. He swallows the pills one at a time and feels nothing, neither better nor worse. 'I don't know,' his mother says. 'We haven't figured out any of that. It's not like in Boston. In Boston the university had a day care. The university here doesn't have one except for little kids. We don't know what's going to happen. We'll figure it out. Don't worry.' He cannot help worrying. They haven't thought ahead, they aren't thinking about him, and now he might be dying. 'Am I dying?' he asks. His mother looks surprised and shakes her head and starts to sob, but manages to say, 'No, no, no. You're not dying, sweetheart.' She waves her hand in front of her face as though she's trying to wave away the crying; he knows she's lying because this is what she does whenever she lies: waves her hand in front of her face, trying to distract him from the truth on her cheeks and in her eyes and flowing out of her nose. 'You talk for a while,' she gasps, but he has nothing to say. He sits there looking at her. After a few minutes she stops crying, wipes her face, and puts her hands on his shoulders, squeezing him, moving his body back and forth a little, almost as though she wants to start shaking him. She swallows several times and her jaw is pulsing. 'I'm sorry,' she says, 'the pills are just to make you feel *even better than you do already*.'

7:30 PM: his father is still not home. They put all the furniture back where it should be. This only takes a few minutes. He is surprised how easy it is, how quickly and silently it can be put back in place. It is possible he really did move all the furniture in his sleep and has no memory of doing it: the casters make almost no noise and when the couches and tables and chairs are moving they feel as if they weigh very little at all. After they finish his mother suggests he should begin getting ready for bed, although the sun has only gone down in the last half hour or so. He asks his mother if he can have a play date with Joslyn and his mother says, 'Yes, of course, but we'll talk about it tomorrow.' He knows that unless he reminds her she will forget. His parents do not think about him very much, he suspects. They think about their work, but they do not think about things like the kind of school he should be attending, whether or not he has any friends to play with, or what is going to happen to him during the day once winter vacation begins. He closes the door to his room and locks it, leaving the light turned off so he can look outside at the old white house where a candle is burning in the window. Louise appears. She looks up at him and he raises his hand, moves it back and forth, and smiles. She raises her candle, moves it back and forth, and then raises her hand. He waves once more and then closes the curtains while he changes, putting his school uniform into the laundry hamper in the back of his closet. He hates the blue shirt, red sweater, khaki slacks, and brown leather shoes, which are a shape and color that make him feel as ashamed as when he has to undress for swimming or go to the bathroom and listen to the other boys hissing names at him. In Boston he did not have to wear a uniform to school, and so every day of the week he got to wear gray: gray slacks, gray shirt, a gray sweater in winter, or sometimes a black one to match his black loafers. His father used to say he looked as though he was trying out for a part in *1984*. He did not understand what this meant, and when his father explained that it was a book, he asked how it would be possible to try out for a part in a book. His father had told him to 'stop being so literal' and 'imagine a film version of the book'. He asked if there was a film version of the book and if he could see it. 'No,' his father said, 'not until you're older.' 'Can I read the book instead?' he asked. 'No,' his father said, 'not until you're older.' He is going to see if the school library has a copy of the book but he suspects it will not. The only books they have are children's books, and half the library is only open to students in grades five and six, and only then if they have parental permission slips. All this has been explained to him. He knows not even to go into the part of the library with red carpeting. If he does, he will receive an automatic fine of twenty-five dollars because 'violations of library policy are taken very seriously,' Mrs Taylor explained during his orientation tour. The library, like the rest of the rooms in the school, has a large black glass hemisphere in the ceiling. Mrs Taylor pointed at it and then pointed at him. She shook her finger and smiled and said, 'We'll be watching,' as if it were a very funny joke.

7:45 PM: his mother is reading him a story, although he would rather be reading his own book about the boy going to rescue his father on the planet where everyone has to move and act and speak in the same way. Once his mother leaves the room, he will pull the book out from under his pillow and turn on the flashlight under the covers. His parents do not know that he reads in the middle of the night. They do not know he can't help himself: even if he goes to sleep, he always wakes up a few hours later and feels compelled to read. If he does not read, he believes he will die: he has believed this since long before discovering, today, that he is actually dying. His mother is reading him the final volume of *The Lord of the Rings*. She tells him that when he is older, he will be allowed to see the movie versions of the books. 'Can I try out for a part in them?' he asks. 'No,' she says, laughing, 'they've already been made.' 'But they could be made again,' he says. 'I suppose they could,' she says. 'And if they are, then I can try out for a part in them.' 'I suppose you could,' she says, and turns out the light. 'Who would you want to be?' He pretends to think for a moment. 'Frodo.' Only when the light is out does his mother lean over to kiss him on the forehead. He has never been asked to go to bed this early, not since he was much, much younger. His mother's face is wet. Her crying exhausts him. He wants to shout at her to stop crying, to grow up and be an adult. He is the one who is dying, so he should be the one crying, but in fact the idea does not really upset him. He has learned the word 'romantic' and he thinks that dying this young will somehow be romantic because he will become even more beautiful the sicker he gets. He knows he is beautiful because Joslyn told him so last week. She said, 'You know you're pretty like a girl, don't you? That's why they make fun of you.' He asked her if it was a bad thing. 'No, it's not *bad*,' she said, 'but it's different. You don't look like anyone else.' 'Neither do you,' he said, and it was then that he understood they were friends.

9:00 PM: he knows the time by his watch, by the minute and hour hand and the creeping second hand. Some of the students at his new school do not know how to read a watch or a clock unless it is digital. In Boston, everyone knew how to read a clock with hands. He has been listening to his mother crying downstairs in the kitchen. She must not realize how sound carries in the house; otherwise she would not make the mistake of crying so loudly. His father is still not home. He is almost finished with his book and decides to stay up until he turns the final page.

11:45 PM: his eyes are closing every few minutes but he has only two pages to go. The story is ending happily. He is disappointed. Happy endings always disappoint him. He hopes for a last-minute disaster.

11:58 PM: as he finishes the final sentence he hears the garage door open, close, the sound of his father on the path from the garage to the back door, the back door opening, his father putting down his briefcase in the drop zone, his mother asking his father where he has been and what took so long, why he did not call again to tell her how late he would be. He hears his father telling her to lower her voice. They talk for a long time, at first about Louise in the condemned house next door, and then in voices so low that he cannot hear what they're saying, but when the crying starts again he knows they have been talking about him. He is certain he must be dying. He is no longer certain it will be romantic. He fears it will be painful. He fears pain more than death. His stomach is upset and his throat grows cold and hard.

★     ★     ★

12:35 AM: his parents go to bed. They close their door and he can hear the lock click into place. Some nights they lock their door. Some nights they do not. Usually they lock their door only when everyone is going to bed early, so the locking tonight is unusual. They are going to cry: they want privacy to cry together, in expectation of his imminent death. It will be important to make it romantic and beautiful so it is not so hard on them.

—:— AM: he does not know what time it is. The sky is dark and his door is open. He can hear the man breathing in the room. He can hear his parents both snoring in their own room. He does not want to turn over to see where the man is, because he fears the man will see he is awake and attack him, hit him, drag him out of the house and kidnap him. If he pretends to be asleep, the man will leave him alone. In Boston, his greatest fear was that a vampire or witch would come into his room at night, come floating just above the floorboards and bend over to – he never knew what it was they might do to him. He knows now that those were childish fears, since there are no vampires or witches, at least not witches like the ones he used to imagine. He knows now, for the first time, what real fear is: it has the same feeling as thinking about school and Mrs Pitt. His stomach churns, his heart roars, he wants to vomit, hide, become invisible. He wants to scream but he can't find his breath or his voice. He is frozen, his body won't move, he cannot move, he cannot speak or scream. He wants to jump out of his bed and run into the hall and lock the man in his room and scream for his parents to come and see that the man exists, that he is right there in the bedroom, *right in the midst of them*, to see that the alarm makes NO DIFFERENCE AT ALL because even with an alarm, this man has ways of getting into the house that might as well be magic. He is aware of a warm breeze on his neck and then a sound that goes with it and he knows the man is right there, leaning over him, breathing onto his body. The man's rough fingers are suddenly on his head, touching his eyelids and eyelashes, combing through his hair and down to his scalp, picking up his hands to touch his fingers, as though the man is trying to identify all the separate parts of a machine. When the man's fingers touch his eyelids again he begins to shake and the water shoots from his eyes and nose. '*Carson*,' the man says. '*Carson*. Carson. CARSON. Are you alive?' The man's hands are on his back, gripping his shoulder, shaking him, as if the man were trying to wake him up. He's either going to throw up or he's going to scream. '*You came back. You came back*,' the man says, pulling him over. He looks at the dark man and screams, screams a short choking cry right into the face of this giant. He tries to form words, to say, 'I'm not Carson,' but the words will not come. He screams again but feels strangled as the man looks at him, eyes suddenly wide and terrified. The man opens his mouth, lets go of his body, and runs from the room.

2:00 AM: he is shaking, waiting for his parents to come. He looks at his watch. His parents do not wake up. Sometimes they wear earplugs because they both snore and if they don't wear earplugs they can't sleep. This must be one of those nights. He would have to pound on their door to wake them. It is a stupid thing to do, wearing earplugs when someone could break into the house or when your child might be screaming for help. He is too afraid at first to get out of bed and follow the man. He can hear the man walking down the stairs, *thump, fmmp, thump, fmmp,* and then a creak. After a moment he decides he has to follow the man to see where he goes. If he can see where the man goes, then he will be able to show his parents, and then they will have to believe him. His teeth are chattering and his whole body is trembling but he drops out of bed and puts on his flannel robe. Tiptoeing to the door of his room, he peers around the edge of the door and looks out into the moonlit hall: it is empty, the man is not there; he must have gone down the back stairs. This is a man, he understands, who only comes and goes by back stairs, back doors, who does not present himself at the front of anything. He slides his bare feet along the whitewashed floorboards and pauses at the top of the back staircase, looking down into darkness. No shapes are visible in the middle of the staircase, but the light from the kitchen falls on the bottom few steps. The man might be hiding in the shadows in the middle of the staircase, waiting for him to come, to grab him in his arms and take him away. Before leaving his room he put his flashlight in his pocket. If he turns it on and the man is there, then at least he will be at the top of the stairs and can close the door to the staircase, scream for his parents, run to their door, and bang until they wake up. He pulls out the flashlight, hesitates for a moment as he thinks about what he will have to do if the man is crouching there in the dark, waiting for him, and then pushes it on, his hands trembling. Although the staircase is empty he hears a thin creak recognizable as the sound made by the top step on the stairs to the basement. The man must be going down to hide in one of the dark corners full of boxes. He knows he should pound on his parents' door and beg them to come, but he fears if he does the man will disappear entirely and once again no one will believe him. Taking the banister in his other hand, he turns off the flashlight, half-swinging himself down the stairs, trying to put as little weight as possible on the wooden steps so the man won't know he's coming. The man's smell has taken all the oxygen out of the staircase and he gags, gasping for breath. It is a smell like the boys' locker room at the pool: wet and cold and clanging: bleach and all the mold and mildew bleach is supposed to kill but has not. In the kitchen he stops, listening for sounds from the basement. He hears the scraping of wood against concrete and knows the man is there. If he could close the door and lock it and be sure the man would not escape then he could summon his parents to see the proof of the man's existence. But the door to the basement has no lock and he is unsure whether the man might have some hidden escape route out of the basement, through one of the windows. He knows the windows have latches and locks, so it is possible this is the way the man is coming and going. He does not think the alarm people remembered to put sensors on the windows in the basement. He followed them around when they were installing the sensors, disguising them in the upper corners of rooms, placing them on windows and doors, and he does not remember them installing sensors on the basement windows. Realizing this he feels a momentary sense of relief that he has figured it out: the sound of wood against concrete must have been the man dragging a ladder to one of the basement windows. But he has to hurry if he wants to prove this is true. A different part of his mind takes over, one without fear: he turns on the flashlight again and runs down into the basement, turns on the overhead lights and waits as they flicker, revealing the huge space with his mother's workshop in one corner. He spins around into the open pantry tucked under the stairs, but it's empty, the whole basement is empty, the windows are closed, and the only ladder in the house, which was left here by the former owner, is hanging on the wall, suspended in space, its wooden legs dangling far from the concrete floor. There is nowhere for the man to hide. The space is clean, empty, polished. In one half there is carpeting and a bar, and in the wall a plaque that says PAUL KROVIK BUILT THIS HOUSE. He runs his hand over the engraved letters and the angle of a 'K' bites into one of his fingers, pierces the skin, and draws out a drop of blood. The man must have been tall enough to pull himself up through the window, or perhaps he had a rope to climb, a rope he took with him, closing the window when he left. Blood is salty, setting his teeth on edge like spinach. From behind him he hears the scraping of wood on concrete again and his head snaps around on its own before he even knows he wants to look. The sound came from the pantry. His heart rumbles and his body starts to shake again as he walks toward the noise, but the space is empty and no one is there. He looks at the bare shelves, the floor, the dust on the floor, the shoeprints in the dust, an arc of dust at the far end of the pantry, an arc like the shape a door makes when it swings across carpet. He drops to his knees, puts his hands on the floor, and examines the lengths of wood under the lowermost shelf. Sticking out underneath the panel there is a wooden tab that looks as though it holds up the shelf, but there is a gap, a space between the tab and the shelf. He pulls at the tab and as the panel swings towards him there is a sudden rush of air from behind the panel and in the same moment a cushioned metallic *thump* whooshes like a car door slamming. A noise comes flying out of his throat as he rears up, hitting his head on the shelf above him. He backs up, pulls the panel wide open, and runs his hand over the black metal surface behind it, pushing against it, but the surface does not budge. He tries to understand, does not understand, a part of him knows the metal surface does not belong to the house, is not a part of its foundation or construction, is not what the house looks like behind its white plaster walls. He understands that windows have nothing to do with it: the man is there, on the other side: the panel is just a mask hiding a door.

2:10 AM: he closes the door to the basement and jams one of the kitchen stools up under the knob. Even if the man can break down the door, at least they will know he is coming. His hands are shaking but he pours himself a glass of milk from the fridge and stands in the kitchen looking out at the yard. From the kitchen window he can't see the old white house down the hill; their fence is in the way, and the house is too far below theirs. The angles are wrong: *lines of sight*, a phrase he remembers, the lines of sight are wrong from the kitchen. He puts the glass in the dishwasher and walks through to the dining room. Everything is as it should be. The blinds are closed but he can sense that the space is the way he and his mother arranged it before bed. His parents will never believe him about the man. Even if he showed them the hatch in the pantry, they would open it, see the black metal behind it, and tell him it was just a part of the foundation. Nevertheless, he knows what he knows.

4:53 AM: since coming back to bed he has not been able to sleep. His mind works on the white wooden hatch and the black metal wall behind it. He sits up and turns on his bedside light. In the mirror on the opposite wall he can see gray half-moons hanging under his eyes, his hair scarecrowing in tufts and waves. The sickness he feels makes him wonder if the new medicine might be speeding up his illness rather than retarding its progress. It is difficult to imagine how he will make it through a whole day at school, how he will be able to keep his patience with Mrs Pitt, survive the hissing in the restrooms, the looks of the other students who always find something about his appearance to criticize. At first it was his hair, and now it is the kind of shoes he wears. All students are supposed to wear brown shoes, but his loafers are, apparently, the wrong kind, different from the brand that most other students own. They say he walks like a girl: this, in fact, is part of the reason for the toy soldier behavior, perhaps the essential reason: to walk more like a boy, to practice keeping his hips straight because Joslyn told him he 'switches', swaying as he walks down the hall. He knows he did the toy soldier walk before ever coming to the Pinwheel Academy, but within a week of being at the new school he realized those military movements could be put to some orthopedic purpose: he would train his body to walk in the way a boy is supposed to walk, by limiting his range of motion. He has to be careful, however, for sometimes he falls into that knee-locking gait at school and then Mrs Pitt grimaces and tells him to stop drawing attention to himself or he will be fined. At least today there is no swimming or PE, although music class, which comes in place of the others, is almost as bad: because he has a good, high voice, the music teacher, Mrs Schrein, always makes him sing solo parts. The boys say he sings like a girl, the girls – except for Joslyn – suggest he should wear a skirt instead of slacks. When they laugh and whisper Mrs Schrein does nothing to stop them, until finally she loses her temper with the entire class and turns off the lights to make them all sit in silence, threatening that everyone will be fined for misbehavior. It is impossible to see how he will make it through the day. Perhaps he has a fever and his parents will let him stay home, except he knows one of them would have to stay home with him; this was never a problem in Boston. When he was sick in Boston he would stay in Mrs Cuddebank's apartment and sleep all day, waking up only when she brought him soup or medicine, or when her own children got home from school. Sometimes, his mother used to say, it felt like Mrs Cuddebank needed more looking after than he did but not much could go wrong in an apartment as long as there was an adult who could keep him away from danger and phone an ambulance if he became seriously ill. His father said there was no reason to worry so much, and that saying those kinds of things in front of a child will only make the child feel endangered or, worse, exceptional. He has looked up ENDANGERED and EXCEPTIONAL in the dictionary. It is true that he feels himself to be both things: sometimes in danger, and frequently, more often than not, unusual, special, even, perhaps, *abnormal*. Here in this new place, his parents have not figured out what to do if he gets sick: more proof of them not thinking about him. It will be better if he dies quickly and they can move on with their lives. Dying will also free him from the Pinwheel Academy and Mrs Pitt and Mrs Taylor and all the students who look at him and see only someone who is not like them, who walks in the wrong way, wears the wrong shoes, speaks with an accent and a voice that is strange to them. He understands they are afraid of him, but he does not understand why: he looks at himself and, apart from the gray half-moons and the scarecrow hair, can see nothing frightening about his appearance. Of course their fear is not only to do with the way he looks but also to do with the way he acts: how he speaks, how his answers to questions are always correct, how he raises his hand to offer comments and thoughts that Mrs Pitt never knows how to handle. On several occasions he has said things in class that even Mrs Pitt does not know and she has been forced to check his answer on the computer, and then, with a frown, will say, 'Copley's right, but . . .' and try to dismiss what he has said in a way that is never convincing. When he dies he will miss his parents and Joslyn. He will miss Grandpa Chilton, his mother's father, but he will not miss Grandma Ruth and Grandpa Arthur since they have never been warm, never like the idea of grandparents suggested in books. Apart from those few people, he will miss no one else when he leaves the main rooms of the house of REAL LIFE to explore the rooms that are not at first visible but which he is certain are there, opening out from the back of his parents' closet, unfolding through metallic darkness beyond the white wooden hatch at the back of the pantry, rooms into which he will disappear and never return. Looking at himself in the mirror, only the top of his body visible from where he sits in bed, his vision blurs and doubles, the two images separating and moving away from each other. Watching his two selves divide, he believes that one of them waves to the other.

5:00 AM: when his alarm goes off he gets out of bed, his body shaking, as though it has not stopped shaking since the man breathed onto his neck, touched his face, examined his fingers, gripped his shoulder, called him by a name not his own, demanding to know if he was alive or dead. He stands in front of the mirror looking at his stomach and chest, at the loose waistband of his pajama bottoms, at the furrows between his ribs. He wonders if he is, as Dr Phaedrus suggested, *undernourished*. He looked it up in the dictionary when they got home – that and a number of other words he heard Dr Phaedrus say to his mother through the door when they did not imagine he was listening or could hear.

5:23 AM: raising his arms above his head, he stretches, looking at the way his body elongates, the ribs protruding, his stomach scooping into itself. As he is doing this he becomes aware of noise outside. He takes a t-shirt from his closet and puts it on before opening the curtains to look out the window. Although it is still mostly dark, under the streetlights he can see a large yellow excavator and a matching dump truck on the front lawn of the old white house, and a black van with the initials of his father's company printed on its sides and hood. Six men in black EKK uniforms with helmets and vests and guns come out of the truck. Two go to the front door, two to the back, and one on either side. Because the men are from EKK, because he told his mother yesterday that Louise was living in the house, he is certain his father must have made this happen. He runs out

338

of his room and across the hall, banging on the door of his parents' bedroom over and over again, shouting, 'I HATE YOU, I HATE YOU, I HATE YOU!' As the door opens he turns and runs down the front stairs, hearing his mother and father come after him, shouting his name, his father's voice flying on wings of flame.

Maybe the boy was trying to warn me, raising his hand, that little ghostface at the window. I don't know what these men expect me to do. They could yell come out with your hands up, but since the city put the big black lock on the front door I can't come out in the most logical way, and if I go out the back they'll think I'm trying to escape.

From my place on the boards I listen: wind, heavy boots on the porch, the idling of their engine outside, sirens in the distance, and now, the men fumbling the lock, the screen doors at the front and back whining open and closed. They must have the wrong code. One of them, his face a black visor reflecting the window and me, a genie, trapped tiny within, looks inside from the porch, shining a flashlight, and shouts to the others, 'She's on the floor. She might be armed.'

'Land sakes, you fools, I'm not armed!' I scream, holding up my hands, palms to the front: read these open tracks with your blind flashing faces.

The men give up on the front entrance, circle round to the back, kick in the kitchen door. I try to hold my body stiff as they spill down the hall, a storm of jet-black vermin surrounding me, shouting, 'Face down, hands where we can see them,' until I extend my body, roll onto my stomach, hands at my sides. One of them pins my head, another clamps my feet, one holds my right hand, the other my left, and then they bring the two hands together behind my back, truss me up with plastic ties, haul me to my toes, pulling my arms almost out of joint. I bite my tongue, refuse to scream. I don't know if I'm being arrested or evicted: no reading of rights, no actual police. I know who they are. Welcome to town: this city is privatized.

So with two of the men leading the way, the other four drag me out the rear of the house. I struggle, scream, and as they pull me through my back door, across the porch, out to the garden and around to the front yard, I see the machine moving on its tracks, cutting into turf, bringing up clods of soil through long-tailed ryegrass.

That skinny little child is screaming in the street and his parents are next to him now, putting hands on his shoulders and arms, small woodland animals emerged from their hollowed-out trunks and warrens, looking like dawn might scare them back inside.

There are hands on my own arms, hot hands, bloody stumps chewed down to nothing on one set, the others perfectly pared, French manicured, and those are the hands that pinch hardest. No misgivings in that man's mind about the work he does. Mr Chewer doesn't grip as hard. I can tell from the way he shifts and shuffles that he knows something's wrong with this assignment, a private action on behalf of an imaginary public.

Sun begins to shoot over the treetops, bouncing gold off the barn's shingle roof, and then comes a sudden passing shower, burst of waters through slanting light and an apparition of color haunting the air: rain and early sun mixing, come together for a moment before the wind blows them apart.

The new neighbor man approaches, whipping out his wallet, flashing identification, talking to visor-faces with their strong hands and their strong-arm car, saying they should let go, there's nothing more to be done, I pose no threat and can do nothing to stop them. What does he know about the kind of threat I pose? I bite my tongue again. This, surely, is the neighborliness I always missed.

These latter-day storm troopers give me ten minutes to go back inside and take whatever I want to save: jewelry, letters, my notebooks, the albums and frames full of photographs, files of a life, ledgers of the farm, the only history I have left. Mr Chewer volunteers to escort me into my own house, and the little neighbor comes with us. The guard cuts me loose and the two men stand now in the kitchen, securing the exit, as I make a pile of my life in the hallway, all cold concentration. Forget nothing, Louise. Check each room, open every drawer, pack all your clothes, your documents.

'I need more than ten minutes. Give me half an hour. That's all I need,' I say to the men, aware of my voice veering off its track of composure even as I try to hold it steady.

Little neighbor man looks at the guard, his visor up, and the guard nods, speaks through his walkie-talkie to the others outside. I move from room to room, filling four suitcases and an old steamer trunk, taking more than I would choose to keep under rational thought, fearing I might later regret some minor loss. I raise loose boards and prize out the cache of Kennedy half-dollars I once collected in belief they would one day bear value greater than their mark. Pens, blank paper, cards and gifts from forty-three years of classrooms go into cloth sacks. Kitchen utensils from Mama and Grandma Lottie go in the cast iron pot. A rope braided by my great-grandmother coils up in a bread bin Donald made when I was pregnant. As I pack, I look down, wondering why my hands are wet; realizing the source, I keep working. There is no way to dry them now. The water rises in silence but flows, unstoppable, a spring opening up to cover the land. Watch me fill the world with my deluge. I am the sea-dark spirit, shaken to torrent.

There is so much to carry I cannot do it alone. With my purse on one shoulder I grip the photo albums against my stomach and watch as the guards all return looking humbled, every one of them, as they cart my life to the curb. They lead us off the property, holding my arms again, the child whimpering against his mother, while the rain slaps faces in passing showers. Standing on the lawn of the Krovik house, we watch as the machine approaches, raising an arm to tear off a corner of my porch with its bucket, reaching again, ripping a gash, opening wide all that should remain private: couches, tables, wallpaper and drapes, sheets and blankets, the oddments of a life. Fragile as balsa my house splinters, collapsing under the moaning hydraulic arm. The house is my Corsican twin: each blow she suffers pulls a sob from my throat. I cover my eyes and feel the child reaching out to take my hand. 'Can I help you?' he asks. 'Can't we make them stop?'

'No, we cannot make them stop,' I say.

In the lull between movements of machinery I hear a rushing in my ears, panting breath, my voice claggy and clotting, words so distorted I don't know what I'm saying, or if the source is even my body. A voice that might be mine, or a multitude, suddenly hollers: *house, home, theft!* Forget the connections, truncate the syntax. Broken apart and wet to the skin, water pools at my feet. Bare feet. I have no shoes. I stand in the waters I summon to wash away this collapse and demise. I scream against the wantonness. If they hoped for an adversary they have created one, kindled me out of soft dry wood, leaf mold, the desiccated moss of forest floors. Lord knows my house could have

344

been moved, lifted off its foundations, put somewhere else on that great patch of empty land Krovik cleared, quartered, and failed to fill.

In less than ten minutes there is nothing but a heap of wood, glass, metal: splinters of things once whole. I can no longer name them. To name what no longer exists is a form of conjuring I cannot muster. I watch the workers – two thin young men, a middle-aged fat woman with a ponytail – collect the damage, put it in trucks, cart it away.

'*This is carnage!*' I scream, glimpsing the pile of plants and vegetables uprooted from the kitchen garden.

Mr Chewer says someone reported an intruder: me, an intruder on my own land. But it is no longer mine. The father of the child nods, trying to be reasonable, says he'll take responsibility, as if I ever needed a man to take responsibility for me. I start to protest but decide it might be better to let myself fall under the protection of this little mole-man than to go to wherever my brigade of mirror-faced fools might deliver me: some private prison, unseen and unlooked for, unable to reach anyone from there. They would have me disappear. Grips loosen on both arms and I feel the blood run back into my hands, a flashing physical cosmos as the circulation returns to my fingertips. And then they give me a push in the direction of chubby nocturnal father who squints in the dim light, rain coming harder now, turning the last stand of Poplar Farm into a mud wallow putsch. The mourning of it, the weeping and keening, the foot-stamping grief, all of that will have to come later, in private, not before these men. I shall beat the ground, shriek to the trees who remain, call the submerged world to rise up and fight on my side.

Through the holding and restraint the child has not let go. His parents help carry my salvaged belongings and, silent, the boy leads me up the lawn into the Krovik house that now belongs to these small creatures. The boy tells me to come in, invites me across the threshold. My gut rumbles with visions of rocking-chair mothers and shower-curtain victims, of high contrast shadows and screaming violins.

Once inside I catch my breath. All is whiteness, nowhere for the eye to set down and relax, every-thing the whitest of whiteness. 'It's okay,' the child says, 'I'll explain later.' I look into his eyes and see he has already decided how things will be.

'We thought we should get your stuff out of the rain,' the father says; he and the mother make trips back and forth from the street to the house. I watch my life piled up at my feet.

We do not let go of each other, the boy and me, not yet. I can't even say what I feel for him but it's there, right away, sparkling in the harmonics of his voice, and not just in those: an energy comes out of him, signals surging through his grip, messages and motives and words: data transfer, they would say today, this child communicates through touch alone. Messages are fuzzy,

346

unreadable, too much interfering noise over the signal, but I can see, hold his hand tight, trying to get all I can, letting him know I'm trying to read, hungry for his message and the keys he holds.

They sit me down in the den with a cup of coffee and stand dripping with rain, clutching mugs themselves, the three woodland people in their wet pajamas.

'This all used to be my land,' I say, my voice settling back into itself, 'until I sold it some years back. And now the city has taken my house to build a turning lane and widen your street into a boulevard, replace all the cracking asphalt that the fool who built this neighborhood didn't lay right in the first place.'

'Do you have anywhere to go?' the man asks.

'You have to understand, my people lived on this land for going on a hundred and fifty years.'

'I'm sorry,' the man says. He shakes his head, as does the mother, but they do not want a history lesson. They have busy lives, want to be rid of me quick. 'Do you have any family you can stay with?'

'My daughter lives in California. Poor girl never loved this land and got away fast as she could.'

'Could you go live with her?' the man asks.

'We don't have an easy relationship, and in any case, I can't bring myself to leave it, not yet. I'll camp in the woods if I have to, or pitch a tent in those fields.'

They must already think I'm a crazy old woman,

ranting as I did. Mine are not the ways of the world today, and gentle as they act, these are not the kind of people who understand a connection to land. On the faces of the adults there is only confusion, looking at me as though I have come out with some fragment of ancient lament:

*She was the daughter of a free farm man,*
*Oh the land and fire.*
*The only daughter of a free farm man,*
*Sold her lonesome heart's desire.*

I find song bubbling up on my tongue, look fast for sand to stop the melody.

*His land no longer kept her safe at dawn,*
*Oh the earth's on fire.*
*That land it couldn't save her heart no more,*
*Called for flood of purging fire.*

'I'm sorry,' I say, 'I'm not – you must think I'm cracked.'

'Not at all,' the man says. 'I'm sorry.'

'You don't have to feel guilty. It's not about you folks. I'm an old woman who made her decisions freely.' Even if I had no real choice, even if the choice was dictated to me: by time, by laws, by debt and circumstance, by the unhappy curve of history's low arc.

Even as I drink my coffee with one hand the child has gone on holding the other.

'Copley,' says the father, 'let the woman go.'

'It's okay,' I say, 'we're acquainted.'

'So you two really have met before,' the mother says.

'We introduced ourselves through the fence, isn't that right?' I say to the boy.

'This is Louise,' the child says. 'She should live with us. We have room. She can't go camping with all her things.'

He reminds me of boys I taught, bright ones easy and eager to please, the kind I always knew I could trust more than others.

'Can I just ask,' I say, turning my face to the father's dark eyes, 'how you got those men to let me go?'

Little woodland father looks uncomfortable, caught in a sudden foot-shuffling shame, staring at the white floor, the white walls, out the window. 'They work for my company,' he says. 'I mean – it's not *my* company.'

'But you pulled rank.'

'In a manner of speaking.'

'I bet you're in a corner office.' More foot shuffling, and now he won't meet my gaze, as ashamed as that guard with chewed-up fingernails, embarrassed by the kind of company he works for, a business that strong-arms old women out of their homes when they resist. He doesn't realize I was teasing.

'Would you like to take a shower?' the mother asks. I've managed to wash each night with water heated on the fire, keep my clothes clean, and have never been a smelly body. My hair, though, it must be a horror show, twisting into a copse of cliff-dwelling trees.

'No, that's very nice of you, thank you, but no. I should be going.'

'Where will you go? Do you have a car?' the man asks.

'I had to sell it. If you could call me a cab.' I don't know how much money I have in my purse, and little idea where I might go. I grip at my seams but feel them beginning to give under the strain. I am an only child in old age, an adult orphan, a widow, my own child so distant I might as well be childless. I am the last tree standing on a clear-cut slope, the saws all pointed at my feet.

'If you'll excuse me,' the woman says, 'I have to get ready. I have an early appointment.' As the mother goes upstairs the man and the child sit staring at me.

'Sorry to take up your time,' I say to the man. 'Thank you for what you've done. I think they would have arrested me and then I'd never have heard the end of it from my daughter.'

The man offers me the phone and something to eat, says I must be hungry, and when I decline he insists, takes me through to the kitchen, sits me down at the counter and makes toast with nice bread. There's a jar of jam, an expensive brand, and then the man starts asking questions: how old my daughter is, what she does, where she lives in

California. Asks me if I've ever lived anywhere else, or if I've always lived here.

'I was born in that house, grew up in it, lived in it with my husband and my parents until they passed away. I raised my daughter in that house and lived there with her and my husband until she grew up and moved out and then until my husband died. In the years since Donald's passing I've lived there on my own. I was supposed to be out a few months ago but I refused to leave. I fought it for a long time.'

'Were you a farmer?'

'My late husband was the farmer, but I did a fair amount of the work. I was a schoolteacher for almost forty-five years until I retired. If they'll let me I think it's time to go back to it, now I've got nothing else to think about. Besides which I've just about spent myself down to zero fighting the city. I have Social Security and a small pension and that's about the sum of it. I suppose I'll have to phone my daughter, and go live with her. I went to California once. Didn't like it much.'

I can see the man thinking and then he excuses himself, goes upstairs, and I sit with the boy, eating toast and drinking coffee. He pours a glass of milk, makes himself a bowl of cereal, asks me if I want any. Good manners, tidy habits, dream of a child. These people don't know what they have in such a boy.

The man comes back, asks me if I'd like more toast, tells the boy to go upstairs and get ready for school. Strange to be sitting here, in this house I have abhorred, eating and drinking, being looked after by people I do not know, my belongings damp and dripping just inside their front door. When the man clears his throat I think: here it comes: a quick shock, time to leave. Extend the hand of hospitality so far, then yank it back when the burden curls into strain.

'Louise, I don't know how to say this the right way.'

'No need. You've been very kind. I'll be going now.'

'No, no, it's nothing like that. Sit down,' he says, refilling my cup. He seems to be searching his head for the right words, how to tell me to stay another ten minutes but no more. 'Would—' he begins, stops, stalling out. I look at him and can't imagine what he wants to ask. 'This is going to come out the wrong way. You're going to misinterpret it. Please don't. Just—' And then he says it in such simple words: 'I wondered if you'd like a job.'

He sees someone in need and wants to offer a handout that isn't one, imagines me capable of scrubbing and vacuuming, cooking and washing, ironing and bed-making. Not a chance, not for anything, not for living here and eating free, no way will I play the maid he wants to make me.

'I don't know what you might be thinking, but I'm no cleaning lady.'

'No, no,' he blushes, hands slicing back and forth

over the counter. 'Oh God, I'm doing this really badly. What – I mean, my wife and I wondered if you would be interested in working as a tutor, a . . . caregiver, too, something a little old-fashioned, like a governess, if you know what I mean.'

'Sure, I know what you mean. I've read the books. But my umbrella does not fly, and if there's a madwoman in your attic or ghosts to battle you can count me out.' The man looks confused, as though he is already thinking twice about his offer. 'Jokes,' I say, 'just jokes.'

'No, that's fine. My wife and I don't mind jokes.'

'So it doesn't matter if I can't fly?' I say, unsure whether I feel as though I'm joking or not. I can hear the noise of my home's destruction, feel the loss of the only place I have ever truly been myself, and this man wants me to think about a *job* looking after his son. They could hire anyone. Maybe he thinks he can get me cheap.

'Flying, no, indeed, that's not a requirement.'

'And there aren't any crazy people hidden in this house?'

I think I see him hesitate for an instant, but he shakes his head, 'No, no, no. No crazy people.'

'And no ghosts of former servants haunting your son.'

'We've never had anyone work for us, and besides, who believes in ghosts?'

'Well, that's okay then, isn't it?'

'You mean you'll do it?'

'I'm still thinking on it,' I say, for this is the

truth. My mind is more than a little divided: the better part of me hovers down the hill, examining the ruins of my world. 'Tell me more. Convince me I should work for you.'

'Right, uh-huh – well, I guess it's clear to my wife and me that Copley likes you, and that for whatever reason he already feels very attached to you, and that's – you have to understand how unusual that is for him. He is a deeply shy little boy, and the move has been hard on him. He's having a difficult time adjusting to his new school, and since you were a teacher, it seems like it could be a mutually beneficial arrangement. And you would be welcome to live here.'

'In truth, Mr Noailles, I don't know whether to be insulted or dumbstruck.'

'How's that?'

'Just tell me what kind of man offers a total stranger a job looking after his child?'

'I—'

'This is not what I imagined when I thought of returning to teaching.'

'No, I guess not.'

'But let me get this straight. You're looking for someone to do a little looking after and a little educating as well. Some kind of private tutor with bells on. A nanny with knowledge.'

'Yes, that's about right. And you'd have days mostly free while Copley's in school. It's just around the corner really. Since we moved here my wife's been leaving work early every day, but that can't continue. Weekends would be entirely yours and we could even arrange for you to have use of a car.'

'All this because you're in a *bind*,' I say, seeing it's a little more complicated than charity. 'So I'd be doing you a favor while you were doing me a favor.'

'How would I be doing you a favor?' the man asks.

'By giving me a job I need as well as a way to stay on this land.'

'I see,' he says, 'yes, I can understand that.'

I have not even seen the rest of the house, the cupboard where they might wish to keep me hidden from their glossy friends and colleagues, the way I might be made to disappear when company arrived, left to usher the child up to his nursery, to feed him bread and milk and read him stories while his parents play. I want to know terms, money, rights, responsibilities, have a clear understanding of what I might be accepting, the regime to which I would be succumbing. I'm not even sure I could sleep in this white house, knowing what I do about the man who built it, the meanness of his ways, how his machines rolled over and ruined the land. And yet, there remains the promise of the woods, a renewal of my stewardship, a way to look over and watch out for the dark spot in the lawn, where trees and the dead lie waiting. Perhaps this offer is a reminder of the obligation I bear, the story remembered, the

355

responsibility to tell it, to teach. If the student presents himself, is it not the duty of the teacher to answer?

We talk money, hours, references, look up the numbers of past colleagues. He phones them and then makes other calls as well. 'You're giving my name. To whom are you giving it?' I ask, as he waits on the line.

'My company,' he says, 'there's a department. Preliminary background checks.'

So I accept his offer, with conditions: I will provide further character and professional references; they will order a comprehensive records check to prove there is nothing about me to fear; I will undertake no housework except preparing meals for the child and doing my own laundry; I will expect a clear and written statement of their expectations of me and rules for the child; I do not believe in corporal punishment (neither do they); I will enter into the proposition for a two-month trial period, at the end of which we will all decide together, the child included, whether it is a workable situation. If it is, then the terms will be reassessed every six months thereafter and either party can end the relationship with two months' notice.

The man listens while I speak, nodding. 'All of that sounds reasonable,' he says.

'You don't want to discuss it with your wife?'

'I'll discuss it with her in detail tonight. For now, though, do you want to come with me to take

Copley to school, so you can see where it is? And I'd like to pay you an advance on the first month.'

'That would be very kind,' I say, wondering just what I think I'm doing, throwing in my lot with these strange people in the monument to everything I have lost.

The woman leaves first, saying, when she hears the tentative agreement, how pleased she is that I will be 'joining' them, as if they were a church or a cult. I wait in the kitchen while the man and boy get themselves ready and then we all tumble out of the house, the father setting an alarm and locking the back door. The car smells of newness and control. Little eyes watch me from the backseat.

'You know there's a shorter way to get to school through River Ranch, or whatever they call it now. It's close enough to walk. I can easily pick him up each day on foot.'

'That would be wonderful,' the man says. 'It would be such a help. We're still a little lost here.'

I take note of the careful phrasing: I am 'helping' them, doing them a 'favor', 'joining' them, everything to make them feel less uncomfortable with the idea of employing me. I never thought I would work for white people, not like this, not putting myself into their service. This is not the same as classroom teaching, working for the state, for the good of all people, instead of the *few*, the *rich*, the *privileged*. I never thought I would go into service on land that used to be mine, a *mammy*, my brain spits up the word, wet with bile, a *mammy* back on the land my people inherited, land I looked after all those years, a *mammy* with more than a little *obstinacy about her*. What an undoing, what a hard, sharp unraveling of all my people built.

The child's school is a carousel blocked out in rainbow colors with a tower at its center and a skirt of concrete all around but without any horses or carriages to ride, nowhere to hold on, no trees either. While the man walks the boy to the door, I wait in the car knowing I cannot continue thinking of them as the 'man' and the 'boy'. They are people with names: Nathaniel and Copley. To name is to acknowledge something more than presence, to know them as people with worries of their own, fears and regrets and desires. Nathaniel and Copley and Julia. No, that sequence of names seems wrong. Copley, Julia, Nathaniel: that is the true order of their private parade, the child leading us towards whatever fate will become of us all.

# PART II

# BURROW

He sees it over and over, the boy asleep, still as a corpse. To be sure, to know if it was Carson or not, he felt he had to take apart that small form, to see whether the roots might have been blond, the eyes the same color as his own, the fingernails chewed down as his son's always were. But the child did not seem to be Carson, or perhaps Paul could not see clearly enough in the dark to be sure. And then came the scream, the flight, the boy approaching the hatch, crouching down and crawling to his hidden entrance. Though he can't be sure, he thinks he closed the containment door in time, an instant before the child could see the corridor of the bunker laid out beyond the pantry. The scream rings in his head, the shriek of a child that could flay skin from a man, a cry less human than animal. He will be haunted by the memory of that face: a mask distorted, stretched tight, the body cold, stone-hard, rigid in sleep, not at all like any child he has known, an offspring of some unholy union. Even in the midst of that scream, which seemed to last for hours, unrolling around the room, echoing down the deepest tunnels of Paul's head, the parents did not wake. If that is not unnatural, nothing is.

Now that the boy has seen the hatch he may lead others to its location. Something else must be done to safeguard the bunker from any possibility of penetration. The answer is to construct a kind of baffle at the pantry end, comprised of a three-dimensional series of false walls and dead ends that no one else will be able to navigate, so complex that anyone attempting it will lose themselves in its tight turnings before they even know they are stepping into a field of deception: it must be protection as well as trap. In the bunker's extra bedroom, the one intended for Carson and Ajax, there is leftover lumber and other supplies: nails, screws, the parts of the now dismantled bunk beds, and his remaining tools – a band-saw, drills and hammers, everything needed to build a barrier over a length of twenty feet from the containment door, reaching from floor to ceiling: an obstacle that will require climbing and descent to navigate. It will have to be mapped during construction or he might risk getting lost and spending days trying to find a way out. Plans! First the plans: design his warren and keep the plans hidden once the project is complete, secreted in the opening of the ventilation shaft, behind the grate, pasted flush with the curves of the pipe, where no one would ever think to look.

In the hours after shutting himself inside,

fancying he can still feel the flesh-freezing breath of the boy on his hands, he sketches a rough design: there will be only one way to get through and all other openings will lead to side alleys that stop after a short distance; a trap door will drop a man eight feet to the floor; a section of crawlspace will be studded with shards of glass cemented against the wood. All of it must be dark, unlit. With the plans finished, he gathers his materials, takes measurements, draws chalk lines in the hallway, leaving enough room for the containment door to swing wide open.

After hearing the thump of two cars the next morning, listening for the rumble of each one reversing down the driveway, and sensing no more sound or movement in the world above and around his burrow, Paul begins with the sawing and drilling, the masonry bit chewing through sheetrock and then, deeper, into the cinder-block walls, the struts sliding into their places. By the end of the first day he has the frame skeleton in place. Another night, the thump of two cars arriving, farther apart in time than during the morning departure, the garage door opening and closing twice, and then the long night of sitting alone in his kitchen, eating his ration of rice and beans, listening to music on the portable stereo that is his only entertainment. He wishes he had thought of running an antenna for a radio out through the ventilation shaft, but this now seems like nothing more than a distraction from the important business at hand. The only music he has are albums from his childhood on old tapes whose sound is warped and discs that skip and jump, catching themselves in jarring repetition: *I-I-I-I-I-I-I dream-eam-eam-eam-eam-eam*. Such songs return him to high school dances, throwing him down the long hole of his recollection to years when he could walk anywhere feeling as though the world watched him with awe instead of suspicion.

On the second day, working with a headlamp, he cuts and lays sheets of plywood to form the walls and passageways in his obstacle course. He is a beast in a burrow. Not a rabbit in a warren, but something fiercer, with victims of his own: a badger in his sett, with long claws and a hard snout, an old male never seen outside in daylight, lurking and stealthy and clever. By the end of the second day the obstacle is finished and he collapses on the couch across from the kitchen before forcing himself to eat. Eating means standing, preparation and attention. It demands thinking about the body, the needs of stomach and bowel. An ideal body would have no needs, would simply be born, grow, flourish, and function, fuelled by nothing but sunlight. His waist is getting narrower, the excess pad of fat around his body disappearing, returning him to an image of his younger self. As he stands stirring his ration of beans and rice, he suddenly thinks he hears a scratching noise. Turning off the burner he drops the wooden spoon into the pot and listens but hears nothing other than his own breath, the strike of his heart, and the sound of his fingernails scratching across the counter.

It is illogical to fear a child: this maze is just a matter of common sense, guarding against the possibility of further discovery. The trips to the boy's bedroom were folly, a risk of his liberty and life. It was a momentary failure in his vigilance, although part of him suspects that vigilance is an illusion, his guard always slipping, imperfect, failing to see the weakness in his designs, the way he has left certain approaches unprotected. Blind spots proliferate: there are ever more numerous ways for people to surprise him. A hobo or hunter could stumble upon the cellar doors in the woods with their flimsy lock, break it open, descend the stone stairs, and discover the rear containment door. None of it is as well camouflaged as it might be. What he needs is a second obstacle at the back, but then that would eliminate the possibility of an easy escape if the entrance from the house were breached and the bunker invaded. As he eats, the smell of the woods comes into the kitchen, sucked down the ventilation shaft, the warm dry damp of cool dead leaves. He inhales the scent, seeing himself with his father in the woods, rifles on their shoulders in unmoving pursuit, finding those sleek brown bodies even when the creatures thought they were safe and alone, hidden in a tangle of trees.

'Carson? Son? Is that you?' he speaks down the phone. Through the white noise of static he hears a cry and then words.

'Dad?'

'Is that you, son?'

'Mm-hmm.'

'How you doing, buddy?'

'Okay. Do you wanna talk to Mom?'

'No, king, I want to talk to you. How's Florida?'

'Hmm.'

'How's the new house?'

'We're not in Florida.'

'What do you mean you're not in Florida? Where are you?'

'I think we're dead, dad. We're all dead.'

The phone is dead. There is no reception underground, no dial tone, no sound whatsoever. He dials numbers but nothing happens, and yet the voice keeps coming back to him. It is not the first time he has heard his son speak when technology has failed.

He wakes in the kitchen chair, the pot crusted dry before him, grains of cooked rice turned to hard shrunken bullets. His watch tells him he has slept through at least one night. When he goes to examine his maze he realizes the obstacle is inadequate, its puzzle too simple. Straightaway he begins disassembling the boards and joists, spends the rest of the day taking apart the skeleton, and then without pausing to worry whether he might be heard by the people in the house above he starts rebuilding a more complex structure based on the pattern of a double helix, with only one of the two strands penetrating the heart of the bunker, the other doubling back on itself and returning to the point of origin. In the process of building this new structure, so much more complex than the first, he gets lost for an hour and a half, bumping his head against boards and beams until he becomes aware of blood smeared on his hands and clothes. But this must be a good sign. If blood has come, if he can lose and injure himself in a plan of his own creation, then this must prove he has crafted a puzzle that only the most determined and most intelligent, perhaps even the luckiest – luck would have to play a part in any successful breach – invader might ever solve. Still, something is lacking: from the entrance to the pantry anyone can see his maze is a man-made structure. He crawls back through it, emerging into the open space of the bunker, and exits through the rear containment door, propelling himself through the old stone storm cellar and up the steps into the cool night. Moonlight is everywhere above him. He drops to his knees, puts his palms on the soft wet earth, and on all fours he collects branches, twigs, moss, dried leaves, everything he thinks he needs, carrying it all back into the cellar in great armfuls. Lying on the floor of the bunker, his materials look inadequate, and so throughout the night he ferries in buckets of soil, leaves, and rocks, pushing the loads on all fours up and down through his obstacle and depositing everything at the far end where he stamps it into place, thumping with his fists until his hands are raw, and then embellishing the dirt with rocks and branches, twigs, moss, and leaves, to suggest an underground cavity of natural design – if not a creation of the earth itself, then something made by one of its less human inhabitants. He stops only when, coming out into the woods once again, he finds the eastern sky turning red. Anyone who might investigate the pantry hatch, who managed to overcome the containment door, would see that beyond it there lies nothing but dark territories of earth.

Leaving his muddy clothes in the hallway he stands for an hour under the shower, his body slender and hardened by walking the city, by the poverty and monotony of his diet. When he is clean and dry the pain surfaces. In the mirror he sees the damage to his forehead and scalp, the places where the flesh has opened. The bleeding has stopped but when he leaves the bathroom he finds the chaos of his frenzy: blood and soil and leaves, gravel and stones and tree roots littering the hallway, the living space, the doorways and throughways. He is too exhausted to clean and instead stumbles into his bedroom, to the double mattress that almost fills the space, where he once imagined holding Amanda through the apocalypse he believes is still imminent, perhaps already in the first hours of its unfolding. If we are not in the final chapters of our history then we are at the end of a particular volume, unable to predict how further installments may unfold. What is certain, he thinks, is that the future will not be one of societies and unions, but of individuals, small family units, fighting to protect their own interests, in the last hours before the ultimate end.

On his bed he sleeps rolled up in down comforters. Waking only to piss, he is careless of his excretions. Sticky and cold he rolls to a place of dryness and warmth. Hours and minutes dissolve and recombine into new units whose quantities mean little to him. With no radio reception underground, days pass uncounted, if, indeed, days are passing at all. Days are secondhours, hours are minute-years. A moment is millennia. c, circling my track, caught in my own dead ends.

Emerging from his stupor there is a new and terrible clarity. Hunger hollows his stomach, and climbing from his stained bed he discovers the filth and chaos again surrounding him. He puts clothes into the washing machine, begins sweeping up the largest pieces of refuse, carries buckets of it out to the woods. With his garbage cleared and dispersed through the trees, he vacuums and dusts, scrubs the floors of the bunker, sponges the kidney-colored walls, and begins to reorganize the kitchen. After taking a new census of his stores, he discovers there is only enough food remaining for a month if he is careful. He never would have been able to provide for his family, but it seems impossible that his calculations could have been so flawed! Again he counts the cans and boxes, mistrusts his totals, counts again and again, and only after he has counted everything more than a dozen times does he know just how short his supply remains. He reduces his ration by half, although hunger is acute and he fears it may already be affecting his thinking.

He needs a job, he needs money, but he needs a house, *his* house, he needs to regain it first, but first he needs a job, he has to have the house in his possession to prove his ability to build other houses, he needs money to reacquire the house, needs the house to acquire money, needs the money and the house to fight for the return of his family. Without the house he has no address. Without an address he will never be able to have a house. The house comes first, the house above all is the greatest of his immediate needs, the house and then the money to acquire it, the money and then the house, the house, the house always, first and last, the house to win back his sons. Count the cans and boxes of food: twenty times, forty times, again, again, spend days counting and eating as little as possible, barely sleeping, mistrusting the accuracy of those sums. Each time, only a month of food remains, and only then if the appetite is kept in check. What seemed an outrageous quantity of supplies when first acquired now seems pathetically meager. He knows he must eat. To eat he must go in search of more food.

As a boy, his van to school always drove past a store called GUNS & AMMO. It was brick, one-story, had bars in the windows, and looked like an Old West version of the local jail. His father never went there, always acquiring his ammunition at an outdoor leisure warehouse with high ceilings and large windows and walls covered with hunting trophies, but when Paul thought of guns and ammunition, he could only see the old redbrick building on a corner of a once respectable neighborhood across the street from a municipal golf course. He never saw anyone go into or come out of that store, and the lights were never on, but it must have done business. It has been closed for years, the windows boarded up with plywood painted offal-red, the bars across the doorway locked and chained.

He has no hunting permit and too little money to acquire one. Already outside the law in a fundamental way, going after an animal that exists in such large numbers it is considered a pest does not seem like a serious offense. Hunting at dawn and at dusk will reduce the risk of being detected by enemies, who are consistently expanding in their numbers until it seems that anyone encountered can only be an enemy: the possibility of friendship, even of tactical alliance, is dead. His mother might still be a friend, but he is unsure if he can trust her. He has not been in touch since he last went to see her for lunch, walking back and forth across town. The messages that appear on his phone when he emerges from the bunker into the woods are always from his mother, asking if he is okay, if he could call her back *just whenever you have a minute, you know, okay* chiquito, *bye-bye.* The *chiquito* gets on his nerves; it started when he was small, because he *was* so small, and then turned into a joke when he became anything but *chiquito*.

With the phone silenced and resting in the pocket of his camouflaged hunting vest, he climbs a tree and waits for the deer to come, and if not deer then turkeys, and failing all else then the lower links of the woodland food chain, the rabbits and squirrels and beavers that might be skinned and gutted and stuffed into his chest freezer, the gophers, mice, and voles. The first evening there is nothing, no animals of any kind except robins and sparrows, crawling beetles and buzzing flies, but before dawn the next morning he spots a doe and cuts her down with a shot to the head that she never hears. As his father taught him, he guts her, hidden in a sheltered thicket of fir trees. Before the sun is up he is back underground, the young doe's carcass on the concrete floor of the hallway where he saws off the legs, skins the body, and cuts it into pieces he can freeze.

The butchering and cleaning takes the better part of the morning and with the hours remaining he goes back to inspect his obstacle, deciding to paint the wooden walls and passageways black. Before his retreat he left cans of paint in the basement of the house. He will wait until night, when the people have gone to bed, and retrieve the paint, which he is certain will be there in the corner where he left it. Before he can attend to the paint he returns to the woods with his rifle and subsonic ammunition, his suit of camouflage, suppressor, and knife. He climbs a tree to wait and in the passing hours he tries to phone his wife. He calls every cell phone number for her he has ever known, since they first met. All have now been reassigned: he talks to young men and old women, to black people and white people, a woman who speaks only Spanish, a man who shouts into the phone and threatens to call the police, an order of nuns, a gas station, a liquor store. He dials directory assistance as he has on countless occasions but there is no listing for his wife or her parents anywhere in the country. Knowing he will be unable to find them, they have nonetheless done everything possible to keep him even from speaking to his boys. Amanda is no longer the point. He understands there is no hope of recapturing her, but he might yet be able to save his sons. As soon as I have a thousand dollars, I will leave this place to find you, making my way on foot if I have to. I will sell myself to survive: if not my labor then my body. I will march across country to find you, boys, and I will bring you back to this house where we will live out our days.

Just after sunset they appear: a buck and a doe. They are cautious, their noses raised, perhaps already scenting his body and the threat of the rifle. He takes the buck first, and though the doe startles, he catches her before she can flee. The moon is no longer full but it is bright enough that he can manage the gutting in the dark. He hauls the buck into the bunker and returns for the doe, but by then he is too exhausted to skin or butcher and goes to bed, still dressed in his camouflage, remembering only in the middle of the night his plans to paint the obstacle. Shaking himself awake, he crawls from bed and out into the hallway, then up into the passage that will take him through to the containment door. By now he has learned how to move through it quickly, knows the turns he must take, when to duck his head, when to lunge over the trap door that opens to a drop of eight feet. At the containment door he listens and checks his watch. Satisfied that the house is silent, he swings wide the door and edges open the hatch, finding the basement on the other side in darkness.

Again the house feels different, colder, and as he turns on the lights he sees that, like the rest of the house, the basement has been painted white, floor to ceiling. He looks for the plaque he mounted on the wall and discovers that, although still there, it has been painted over as well, the recesses of the engraved letters clogged with paint, words legible but only from an angle. It is dustless and sterile and no longer feels like a basement. Other than the woman's workshop space, the room is empty, and this emptiness, as so much else about what these people have done, fills him with dread. There is no place to hide. On the far side of the basement, where his cans of paint should be, there is a large metal cage, five feet by two feet by three feet high, made of heavy-duty steel mesh and secured with a padlock. Inside are the cans of paint he left behind before retreating to the bunker, as well as the leftover paint from the work done by the new owners. He was a fool to leave anything behind in the house.

Panting, his clothes soaked with sweat, he follows the light of his headlamp back through the obstacle but after only a foot or two the lamp goes out and he has to proceed in darkness, trying to discern any hint of light from the other end. There is a groaning and clunking in his ears, a rushing like water through pipes, throwing him off the path he made until, before he knows it, he is in the field of broken glass, his hands lacerated and bleeding, spreading a stickiness that keeps pulling him back into a suction lock with the wood beneath him. In retreat, he crawls backwards, tries to remember how to escape from the field of glass, forcing himself to recall which turn to make, whether to go up or down at the fork: he goes up, pulling his body along the plywood surface, sniffing the air ahead in search of his own scent. As he climbs, a catch picks at the back of his mind, and then, as the memory rips itself open, he feels the wood give way beneath his weight: a whoosh and a judder and his head banging against boards, the wind pushed out of him, a fall of eight feet before he knew he was falling, but the fall itself is interminable, the boards and joists and timber passing him, all the detail of his construction visible, the poorly finished nails, the hurried carelessness of his work, the shoddiness of the materials, a sticker of a rocket ship on a board that was once part of the bunk beds intended for his boys. Wheezing great gasps, drowning, he rears back, hitting his head against a two-by-four beam. The headlamp flickers, bringing the tunnel into view, and he sees a familiar section, knows he must go forward, turn right, double back, take the first left, climb again, take the second left, the third right, and then prepare to descend the ladder into the bunker hallway.

There is a fault in his memory. He thinks he has made the correct turns but finds himself back at the beginning after what feels like an hour of crawling in tunnels scarcely wide enough for him to pass. He turns on the light above the containment door, removes his clothes, examines himself. The cuts on his hands are deep, the shards of glass may have severed tendons, his clothes are heavy, soaked with blood and sweat. Without the clothes he will move faster. It is impossible to traverse the obstacle without starting from the uppermost of the two possible entrances. The earth around them has been packed and repacked, the roots, twigs, leaves, and stones now settled into their places:

holes in the ground, holes in the earth, nothing about them appears man-made. That was his mistake, not starting through the topmost entrance. He pulls himself up and into the darkness. Naked he can move faster, concentrating on turning in the right direction, remembering when to go up and when down, left or right, and then, after no more than five minutes, he is back in his hallway, sweat cutting camouflage through the coating of blood and dust that encases his skin.

In sleep he dreams of leaving the bunker by the rear exit, walking through the old stone storm cellar, up the stairs, into the woods, and as he steps onto the woodland floor his clothes fly from his limbs, the cotton shredding in a sudden wind that scrapes the hair from his body, scouring him until he is hairless, his skin withering, aging all at once under the force of the elements, his body declining, bones becoming brittle, spine shrinking and curving in on itself until he can no longer stand upright but must crawl, always on all fours, sniffing the ground, unable to raise his head high enough to see the path in front of him, and as he crawls, head swaying left and right, his nose to the ground, he turns to look back at the burrow entrance where he sees a great dark shadow approaching through trees, shifting, elongating, plunging through brush and down stairs, discovering his retreat.

He wakes, the down comforter speckled with

dried semen, blood, sweat. The pelt covering his chest and head is still there, his long eyelashes twitch, a week's worth of beard stipples his face. There is no time to shower. Taking the dream for prophecy, he dresses, arms himself, flees the bunker. From a hiding place high in a tree, he watches the entrance to the cellar. Although he cannot remember when he last ate, he is unaware of hunger in the first hours of his watch, seeing nothing and no one apart from squirrels and birds. For a moment he stands, looking out through the thicket of branches. On a hill in a tree more than forty feet off the ground, he recognizes Demon Point, the crest where the land rears up suddenly before dropping again to the river. When the house was still his, he had been able to see the Point from his bedroom. Every year several kids, usually teenagers, would break legs sliding down its vertical flanks of loess, or be unable to stop themselves and go flying to the river, hit their heads, catch on a snag and drown, so people would say, in a way that was at least half-believing in forces beyond the visible, *the Demon got him, see, the Demon got that boy.*

When he is too tired to stand he sits again, straddling a branch as big around as his newly narrow waist, and leaning back against the trunk he is aware for the first time of hunger and thirst, of the dryness of the air after so much rain. The ground is waterlogged, the rough ridged bark of the tree still damp, a smell of wet growth and decay rising up through the branches. In the course of the first day no one comes, and once it is dark he can see so little he has to rely on his hearing. While day is a time of distant machine noises, cars and aircraft, beeping construction equipment and howling sirens, night settles into its natural cacophony of owls, winds, and the leaf-crunching movements of animals he can no longer see. Staring into the navy black ground below, listening, he keeps himself awake. An owl is close, whinnying a long descending note that makes Paul quake and hold himself. At some point he sleeps, stirring only late the next morning when he hears voices and looks down to see the child led by the Washington woman straight to the old stone steps of the storm cellar. He forgot to lock the doors to the cellar, left one of them wide open, and the containment door itself will be unlocked as well. He is as care-less as his father always suspected.

'There used to be a house here, an old house, older than my house was. It burned down a long time before I was even born,' he hears the widow say.

'And this was part of the house?' the boy asks, as the two of them pull more branches away from the entrance.

'This is all that's left of that place. Deeper in the woods, closer to the river, there's a chimney and a fireplace, all made of stones. That belonged to a log cabin once upon a time but the walls fell down and rotted years ago. My mother would take

379

me there and we'd sit inside on a hot afternoon because it was so cool and quiet. Deer used to come up to the window and stare at us.'

'Can we go down there?' the boy asks, pointing into the cellar.

The woman opens the other door and leans into the dark cavity. He does not breathe. If her vision is acute enough to see in the dark she will discover his lair. A moment later she comes back up.

'Better not,' she says. 'The ceiling might not be safe. Come on, I'll show you the chimney.'

He exhales as the two of them walk north through the woods, disappearing beyond his sight. The widow will have seen evidence, the marks of human presence on the floor of the cellar, on the steps, all the scratchings and leavings, smelled odors of body and breath. He waits until they return, the boy and the widow, walking up to the fence he built, placing a key in the lock, letting themselves into the backyard and locking the door behind them as if they expect the arrival of savages.

Struggling for breath he props his back against the trunk, dizzied from watching the woman and child and knowing they were never aware of him. If he could watch them, vulnerable as they were, then anyone might be watching him. Even if he managed to get back into the cellar, someone might follow him, see him enter, discover his hiding place, flush him out. All it would take is a muffling of the ventilation shaft hidden in the hollowed-out trunk that stands not twenty paces from the stairs to the cellar. They could smoke him out, gas him, force him to come fleeing into the open where there would be no choice but to present himself armed, to go out battling for his liberty.

Only when his legs and arms go numb does he move them, adjust his position, climb to a lower, broader branch, nearly falling as he grapples down the rough trunk, feeling the weight of his body pulled backward in space. Planting a foot, he clings, grasps, pivots, slides his legs around the new branch, heaves in air, and notices the sun is setting, the world turning red, air throbbing with this new coloration, the forest distorted, the greens popping neon, fluorescent, a patch of red label on his shoes shimmering as the woods are suddenly full of deer, a few at first, the forerunners, darting a path through trees, flying, and then dozens more in stampede as he takes aim, the suppressor muffling his shots, bodies falling, others coming faster, in panic and disorientation, piling up, a carnage of brown and white flanks, some still bellowing, eyes rolling, staring up at him as the lights go out, the wind picking up, clouds cantering in from the west, the first fat and acidic drops forcing him from the tree, half sliding down the trunk to the ground where he surveys his kill.

One by one, he guts them and carries each body down to the storm cellar, through the containment door, and into the bunker. He works slowly, rain falling harder, bodies cooling, requiring more work with his knife, a slip in the rain, blood coming now from his own skin. Five deer, all at once, enough to feed him for a year.

As the rain belts him harder, wind driving water through wood, he retreats once again, sealing himself inside the vault. The hallway of the bunker is a landscape of bodies. He cuts off the legs and skins them but lacks the energy to complete the job. At the stove he cooks rice and beans, eating from the pot as he looks at the carcasses, imagining how he will butcher and freeze them, find ways to preserve all that meat; some of it will have to be cured or go to waste. He eats two days' worth of rations until he feels sick, and then, before he can even turn to the carcasses, he stumbles to his bed, strips off his wet and bloody clothes, watches the trickle of blood from his arm slow and stop, its browning crust caked across his skin, a smear on the blankets, a track, his eyes burrowing into the path that cuts through the folds of his comforter, a lane through hills, a red trail into darkness.

When he wakes he turns over and sleeps again, forgetting his dreams. In the moments of waking he wants only to return to the red path and follow his bloodline back to mountains he has never known.

A high whine screaming through the bunker wakes him. Climbing and tripping through deer carcasses that emit a tart-sweet smell of decay, he searches for the source of the noise, but everywhere it has the same intensity, a bright screeching drone, like the scream of the child. Or perhaps it is not whining so much as some watery rushing, surging up from beneath the bunker, the aquifer rising to engulf him. Or else it is something alive in the walls of the bunker itself, between the concrete and lead lining, and the only answer is to dig, to find the source. A drill will make too much noise, the people upstairs would notice, but a spoon, a spoon will work, cutting into the walls. He finds a spoon in the kitchen's utensil drawer and begins scraping away at the corner of the hallway closest to the rear containment door, sensing the noise might be loudest there, that in fact there is a shift of intensity and pitch, a higher gurgling-whine, a rotating whooshing. He scrapes and scratches, wearing down the spoon, creating a small mound of dust on the floor. For the first time since rising from his bed he notices his nakedness, the stains of blood and dirt still traced along his arms. He has defecated and urinated on the floor as the noise, growing in intensity, exploding up through the walls, penetrated his brain. It is not water, nothing mechanical or electronic, not a whine, not a gurgle, but that same terrible scratching and clawing noise he has heard in the past, a beast from deep in the bowels of the earth rising up, breathing in and out, clawing through the ground surrounding the bunker, approaching, circling, scrambling in fury against the lead lining, clawing its way in, piercing the outer shell. He stumbles backwards, tripping over the carcasses, sliding between them, the hunger erupting out of his gut, tearing into his mouth, his hands reaching, shredding, pulling away a strip of flesh from the carcass closest to him, his fingers bringing it to his mouth, the flesh on his tongue, the tart-sweet odor, and then a sudden blackness and night.

# PART III

# FALL

4:53 AM: he stares at the red numbers on the clock radio. Individually they are masculine but 4:53 is somehow feminine. It has to do with adding them all together, or multiplying. Either way, the result (12 or 60) is feminine. This is not something he has to contemplate. He knows the time is feminine before he is conscious of making calculations. He wonders if three men make a woman. It calms him to know there is now another woman in the house, although he is still unsure if he can trust her. She has told him to call her Louise. His father thinks this is too familiar and wants him to call her Mrs Washington. During the day, when the two of them are alone, he calls her Louise. As soon as his mother or father gets home, he has to remember to switch to Mrs Washington. He asks her one day at dinner if she is related to George and Martha Washington. She laughs and says no, but her husband might have been since he could not tell a lie. He turns off the alarm before it can buzz. It is a Friday. He is in no hurry to get ready for school.

★   ★   ★

4:58 AM: he turns on the light and picks up the book he is reading. He has finished the book about the boy who goes in search of his father on a distant planet and is now reading its sequel, in which the same boy becomes very ill and his sister has to shrink herself down to sub-molecular size and enter his body to save him. Like the boy in the book, he also has a mysterious illness, a battle going on inside him, but unlike the boy, he has no sister to save him. His father says he should spend more time outdoors in the backyard, climbing trees, but the trees are tall, and there are no branches anywhere within reach. Last weekend his father tried to help him climb, giving him a boost so he could touch the closest branch. As he was reaching for the branch to pull himself up his arms began to shake, and then his legs, and they shook so hard he lost control of his body and found it squirming out of his father's arms, dropping to the ground. He turned his ankle and began to cry. 'Come on, Copley,' his father said, 'don't be so afraid.' Sitting on the wet grass, looking around at the world, he did not know how to say to his father that he was afraid not just of heights, but of the open space around him, so wide it seemed ready to consume him, to take him in its gaping jaws and replace him with itself.

5:10 AM: he watches himself in the shower, looking at his head, his feet, his elbows, the backs of his knees, seeking himself in the body he no longer recognizes as his own. Only when he glances into dark corners of space does he sense something that looks like his thoughts. Empty space has consumed him. He now belongs to space.

8:02 AM: he and Louise eat breakfast together but do not talk. He wants to speak with her but every time words begin to form, rising up in his head like buildings, before he can place them on his tongue they flatten and slide away, filling his throat with debris. It is not a question of having nothing to say. He has many things to say. He feels as though he came into the world to speak, to name, to describe things in the way he sees them, but something is now stopping him, either the illness or the pills that are supposed to make him better. The pills might, he thinks, as well as being a remedy, also be a kind of poison. After the last time he thought he saw the man, and followed him into the basement, discovering the short door at the back of the pantry hidden under a shelf, he told his parents. 'I saw him again,' he said, 'and I know where he lives. He's behind the pantry.' His father told him to stop making up stories, but the following evening, while his mother was working down there, he took her by the hand and pulled her past the empty shelves. 'There, under there, he lives down there. Look, please look.' She leaned over, crawled under the shelf at the back of the pantry, and felt the wooden back wall of the unit. 'Pull it,' he said, 'pull the handle.' 'There isn't a handle, Copley.' 'The tab, the thing holding up the shelf.' She huffed, she was impatient with him, he understood this. He asked her again to pull it. 'I'm pulling it but nothing's happening,' his mother said, backing out from under the shelf and dusting off her hands. 'There isn't anything there, sweetheart. You've been having such vivid dreams, haven't you?' She told him that now, in not too long, dreams like that would stop. He wonders if she meant they would stop because he is going to die, especially now that the words are flattening out and slipping away. 'Are you looking forward to school today?' Louise asks. 'No,' he says, 'I hate school here.' She holds his hand. 'Try to find something good,' she says, 'it won't be forever.' This is all she can ever tell him. It won't be forever, he knows, because he is very sick and he is dying. His parents know it, his doctor knows it, and even Louise knows it, but all of them are refusing to tell him the truth.

12:40 PM: he sits across from Joslyn at the end of their usual table in the cafeteria gym. Lunch today is fish sticks with tartar sauce, peas, carrots, and fruit compote. Ethan, one of his tormentors, has not been in class all week, and this morning Mrs Pitt removed the nametag from Ethan's desk. Joslyn, who lives across the street from Ethan, says the family disappeared over the weekend. 'And on Monday, the house was boarded up.'

'What do you mean boarded up?' 'There were boards nailed over the front door and all the windows.' He wonders what kind of neighborhood Joslyn lives in. He has never seen a house boarded up, except for Louise's house, and in that case it did not have boards, just a big lock on the front door. He has told no one at school about the man in his basement but he decides, now, that he should tell Joslyn. 'You mean *living* in your basement?' she asks. 'That's right.' 'And your parents are *letting* him live there?' 'No, they don't think he exists. They think I'm making it up. My father says I read too many fantasy books.' Joslyn looks at him as she chews her food. She is careful when she eats and he likes this about her. She chews each bite fifteen times, more if it's something tough, but never any less. She eats slowly and is always done just before the lunch period is finished. Sometimes this makes him anxious, because he's afraid she won't throw away her trash in time to line up for recess and then she'll get a fine. 'What's wrong with your voice?' she asks. 'What do you mean?' She wipes her mouth with her paper napkin, puts her hands down on the table, and leans over to whisper to him so the girls sitting next to them won't hear. 'You're talking different than you used to.' 'Different how?' he whispers. 'Like you're dead.' 'Like a ghost?' he asks. 'Not like a ghost. Like you're dead.'

*   *   *

12:55 PM: he and Joslyn have formed a habit of walking the perimeter of the playground. Most of the other kids are busy with games, and they've discovered that if they keep moving rather than trying to sit in one place, the others are less likely to bother them. The usual games are going on: older boys playing basketball, a group of girls bouncing basketballs in time, hop scotch, jump rope, kids on the play equipment, the security guards watching everyone. As they approach the far side of the field he sees someone outside the school grounds, across the street, walking. Because it is strange to see an adult on foot in the area, they both notice the man, who seems also to notice them. They stop and stare at the man, who slows down for a moment before speeding up and starting to run until he disappears around the corner. 'What was that about?' Joslyn asks. 'It was him. I think it was him,' he says. 'What are you talking about, Policeman?' 'That was the man who lives in my basement. I recognized him.' Joslyn looks at him, pushing out her lips, narrowing her eyes. 'Are you soft or something?' 'What do you mean *soft*?' 'Are you crazy?' 'I don't know. I think I might be dying.' She laughs and takes his hand and drags him forward. 'If you're dying then I'm already dead,' she says, 'and I can tell you that I'm as alive as those trees.'

1:32 PM: Mrs Pitt is in the middle of social studies. This week the lessons have been about citizenship and government, about the importance of rules and regulations, of obeying orders and signs. Yesterday she asked them what would happen if nobody paid attention to signs. 'What if people ignored traffic signals? Stop signs? Crosswalks? What if drivers didn't follow speed limits? What if the bus drivers ignored the bus stops?' He understood there was only one true answer to all her questions. Signs and rules have to be followed or else there will be nothing but chaos, and chaos, Mrs Pitt has explained to them, is another word for evil. He has looked in the dictionary at home and this does not seem to be true, not true at all. He raised his hand and asked Mrs Pitt, 'What if a sign is wrong? What if it's pointing in the wrong direction?' 'That doesn't happen very often, Copley.' 'And what if a rule is wrong?' 'I don't know what you mean,' Mrs Pitt said, 'a rule can't be wrong.' 'But what if it is?' 'That's enough, Copley. I'm giving you a warning.' Today they are talking again about rules. 'We have to have rules,' says Mrs Pitt. 'It's important to have rules at home. What are some of the rules you have at home? Max?' 'I have to brush my teeth before bed and after breakfast,' says Max. 'Very good,' says Mrs Pitt, 'and if you didn't brush your teeth you would get cavities.' 'What about you, Emily?' 'I have to ask permission before I go outside.' 'Very good,' says Mrs Pitt, 'because if you didn't ask permission your parents wouldn't know where you were, and because you're not old enough to know whether or not it's safe to play outside.' It goes on like this for five minutes; he checks his watch, and although he and Joslyn both raise their hands to offer answers (he is going to tell the class about the rule that allows him only half an hour of television a week), Mrs Pitt ignores them. 'Very good. Hands down. Now what we're going to do is think about some other rules we can create for the classroom. We already have lots of important rules, about being quiet and lining up and following directions from Miss Fox and me, but I bet you can think of some other good rules, maybe even rules that I haven't thought of.' The room is silent for several moments, Mrs Pitt walking back and forth across the front of the room, Miss Fox standing at the back, the rain flinging itself against the windows. At last Austin raises his hand and Mrs Pitt calls on him. In the past week, Austin has taken the lead in whispering to Copley during bathroom breaks. Yesterday, Austin came into the stall where Copley was trying to urinate and pushed him against the yellow tiled wall. 'What are you doing in here?' Austin asked. 'Why don't you use the urinals like a normal boy? Are you even a boy?' When Copley did not answer, Austin pulled at his pants, whispering, 'Let's see if you're a boy.' The only thing that saved him was Mrs Pitt shouting into the boys' bathroom to ask what was taking them so long. Now, waiting for Austin to tell Mrs Pitt and the class his idea for a new rule, Copley has a

394

sense it will be something to do with him. 'I think that only real boys should be allowed to use the boys' restroom and only real girls should use the girls' restroom.' Mrs Pitt looks at Austin and writes on the board: 'Boys in the boys' restroom, girls in the girls' restroom.' 'Yes, Austin, I think that's an important rule,' says Mrs Pitt. 'So does that mean Copley won't be able to use the boys' restroom now?' Austin asks, and everyone except for Joslyn, everyone including Mrs Pitt, laughs. 'We'll just have to help Copley straighten up,' says Mrs Pitt, raising her hands to quiet the room. 'I'll count on all you other boys to help him do that.' 'But he isn't even a boy,' Austin says. 'That's enough now, Austin. Who can think of another good rule for the classroom? Emily?' He feels dazed and dizzy and the world turns red. Miss Fox catches his eye, smiles through a frown, and seems to say without speaking that she is sorry. He tries to think of something to say but the words rise and then flatten, sliding back into his throat, wreckage building up, clogging, rusting. He looks out at the dark day through the slats of the blinds and puts down his head on his arms, crossed on top of his desk. 'Head up, Copley. Back straight. This isn't naptime,' says Mrs Pitt, and the lesson continues.

3:25 PM: it is swimming today and they have started a unit on diving. In Boston, his swimming teacher had already taught him to dive before they moved and he has been looking forward to this. In the boys' locker room Austin sneaked up behind him and whispered in his ear, 'You're supposed to be in the other locker room. It's a classroom rule. Let's see what's there. Are you a boy or not?' Mr Bruce shouted at Austin to 'knock it off' and Copley was able to change into his swimming suit without being seen. Now it is his turn on the diving board. Mr Bruce and Miss Connie are in the pool with the students who have already done their dives. Behind him, on the concrete deck surrounding the pool, are the rest of his classmates. He has no fear about doing the dive. He remembers what his swimming teacher in Boston taught him, and he knows he can dive well. As he approaches the edge of the board, Austin shouts from the far side of the pool, 'She's going to fall!' He jumps, and in the moment his feet leave the board, he knows his form is wrong. His knees bend, his legs scissor, his arms go wide and wild, and he can see the surface of the water rushing into his face.

3:28 PM: he is on his back on the concrete at the side of the pool and Mr Bruce is leaning over him saying his name: 'Copley, Copley, Copley, *Copley.*' He is fine. He opens his eyes. He tells Mr Bruce he is fine. He hears Austin shout, 'She belly-flopped!' He looks down on himself from a high corner of the building and sees, for an instant, a shiny red disc on the concrete under his head.

★   ★   ★

396

3:55 PM: Louise is waiting just inside the front door of the school, arguing with the security guards over a piece of paper. It is not the first time this has happened. He does not know what is on the paper, but when he approaches, the two men look at the paper and look at Louise's driver's license and then one of them says, 'Okay, you look like your picture.' Louise takes his hand and they both open their umbrellas for the walk home. It takes ten minutes on foot to get from the school to the house, cutting through River Ranch, the Demon Point nature reserve, and the woods behind their house. He likes coming home this way, through the gate into the backyard. It feels secret, hidden, protected from the neighbors, although he has met none of them and knows nothing about their lives. If they are anything like the students and teachers at his school, he does not want to meet them.

4:30 PM: while he changes out of his uniform and puts on dry clothes, Louise makes him peppermint tea and they meet in the playroom on the top floor. He thinks most clearly at the top of the house and his tongue moves faster, getting the words out before they flatten, slide, and collapse. He tells Louise about his day at school. She shakes her head and says, 'I can see why you don't look forward to it. I'll speak to your parents.' 'You know I could fly if I wanted to,' he says, putting his hands on the glass of the

397

balcony doors and looking out at the sodden platform. Wet ashen drapes sweep across land and houses. 'What do you mean?' Louise asks. 'If I thought hard enough I could fly. It wouldn't be difficult. I don't weigh very much. I could. And anyway, weight doesn't matter.' Louise puts her hands on his shoulders and turns him around. She kneels down in front of him so they are face-to-face, and then takes both of his hands. 'I want you to promise me,' she says, 'that you won't do anything of the kind. I want you to promise me you will not jump off of anything anywhere. Flying is for birds and insects, not for humans. I know what a bright boy you are, Copley, and I want you to think about this like it's a math problem. It does not add up, your body and the air and high places. You understand?' He nods but knows she does not understand. He tries to tell her without words, to show her the way he has already left his body, the way he is watching both of them from outside the window. 'Watch yourself,' she says. 'I am,' he says. 'I'm always watching myself.'

9:22 PM: although he is supposed to be in bed he has crept onto the landing to hear the conversation in the kitchen. The voices of his parents and Louise rise up the back stairs, their words all coming with such ease and speed that he knows this is the way people are supposed to talk.

Louise: 'He's being bullied by the other students, and by his teacher.'

Mom: 'Bullied in what way?'

Louise: 'Teasing, name-calling. Picking on him, making an example of him in class.'

Mom: 'He's told you this?'

Louise: 'He's been dropping hints since I came but today it all came out.'

Dad: 'And you believe him? You don't think this is just another one of his tall tales?'

Mom: 'Nathaniel, please. Calm down.'

Dad: 'I'm perfectly calm. I just don't understand how Louise can listen to someone who is so clearly a practiced and talented liar and fail to see that anything he says can't be trusted.'

Louise: 'I don't know why you chose that school, but I'd move him sooner rather than later. There's a perfectly good public school two miles away where an old friend of mine is the principal. You'd have no trouble getting him in there.'

Dad: 'The reason he's at the Pinwheel Academy is because it's funded and sponsored by my company. If I didn't send him there it would look weird. And frankly, I can't believe EKK would have anything to do with a school that allowed bullying. We're an equality-minded organization. And if there were *real* bullying going on, then the security cameras would catch it. Do you see bruises on him? Do you see injuries? He's fine. If he were really being bullied, we'd know it just by looking at him.'

He doesn't need to hear more. Nothing will change. He will continue at the school through the rest of his dying days and his parents are not going to save him.

11:15 PM: he fell asleep for an hour and has now woken from a dream he might call a nightmare. He was bouncing on the end of the diving board but did not want to jump because Austin and Ethan were in the water below, calling out to him, saying 'she's going to fall'. He leapt into the air, flipped, and made a perfect dive. As he swam back up to the surface, their hands reached out to hold him down, pushing his head underwater, and he ran out of air. And then, when he felt as though he was going to die, larger hands gripped him around the waist and pulled him away, deeper underwater, and then up, backwards, dragging him out of the pool. He sucked in air, spat, shook the water from his ears, and squirmed around in the hands that had saved him until he could see the face of his rescuer. It was the man from the street, from his basement, the giant who lifted him up on the lawn and carried him back inside.

12:30 AM: everyone has gone to bed, the lights are out under the doors. Though he knows he should be afraid of whatever lurks behind the pantry wall, he tiptoes down the back stairs, through the kitchen, and into the basement. At the far end of the pantry, he wriggles down under the shelf, and knocks against the short door that he knows is there, although he cannot see hinges or anything else to prove what he knows. His knuckles rap softly against the wood as he whispers, 'Help me. Please, help me. Help me.'

'W'hy do you keep siding with him?' he asks her. She's still wet from the shower, running a towel round her head. Julia has always been thin but in the last month she has started to look even thinner. He can see all of her ribs, the bony knot of her sternum, the arc of her clavicles. To look at her body you would never say she had given birth. The towel hangs over her face as he asks the question. She whips it away and looks at him, her eyes dark and sunken between cheekbones and brow.

'What are you talking about, Nathaniel?'

'Why do you always side with Copley?'

'I don't know what you mean,' she says. 'Are there sides? I don't side with Copley.'

'Every time we have an argument you side with him. He's always right.'

She sidles past him into the bedroom and flicks through the hangers on her side of the closet. It would be easy to push her inside, close the door, and then she'd see how serious he was.

'Don't put me in the middle, Nathaniel. If you

402

have problems with Copley you need to work them out on your own.'

'You sound like my mother.'

'That's not fair. You have no right to say such a thing.' She puts on a bra and underwear, steps into a pair of black slacks and sticks her arms through the holes of her beige blouse. All her clothes hang loose on her. He is sure they used to fit.

'You sound *exactly* like my mother. Don't your books say parents should be united? You try to be the kid's friend when he doesn't need a friend, he needs authority.'

'He does need a friend, Nathaniel. In case you haven't noticed, he doesn't have any friends. We haven't done anything to meet our neighbors. He asked me if I could arrange a play date and I haven't even helped him with that, so don't tell me I'm siding with our son against you. This is not a competition.'

'You let him get away with murder, Julia. That kid could walk in here right now, hit me in the gut, and you wouldn't do anything. You'd tell me it was *my* fault.'

'What's got into you?'

'You're like a team, you and him and Louise, all ganged up together to run this place. I don't know why we ever hired her.'

'It was *your* idea, Nathaniel. And I think it was a good idea. I admit I was skeptical but she's been wonderful with him so far. Even if he hasn't stopped acting out at home, at least there haven't been any more problems at school. He seems less troubled, don't you think?'

'I'm not at all convinced—'

'Has he spoken in that weird voice?'

'I – no, I don't think so. But that's as much to do with the drugs as anything else. I'm talking about relationships, Julia, and when it comes to relationships, the three of you are this tight little unit, all aligned against me, because I'm the one who tries to impose order and discipline and rules. Louise is always telling me the kid needs more freedom. I never should have hired that woman.'

'Then why *did* you?'

'Because there was no one else!'

He almost says, *because you refuse to stay home and look after our son*, although this is not, in fact, what he thinks. He cannot tell Julia he hired Louise Washington on the spot because when he saw her sitting in their kitchen, dispossessed, turfed out of her house by agents of his own company, he remembered a woman from his past he had nearly forgotten, the black woman who was briefly his nanny as a child while his mother went to study in London for six months. He was only six at the time, and remembers calling her Mozelle, although when he later asked Matthew about it his brother insisted the woman's name was Maisie. Louise instantly reminded Nathaniel of Maisie or Mozelle, of her quiet, challenging presence, and of the way she had hugged him, saying what a tiny boy he was for his age. 'Like a little munchkin,' he can hear her saying, 'a chubby

little munchkin running away from the wicked witch.'
Looking at Louise, seeing Mozelle, he had also seen
the shadow of his own guilty conscience, his aiding
and abetting and association with a corporation
capable of evicting an elderly woman who wanted
nothing more outrageous than to remain in her house
– that was as much as he could explain to Julia. When
he'd heard that she was living there, he had assumed
a straightforward case of trespass, nothing more. The
truth, when he learned it from Louise herself, had so
devastated him that he could see nothing else but to
offer help in the only way that seemed just.

As the weeks have passed, and he sees more of
Louise, of her quiet, lurking ways, slipping up and
down the stairs, front and back, the way she can
suddenly appear in a room without warning, he has
remembered another thread of Maisie-Mozelle's relationship with his family. The woman had a brother
or husband, a male relative at least, who sometimes
came to pick her up when she went back to her own
house on weekends. The first time this relative came
to fetch her the doorbell must have been out of order,
because the man, in dark brown overalls, with a tight
spherical afro, came round to the back garden,
bounding through deep January snow, and knocked
furiously at the window to be let inside.

'Well, now we have her, Nathaniel, and as far as
I'm concerned she's here to stay, for as long as
she wants,' Julia says, leaving the room and closing
the door behind her. It was not a slam, but neither
was it uninflected.

As Nathaniel gets dressed alone in the bedroom, he thinks perhaps the man he remembers approaching their house in Cambridge through the snow one January afternoon came again, another time, returning where he was not wanted. He remembers an evening in the summer after Maisie-Mozelle had stopped working for them. Nathaniel and his brother sat on either side of the long dining table, his parents at opposite ends, blue candles blazing. The curtains had not been drawn and they were eating in silence, looking out on the twilit backyard, when the doorbell rang.

His father turned to his mother and said, 'Are you expecting anyone, Ruth?'

'My last appointment cancelled.'

Arthur Noailles put his napkin on the table, stood, and went to answer the door. He remembers his father sounding surprised, uncertain, and then Nathaniel and his brother and mother listened in silence as an argument escalated, culminating in his father shouting, 'We never promised Mozelle a permanent job! It was always going to be a temporary thing! You have no right to disturb my family, mister!'

There was a sound like a scuffle and he remembers – or perhaps he imagines – that the other voice shouted, 'But my wife needs that job! You can't just hire a person and let her think she's gonna work for you forever and then six months go by and you let her go. It isn't right, sir. I'm telling you it isn't *right*.'

The door slammed. His father came back and

sat down at the dinner table, put his napkin in his lap, and the doorbell began to ring.

'*Mister* Mozelle, I take it,' his mother said.

'The one and only,' said his father. The doorbell rang for at least five minutes and then stopped, abruptly, and his parents both exhaled. His mother was just standing to clear the dishes when Nathaniel saw the man appear in the backyard, suddenly revealed by the motion-sensitive porch light, approaching the house, walking up to the dining room windows, and hammering in fury until the glass split and blood trickled down the panes.

In the kitchen at 2001 Abigail Avenue, everyone speaks at once:

'Do you have your homework?' Julia asks.

'They're in the drop zone.'

'Why shouldn't I call it the drop zone?'

'Yes, Copley, ask Joslyn for her number so I can call her mother.'

'Where are my keys?' Nathaniel asks.

'Please don't call it the *drop zone*.'

'Because it's a horrible neologism that signifies nothing. Don't shout, Copley.'

'You're assuming she only has a mother?'

'It's in my bag,' says Copley.

'Yes, please.'

'Can I ask Joslyn to come play?'

'CAN I ASK JOSLYN TO COME PLAY?'

'But you weren't listening.'

'We've got it all in order. You want some more toast, Copley?' Louise asks.

'I think I saw them in the hall, Nathaniel.'

'You'll have to ask your mother.'

'Did you hear that?'

'Why shouldn't she have a mother?

'It's just the computers, Louise. I left them running.'

'Don't go there, Nathaniel.'

'Don't be ridiculous, Nathaniel. Louise and I manage Copley's schedule.'

'Yes, it's already in his bag, Louise, thanks for remembering.'

'You're being totally unreasonable, Nathaniel, and in any case this is not a conversation we should be having now, particularly not *devant l'enfant*.'

'What about a father?'

'Answer me, Julia. Why shouldn't the girl have a father? Are you assuming she's the child of a single mother just because of her—'

'And would you explain to me, Louise, why Copley should have to ask his mother about a play date and not his father?'

'This is exactly the triad of solidarity I've been talking about, Julia. Enough with the man, Copley.'

'I've had enough. I'm going to work. We'll discuss this tonight. Goodbye!'

'Hear what?'

'She has a mother.'

'She has a father, too. He's a radiologist.'

'No. Yes. What is it?'

'It's not a *date*. It's just *playing*. It's not like a date. It's not like we're dating. What schedule do I have? I don't ever go anywhere but school and the doctor's office.'

'It's the man.'

'What's a triad?'

'I know what that means. We sang *Il est né le divin enfant* last year at the Lab. I know

'I don't know. I thought I heard something downstairs.'

'That's a big word.'

'There it is again.'

'Do you hear that?'

'I'm sorry, Nathaniel, I didn't mean to suggest anything. Julia, have you signed the permission slip for the field trip?'

'Doesn't sound like computers.'

'Have a good day, Nathaniel. Don't forget your umbrella.'

'Nathaniel!'

'Don't slam the door!'

you're talking about me.'

'I know you were talking about me.'

Alexander reveley's meeting with the executives of the Security and Corrections division is announced only half an hour before it begins. The EKK CEO and heir of the South African branch's founder sits at the far end of the long black boardroom table, dressed in black, with black hair, and eyebrows that point down to his nose in a V, matching the widow's peak of his hairline. He wears a deep tan and a third of the way along his thin arm is a fat gold watch. As the room fills, Reveley twitches, crossing first his left leg over his right, then right over left, perching at the edge of his seat, pushing it back and forth, paging through notes, crumpling in on himself, doubling over the table and bursting into a spasm of sudden movement, bouncing the balls of his feet against the floor. Nathaniel looks at him and thinks of a long-legged spider reacting to electrical stimuli.

When all the seats around the table are occupied Reveley begins speaking, but throughout the subsequent hour he never makes eye contact with any of his officers.

'What I want to sketch here is a topography of the future security landscape. There will no longer be such a thing as private *qua* private.

Private is now public, in the interests of security, the private must be revealed to be within the ambit of the public, always visible to the public *qua* public, the public constituted at its primary stratum by governments, corporations, and security-surveillance entities, and at secondary stratum by ordinary citizens, beneath which there is a permeable membrane dividing the public from the non-person, the disenfranchised, the disenfranchised *qua* criminal, the non-voting, the non-politically active ex-citizen, who self-abrogates citizenship through criminality, removing himself from the protective liberty of public status to the total restriction of the carceral. The house *qua* home is no longer a space of privacy. The only privacy that remains must therefore be the privacy of governments and corporations for the good of the public, for the security of the public, for the security of the public *qua* franchised citizen living a transparent life.'

Reveley's wallet falls out of his pocket. He looks at it, notes its place on the floor, but continues speaking without pause. Later, a gold lighter falls out of the same pocket but on that occasion he does not even seem to be aware any loss has occurred. As he speaks, his eyes tunnel into the table, piercing black pupils making more connection with the furniture than with his audience. It is difficult to tell if he is nervous or merely oblivious, although his hands tremble as he turns the pages of his text. At one point he loses his place, goes silent, spends several minutes trying to find it again. Nathaniel cannot decide if the head of his company is a moron or a genius.

At the end of the hour Reveley puts down his text and, without looking at anyone else in the room, asks if there are any questions. Maureen raises her hand and Alex nods in her direction.

'Thank you, Alex, for that extraordinary illumination of the way you see the landscape of security *qua* surveillance evolving. I wonder if you could communicate to everyone else how you envision this manifesting in a given sphere – say, the domestic security product range for instance.'

'Wasn't it clear?' he asks.

'I think a little more elaboration would be helpful for those who don't have your comprehensive grasp of the subject.'

'What business are we in here? If my executives don't have a comprehensive grasp of the subject then we might as well go home,' he says. 'You might as well all retire to your gated communities and let some real professionals take over, hey?'

'It's just that what you're proposing is so visionary,' Maureen says, her voice quavering, 'that I fear some of our newer and more junior associates might not entirely have grasped the finer points of what you're proposing.'

'Oh, right,' he says, scratching his neck. '*Ja,*

411

okay, well – . Right! Here it is. It's really quite simple. As a company our new mission is global transparency of the second and third tiers, meaning the public that is the ordinary citizen, and the incarcerated population comprised of the ex-citizen. The only tier that retains privacy, and this has to be the case for the sake of global stability, is the top tier, made up of governments and corporations, which will become increasingly indistinguishable from each other. So total transparency of the second tier, for instance, Maureen, begins with something like the surveillance of the self, or the home. Burglar alarms are unexploited tools. Motion sensors can only tell the global security infrastructure – in other words the first tier – so much about what's happening in a given domestic or commercial space, am I right?'

There is a murmur of cautious assent around the table.

'Imagine wedding motion sensors to surveillance optics, so the technics of a given security system work not just to identify intruders, but also and not exclusively to monitor the health and wellbeing of the citizens it is employed to protect. So, if you have optical and audio surveillance of the home, what then becomes possible is a holistic analysis of domestic health, climate, spending, energy and food consumption, sleep patterns, work patterns, brand preference, time allocation, interpersonal activity, hygiene, nutrition, etc., as well as the more traditional armature of property and bodily security from external harms. How can we assume the threat is always peripheral to the home? That's at the heart of this reconception of security architecture and purview, and the belief that people will want the benefits of security systems that help them live better, healthier, safer, more productive lives, in which they can see their own place in the system, in which they could, perhaps, even compare their habits with those of their neighbors, or a family in Springfield could compare their lives with a family in Bangalore or Beijing or Johannesburg, living in real time, entirely out in the open, with everyone else in the world. That is the future of security.'

Nathaniel has taken notes throughout Reveley's presentation; at the end, when it all becomes clear, he feels dizzy, intoxicated by the landscape envisioned. *This*, surely, is what the future should look like: not just governments and private corporations monitoring security, but anyone anywhere checking up on their neighbors, friends, associates, peers, even strangers, to see that everyone is living responsibly, all the time, waking or sleeping.

After the meeting, Maureen steers Reveley towards Nathaniel. Up close, he can see that there is no visible division between the CEO's pupils and irises, or rather that the pupils are fully dilated, making the irises disappear. Whatever the cause, the effect is like looking into a tunnel, and finding one's own reflection deep inside.

'Alex,' Maureen says, 'this is Nate Noailles, who joined us recently from the Boston office. He's doing amazing work in corrections rehabilitation. A very fast mover, going great guns.'

Reveley's skin is so tight his pores are invisible, age impossible to discern, although anywhere from thirty-five to fifty-five seems likely. 'Of course, Nate. Maureen can't stop talking about you. Great work. We have our eye on a place for you in Switzerland. Make it work here and the job is yours for the taking. VP of Global Rehabilitation. That's what I see for you.'

Nathaniel shakes Reveley's hand, musters his glossiest tone, and thanks Alex 'for the opportunity to do such exciting and important work'.

'We're grateful to *you*, Nathaniel. We need responsible officers, people who understand that the way they live their personal lives, at home, is a reflection on the work they do in the corporation, and out in the world. I think you already understand that. I can see, looking at you,' Reveley says, his pupils seeming to grow ever larger, eclipsing even the whites of his eyes, 'that you are entirely in sync with the aims of this organization, with the way we see the future of our place in the world.'

'Yes, Alex, that's absolutely right. I am totally on board,' Nathaniel says, doubting that Julia would ever countenance a move to Switzerland.

'There could be a position for your wife as well, you know. We need top scientists, people who can activate the kind of technological advances neces-sary to realize the surveillance possibilities we haven't yet unlocked,' Reveley says, nodding his head, black eyes hypnotizing.

'I'll be sure to mention that to her. She's a great scientist. She does amazing work. Mostly not to do with surveillance, though. She's more inter-ested in assistive technology, for the disabled and elderly.'

'What could be more assistive than domestic monitoring? What I'm saying, Nate, is that it would be good to have both you and your wife on board. We're a family company. We like to have families involved from top to bottom, through and through. It's not just a matter of company philosophy, but also one of corporate security. We'd love for Nathaniel and Julia and Copley Noailles to be an EKK company family. We want all of you involved, so let's keep in touch,' he says, slipping his smooth hand once again into Nathaniel's own.

Nathaniel thinks back to that moment in Maureen's office, when her hand slid along his leg, when he failed to respond to what appeared to be a sexual provocation. Perhaps that moment was designed to gauge the kind of man he might be, a test he undoubtedly passed. He is aware that only a few months ago, if he had discovered the company knew half what it seems to about his family, he would have been surprised, perhaps even alarmed. And yet now, high inside the national headquarters, with the shimmering promise of ascension to even greater heights, the feeling overwhelming all others is that he must find a way to bring his family into line.

The waters have risen, or fallen, fallen to rise, autumn rainfall bringing them up, rivers engorged, coming down from the high west, meandering across borders, state lines, down inclines, a surge of whitewater coming, the browning of the water as it collects silt along its course, rivers swelling, great muddy veins of hypertension, clogged and closing in, spilling out over the earthen levies, breaking through, inundating the low-lying counties, the pancake flats of bone-rich farmland, the quick, dark earth, all of it coming back up, rising.

Standing with Copley at the window of his playroom at the top of the house we look out on the neighborhood, water drip-dripping from the ceiling into a large plastic bucket I have to remember to empty every few hours during the day. In becoming a tutor I have also become a skivvy. Other leaks and buckets ping through the bedrooms and all the rooms on the ground floor, the whole house an upturned sieve, the outside coming in through numberless cracks and fissures, water running along corners and seams, turning white from the powder of plaster and drywall, milky with gypsum. A crow perches on the balcony railing, shakes its body, spreads its wings, looks at us and lowers its head, breathes out a mewling cat noise, laughing.

I remember past floods, the way our creek would fill, spilling out over crops, but there was never water so deep as this. The road is dry but across the street the unfinished foundations have turned into treacherous swimming tanks for wild creatures of the woods, and the houses to the west, at the lowest point of the land, have seen water lick around doors, swamping basements. No drawbridges to lower, no way out but wading or boating. People in those houses have left already, evacuated, while these forest folk sit tight, rest easy on their hill, sandbagging all around the front except the driveway. 'We'll do it last,' Nathaniel said, looking out at the abandoned properties, the red alarm boxes flashing for now, until some electrical short circuit renders them unprotected. I shook my head, warned him: 'Sometimes the water won't wait. I've seen floods before, but never like this. Never so fast, never so widespread.'

I keep a bag packed, ready to go at the moment I hear water cross the road, knowing I can escape out the back gate to higher ground in the woods, up the ridge and all the way to Demon Point, wait there until the waters recede or give myself over to them, letting all that I've conjured consume me.

After that first meeting, Copley's hand flying out

to welcome me into his house, his parents asked him to give me a tour. He took me from room to room, naming spaces: 'the living room', 'the den', 'the dining room', 'my parents' room', 'my room', 'the playroom'. He pointed at the basement from the top of the stairs in the kitchen, as if he didn't want to descend into its dull ivory glow.

I am responsible for administering his medication at breakfast and dinner, and I have no doubt that the pills are making him withdrawn, sour, flattening him, wrapping his movement in tight-wound muslin heavy with starch. Last night I thought I heard a noise from his room but when I went to check he was sound asleep, his body so rigid he might have been dead; even his eyelids were blast-furnace forged.

On the day of my arrival – a day that was, for me, also one of final departure – they made up a bedroom for me next to Copley's, a room among many that all feel like being trapped inside a series of squared-off, hollowed-out eggs with windows and doors, a clutch of people waiting to hatch out of their collective confinement. There is nowhere to go in this kind of rain, no way to travel except by car, which, despite their promises, I do not yet have at my disposal. From the beginning, at unpredictable times during the daylight hours I spend here alone, I have heard noises whose source I cannot locate: the sounds of distant construction, doors slamming, water running. The day after I came, Copley said to me in a whisper, even though the two of us were alone in the house, 'Things happen.'

'What things?'

'The furniture moves.'

I felt the hair on my neck stand up.

'What do you mean it *moves*?'

'At night. We go to bed and everything is normal and when we get up it's not.'

'Ghosts?'

'No,' Copley said. 'My parents think it's me. But it's not. It's *him*.'

'Who?'

'The man in the basement'.

My first thought was Krovik, but I knew it could not be possible. I have looked there myself, went down one evening when Julia was working, hunched over the strange tools and metal limbs, the case filled with glass eyes. 'See, the pupil is a camera. It doesn't have to look like an eye,' she explained, 'but it makes interaction less alienating.' I wonder if the boy might be inventing to cover his crime, seeing the components of his mother's work as a man with movement and agency. Or perhaps he is thinking in substitutions: a fantasy man in the basement in place of the only other man in the house: his father.

When I saw him that evening, I looked at Nathaniel Noailles sitting at his computer in the office created from the remaining spare bedroom, humming and sighing over his work, the swish and twirl of his chair, the rage in his shoulders, and wondered if he was altogether present. The following morning I listened to hear if there might be an off-key chord in the music of his voice, looked to see if the balance of color in his eyes and skin and hair betrayed a deeper instability, if it might be possible to imagine him sneaking around at night, moving sofas, blaming his tricks on the child. I know he does not want to live here, does not believe they should have moved from Boston, and is searching for a way to force their return.

As Copley said, things have, indeed, started to happen. One morning I found the faucet running in the kitchen sink and all the burners on the stove red hot, the freezer and refrigerator doors open on another. After a day of shopping – the four of us all going together on a Friday evening, as if a trip to the mall were a leisure activity – two loaves of bread went missing the next morning and the milk had all been poured into the sink, the cartons left dripping from the counter onto the floor. After that, Nathaniel took me aside.

'Copley's been having some problems. That's why he's medicated. That's why he goes to the doctor. We're trying to deal with it.'

I looked at Nathaniel's eyes, the cushions of soft skin around them, searching for deceit in his face.

'He tells me he hasn't done any of this.'

'He has problems with truth. With reality and fantasy. Dr Phaedrus—'

'I believe Copley, Nathaniel. Your son's not a liar.'

421

He looked at me as though he did not understand.

Each day I walk in the rain to pick up Copley from school. Each day the EKK guards at the Pinwheel Academy demand to see my identification and the letter from Julia and Nathaniel confirming that I am empowered to escort their son from school to home. Each day Copley says less to me, seeming more withdrawn, not as verbal. He holds my hand but speaks only when I ask him a question. We walk from school, through River Ranch, sometimes along Poplar Road, past the gravesite of my home, the city's construction stalled by the rain, and up Abigail Avenue. Alone in the house I make him a snack and read to him. He wants fantasy and horror. We finished *The Return of the King* and now he is demanding *Frankenstein*. I worry the book is too advanced for him, but he listens and does not fall asleep or squirm and after an hour of reading he sits to do his homework before dinner. He never complains. He never throws tantrums. Each day he does his assignments, checks his work, shows it to me, and if he is having problems, which is almost never, I try to send him in the right direction without giving him answers. Mistakes are ones of speed rather than ignorance. If I point out that an error has been made, most of the time he can find it and correct it on his own. In four decades of teaching, I can remember only one or two children as bright as Copley Noailles.

Each day during the week I make his dinner and give him his medication. I look at him and look at the pills and he looks at me. I smile in a way I hope communicates more than I feel I can say: I am giving you this poison because I have no choice, but I know it is doing you harm. He nods, takes the pills, and swallows.

In the last few days, the nocturnal disruptions have become more acute: dining room chairs pushed against the wall, windows opened and rain driving in, curtains and blinds torn down and cut into pieces, rugs rolled up and shoved into the fridge, all the cupboard doors in the kitchen opened, the television turned on, the stereo tuned to static, the art taken down and all the glass in the frames smashed.

'He's done this before,' Nathaniel says, 'this kind of furniture thing. He's an inventive child. We should have warned you. I feel like we've lured you into a living horror. That's what it's beginning to feel like to me. That's why I spend so much time at work, Louise. *My life at home is a living horror. Do you understand that?*' His voice is high and strained and his eyes bulge as he juts out his jaw at my face.

I shake my head and step backwards, trying to puzzle out what might be happening. 'I can go when I want. And if it gets too much, I *will* go, Nathaniel. But for now, I don't believe that Copley's doing any of this.'

'What do you *mean*?'

'I don't know what I mean, but I don't believe that a child like Copley could do half the things you think he's doing.'

When these conversations happen, Julia absents herself, leaving the room or simply refusing to speak, as if she also doubts her son is a midnight demon stalking his family.

Each morning I wake bracing for a new outrage. The vandalism was confined to the ground floor until yesterday, when I woke to find the contents of the linen cupboard emptied into the upstairs hall and spilling down the front staircase, sheets and towels twisted together into a long rope, tied at the end into what I can only describe as a noose. Copley could not have done it. The materials were tied too expertly, the noose too clear in its forma-tion: a functioning knot that slipped like rope and held fast when tugged. For a moment I thought of putting it all away, untying it and folding the sheets before anyone else was up, but then I decided that they *should* see, or at least that if Julia did, she would understand. Nathaniel told me he grew up boating with his father off Cape Cod. The man knows how to tie a knot.

When the sun comes out again, if it comes, how blinding this house will be, its white surfaces throwing light back in our faces. Julia insists that shoes are always removed on entering the house, to keep the floors white. A cleaner comes once a week, hooks up the hoses to the central vacuuming system, an inlet in each room, scrubs off any streaks or scuffs, dusts, wipes the mirrors and cupboards of fingerprints, arranges everything into perfect order. The cleaner speaks no English and I do not know where she is from, whether she might speak Spanish or Russian or Inuit, Arabic or Urdu or Kazakh. She works for a company that sends cleaners all over the city, a tribe of women who are known for their silence and efficiency, for their white slacks and red smocks and matching cars. After the first week, I stop trying to make conversation, allowing the woman, whose name is Di, to go about her business and finish her work. She does not look happy. She wants to arrive, to work, to eat a sandwich at noon, to go home at five, to come back the following Friday and repeat the pattern, as she must repeat it at other houses on other days of the week. I try smiling at her, but she does not smile back. Today I ask her if she would like a piece of the pumpkin bread I baked for Copley, but the woman shakes her head, says, 'Green card. I win lottery,' and goes back to work, tucking her artificially blonde hair back up under her blue cotton head-wrap. Next time we will not speak, not even nod in acknowledgement of each other. I must attend to Copley and nothing else. The boy requires all the attention I can muster. Not because he does anything wrong.

There is nothing wrong about him except what the pills I must administer are liable to do.

I call out to my mother but she no longer speaks to me. My people have gone deep, submerging themselves to wait out this era. I move in silence, with only my own voice to accompany my thoughts. Living in this house has changed my thinking, making it colder, harder, iced over, while a warmer current flows somewhere deep and still alive: I have to think in this way to stay alert, to stay alive, to watch out for the child. I try to sleep lightly, listening for sounds, but whoever or whatever is terrorizing this house does so in a way that never wakes me. I have tried to stay awake, sitting up in the chair in my room, reading a book, rewriting my account of the Freeman ancestors and Mr Wright, but I always falter, lids heavy-drooping, spine going late-wilt limp. In the rounded interior of my bedroom I have recurring dreams that my blood is being drained away, tubes tapped into my arms, snaking down and out of the room through the central vacuum system, tubes disappearing into the portal just above the slope where the wall slides into the floor.

Copley tells me the house did not look like this when they moved in: 'It was like other people's houses. My parents wanted it to look like our apartment in Boston. When I have dreams about being at home I'm still in the apartment. And then I wake up here.' He is unfailingly polite, reserved, self-contained, all of his processes and emotions hidden behind his face, which almost never betrays any emotion, not even pleasure or happiness. Expression of sentiment is unusual and confession of this kind truly rare. If he enjoys the food I prepare he does not show it, does not laugh at my jokes. I've learned not to take it personally, recognizing that Copley would be like this with anyone, and is just like this with his parents after I go to bed or when I leave them alone together for an hour in the evening. His voice is flat, monotonous, without affect. It is a house bled of joy, deprived of laughter, and except when I sing or turn on the stereo, a house without music. Di works in silence, the vacuum cleaner itself silent, its machinery hidden in the basement in a soundproofed cupboard the shape and size of a coffin. I move through these rooms lost in a space that feels as much mausoleum as maze.

Because the rain has been constant for weeks, apart from walking back and forth to school, Copley and I have been outside to play only once, for a walk in the woods. We looked at the old storm cellar, the ruins of the chimney and fireplace in the trees, and in the backyard the granite slabs marking the place where two bodies lie.

'Why are the stones over there if they're supposed to mark the sinkhole?' he asked.

'Out of fear they might also be consumed if the hole broadened out to take more of the land.'

'What are the stones for?'

'History.'

'I don't understand,' he said.

'They're for remembering. And you remember this, like I told you through the fence. Don't ever walk on the compost heap. It's like quicksand. It could swallow you up.'

We spend wet afternoons indoors occupying ourselves with drawing and reading. Each Thursday night, either Julia or Nathaniel takes the garbage cans out to the curb. Today, as the sun goes down, Copley and I watch the garbage trucks, one for household waste, the other for recycling, each truck equipped with a mechanical arm that extends, grips the container, lifts it in the air, raises it up over the truck's stomach of waste, and empties it before returning the bin to the ground, the driver never leaving the cab of the truck.

'Used to be, there were three or four men on each truck, one or two in front, one or two hanging off the back. Someday soon I bet there won't even be a driver. The truck'll drive itself, pick up whatever it sees fit to throw away, whether it's in a trashcan or not.'

Copley looks at me, eyes wide, hazel-green crystals surrounded by milk glass. 'Machines are smart,' he says, as if he knows something I do not. We go back to drawing on the floor of the playroom at the top of the house, the rain shifting its aim, peppering the windows with liquid shot.

'What are you drawing?' I ask, looking at his careful depiction of men in hats holding cartoon bombs out of doorways and windows, dropping them on an empty street.

'Terrorists,' he says.

'Why terrorists?'

'They're bombing things.'

'And what's that in the sky?' I ask, pointing to a small black mass of lines in the upper right-hand corner of the white page.

'One of our drones.'

'And what's the drone doing?'

'Bombing the terrorists.'

I remember when children drew gardens and parks: a band of green for the earth, flowers and trees sticking up straight, birds and squirrels and dogs, outlines of cloud, a personified sun, a band of blue at the top of each page to signify sky. Children today know too much, should be protected from some knowledge. He turns over the page and starts a new drawing, a room, a bed, a child in the bed, a door, fat legs, a fat body, a tall fat man with mechanical arms coming through the door, a tall fat man with mechanical arms dressed in a suit and carrying a briefcase who bears a certain resemblance to Nathaniel, the monstrous creature menacing the boy in his bed.

'Who's that?' I ask, pointing at the child in the drawing.

'A little boy.'

'And who's that?' I point at the figure with robotic arms.

'The man who moves furniture.'

The man who moves furniture: who ties nooses from bedclothes, lives in the basement, is born from the elements of Julia's workbench, who shadows the boy's nightmares as a mask for his father. I can see no other explanation, given the security of the house. We move freely within it, but any breach, any coming or going between inside and outside, would trigger alarms to bring down the neighborhood. No, I am convinced the monster is a man who may not even be conscious of what he is doing, who perhaps believes himself as blameless as a child.

A friday morning in late October. The vandalism evolves. If any part of me doubted Copley's innocence, this new development is something he cannot have done. As usual since coming to live with them, I am up first in the morning, showered, dressed, down the stairs to make my breakfast before the family is up. I empty buckets because the roofers have not or perhaps cannot come, the rain never stopping long enough to fix the leaks. I make coffee, falling back into habitual rhythms, looking out the kitchen window at the mess of muck where my house used to be, the work still stalled because of the weather. I grind the coffee in their slick black machine, boil water in a stainless steel electric kettle, brew it in a French press, drink it black, five minutes elapsed from pouring to reach the optimal temperature for drinking. I would read the paper but these people do not subscribe. Listening to news on the radio, I think about the day to come. I do not even notice what has happened until I open the white curtains in the white living room and see it, all that white furniture pushed up against the walls, and in great bright red arcs, gouts of ketchup sprayed across the floor, ranging from wall to wall, climbing up those egg-interior curves, crisscrossing and cross-hatching the white room.

I drop my coffee, hear the mug catch and smash, am aware of the warm liquid splashing against my legs, making brown marks on the white boards, a single drop flying up and landing on the back of the white couch. Copley could not have done this. I go back to the kitchen for a towel, return to wipe up my coffee, collect the pieces of mug, put them in the trash compactor before Julia notices, because the woman gets twitchy about breakages. It's only an inexpensive mug, white like all the other china and crockery, no decoration or embellishment on it, but Julia will have fits if she discovers one is broken. I bury the fragments under paper towels and food scraps.

To whom is the message directed, for message it must be? I can only think, given the noose on the stairs and now this, that it must be meant for me. But if it is, then why is it in the living room and not against my door? If meant for me, then surely it should be directed at me alone, instead of in the space that, not for nothing, people in these parts still call 'the family room'.

431

For all my talk of the dead, I do not believe in ghosts, not in the usual sense, but nonetheless I wonder if a kind of haunting is at work. From the kitchen I look at the place where the land lies in a dark depression, to the side of which rest the two granite slabs. I have not explained the spot to Nathaniel and Julia, never explained it to Krovik, but somehow the man understood it should not be touched, that to dig too close would tempt and tease an old and angry history. Through the veils of rain I can see the depression has changed: no longer concave, it has pushed upward, expanding, a boil on the earth craving a lance, all that dark river water trickling down, deeper waters rising to fill the half-filled void, drawing history back to the surface.

In the rain's lull I rush out under the eaves of the garage, stepping on land thick with unnatural lawn, and find a long leafless stick fallen from one of the cottonwoods. I poke at the swollen place where grass will not grow, disturbing that dark wound, and as I feel the stick penetrate the surface, sliding through a layer of fallen leaves, there is a sudden shift in tension, a trembling tug as it slips from my fingers and slides, sucked down fast by the earth.

*A Brief Analysis of My Present State of Mind*
*by Professor Julia Lovelace-Noailles*

*Intention:*
The following text I have written for myself and for
any future health professional I may need to consult,
as well as for my son, assuming I predecease him,
and any issue he may eventually produce. It is
a document both for my own improvement and a
historical curiosity for those I will eventually leave
behind, or for the scientific community, if my life
or my work is believed, ultimately, to hold any lasting
interest. Nathaniel, if you are reading this, do not;
it is not for you. Copley, if you ever read this, I hope
you do so in better health than you find yourself at
the moment. I know these pages may be painful for
you to read, but it is solely in the interest of forensic
truth that I say everything I do, my perspective being
but one of several possible.

*Immediate Concerns:*
1. Copley
2. Nathaniel (our marriage)

433

3. The ('new') house
4. My father
5. Nathaniel's relationship with his parents

*IMMEDIATE ACTIONS & POSSIBLE SOLUTIONS:*
1. Copley: talk therapy & psychopharmaceutical regime
2. Nathaniel/Marriage: couples therapy
3. The house: quotes for new roof and remedial work on siding
4. My father: investigate long-term care facilities, explore independent/assisted living
5. Nathaniel & his parents: encourage him to undergo individual therapy and sever all contact with his parents

*PERSONAL MEDICAL HISTORY:*
No surgeries. Natural childbirth. Occasional treatment for seasonal allergies. Less than half a dozen prescriptions for antibiotics over the course of my life to date, with no adverse effects. One broken toe, but no other serious bodily damage aside from a brief bout of tendinitis in my right foot at the age of twenty. At thirty-nine, I show no signs of menopause. Sex drive optimal, cycles all regular.

*CURRENT MEDICATIONS:*
No prescription medications taken. Multivitamin, Vitamin D3 supplement, Vitamin C and Zinc supplements during rhinovirus season.

*BELIEFS:*

1.  I am surrounded by crazy people (my computer tells me this is a passive-voice construction, but I cannot put the crazy people before myself; I am at the center of a community of madness, or incipient madness; I refuse to see the crazy people first, as those who define what I am or may yet be; I come first, I find myself, on this journey, suddenly surrounded by them, plagued, followed, pursued). My son is crazy, my husband may well be crazy, and even the woman we have hired to look after our son appears to be crazy. She tells me that history is ready to explode from out of our yard, from beneath the compost heap. I told Nathaniel I didn't think it was a good idea to hire someone who had been living illegally in a condemned structure without any utilities for goodness knows how long but he insisted that he felt a certain responsibility for the actions of his corporation, even those carried out by a division entirely separate from his own; he also said that he could see Copley had an immediate rapport with Louise and it might be just what we've been looking for to help him snap out of the strange behaviors that have arisen since moving from Boston. Although I have grown to like her and believe she is good for Copley, so far bringing Louise Washington into the house has done little to ameliorate my son's behavior, which remains robotic in a way I

cannot help thinking is intended, consciously or not, as a criticism of his mother, because it is my work that has brought us here, to this city and this house that we are growing to hate in our individual ways. (Nor does the medication seem to be having a positive effect. Quite the reverse, in fact: Copley's physical affect has become, if anything, less human the more medication he takes, and under Dr Phaedrus's supervision the doses have been steadily increasing.) Even I can now see that buying this house was a mistake. It was poorly built and poorly finished, and no amount of internal redecoration, of which we have done more than most would dare, is going to make this anything like the apartment in Boston we loved and where we were, I know, happy beyond our rights. Now that the roof has started to leak and the siding is coming away from the north-west corner of the house, I can see how this place could easily gobble up all of our savings, most of our disposable income, and leave us still unhappy within it, trapped in a house in a market where houses are not selling. Nathaniel complains that it does not feel like a home, but instead like a soundstage or series of hospital waiting rooms, and even though I often have a similar feeling, I resent him every time he voices these doubts. A house does not magically become a home. Goodness has to be put into it, weekly if not daily. We are too absent here, or at least Nathaniel is, spending more and more of his life in the office under the gaze of a boss whom I believe he desires as much as he fears, a woman who, along with this house and the weird jollity of the people in this city (despite the flood engulfing them), is making a formerly sensible man crazy. Thus, this belief is both simple and horrible: my child is mentally unwell, diagnosed with psychotic depression, and consequently medicated with pills that seem only to remove him further from my affections, and my husband is also apparently unwell. I have no proof for the latter presumption. These, in fact, are not beliefs so much as truths, of whatever quality or degree. The belief is this: that I am responsible in some way for their illness or apparent illness. Increasingly, I worry about my own sanity as well, as if the house itself, and the land on which it stands, were poisoning our minds. Nathaniel and I used to joke about people who might be 'certifiable', including his parents and my late mother; I can no longer joke about mental illness when my son is not just certifiable but *certified*, diagnosed with an illness his doctor says is likely to require long-term medication. He already has the thousand-yard stare of the medicated mind. Louise looks at him and says to me: 'There's nothing wrong with him that a daily walk in the woods and a little homegrown food won't cure.' I want to believe her homespun advice, but the rain does not stop, the gullies that were dry when we moved here a month ago are practically rivers, and I have had to change my route to work to avoid the spreading flood. How can I allow my child to go venturing out into the world on foot, even under Louise's supervision? Bridges have been washed out and five people have already died in the city, which, if we are to believe the aerial photography, is now a series of islands: some small, others large, surrounded by water that is alternately coursing and stagnant, the low-lying north–south highways turning into torrents, the neighborhoods around us a vast and spreading lake. Two bodies remain unrecovered. On the way to work I passed a half-submerged stretch of interstate. An island of overpass was the only dry spot and on the island was an encampment of tents and make-shift shelters. An inflatable boat appeared to be bringing more people to the site. I learned later that those are the homeless who have been displaced from their previous shelters *under* the overpasses and bridges, who had no choice but to escape the flood by going out into the rain. I dream of bodies floating through the city. Last night I dreamed that the unfinished foundation across the street became filled with corpses, a drain pulling all the flood's victims, the animals who walk on two legs as well as four, down into its depths.

2. My marriage is not what I believed it would be. I love my husband. I miss him during the days at work. I look forward to seeing him each evening. I look forward to seeing him in the morning in the moments before I open my eyes. But the man I want and hope to see is no longer the man I find before me. When I dream about sex I dream about him, the familiarity of his body, which is homey in a way that comforts rather than arouses: he is not an Adonis, not a man of great physical beauty; he does not go to the gym or run or do anything to look after his physical health; he has let himself go since we first met, when he was perhaps chubby, although hardly fat, a man of small stature who had never thought about diet or exercise and who, after the age of thirty, began as so many do to slip into the saturation of this country's appetite for overindulgence, walking only from one form of transportation to another (car to elevator, escalator to car, moving walkway to airplane, monorail to taxi), eating more calories than he needs but which his body has been trained to demand. I do not dream of hard-bodied men with chiseled features and deep tans. I dream of goodness and warmth and (what shall I call it?) *nominal* attractiveness, the qualities about Nathaniel that first drew me to him. The goodness I believe is still there, but the warmth has cooled, its energy drained by his obsession with what

he regards as the mistake our move from Boston entails. Our sex life is reserved but mostly still fulfilling; I supplement my needs in private, in the bath, and even, on one or two occasions, in the basement at night after everyone else has gone to bed, observed only by my machines, who, for all I know, will learn from their observation of my behavior. But even then I think of my husband, I visualize his face, imagine his mouth against my body, drawing tremors from my gut, turning the gears that make me arch my back, sensations I am able to summon more powerfully alone. (I don't know if this is his failing or mine, or if failure is not a factor in these phenomena, if it is simply a matter of chance and physiology united with behavioral psychology and cultural aversion: Nathaniel has a small, inexpert mouth, flinches when I look down the length of my body and nod, asking without speaking for what I most want him to do, what he is so bad at doing, but for which, even at his worst, he makes me long, warm wet human tissue being more desirable than cold slick silicon brought to life through an artificial power source.) And then, too often, when I do see him after these separations of space or consciousness or temporality, I find myself disappointed, not because of the way he looks or the person he is, but because he returns to the same narrative we now seem unable to escape: the house, and all that is wrong with the house. This disappointment and frustration has only surfaced since we moved from Boston. I cannot remember ever being truly disappointed with Nathaniel before the move, except in the weeks leading up to it, when I could see him already deciding we had made a mistake, second-guessing a decision I believed, and that I continue to believe, we reached together. He now says he never wanted to move; he claims he told me it was a bad idea, but I do not recall ever hearing him say such a thing. My own career may have spurred this migration, but I did not force it on Nathaniel, I did not dictate to him that we had to leave Boston. Rather, I presented it as an option, because my new job was in the same city as his own company's national headquarters and it seemed then (perhaps less so now) to present an ideal opportunity for us to progress. Granted, we would undoubtedly have advanced along different lines if we had remained in Boston, where there are more and objectively better universities than there are here, and where there are more and objectively more interesting other kinds of work Nathaniel might have done if he had chosen to move on from his company. When we talk to each other it no longer feels as though we are speaking the same language, or else we are using different dialects, always accusing the other of misinterpreting what we say. I misinterpret his panic

441

as aggression, he misinterprets my absorption with work as *froideur* and sexual disinterest, while I interpret, wrongly or rightly, his growing obsession with his own work as sexual attraction to his boss. There are moments when a silent and invisible interpreter seems present between us, when fluency flows once again and we understand each other as completely as two human agents with entirely private senses of language specific to their own socio-geographic and familial contexts can possibly manage. No one speaks the same language. This is a planet of X billion languages. There are, I would hazard, verbal *structures* and *vocabularies* – the things we call 'languages' – but the common speakers of any one of these will use the structures in different ways, bending and breaking them to fit their needs, and employ the vocabularies with their own private dictionary of associations and understandings that no one else will ever wholly understand. When two people understand each other in a way that feels genuine to both of them, even for a few minutes or hours (what a gift if they have years of this kind of understanding), it is something like a miracle. Nathaniel and I still have minutes, sometimes even whole hours, of what seems like near perfect understanding. I listen and believe that I understand. I reply and feel as though I am understood. There is no need for further explanation or elaboration or

442

rephrasing. In times like these the meanings conveyed are often simple: talk about transportation, about food, about schedules. The value of understanding such small matters is not to be underestimated, and knowing I can speak and be understood about the most basic actions and contents of our daily lives reassures me, pulling me back from the edge of feeling as though I am about to fall into a miasma of isolation, where only the machines I create can understand me because I have programmed them to speak and understand in the way I speak and understand. In these times of apparent fluency with Nathaniel, I have to concede this is only my *sense* of the tenor of our exchanges; I cannot speak for him since so often I cannot even speak *with* him. I have no idea whether he feels understood, or that he understands, or if he feels as though he is moving through a world in which he is the only true speaker of his own private language.

3. I believe that the house is a major part of the problem. The house is driving each of us insane. I am alone in the basement now, and think that I hear a noise, not from above, but from behind, as if it were coming from the ground itself, a churning thud, or series of thuds. I focus my attention on the computers in front of me and on the machine the computers direct. I give verbal commands, I

watch as the machine tries to complete them, learning from observation of its surroundings and from whatever it can discover online. I ask it to make me a cup of coffee and for the first time ever it completes the task, although the coffee is weak. As it delivers the coffee to me in a hand more finely articulated than my own, I hear a noise again, but instead of a deep thud like I heard a few minutes ago, this one is a high-pitched whine, almost mechanical itself, like a dentist's drill boring into enamel, the screech of metal against some softer substance, shrill and wet. I listen at the walls but the noise stops, or my sense of it stops. I look at the machine and it looks back at me, tilting down its head, turning left to right, waiting for me to tell it what to do as it listens and observes the room, the noise, and me. I ask it if it hears a noise, knowing that its auditory senses are more acute than my ears. 'Yes,' it says in Copley's recorded voice, 'I hear a noise.' I ask it if it can identify the source of this noise. It pauses, turning from side to side as we wait in silence. 'I think it is a drill,' it says. If it could walk, I might ask it to investigate, although there is nothing here I cannot see: the basement is a white space, its limits visible, nothing hidden except the pantry, and I can look behind me into its space and be sure there is nothing inside but empty shelves, which I know I should fill in case of emergency. There is no one here but my machines and me. If there is a drill, it is coming from a distance, perhaps all the way from the next-door neighbors' basement, but not from this house. Nathaniel, Copley, and Louise are all upstairs in bed. I heard a noise and the machine confirmed what I thought I heard, although that proves nothing except that I am not hearing imaginary sounds, only sounds whose origin I cannot locate. But then there is the greater question, the problem of the continued disruption to the house. Copley has the strength and strangeness to move furniture, but the noose of bedclothes seems beyond the capabilities of a boy who, for all his intelligence and physical control, failed to learn to tie his shoes until last year, a boy who has always had difficulties with buttons and laces and ties, who prefers zippers and snaps and Velcro. There are, then, only two other people who might have tied the noose, and, assuming Copley is wholly innocent, moved the furniture on countless occasions, wasted food, electricity, and water (despite the solar tiles the first power and water bills were astonishingly high). The two suspects are Louise and Nathaniel. I should, by virtue of loyalty, assume Louise must be the culprit, except that the first incident occurred before she came to live with us and it seems not only unlikely but also impossible that she could have entered the house then, bypassing the alarm.

All this means that my husband must be the one who is terrorizing us, and yet at each new assault Nathaniel looks as wounded as I feel, though unlike me he believes – and is very vocal in his belief, even faced with the newest incident – that it *must* be Copley because there can be no other logical explanation. I wonder about the rigor of his logic. And then I realize with horror that there is another possible suspect: me. I work my way through the front-line symptoms of schizophrenia, but believe myself clear and healthy.

a.  I don't hear voices; my thoughts do not echo in my own mind.
b.  I have no delusions of control, no belief that anyone is modifying my thoughts: injecting their own, taking mine away or disseminating them for anyone else to access.
c.  I do not believe that I have any symptoms of heightened or altered perception.

And yet the strangeness of the events that have taken place since we moved here is so acute, any explanation so impossible to reach, that I am moved to wonder whether I might be suffering from some dissociative disorder, a derangement that might allow me to commit these domestic atrocities, if this is not too strong a word for what is happening, and have no conscious awareness of my actions. The ketchup is a mystery like all the others, because we never have ketchup in the house. I look through my recent financial records, hoping to find evidence of a purchase at a grocery or convenience store, but there is nothing on the statement I cannot remember, and no occurrence of ketchup on any of the recent grocery receipts. I feel relieved and at the same time long to find proof that it *is* me who has done these things because it would mean it is *not* Nathaniel and it is *not* Copley: to implicate myself is to exonerate them, to be able to go on believing in their goodness as people, in their health and sanity and morality. When I heard Nathaniel interrogating Copley about the most recent bout of vandalism all I could do was remain mute, on the verge of shouting out – although I do not believe it for a moment – 'I did it!' I want to love my husband, I do love my husband, but with each new event of defacement and disorganization I believe more firmly in only two possible explanations: my husband is either sick or evil, either profoundly mentally unwell, or a cruel genius, so capable of deceit that he only ever looks innocent.

4. Fathers are the root of all evil. Nathaniel does not come from a healthy family: I know what his father did to him when he was a boy. I know that charges should have been pressed a

long time ago; if Nathaniel had the courage he could still do so and, if nothing else, put to rest the memories that plague him. Last night when I came to bed he was already asleep. I closed our bedroom door, locked it, took a shower, dried off, put on pajamas, turned out the light in the bathroom and crept across to our bed, but Nathaniel was already snoring. I slipped under the sheet and bedspread, rolled up my earplugs and stuffed them into my ears. I closed my eyes, I tried to go to sleep. I counted backwards from 1000 in French and knew when I was still awake at 322 that the counting was not going to work, Nathaniel's snores punctuating every three or four numbers. Then, around 200, he turned over onto his side, back to me, the snores stopping, and I never reached 0. I dreamed that Nathaniel was on top of me, inside me, but I could not open my eyes. I touched his back and buttocks, gripped his arms, trying to shove him off, and although I knew it was him he felt unfamiliar: harder, thinner, muscular, his skin smooth where it should have been hairy. I dreamed that a hand was clapped over my throat and the sex was brief and brutal and painful. I woke up at 2:37 to the feeling of a distant thud, a vibration rather than a noise, and sat up in bed. I was wet and my pajama pants were around my knees. The dream was not only a dream. Nathaniel has never done this to me before, at least so far as I am aware. Perhaps he thought I was awake – perhaps a part of me was. But on waking I was alone, the covers all in order, as though Nathaniel had slipped out of bed and smoothed them back into place. I waited, breathing fast, wondering if I should go investigate, until finally I threw my legs out of bed and tiptoed across the floor. Our bathroom was empty and dark, the door to the hall standing open. The landing was dark, the doors to Copley and Louise's rooms closed, the rain spitting against the windows. The door to Nathaniel's study was closed, the light on inside. I pulled the plugs from my ears and held them in my hand. I thought I heard him typing. I knocked on the door but he did not answer, and at that time of night I did not want to wake anyone else. I was hyperventilating from shock, and as I walked down the front stairs, trying to steady my breath, I saw a dark shape in the shadows of the foyer, or perhaps not a shape but only a shadow. I stopped and the shape moved, disappearing into the dining room, although I heard no noise accompanying the movement. For a long time I stood on the stairs, unable to move, certain I saw the shadow return, shift, move backwards and forwards, sway and convulse, although it had an indistinct outline, amorphous and globular, and resembled nothing so much as condensed smoke. As I stood watching the silent shape I

449

was reminded of Nathaniel's stories of his father, which he told me only after we were married, about how he lost certain senses when his father entered his bedroom at night, how his vision became dulled, outlines blurring, his hearing dampened, voice choked, tongue ashen-tasting, those four senses receding as his somatic senses became more acute, making him painfully aware of his bodily position, the heat of his father's own body, the sharp and dull pains Nathaniel suffered, a hand clapped over his mouth, sealing shut his lips, another one over his eyes. His father raped him repeatedly. I do not think Nathaniel has called it this, but there is no question in my mind that rape is what happened, whether or not penetration occurred. He told me that in the days following such events, the sensory dampening continued, so that everything and everyone became blurred: he could only see his father, the great man and scholar, as a dark shape moving through the house like a thundercloud. My own father was never cruel or abusive or criminal in the way that Nathaniel's father was and still threatens to be, but that is not to say my father is innocent of any wrongdoing, for how can any parent be completely good? His failure was to pretend, even though I, at six years old, found my mother hanging from the chandelier in the front hall of our house, that Mom had left him for another woman, a fiction that hit upon a kind of truth, although I was too young to understand it at the time. He did not attend the funeral and prevented me from attending; all the events of her death and mourning were placed in the hands of her two sisters and grieving parents while my father and I played a grotesque farce according to which Mom, the youngest and brightest of her family, had run off to live in San Francisco. Young as I was at the time, there were moments when I believed this might be true, thinking that to hang oneself in the home was to effect a kind of transcontinental migration of the mind into the body of someone else. I imagined Mom in a body almost recognizable as her own, but with red hair instead of brown and thin curves instead of round ones. I was ten before I understood completely, comprehensively, that my mother was in her family plot in Portsmouth, reverting to dust, and not living a queer new life with another woman on the opposite coast, and when I realized this was the truth, I began to hate my father for persisting in the fiction of her leaving him. As his own health declines, it is difficult not to feel sympathy for the blow my mother's suicide struck, but I still cannot bring myself to want him anywhere near me. A visit once a year is more than enough because each time I see him there is a moment when the old fiction gets aired again, with him speculating about the life he imagines Mom leading in San Francisco, 'in the Marina District, probably,' he'll sneer, 'with her new "family"'. I huff and lose my temper and say to him, 'Enough already, dad. She killed herself and I found her. I saw the body. It had nothing to do with us. She was sick.' I wondered, looking at the shifting darkness below me in the hall last night, whether I too might be sick, or if it is in fact my husband, as I believe now in the daylight (such light as there is in this endlessly rain-shadowed city), whose illness is undoing us all. At last the shape disappeared and after several more minutes of standing, listening to water drop into buckets scattered around the house, sounds I had not registered up until that point because they have become, in the last week or so, a constant accompaniment to our lives, I heard a noise upstairs. But instead of moving toward the noise, I went down to the ground floor, circling through the living room, the dining room, the den, the kitchen, looking out onto the back porch, expecting to find some new outrage, the furniture stacked up on itself, the food in our refrigerator thrown on the floor, shit smeared across the walls. There was nothing. Everything was in order, the refrigerator humming but no other noise, no movement. The lights in the basement were off, the doors locked, the security system armed. I made a cup of warm milk and drank it in the dark, holding myself, trying to decide how I would address the events of that night the next morning. When I was ready I went back upstairs by the rear staircase, found darkness and silence, and the door to our bedroom ajar. Inside, Nathaniel was in bed, snoring, and the sight of him there, where I knew he *had not been* only half an hour before, made my legs soften, my spine curve in on itself. I slumped against the wall for a moment, listening, still gripping my earplugs, and then went back to bed, although I could not sleep again and got up first this morning, determined not to have any time alone with him, no moment when I could look at my husband and ask what he was doing, why he was walking the house at night, why he fucked me when I was sleeping. Then I realized I had no proof he was doing anything of the kind, except my belief that he was not in the bed when I woke in the middle of the night, that my own body was wet, that I had both a dream and a lingering physical sensation that suggested we had been intimate. I have incontrovertible proof for only one conclusion: last night *I* was the one walking the house, seeing phantoms that might or might not have been there.

5. Mothers, I know, are not always good.

  a. I have difficulty saying that my mother was bad. She was depressed, certainly, and,

453

given what I have been able to extract from her surviving sisters, she was also in all likelihood suffering from some form of what is now described as bipolar disorder. My aunts, Cassandra and Helen, told me only last year about the way my mother fell into a prolonged depression when, although she was accepted to Smith, my grandmother refused to let her go, instead keeping her home to help look after their father. 'Isidora was the brightest of the three of us,' Helen told me, 'and no one deserved to go to college more than she did.' 'Such a good student, always,' Cassandra said, 'never missed a day of school. She even timed the chickenpox to occur over summer vacation between second and third grades.' But instead of going to college, as she should have done, preparing for a career in any of the subjects in which she had excelled as a girl, she stayed home and looked after her father, a New England patriarch who had inherited all his money, the baby of his own family, spoiled and moody and incapable of even making coffee for himself. My mother and grandmother took it in shifts to look after him, tending to illnesses that were never diagnosed but always excruciating: pains in his legs and feet, pains in his back, a persistent cough, a general malaise that kept him orbiting his bedroom and study for thirty years, moving from bed to couch to the bathroom down the hall, almost never changing out of pajamas and dressing gown and slippers. My mother and father met on the beach one summer, or at least that is the version I know from my father. My aunts have no idea how the two met: 'Your father came to the house one day and asked for Isidora's hand. Our parents were many things, stubborn, backward looking, but they were not inherently cruel. They could see that Chilton and Isidora were in love and our father gave his consent,' Helen explained, although Cassandra interrupted: 'You could see it was somewhat grudging. Helen says they weren't cruel, and perhaps that's true in a way, cruelty was not the overriding character of their interactions with us, but they were certainly capable of cruelty. I felt the willow switch more than once, and when I brought home my first beau, who went on to be president of a bank and later a state senator, my father escorted him out the front door because his shoes weren't shined.' My mother's manic spells, my aunts told me, only came after the marriage, when my parents set up house in Portsmouth, my father driving to work in Durham while my mother tried to keep order in a house that needed constant attention; a house, I cannot help thinking, not so unlike the one Nathaniel and I now own: recently built, but already falling down. 'It was the house that drove her mad,' Cassandra continued, 'trying to keep up something that never should've been built in the first place, at least not where it was, in the middle of a *swamp* for heaven's sake.' 'It doesn't work that way,' Helen interrupted, 'mental illness, I mean. A place can't make a person crazy. Crazy is in the blood, in the genes, I mean look at Daddy, Cassandra. Crazy is a wind that blows through the generations, not just a momentary storm. Your mother had her first breakdown after you were born, Julia. Terrible post-partum blues, and then when you started walking, the manias returned. She was so worried you'd walk yourself into harm that she tied you down in the crib and flew round the house taping and retaping foam padding on every corner, sharp or dull. Your father was beside himself. He tried to talk sense into her, and managed to do so to a certain extent.' 'The depressions just got *worse*, Helen,' Cassandra interrupted. 'When the mania went it never came back, but Isidora kept sinking deeper and deeper into that swamp until she couldn't see any way out of it except to hoist herself up by the only means she could find.' The image shocked me, not least because I had always thought of my mother's suicide as an act of aggression against my father and me; I had only occasionally stopped to think that we might not have played a part in her actions except as extras to fill out the back of the stage in a crowd scene, powerless to revise the conclusion she wrote without ever consulting the two of us. Even before she died, I grew up without a mother. For the first six years of my life, there was a woman who lived in my house, who lifted me from my cot in the morning, washed me in the bath, brushed my hair, put me in immaculate dresses, fed me bland food, and tied me to chairs, put me in playpens and never allowed me to go outside unless I was with her, wrapped my head and arms in foam padding tied with elastic bandages, little bells glued to the backs of my shoes and slippers so she could always hear where I was if she lost track of me for a moment. Her name was Isidora Crutcher Lovelace. I survive her. And what she was, what she did to me, I think now, was no fault of her own.

b.  For a portrait of truly bad mothering, one need look no further than Nathaniel's mother. When I first met Ruth and Arthur Noailles, neither said anything to me directly, and up until our wedding day Nathaniel's father never spoke to me; even since then we speak only telegraphically, yes-or-no questions, brief greetings and farewells. I know the man is evil and I will have him nowhere near my child. I encourage Nathaniel not to see them, and finally decided Copley would never see them again, not until he is old enough to defend himself, by which time Arthur, I hope, will be dead. All real communication has always been through Nathaniel's mother, who dismissed me on first sight as 'a backwoods tomboy', and suggested he could do better just by throwing his hand inside any of the sorority houses on campus and grabbing the first plaid skirt that presented itself. Apart from the many horrors Nathaniel himself has told me about his mother's behavior, there is one story I have heard only from his brother, Matthew, and which, at Matthew's request, I have not discussed with Nathaniel. Matthew confided in me in the hope that it would help me appreciate things about Nathaniel that perhaps even he himself does not understand. I am still of two minds about whether it would help him to know the story, or do him more irreparable harm. He knows his mother subjected him to analytical interrogation recorded on a daily basis from the moment he was old enough to hold a coherent conversation, and that these 'sessions' fed directly into her published research. What he does not seem to remember is that in his earliest years she all but used him as a subject of psychological experimentation, while Matthew looked on, bewildered. The experiments were a variation on others, undertaken earlier in the century, in which children were exposed to adults beating up an inflatable doll and then themselves given the chance to play with the same doll. 'In our mother's case,' Matthew explained to me, 'she experimented only on Nathaniel. Although I suppose it's possible she did the same thing to me when I was very small and I have no memory of it, or have merged the memory of my own experience with the memories of watching Nathaniel make his way through these set-ups. In Mom's version, she and Nathaniel, who was three at the time, made a doll together, the size of an adult man. They stuffed newspaper into panty hose to make legs, which were then placed inside a pair of my father's cast-off khaki slacks. They filled one of dad's old thermal underwear shirts with more newspaper to make a torso and arms, then clothed it in one of dad's cast-off dress shirts. This was all pretty straightforward, nothing very sinister, and they were doing it around Halloween, "making a scarecrow" for the front porch, as my mother put it. It

459

was with the making of the head that things turned weird. They inflated a pink balloon and covered it with papier-mâché, which was allowed to harden and dry before being painted a sickly flesh color, and carefully pasted on a photocopied image of dad's face, taken from a recent academic portrait, so the scarecrow was explicitly an effigy of our father. In this whole process, I wasn't allowed to participate. They did it on the back porch and I was locked in the kitchen, told to do my homework, even though I was too young to have any. When the scarecrow was finished, my mother sat the figure upright in a lawn chair and looked at it for a long time, while Nathaniel also looked, and then she said to him, "Sometimes I get so angry with your father. And you know what I do when I get angry? I want to hit him." There was a baseball bat on the porch and she suddenly picked it up. "I'm feeling angry with him now," she said, and she took a swing at the scarecrow's head, which was attached to a broomstick that had been shoved into the torso. The papier-mâché head, brittle as it was after drying, cracked open like a piñata. She hit it again and again until it was in shreds, and then she started to punch the stuffed body, tearing it apart and strewing the newspaper all over the porch while Nathaniel watched. Our mother was in a frenzy and Nathaniel looked like he didn't know what to think. When she was finished, she smoothed back her hair and said, "Oh dear, it looks like we'll have to start all over." So they began the process from the beginning, but unbeknownst to Nathaniel there was a second head already prepared, which she brought out from a box in the corner of the porch. When the second scarecrow effigy was complete, seated in the lawn chair, she excused herself, leaving Nathaniel alone with the simulacrum of his father and the baseball bat, which was too big and too heavy for him to handle. He tried to pick it up but couldn't swing it, and then he noticed a smaller bat, a toy plastic one, on the other side of the porch. He went for the plastic bat and ran at the scarecrow, walloping its head with the pasted-on image of our father's face until it began to crack apart. When it failed to break in the same way as the first one, he dropped the bat and pulled the scarecrow onto the floor and began stomping all over it while my mother watched from the kitchen, taking notes the whole time. As I remember it, this happened once a week, usually on Friday afternoons, for more than six months. When it got too cold to do it on the porch, she relocated to the basement, and the scarecrow turned into Santa

Claus, and then the Easter Bunny, and finally Uncle Sam. Sometimes the figure had my father's face, but sometimes it had Mom's, or even mine, and with each subsequent iteration of the game, my mother's beatings and Nathaniel's abuse of the dolls became more violent, until, by the end of it, they burned two effigies of dad in the garden on the Fourth of July, while he was at an academic conference in New York. When the fires burned out, smoking fragments of material were strewn around the lawn and my brother, who hadn't even turned four, was sobbing uncontrollably.' After Matthew told me about these 'experiments', I went looking through Ruth's publications for any indication that she might have used her findings, such as they were, and came across a long article she published in the early 1980s, in which she claimed to have undertaken a similar study on a group of thirty children.

c. Nathaniel and I came together, in part, as survivors of our childhoods. We described ourselves to each other in those terms. And in leaving Boston we are both, in our ways, fleeing from our parents. I believe that I am a good mother. I believe that I am neither like my depressive mother nor my abusive mother-in-law. I believe that I am nurturing and fair, and that the ways I have

involved Copley in my work are not exploit-
ative. He enjoys recording the lexicon and
we discuss the meanings of words that are
new to him. As a result, his vocabulary is
far beyond what is normal for his age, as
though there is anything truly 'normal' in
this world of constant and subtle and highly
individualized variation. Yet I wonder if I
have bewitched myself into believing that
I am good. Perhaps I work too hard,
perhaps I should stay home instead of
trying to have a career, although the idea
fills me with dread. I would die if I gave
up my work. I wonder if the ways I have
involved him in the production of my
research, ways that I tell myself are merely
temporary, because his voice will be replaced
in time with the voice of someone else, a
professional, someone paid to express words
in a neutral, natural way, are in fact forms
of exploitation no less serious if less
disturbing than what Nathaniel's mother
did to him. I hear noises and I ask the
machine to confirm what I believe I hear;
I fail to trust my own senses, and, on some
occasions, the machine is unable to confirm
what I think I have heard, or even that there
was anything *to* hear: 'I can hear you
breathing,' it says in Copley's fragmented
voice. 'But can you hear anything else? Can
you hear any noise that I am not making?'

I ask. It thinks for a moment, looking at my hands, my body, I even stand up in front of it so it can have a clear view of my entire person, and know I am not making a noise under the counter, and then it says, 'No, I cannot hear any other noise.' I check its sound sensors and, holding my breath and keeping my body completely still, confirm that they register nothing. If I am hearing noises that do not exist, then there must be something amiss in the way my own brain is firing, even if it is not mental illness as such. I hear noises, I see moving shadows, and I have no way to confirm these phenomena are 'real' in the sense of their occurring in a way that others would be able to verify, and not just manifested by my mind. When I sleep do I sleep soundly, or do I rise from the bed and fly through the house, putting my hands to mischief I never remember when I wake? No. I would leave behind evidence for my waking self. I have to believe that if I were the agent of our distress, there would be a sign: a trail of crumbs leading me back to my own guilt. There is no such trail, at least not one pointing in my direction.

6. I fear my husband and I fear for Copley. Nearly a week has passed since I began this document, the night when I believed I woke to find myself

alone in bed, when I went in search of answers and found only the dark shape at the bottom of the stairs. When I spoke to Nathaniel about it the next morning, he flew into a rage: 'You're accusing me of rape,' he said. 'I am accusing you of nothing. I am asking you if we had sex last night.' 'I was working. And no, we didn't have sex. I wouldn't – you have to believe I would never violate you, Julia.' I wish I could believe him. After that morning, when everything was in order, the house calm for a brief period, the incursions have now resumed. Nathaniel looks at me as if I were the guilty party, while I look at him in the same way, more convinced with each passing day that I must be right. The changes I now find each morning have turned from the dramatic to the subtle, so that I wonder even if they are intentional. A brush that I am sure I left next to the sink in the bathroom I find lying on top of a stack of my sweaters in the walk-in closet the next morning. The long-missing window keys suddenly appeared in a drawer, and windows that have been closed end up open, rain flashing in through the screens to soak the floors. Doors I am sure I have locked are unlocked in the morning – not open, but susceptible to opening. We all come home one day, the four of us having gone out together to a movie, to find the back door unlocked and a candle burning in the living room next to a

465

framed photo of Copley. I do not remember lighting the candle, nor do I remember the candle being next to his photograph, but Nathaniel assures me it was just an oversight, forgetfulness, because he and I are both so busy. (Later I ask Louise and she shrugs, looks concerned, says she does not remember the candle even being in the living room. During the movie, I recall, Nathaniel excused himself to buy more popcorn. He was gone for almost half an hour and then returned empty-handed, saying he'd been to the restroom.) On the weekends, there are endless phone calls from numbers I do not recognize. Whenever one of us answers, there is a brief pause before the caller hangs up. I have checked the numbers and they all belong to payphones, scattered across the western half of the city, none of them more than a mile from our door. I feel my gut contract every time the phone rings, and threaten to have it disconnected. I know that Nathaniel cannot be making such calls, but perhaps, I think, it is unrelated to the other 'events'. All of them, it seems clear to me, he *could* have done, and not only that, given the other factors, he *must* have done. What I do know, and what I cannot ignore, is that it is my duty to protect Copley from a father who, not an hour ago, hissed into my ear, 'I hate that kid. I'm gonna kill him.'

His wife believes he is being driven to collapse by Maureen McCarthy and by the expectations of working at his company's national headquarters, but in fact Nathaniel has found himself distorting the weight of expectation he is facing so he can spend longer hours in the office that has become, along with the work itself, a refuge and release from the horrors of home, even though the nature of his work produces a certain amount of distress. The longer he is on the project, marveling at the genius of Maureen's vision for a criminal-labor populace subject to a form of permanent incarceration either inside or outside the walls of a prison, providing units of production for EKK while minimizing their criminal activities, the more it seems to make sense. Perhaps, he thinks, some people simply are criminal in a fundamental, immutable way that, for all he knows, might even persist at the genetic, cellular level: a selfish impulse passed down through the generations, across continents, compelling bearers of whatever gene it might be to take what is not theirs. He will find ways to safeguard against any exploitation in the system, to ensure that those who are innocent remain untouched, to allow for redress if miscarriages of justice occur. It will be important to retain the possibility of total rehabilitation. Assuming criminality might in fact be innate and the first visible crime committed a form of self-identification by the criminal that he *must* enter the corrections rehabilitation system (in other words to take up his rightful place, a place reserved for him, in which his own purpose in the world becomes clear), then the permanent monitoring of anyone who has been convicted of a crime, even after they have served their sentence, seems not just logical, but natural. It is the only way truly to protect the law-abiding, who are themselves, of course, also a natural group. Nathaniel has taken to heart one of Maureen's favorite maxims: *Anyone who doesn't believe in freedom at eighteen is a fascist. Anyone who doesn't believe in security at forty is a criminal.*

The moment he is alone in the company car, pulling out of his garage, he can begin to feel the agitation and anger that have accumulated in the hours at home disperse. Even though he is ignored by his wife and son (who do not wave from the window, never mind stand outside and wish him well the way he and his brother did when Arthur Noailles left each morning; whatever their private feelings about the man, they maintained a performance of respect), watching the garage door go down, smelling the filtered air come through the vents, a recorded female voice welcoming him by name and reminding him to fasten his seatbelt, the hatred towards his son that has been growing since before the move begins to settle into a feeling closer to annoyance, disinterest. He will speak with Julia about asking Dr Phaedrus to boost the dosages again and increase the therapy sessions to twice a week. The EKK health insurance is generous and, even if it were not, they can easily afford whatever it takes to get the boy behaving like a normal child again, before there is any further disruption at school or damage to the home. There can be no question that Copley is the one at fault, the little brat marching through their lives with his automatic movements. It is nothing but sociopathic behavior – the daytime manifestation of the chaos he unleashes at night. If it doesn't stop soon, Nathaniel is going to have to take more serious action: an outside lock on Copley's bedroom door, for instance, or, if Julia won't agree to that, then hidden surveillance cameras, whatever it takes to prove to his wife that their son is the monster in their midst.

He turns on soft ambient music, and to avoid the flooded neighborhoods takes the freeway hot lane (faster commute, nominal cost, no junkers or trucks), arriving in only twenty minutes at his reserved parking space in the executive underground garage. Artworks hang on the concrete walls and, if he is late for a meeting, one of the attendants will park the car for him and he can

469

dash from the driver's seat through the palm-scanning barrier and into the elevator that takes him to the twentieth floor, his oasis of gray short-pile carpeting, potted plants, and glass doors that slide open and closed with the wave of a hand over motion sensors and never so much as a whisper of sound.

Because she worked overtime last night to help him finish the bi-weekly report of their division's progress towards identification of 'insourceable' manufacturing, he has brought Letitia a bouquet of flowers. It is not even eight but she is already at her desk, smiling, professional, grateful, he suspects, for a job with benefits. He knows he should find a way to help her advance out of the lower ranks of administration and into a managerial position; she is well educated, intelligent, makes no mistakes with dictation, her spelling and grammar and typography are all close to flawless. But already he feels reliant on her and does not want to risk a replacement less well versed in the organization and expectations of the headquarters' hierarchy. She has noted all the birthdays of important colleagues in his calendar, reminds him that a small token should be given, makes suggestions for appropriate gifts, undertakes the ordering on his personal credit card and keeps the receipts, reminding him they all count as tax-deductible business expenses, which he should not fail to have his accountant claim next spring.

In the last several weeks, despite his misgivings,

he has taken to phoning his mother each morning out of a sense of desperation. She has booked him a regular slot in her schedule.

'Hello, Nathaniel. You sound hungover.'

'I'm not hungover. I didn't sleep well.'

'Is your wife still snoring?'

'Yes, Julia still snores, but so do I.'

'What have I told you about spreading the blame around, Nathaniel? Look to the source. The source is lying next to you in bed each night. You need to put your foot down and reclaim your place as head of the household. I always said that your wife was one of these forward women who thought that because she has a career she can also subvert the traditional hierarchies that are in place for the very good reason that they work: gender hierarchies keep order, prevent chaos, and let everyone know where they stand, not only in relation to each other, but to the rest of the world. The only blame you bear is in failing to maintain your position in the hierarchy.'

'It's difficult. They've formed such a cohesive block. Every time I try, they stand together. There doesn't seem to be a way around them.'

'Divide and conquer, Nathaniel. You need to separate the child from his mother and enact the kind of discipline necessary to restore order to the family unit. And get rid of the nanny if you can. Remove the person from the home who is disturbing its balance. Everything was fine before you hired her, wasn't it?'

'Not exactly fine.'

'But it sounds like things have gotten much, much worse since she moved in.'

'Yes, I suppose that's true.'

'Then you have to get rid of her.'

'And what do we do about vacations and after school?'

'You've told me your financial footing is sound. So enroll the child in day care during vacations and hire a babysitter for after school. In time, once order is restored, you might think about an au pair – but it should be a *young* woman, someone you can control, not an older person who thinks of herself as your equal or even your superior, which is clearly what this Washington woman thinks. I understand you were acting out of desperation and guilt when you hired her, but pay her a severance and end it. Promise me that you'll act on this.'

'I'll act on it, Ruth.'

'And remind me who you are.'

'I am Nathaniel Noailles.'

'Go on. Start over.'

'I am Nathaniel Noailles. I am the head of my house, husband to my wife, father to my son. I make the decisions, I steer the ship, I cut the path through the forest.'

'Now, tell me, have you still been having those dreams?'

Most of the day is devoted to reading a report on how much EKK spent globally on paint and paintbrushes in the last year. The figure is higher than he could have imagined and it occurs to him, from previous research, that prison labor produces the majority of all paint and paintbrushes on the market in the country, which means, in all likelihood, that EKK is effectively paying either the government or some rival corrections corporation for paint and supplies it could be producing in its own prisons at a much lower cost. A day does not pass without him discovering a fact of this kind. In the end the question will be: what are the things that inmates can produce that will both save and make the most amount of money for the corporation? Paint is unlikely to be the answer, although it is a good place to begin. Circuit boards, telecommunications equipment, these are also possibilities, but the area that excites him most is the possibility of prisoners manufacturing domestic law enforcement drones, which, if his research is correct, could be mass-assembled in relatively little time, equipped with surveillance and other equipment, including crowd-control taser and baton rounds, and either used by EKK itself or sold on to local governments across the country and around the world. Extraordinary machines, some no larger than a hummingbird, once they reach cruising altitude they are as silent as the glass door to Nathaniel's office.

In the process of undertaking this vast research project, Nathaniel has begun to have other ideas as well, about a new regime of prison life that would introduce more regimentation and restriction: requirements that prisoners rise at five in the morning regardless of the season, and that they work a ten-hour day with lights out at eleven in the evening. In the hours when they are not manufacturing or sleeping, they will be given cleaning duties around the prison and compulsory education, as well as a total of one hour for eating, forty-five minutes for personal hygiene, and thirty minutes for religious observance, all at appointed and immovable times. Their days will be spent in monastic silence, with speaking restricted to working and religious hours and even then only when necessary for clarification, compliance, or ritual. Periods of hygiene, cleaning, and eating are to be conducted in silence. Any infraction will lead to a sixty-day extension of their sentence (a fact, Nathaniel is pleased to note, which is bound to result in higher profits for EKK). There is no place for recreation in Nathaniel's new schedule, the idea being that the cleaning duties will be physically strenuous, requiring the lifting of large buckets of water, scrubbing, mopping, and sweeping. In the past, in the barbaric history of this country, prisoners were punished through pain. In the enlightened present, they are disciplined through a curtailment of rights and freedom, and through the enforcement of productive labor. If that is not progress he does not know what is.

Nevertheless, one thing begins to concern Nathaniel. In an age in which so many people – the free, the innocent – struggle to live comfortable lives, prisoners under his notional executive supervision might, in fact, be better off than many of the people outside, so that committing a crime and submitting oneself to punishment could be seen by the underprivileged as a way of having an *improved* life: more stable, better fed, better housed, and of longer duration than would ever be possible for them if they remained free.

Late in the day a memo circulates from the Vice-President of American Operations. In the clearest possible language, it suggests that all employees registered to vote should, in the upcoming election, tick the box for the candidate who is on record as looking favorably upon corporations such as EKK. Failure to elect the right candidate from the right party could, the memo explains, imperil the jobs of countless EKK employees, from the bottom all the way to the top. 'If security is what you want,' the memo concludes, 'then defense of your very own job security should be at the heart of your voting choice.'

On his way home the traffic is so heavy that even the hot lane is slow, and as Nathaniel creeps along he looks across to the encampment of homeless people on an island of overpass to the north, surrounded by floodwaters. They have erected tents and makeshift shelters. A fire burns in a trashcan. Although they would be better off inside, the homeless shelters – those that have survived in the current economy – are all over-crowded. He makes a mental note to check on the rigor of municipal vagrancy laws.

'I am Nathaniel Noailles,' he says to himself, repeating the mantra his mother has taught him. 'I am the head of my house, husband to my wife, father to my son. I make the decisions, I steer the ship, I cut the path through the forest.'

'Have you spoken to Julia yet about your longer term plans, about Alex's vision for your place in the company?' Maureen asked him earlier in the day.

'She's been really busy. We're going through some things at home. Our son has been having problems at school. But it's on my mind, believe me. I can't stop thinking about it. I'll speak to Julia soon.'

'*Have* that conversation,' Maureen said, squeezing his arm. 'Bringing her into the fold will do wonders for your career, and for your family. We want all three of you under our canopy.'

Two young men from the yard service move their machines over the wet lawn during the first lull in the weather Nathaniel can remember for weeks. It will be the last mowing before winter. The cut grass clumps and clogs the mowers, the men struggle with their equipment and one of them, the younger of the two, keeps glancing at the flood on the other side of the street, at the rushing torrent between the house of his employer and his employer's neighbor, as if he believes the water will rise fast enough to take all of them with it. The men are both tall, blond, muscular in a way Nathaniel never has been, and because it is an unseasonably warm October day, both are wearing baggy basketball shorts and oversized red jerseys whose sleeves have been cut off. What remains of the shirts has the quality of a loose smock or tunic, the sides of the men's upper bodies all but uncovered and looking oddly vulnerable in spite of the muscular armor they bear. It takes the two men an hour to mow the front and back, to edge the lawn around the paths and driveway, to suck up the stray trimmings and the accumulations of fallen leaves into their agri-industrial vacuum bags, and shave the shrubs with electric hedge-trimmers. They skirt the northern edge of the property, leaving a swath of long grass closest to the stream. Watching them, Nathaniel thinks of his own father cutting the grass, Arthur Noailles in baseball shorts and tank top, making a brow-fixed assault on the lawn and the hedges, and then the stench of gasoline and cut grass and adult male sweat when his father came back in the house and sat, wide-stanced in the kitchen, flecks of dirt and grass on his tanned arms, blue shorts cutting into his groin, testicles sheathed in cotton boxers protruding from the cuffs as he drank a beer. Unlike some of their friends and neighbors, Nathaniel and Matthew were never allowed to mow their own lawn as a way of earning an allowance. Maintenance of the yard was exclusively their father's domain, as so much of life seemed to be. With the odor of Arthur's filthy body in his nostrils, he cranes his neck down to his armpits, hoping to find that he smells nothing like the man whose memory brings a shiver of nausea. Under his own arms he finds nothing but the smells of deodorant, fabric softener, myriad individual and conflicting perfumes, all of them, he thinks, poisoning his body while making it fragrant. He is sure his father would say he smelled like a woman.

They are going next door for a barbecue, he and Julia and Copley, while Louise has driven downtown to see a friend or cousin or some other shirttail relative, the kind of person, he suspects, whose association ought to be avoided.

The neighbor, Brandon Edwards, apologized for taking so long to introduce himself and 'his partner and child'.

'Do you think he means the man is his partner?' Nathaniel asks Julia.

'Have you seen a woman? I've only seen the two men, and the little girl.'

'No, I haven't seen any women.'

'What's the partner called?'

'I don't know, and I'm not sure how I feel about this.'

'Don't be a bigot,' Julia says, slipping on a black linen sheath that makes her look even more like a wraith.

'I'm not being a bigot. I'm voicing reasonable

478

speculations. We don't know anything about them and I think it's reasonable to ask questions about the people we're choosing to associate with.'

'What would Matthew say if he heard you?'

The longer he looks at it the more Julia's dress seems too metropolitan for a suburban barbecue; she should be in floral prints, or at least bold blocks of color, but he doesn't know how to say any of these things. He has dressed himself in jeans and a navy blue polo shirt and deck shoes. 'I think you should change.'

'I'm not going to change. I like this dress.'

'You look foreign. You should wear more color.'

'What's happening to you? What do you mean I look foreign? I've always dressed like this. And what do you care if they're two men living together?'

'That's not at all what I'm talking about, Julia. I don't give a damn if they're a couple. If you'll let me explain, what I meant was that the partner, if that's who he really is, he looks like a terrorist. And if that dress had sleeves, a hood, and a veil, then *you* could pass for a terrorist too.'

'Are you kidding me? A man looks like a terrorist just because his skin is brown? What about your brother-in-law?'

'Baldur is half-German. And this man, this "partner" next door, has a beard.'

'And apparently, like Matthew and Baldur, he has a partner who's a man. And he has a child. I think that automatically makes him an unlikely candidate for the potential-terrorist category, but then who am I to judge, since I myself appear to fit that category as far as you're concerned.'

'You can't assume anything these days.'

'What the hell is happening to you, Nathaniel?'

'I don't like the dress. If your husband doesn't like the dress you're wearing you should change. You're going to embarrass me. You look like a vampire.'

'Honestly, Nathaniel, I don't even know who you are anymore.'

Brandon and his partner, Azar, have a brick oven on their terrace, around which the adults have gathered, taking warmth against a sudden midday chill that has blown down from the northwest, while the children play on the lawn, throwing armfuls of leaves at each other, chasing themselves through a disorderly game of tag. Azar is making vegetarian pizzas in the oven while Brandon grills burgers and salmon on the adjacent barbecue. There are salads, homemade rolls, and in the kitchen a table of desserts, a full bar, wine, beer, soft drinks and juice for the kids and teetotalers. The other neighbors are friendly but Nathaniel feels unmoved to make an effort with these people: Cathy and Rob and Janet and Peter and Devon and Dermot and Zach and Molly and Mike and Denise, all of them white, bland, mass-produced Styrofoam slices of life, some thinner, most thicker, globular, pear-shaped and shining with perspiration. There are promises of dinner invitations and

Christmas parties and sledding on the 'empty lot', which is what the others call the acres of undeveloped land to the north. The food, when it comes, is delicious, the pizza as good as anything Nathaniel ever ate on the East Coast. Denise tells him that Azar is a trained chef.

'I'm guessing he *can't* work,' she whispers, 'which is why he's playing stay-at-home dad.'

'But he lives here.'

'Don't ask me,' Denise says, raising her hands, rolling her eyes, 'but I think he leaves the country every few months, comes back in as a tourist. Between you and me, I overheard him and Brandon in the kitchen, and it sounds like his time is already up. I mean they didn't say anything specific, but I got the idea he should've left by now. I don't know how they do it. I feel for them, you know, what with the kid and everything – you know Brandon is the father and Azar's sister is the mother. My husband has some ripe words, but I tell him just to shut up. I go by "live and let live", "each to his own". I don't have a problem with it myself, and they seem to know how to look after the little girl. She always looks real neat, real pretty. Although you have to wonder how they'll manage when she hits puberty.' Fat fingers raise a chip to her mouth. Denise, Nathaniel learned a moment ago, is a dental hygienist, while Mike works in the middle rungs of IT management at EKK, though Nathaniel has never seen him at the office. Between them they just afford to keep up their lifestyle:

481

mortgage, insurance and utilities on a three-thousand-square-foot house (one of the smaller ones in the development), two cars, a snowmobile, annual vacation, birthdays, shopping, gifts, and all the costs involved in raising two children, one of whom is 'on the autistic spectrum'. While Denise talks, regaling Nathaniel with the catalog of injustices and difficulties that have plagued her mostly comfortable life, the nightmare that was their experience of dealing with Paul Krovik – 'a real amateur, a total nut job' – he finds himself staring at Azar, at the man's chestnut-colored skin and carefully trimmed but full black beard, the paunch at his waist, the loose ethnic shirt embroidered along the hem that falls to his upper thigh, the waft of exotic scents coming from the man's armpits and the unusual spices that flavor the pizza, which is not, in fact, pizza but something less European, flatter and spicier and resolutely foreign. He looks at those steady hands and thinks they would be good for fine, skillful work: assembling circuit boards, cameras, advanced weaponry, bombs, flying planes.

'Where is he from?'

Denise shakes her head, chews a mouthful of burger, swallows, and says, food still secreted in her cheeks, 'No idea. Somewhere over there or down there'; she flaps her free hand to the east and then to the south. 'I've never asked. I don't like to pry. He's a *nice* guy. They're both real *nice* guys, and good neighbors. They looked after the kids earlier this year when I had to go to the emergency room. And Sofia's a sweetie. But, you know, it's a big risk what they're doing, I mean, if that *is* what they're doing. I could be wrong.'

As well as the memo directing employees how to vote, there had been another one on Friday reminding them that, as a contractor with the federal government, and as one of the corporations involved in the provision and maintenance of Homeland Security, EKK's employees are expected to report any unlawful behavior about which they may be aware, including the presence of illegal immigrants in their communities, suspected terrorists, and anyone else working against the interests of the country. A phone number was provided for *anonymous reporting of suspicious activity and/or individuals*. Technically, Nathaniel knows, he should waste no time in phoning the number and reporting the suspected presence of an undocumented migrant in his community; looking at the man, the un-American body language, talking with his hands, and hearing the loud voice and raucous laughter, the heavily accented English, it is possible to imagine that Azar whatever-his-name-is should be feared, or at the very least suspected, if not of terrorism, then certainly of breaking state and federal laws – laws meant to protect American citizens, to defend the homeland and secure the borders and ensure the country does not find itself susceptible to attack from within. A man like Azar could be from anywhere, sent by a foreign government to infiltrate American society, to be the least likely looking terrorist or agent possible by a performance of – Nathaniel thinks it before he has a moment to correct his language – *aberrant* sexuality, so that American officialdom will look at him, see a homosexual father with a daughter when, in fact, he is a cold-blooded plotter and schemer, who would, no doubt, sacrifice a child's life, even a child for whom he appears to be a loving parent, in order to bring new horrors raining down on the peaceful acres of neighborhoods just like Dolores Woods.

'What grade is Copley in?' Denise asks.

'Second.'

'Same as Austin. What school?'

'The Pinwheel Academy.'

'*Same as Austin!* What teacher?'

'Mrs Pitt.'

'Isn't that weird? I haven't heard Austin talk about him.'

'No. And Copley—' Nathaniel tries to remember if his son has mentioned the names of any of his new classmates.

'He's sure skinny.'

'You think?' Nathaniel looks at his son, pacing his usual grid on the lawn, staring at his feet, kicking every leaf he encounters, while the other children have organized themselves into a game of Duck, Duck, Goose.

'What's he doing? Pretending he's in *Dawn of the Dead*?'

'My wife says he's still adjusting to the move.' He stops himself from lurching into the kind of excessive sharing that this neighborhood gathering seems to engender. He does not want everyone to know that his son is seeing a psychiatrist, is medicated, and is in all likelihood terrorizing his own family.

'I know a good counselor if you need one. She works in the same building as me. We took Austin to her when he started pulling down his pants at school and she put a stop to that in no time.'

'We don't need a counselor,' Nathaniel snaps, getting up to refill his plate. 'There's nothing wrong with my son.' He knows as soon as he walks away from Denise that the other adults have heard what he said and are looking at him and at Copley, who is walking towards the circle of laughing children, romping through piles of fallen maple and cottonwood leaves. Of course there is something wrong with Copley, which is why the boy sees a psychiatrist, why he is taking a cocktail of medication that would give even Nathaniel's pill-happy mother pause. At the granite counter next to the oven he puts several more slices of the pizza or flatbread or tostada or whatever it is on his plate (they don't do paper plates, these two men, but an assortment of colorful crockery). He turns, finding himself nose to nose with Azar.

'Can I get you anything else, Nathaniel?' the man asks.

'No, thank you, Azar. I'm good.'

485

'Another beer? A soft drink? You understand I'm culturally pre-conditioned to make sure that, as my guest, all your needs are satisfied,' Azar says, his accent thickening. Nathaniel is unsure how to respond and then Azar's face cracks into a smile, his accent modulates, becomes more American. 'I'm only joking, man. Now what else can I get you?'

'Nothing, really. *I'm good.*' As Nathaniel says it a second time, this inane shorthand phrase Americans have adopted to mean, *thanks, I have everything I could possibly need, I don't need anything else at the moment, you can leave me the fuck alone*, screams erupt from the lawn. He turns to see Copley marching into the circle of other children, advancing in a fixed, unwavering course that has him kicking and stepping on small legs and feet and torsos. The other children fall away as Copley continues to the fence, turns, and comes back to pass through what remains of the circle. Julia is already halfway across the lawn and redoubles her speed, intercepting Copley before he can do more damage. Other parents have jogged over to attend to their own children while Julia draws Copley aside, speaking to him, Nathaniel can see, in a firm but kind voice. It is time to dispense with the kindness; surely they have now reached the point where physical discipline is necessary for the boy to understand he can't simply do whatever he wants, oblivious to the happiness and wellbeing of others, without repercussions. The first chapter in

486

a lifetime of criminality, that is what is unfolding in the actions and mind of his child: delinquency, petty theft, arrest, incarceration, drug addiction, release, theft, arrest, incarceration. He does not want his son to stumble blindly into a system never intended for people like him.

There were no recriminations or chastisement, just a sickening array of sympathetic looks and quiet words, people who understood *the difficulty of moving to a new city*. Play dates were offered and Denise scribbled the name of her son's counselor on a paper napkin, while her husband Mike caught Nathaniel's eye, nodded in Azar's direction, and shrugged, as if to say, *should we do something about this, man?* Nathaniel pretended not to understand but began to wonder himself if something ought to be done, especially now that he and a fellow EKK employee were conscious of each other's knowledge of whatever this situation might be. Meanwhile, the party continued as if nothing had happened at all, and for this Nathaniel found himself both grateful and outraged.

As the hours after the party have passed, he wishes that someone *had* made a big deal of it so his son would get the message that you can't just be a creep who walks all over other people without there being consequences. At home, in private, he has suggested to Julia that Copley face some kind of punishment, although it is difficult to know what. They do not spank, they do not allow him to watch television more than half an hour a week, and he seems happiest when left alone in his room, so sending him there is hardly going to discipline him.

'Talk to him, that would be more productive,' Julia says.

'On my own.'

'No, I'll talk to him, too.'

'Together.'

'Fine, okay. Together. But not here. I don't want him to feel cornered or ambushed. Let's take a walk.'

'A walk?'

'In the woods.'

It is the first time Nathaniel has been out the back gate and into the wooded portion of their property, which extends all the way to the sign marking the boundary with the nature reserve. Walking naturally again, Copley takes the lead, waiting only for his father to unlock the gate with a key and lock it again behind them. Julia has proposed exploring the trails that lead all the way to the river and Demon Point.

'I've been here before,' Copley says. His voice is cocky and boastful in a way that enrages Nathaniel. 'There are stairs and a chimney. There used to be some houses here. Louise told me.'

The woods look all but virgin, the trees tall and dense, others fallen and overgrown with ivy, gripped by decay: trees that are inmates in a prison reserve, growing up and out, some of them dying within, collapsing, decomposing, never escaping to freedom, but perhaps giving rise to positive regenerative growth, production of new life and materials on which others will feed. They walk for five minutes to the limit of their property and cross into the reserve. Copley runs ahead until Julia calls him back, telling him to stay close.

'Why?'

'For safety.'

'But it's safe,' Copley says.

'And because we want to talk to you about what happened earlier.' Julia puts a hand on the boy's shoulder, drawing him between the two of them. Why does Copley always have to be in the middle? Why can't he stand to one side? Gripping the boy's shoulders, Nathaniel moves his son over so that he and Julia can walk together, hand in hand, while his right hand steers Copley by the back of the neck. He can feel Julia flinch at the suddenness of the shift, and her hand squeezes his, not cooperative or soothing but itself a kind of punishment, pinching and chastising, making it clear, as if he had any doubt whatsoever, on whose side she really stands.

'What about earlier?' Copley squirms out of his father's grip and walks a few feet to one side.

'The way you kicked the other kids.'

'I didn't kick them. I was just walking. They were in my way.'

'But sweetheart,' Julia says, still not taking a firm enough line, 'you can't do that to other people. They were playing a game and you made a decision not to play. You can't just go wrecking other people's fun because you're not a part of it.'

'That's not what I was doing,' Copley shouts, his body doubling over, one of his feet stamping the ground.

'Then what *were* you doing?'

'I don't *know*.'

Nathaniel feels his patience slip. 'That's not good enough, Copley,' he says, his chest swelling as the old pressures build up inside. 'You have to know what the hell you're doing in the world.'

'Nathaniel—'

'You know what happens to kids like you,' he says, grabbing Copley by the shoulders and spinning him round. He leans over and points at Copley's chest, has a vision of his father doing the same thing to him, on some trail in the Berkshires, in the buzzing humidity of Mount Greylock. 'You've taken the first steps on the wrong road. You're getting in trouble at school, you're making messes at home, you're lying to your parents, now you're hurting other kids. Pretty soon you'll get into more serious trouble at school, you'll fall in with the wrong crowd, you'll disobey us, we'll punish you, you'll revolt, you'll get into trouble with the law and they'll send you to juvenile detention where older kids will do very bad things to you, things you cannot begin to imagine.'

'Nathaniel, that's enough!' Julia shouts.

He ignores her, index finger thumping his son's chest.

'If you're lucky you'll just *barely* finish high school but you can forget about college because you'll have such a bad record that no college will admit you. You'll work menial jobs, you'll have more brushes with the law, you'll probably start doing drugs. And then one day, you'll either get busted for drugs or busted for doing something to support your drug habit, and then you'll go to prison, and for the rest of your life, nothing will ever be the same. Your life will be prison, whether you're inside its walls or outside, you'll be thinking about prison the whole time, about going back in, about getting out, about how far you can push the system before it sends you to the hole. Your life will be nothing, and you'll ruin not just your own life, but our lives as well. You will be a gear in a big machine instead of one of the people running the machine. People like us, like your mother and me and the families we come from, we're the people who run the machine. We're at the top, pushing the levers. We're not the gears. You are not going to be a gear.'

Bewilderment floods Copley's face, and then there is a sudden torrent of tears and redness, the boy wailing, running to his mother, who embraces him and looks at Nathaniel with such hatred and fear that he knows he has done the right thing, the only action that could possibly be taken.

'What's a *gear*?' Copley sobs.

★    ★    ★

Walking in silence they pass family groups, couples in sneakers and jeans and windbreakers, outdoorsy teens in hiking boots with rucksacks. It takes them half an hour to reach Demon Point, climbing a steady path upward through woods until they arrive at a clearing where the yellowish earth is bare and muddy. A sign from the State Parks Department describes the composition of the soil, the balance of clay, sand, and silt, and the landscape visible from the Point, the river basin, the floodplain, the distant hills, the invisible mountains far to the west. Standing near the edge of compressed soil, they look down on the broad river spreading out of its banks, covering farmland for miles, trees poking out from black water, the whole region like a vast swamp except for the steadiness of the current, travelling south and east, broken cottonwood branches and whole trunks of trees caught up in its flow. Imagine all the drowned and displaced animals, the unnamed and forgotten, the homeless sleeping in hollows, unmissed by anyone. When the waters recede there will be bodies.

The boy and his mother solidify their position, separating themselves from him, standing to one side. Although feeling nothing but anger towards his son, Nathaniel fears what life without his wife would possibly mean.

'Look, I'm sorry,' he says, 'I was just trying to make you see how serious it is.'

The boy turns away and Julia glares at Nathaniel, her eyes wet, and he mouths it again, his apology, reaching out for her. She shakes her head, wipes her eyes, snaps her body away from him. Other people are watching. He hates to be noticed. They turn around, falling back into their usual order, Copley leading Julia, with Nathaniel at the rear.

Copley insists on looking for the ruined chimney and stairs. They wander for half an hour through trees but can find no trace of either – proof, Nathaniel knows, that the boy is a liar: lies revealed by facts, by empirical evidence.

Light drains out, distances shorten, the visible world closes in, amber leaves darken except where the last sun flames them into gold. As they leave the reserve Nathaniel tries again to pull Julia and Copley closer to his body, feeling as though, at last, some understanding has been reached and their lives will return to the even and regular course that was their character for so many years, but then Julia pulls away once again, taking Copley with her. There are instants, flashes, even in the course of this walk, when he thinks that his and Julia's lives would have been happier without Copley, that they should simply have carried on childless, focusing only on each other, and that, if by some accident they were childless again, they might start over afresh, newly happy. Grief would mark the transition. He would grieve for his son if he died, for the boy he used to be rather than the monster he has become.

Their rubber-soled shoes make no sound on the

compacted earth where fallen leaves have already been ground to dust by the passage of other feet. Nathaniel looks at the path stretching from the sign at the perimeter of the reserve and leading into the heart of their property. Someone else has been walking here – perhaps only Louise, but possibly others as well. It would be worth extending the fence, enclosing the part of the woods belonging to them, posting NO TRESPASSING signs; if people are accessing his property, he could be liable for any illegal activity that might be occurring, even without his knowledge.

The broad tall man steps out of a triangular clump of firs, looking as startled as they are. There is a staggered, collective intake of breath, a yelp from Copley, and a deep bellow from the man, who wears a suit of green camouflage and carries a hunting rifle slung over his shoulder. The man is at least a foot taller than Nathaniel; he is lean and muscular, his skin tanned, hair dark and glossy, cuts on his face and bandages on his hands.

'Man, you scared us,' Nathaniel says, trying to smile.

'You scared *me*,' says the man.

'Huh. What are you doing back here?'

'I was hunting.' The man steps to one side, revealing the carcass of a deer, collapsed on the leaves, eyes wide and staring. The ground is a mess of blood and entrails. Nathaniel feels a loosening of the ligaments in his legs, a hot flush rushing through his calves and thighs, as though he is standing without protection, buffeted by wind, on the edge of Demon Point.

'I can see that. I guess you didn't realize you were on private property.' Nathaniel keeps smiling as his voice skews high and queer.

'No, I didn't. I thought I was still on reserve land.'

Nathaniel laughs. 'No, no. I'm afraid the reserve ends a ways back there, near the sign. You can't miss it.'

'I guess I'll just take my kill, if you don't mind, and be on my way.'

'That's fine. No harm done. I've been meaning to put up a sign.'

The man nods and smirks.

Nathaniel feels Copley reach out and clasp his hand. He's so relieved by the contact that he squeezes back, trying to be reassuring, all the while knowing that this man with his gun and knife – the blade flashes at the man's trim waist, blood smeared on the camouflage pants – could bring down the three of them in an instant. He decides that they should stay there, standing and waiting, watching while the man hoists the carcass onto his shoulder, and stomps away in the direction of the reserve. When the man is out of sight the woods are silent except for the screaming of jays.

'I think that was the man,' Copley whispers when they are safe in the backyard with the gate locked behind them.

'What man?' Julia asks.

'The giant. The man in the basement.'

'For goodness' sake stop pretending, Copley,' Nathaniel shouts. All the fantasy, the giants, the ruined houses in the forest, stairs leading underground, it is all so exhausting. 'It's not funny to make things up. That man could have been dangerous.'

'I *know*,' Copley whines. 'That's what I've been *telling* you.'

The party at Brandon and Azar's is still going on, music coming from inside the house, the back doors open, spreading a foreign beat through the neighborhood, which Nathaniel knows is against the Dolores Woods bylaws.

The call takes less than two minutes. A woman answers, directs him to give the name – if known – and address of the individual to be reported, as well as a physical description, the nature of the offense, and any other pertinent information. Closed in his study, Nathaniel speaks his neighbor's first name into the receiver, gives the address next door, describes Azar's appearance, mentions that he is widely rumored to be an illegal alien who has outstayed his tourist visa, and that he lives with another man and a small child who are, apparently, American citizens.

'And they're not implicated?' the woman asks.

'The other man isn't, I don't think. He's as American as you or me. The girl I don't know about.'

As soon as he puts down the phone, realizing he knows nothing of substance about the men next door, a sickness rises in his stomach.

Louise returns after dinner looking shaken. Her hair is untidy from being under the hood of her windbreaker, her skin gray, upper lip cracked. After Julia puts Copley to bed, they sit with Louise in the kitchen and offer her a drink, which she declines. She would prefer a cup of tea.

'Because of the flooding I parked near your office, Nathaniel, and took the bus downtown to meet my friend for lunch,' she says, trying to catch her breath. 'Before we reached my stop, the bus was pulled over by an unmarked car. These two men in uniforms got on, but they weren't police, and then I noticed they were from your company, Nathaniel. I thought they were just checking people's tickets but they made the bus driver lock the door of the bus. They told everyone to produce some form of photo identification that proved our right to be in the country. I couldn't believe it. I thought it was a joke and I laughed before I knew what was good for me. One of them came right over and asked for my driver's license and I reached into my purse to get my billfold and discovered I'd taken out all the cards and left them in my other purse. I just had cash and my bus pass. Other people were showing their IDs to the other man and then he got to this Mexican-looking fellow at the

497

back who didn't have an ID and the man in the uniform got on his phone and called for backup. I don't know who he called but another car arrived and two other men got onboard and all this time I'm scrambling through my purse trying to find something to prove I'm as American as I sound. They took the Mexican and put plastic ties around his hands and shoved him in the back of that car and I thought I was in for it too but finally I said to the men, listen, I work for Mr Noailles, who's a big shot at EKK. They looked skeptical but I begged them to phone you. There wasn't any answer so I asked them to phone the company and check to see if there *was* a Mr Noailles and they did and that was the only reason they let me go. I was so upset I got off the bus at the next stop and walked back to the car.'

'That's terrible, Louise,' Julia says. She reaches out to touch the old woman's arm, the alliance as clear to Nathaniel as ever. 'What kind of company are you working for, Nate?'

What gives her the right to call him *Nate*? She's never done it before, not in all their married life. He shrugs, looking at them both, and says the only thing he can think to say: 'They were just doing their jobs. We have a search-and-detain contract with Immigration & Customs. You can't fault them for what they have to do. In fact, you might say they *failed* to do their jobs properly. They shouldn't have let you go until they could reach me to confirm you work for me. These days, you just can't go around without carrying ID, Louise. We have to think about national security.'

The old woman shakes her head. 'All I know is I haven't been treated like that since the sixties. And I thought those days would never come back.'

Louise excuses herself and thuds up the back stairs to her bedroom while Nathaniel and Julia stand in silence. She loads cups and plates into the dishwasher, avoiding looking at him until she has no choice. There's an expression on her face he hasn't seen before. When she opens her mouth, her lips pull tight and her chin trembles.

'Who *are* you?' she says.

'It's been a long day,' he says, 'you're tired.'

'I'm not tired. I'm – in shock. I don't recognize you.'

'I've just been saying what's true. We have to stop living such soft lives.'

He switches on the television in the den and turns up the volume so everyone knows what he's doing, flicking from news to weather before settling on *Saturday Night Live*. For an hour he laughs as loud as he can, even when nothing funny is happening on the screen, and only turns it off after midnight. When he comes to bed he finds the door locked, light seeping out from the threshold into the dark passage. He jiggles the knob, knocks, calls out in a low voice to Julia but she never answers. As the light goes off he kicks the door at its base and rakes his fingernails down the wall.

He makes out the couch in his study and locks himself inside. Just let them try to wake him up in the morning. He'll spend the day alone, ignore them all, show them what it means to be ostracized.

When he finally sleeps he dreams of the man in the woods with the gun and the deer. The man has him on the ground, prone, Nathaniel's hands tied behind his back with a plastic cord, and the man is pulling the jeans from Nathaniel's body. He struggles against the man's grip, trying to squirm away as he feels a cord looping his feet, twining in and out around his bare ankles as the man huffs and grunts, smelling of gasoline and sweat and cut grass. Nathaniel looks up to see a deer hanging from a tree, suspended over a ruined chimney, smoke wafting up as the carcass turns, slowly roasting, its two front legs huge, engorged with blood and throbbing. He feels the man pushing into him, the hard sharp shock of pressure slamming up through his body, skin against his skin, rough and slick.

His father never took him hunting. His father does not hunt. His father would never know what to do with a gun or a deer except to chart the social and manufacturing history of the gun, the legacy of hunting deer and their place in the American diet, the law passed down from Deuteronomy that sanctioned their eating and sacrifice as a species. He opens his eyes to find it is already light – or at least dawn, gray and fog-choked. The dream, like so many of his most vivid nightmares, occurred in the shallowest period of sleep, when his brain was already half awake, mulling and stewing. His father is no hunter.

It is only six but he gets up, goes to the adjoining bathroom, puts on the clothes he wore yesterday after sleeping all night in the nude. There is a stain on the fitted sheet covering the foldout mattress. He removes the sheet, balling it up, and sees that the stain is dark, still wet, and appears to be spreading, turning the pale blue mattress a deep navy. He returns to the bathroom, moistens a towel, and tries to scrub away the stain, succeeding only in making it larger, wetter, more incriminating. Placing a dry towel over the spot, he folds up the bed, putting the cushions back in position. At some point he will need to replace the mattress, although there is no urgency; no one else is going to sleep on it, no one else will bother to open it.

Mulling over the events of Saturday, he feels close to remorse, if not for the intention behind his words and actions, then for the way they were expressed. Aggression has never been his style; if anything, he has sought to bleed aggression from his interactions with other people as a way of being less like his father. He sees now that yesterday was a slip, brought on by fatigue and stress. As much as he wants to believe in the new work he is doing, he suspects it is wrong. He knows that what happened to Louise is wrong, that the right of EKK employees to pull over city buses and detain, however briefly, law-abiding American citizens, demanding they prove their right to be in the country of their birth, on public transit, is at best a legal gray area, although one not without some precedent. The problem is one of style and tone, the overbearing aggression, which is, he fears, poisoning his own way of being in the world. The white leather couch stares back at him and he can see the dark navy stain rising up from the cloth and metal innards, surfacing and spreading along the bleached hide, a blue so deep it is almost black. He runs his hands across the cushions, feeling for moisture, sniffing his fingertips for the ozone smell of his own fluids. Nothing. Dry. Odorless.

It is time to start fresh, to make coffee and waffles for everyone, set them all on a new course. 'I am Nathaniel Noailles, head of the house, leader of my family, captain of the ship.' A good leader admits fault: he will apologize if what he said upset or frightened Copley, and find a way to rephrase his exhortation, explaining that he is only concerned about his son's long-term health and livelihood and wellbeing since he is such an obviously intelligent and sensitive child. He loves his son – no, of course he does.

Thoughts catch and tear; these are the things Julia will want to hear, will perhaps even expect to hear if he has any hope of mending the situation. Put it right, *Nate*, get it back together. Don't be so small, don't be such an insect.

But when he opens the door to the hall, he knows he will not be making waffles and he will not be apologizing to anyone. All along the floor and rising

502

up the walls, scrawled in red crayon, in handwriting that could only belong to a child, are the words GO AWAY GO AWAY GO AWAY GO AWAY GO AWAY GO AWAY GO AWAY GO AWAY GO AWAY GO AWAY GO AWAY GO AWAY GO AWAY GO AWAY GO AWAY GO AWAY GO AWAY GO AWAY GO AWAY GO AWAY GO AWAY GO AWAY GO AWAY GO AWAY GO AWAY GO AWAY GO AWAY GO AWAY GO AWAY GO AWAY GO AWAY GO AWAY GO AWAY GO AWAY GO AWAY GO AWAY GO AWAY GO AWAY GO AWAY GO AWAY GO AWAY GO AWAY GO AWAY GO AWAY GO AWAY GO AWAY GO AWAY GO AWAY GO AWAY GO AWAY GO AWAY GO AWAY GO AWAY GO AWAY GO AWAY GO AWAY GO AWAY GO AWAY GO AWAY GO AWAY GO AWAY GO AWAY GO AWAY GO AWAY GO AWAY GO AWAY GO AWAY GO AWAY GO AWAY GO AWAY GO AWAY GO AWAY GO AWAY GO AWAY GO AWAY GO AWAY GO AWAY GO AWAY GO AWAY GO AWAY GO AWAY GO AWAY GO AWAY GO AWAY GO AWAY GO AWAY GO AWAY GO AWAY GO AWAY GO AWAY GO AWAY GO AWAY GO AWAY GO AWAY.

The graffiti covers the doors of his study and the master bedroom, the floor and walls of the landing to a height of four feet, and on the door to Louise's bedroom, surrounded by the storm of GO AWAY, there is another word, a single utterance, blocked out in black marker:

NIGGER

The only surface untouched by graffiti is Copley's own door.

Nathaniel feels the pressure rise again in his chest, the old rage expanding.

'Copley!' he screams, 'Copley! Out here now! COPLEY!'

503

The door to his son's room opens and the small white face appears, hands trembling. He feels nothing but hate for this boy, wants to obliterate the monster he created, make him disappear, or transform him into something else altogether.

'Stand with your back against the wall,' he shouts. Copley gapes at the vandalism, looking surprised, such a good, mincing little actor. 'Raise up your arms,' Nathaniel says, as Copley starts to whimper. The boy's arms reach above the line of the graffiti. Julia and Louise are standing in the hall now, idiot jaws slack. Nathaniel's hands shake, he watches himself telling his son to go to his room, hears himself tell his wife that something serious is going to have to be done. After the warning he gave Copley yesterday, to have this shit thrown in his face is too much, never mind the offense directed at Louise. The camel's back is broken, this is a hundredweight of straws. Even Julia, he can see, who has been the kid's champion from the beginning, looks at Copley now with confusion and disappointment. Doors slam. Rage pumps him full, fills his veins, his lungs; his temples throb, he sees meteoric silver stars everywhere he looks: the red wax, the time it will take to clean it off, Nathaniel's whole body shaking, his chest inflated, bursting, and then, arising from deep in his gut, a howl that flies out of his mouth, flies and fills every room, shaking the house into silence.

6:20 AM: he sits on his bed, sniffling although he is trying to stop. He hears his father shouting in the hall, 'I hate that kid, I'm gonna kill him.' He believes what his father says and starts to cry, waiting for his mother or Louise to come, to bring him his breakfast. His father is going to kill him, but first he hears him go downstairs. There is shouting in the kitchen, his mother and father, but he cannot understand what they are saying. The door opens and Louise comes in, closing it behind her. 'You didn't do it, did you?' she asks. He can't speak, he chokes and hiccups and sobs, shaking his head. 'Hold onto yourself,' she says, 'and don't worry. It's going to be okay. We'll fix it.' She rubs his back for a moment and then leaves him alone again. He knows it is the man in the basement, the man they saw in the woods with the gun and the deer. He has tried to tell them in every way he knows. He has showed his mother the hatch in the pantry and even then she did not believe him. While he is thinking about how he can convince them he is telling the truth, he lies back down and begins to fall asleep, thinking of the shock he felt when they arrived at the barbecue yesterday and Austin was standing in the middle of the neighbors' backyard. He dreams that Austin pushes him off the diving board and out into space, and as he is falling, he looks down, only to see there is no water left in the pool.

7:10 AM: he can smell his mother sitting on the chair next to his bed. He opens his eyes and pulls himself up to look in the mirror on the opposite wall. His cheeks and eyes are red, his hair angled in waves all over his head. When he sees the image of the boy in the bed at first he does not recognize himself. 'I want you to tell me the truth,' his mother says, 'did you write those words in the hall?' '*No*,' he says, 'I never did any of those things. It was the *man*.' 'Which man, Copley?' 'The man in the woods yesterday, with the gun, he lives in the basement.' His mother exhales, 'Oh, Copley. Come on, sweetie. There is no man in the basement.' He knows she has run out of patience. 'Why don't you believe me?' he asks. 'I want—' she says. He does not understand what she wants. It almost seems like she wants to believe that he *is* responsible. 'Let me show it to you again. Let me show you where he lives.' 'Enough! Copley, honestly, enough already. There are four people in this house. Me, you, your father, and Louise.' 'No,' he says, 'not just the four of us.' 'Stop. You have to stop lying. Do you know what the word means that you wrote on Louise's door?' 'I didn't *write* it,' he shouts, outraged that she would believe him capable of such a thing. Of course he knows what the word means. He has heard other students at school whisper it when he and Joslyn pass. He never heard the word before that, and did not, at first, understand what it meant until he asked Joslyn. 'Don't ever say that word,' she said, 'if you're my friend you won't say that word.' 'I don't understand what it means,' he said, 'why do they call us that word?' 'Not *us*,' she said, 'they're calling *me* that word.' 'But what does it mean?' 'It's what nasty, stupid people call people like me. And it's the *worst* thing you could call me.' That was enough of an explanation. He didn't need to hear anything more than that. He looks at his mother and tells her about Joslyn. He says that he would never use that word. His mother gives him his morning pills and he swallows them. She looks at the bottles and turns them over in her hands and looks at him. 'So you knew that word already,' she says. She shakes the pills and takes them into the bathroom. He can hear her opening the bottles and throwing the pills into the toilet and then dropping the plastic bottles into the metal trashcan. When she comes back, she's smiling but does not look happy. 'No more pills,' she says. 'We're stopping the pills today. That was your last dose.' 'Why?' he asks. 'Because I think they're doing more harm than good. I think they might be making you do things you don't even know you're doing.'

★   ★   ★

8:00 AM: his mother leaves him alone and he takes a shower, gets dressed, and goes downstairs for breakfast. His father and mother are standing up at the island, while Louise is sitting on one of the stools, eating a bowl of oatmeal. 'You come sit next to me,' she says. His father looks at him and says they expect him to apologize to Louise. He thinks that the three of them have been arguing. His mother bites her lip and Louise raises a hand to his father but his father puts up his own hand and pats the air, as if he were a teacher telling Louise to be quiet. 'I want to hear Copley apologize for what he's done,' his father says. Copley looks at the three adults. His father stares at him, his face cut into many small triangles; his mother looks at him and then at the floor, chewing her lip. Louise won't look at him at all and stares out the window instead. He can see there is only one way out of this, even though it means admitting a thing he knows he did not do and would never do. Then he notices the box of crayons that are usually in the activities drawer in the kitchen. His father taps the lid of the box. 'These were thrown all over the floor of the kitchen.' He isn't sure what his father expects him to say in response. He would never leave anything a mess. He hates messes. 'Come on, Copley. Let's hear it.' His father's voice is calm in a way that makes the back of his neck prickle and crawl. 'I'm *sorry*,' he says, 'but I didn't do it. I didn't do *any* of it.' His father throws the box of crayons on the floor and stomps out of the kitchen, shouting at his mother, 'I expect *him* to clean it up. No one else is going to help him!' His mother runs after his father, shouting, '*Nate*, be reasonable. He can't clean it up. It's going to be way too much work. I'll call Di tomorrow and see if she can come earlier in the week.' 'No!' his father shouts. 'I want it cleaned NOW.'

8:30 AM: his mother has given him her hairdryer, a bucket of warm soapy water, and a sponge as big as his head. 'Turn the hairdryer on a small section and heat it up. When the crayon is warm and soft, wash it with the sponge,' she says, looking as though she is about to cry. She watches while he turns on the hairdryer and heats up a postcard-sized section of floor where the word AWAY has been written. His own handwriting looks nothing like the writing in the hall. When he can see the wax beginning to melt he turns off the hairdryer and draws the sponge up out of the water, squeezing it before he wipes it over the floor. He scrubs the melting word, moving feathery arcs of foam back and forth, watching the red wax begin to smear and disperse. He can see that it's going to take a long time to clean the entire hallway. It looks impossible to do in a day.

10:15 AM: he is on his fifth bucket of warm soapy water and has managed to clean a section of floor the size of a bath towel, although there is still a haze of pinkish wax covering parts of it where he could not get all the crayon to come off. As he heats and scrubs, his arms and back and knees and neck all aching, the sweat running along his body, he wonders who the man is that has done these terrible things, who took him up in his arms when he walked outside, who has tried in so many ways to drive them from the house. He has read about ghosts and poltergeists but thinks that neither of these are a way of describing the man. Instead, the man reminds him of a troll or an ogre, a creature who is real and fleshy and wicked, who lives in a dark hidden place, and wants no one to pass over his bridge or disturb his rest.

12:05 PM: his mother comes to check on his progress. He is scrubbing so slowly, barely a quarter of the way along the hall, not even touching the walls or the doors, that she says, 'Okay, time for a break. Come have some lunch.' They eat in silence. He pays no attention to the food on his plate. He puts it in his mouth and tastes nothing but soap and wax. When his mother's back is turned, Louise winks at him and reaches out to touch his hand, which is red and raw, either from abrasion or heat or melted crayon. He does not know where his father is.

1:00 PM: he is still sitting at the island in the kitchen, between Louise and his mother, when his father comes through the back door. 'I think Copley and I should go for a walk,' his father says.

510

'I think we should talk about things.' Although they are not touching, he feels his mother's body grow tense. 'Where are you going to walk?' she asks. 'Just back in the woods, maybe into the reserve.' His father's voice sounds calm and flat. 'Cop and I need to discuss what all of this means.' 'Nathaniel—' his mother begins, but his father interrupts her. 'It's okay, Julia. We won't be long. We'll be back soon. He has a job to finish this afternoon.'

1:10 PM: there is low cloud over the woods and the fog from overnight still has not cleared; if anything, it is growing thicker and more opaque. His father says nothing as the two of them walk to the back gate, which is already unlocked. 'The gate,' he says. 'It's okay,' says his father, 'I was just out here a while ago. I was looking for those stairs and that chimney. And you know what? I *still* couldn't find them.' After his father closes and locks the gate they are alone in the woods, standing in the fog beneath corn-yellow leaves.

1:15 PM: his father leads him towards the stand of fir trees not far from the back gate. When he looks at the house he notices how the trees and fence block the view: he can't see the house and the house can't see him. He looks up through the twisting branches of one of the cottonwood trees. 'You still haven't climbed a tree, have you, Cop?' He shakes his head; the first branches are far above the ground. 'It's really an experience every child should have,' his father says, pulling a coil of rope from the pocket of his coat. 'I want to help you climb this tree.' He watches as his father throws the rope up over the lowest branch, which is five or six times higher than his father is tall, and catches the other end when it comes down. 'Come here.' He steps toward his father, who threads the rope through the small loops at the waist of his jeans, twisting it around his leather belt. His father ties a knot and then another knot and yanks several times on the rope to see if it's secure. 'Okay, so here's what we're going to do. I'm going to pull you up to that branch so you can climb on it.' 'No,' he says, feeling his legs dance, 'no, please, no!' And then, before he can run away, his feet are off the ground and the rope tightens around his waist. He grips the rope above his head but the noose around his waist pushes the wind out of him; he struggles to breathe as his father pulls him up through the air, the world falling away in spinning lurches as his head approaches the branch. 'Now reach up,' his father says from below, 'and when you can, you grab that branch and pull yourself up on top of it. Don't be afraid, I'm holding the rope.'

—:— PM: sliding out of time, he forgets where he is, loses sensation in his body, slips away from his arms and legs, connected only by the head to his body, the two of them suspended in air, rising,

rising, trying to separate from his body, and then a knock pushes his arms and legs back into their flesh, his two heads joining up first, aching from the blow of the limb against his crown. He reaches for the branch, fumbles onto the wet ridged surface, pulls himself up, trembling, the breath coming back to him, one leg over the branch, straddling it, his chest collapsing, arms clutching, struggling to hold on to the wet bark, seeking purchase on the rough edges. He looks for his father down below but the fog whites out the ground and fills his lungs. 'Copley?' his father calls, 'you all right? Stand up so I can see you. Come on, stand up! I want to see you stand up. You're climbing a tree!' He pushes his chest off the branch and sits upright, looks back at the trunk, three or four feet away, and begins to scoot his body in reverse, tightening his legs around the branch as he moves, teetering from side to side, his balance precarious, until he reaches the trunk. He exhales. He inhales. His father hates him. His father is trying to kill him. '*Now*, Copley! I want to see you stand up. I'm not letting you down from there until you stand up on that branch and admit what you did. I want to hear a confession. I want you to stand up and tell me what you did. Copley? Say something!'

—:— PM: it may have been seconds or minutes although it feels like many days of sleeping and waking, of dreaming in and out of consciousness as the fog closes around him, thickening and rising up until it is lying beneath the branch, the surface of a silvery white lake. He will walk the length of the branch, believing that if he falls, he will fall only into water, that he will be able to swim back to the branch, pull himself out of the water, and continue his walk. He knows how to swim, he was always good at the balance beam, his dance teacher in Boston said he walked the most natural straight line she had ever seen. There was a floating log in the lake near his grandfather's house in New Hampshire, which they last visited two years ago during the summer vacation. He swam with his mother out to the log and she held it still at one end while he climbed on top of it, pulled his body upright by gradual degrees, and walked back and forth along its length until his mother let go and he walked for a full minute, she said, timing him, as the log rolled gently beneath his feet on the surface of the silvery white New England lake. Here the tree is holding the branch instead of his mother, so it will not turn beneath his feet. It is wet like that other branch was wet, it has ridges along its bark as that other log had ridges. He can walk its length, back and forth, without having to worry that it will begin to spin too fast, and that he will eventually plunge forward or backward into the void. Not a void, not the air, but water, the silvery white lake of fog on which the branch of the cottonwood floats, a body of water that will buoy him up if he falls.

★   ★   ★

—:— PM: his father's voice is distant and small and he cannot see the man, nor does he believe that his father can see him. All he wants is to be back on the ground. All he wants is for this terror to stop and for the three of them to go back to Boston. He reaches behind him, gripping the rough trunk as firmly as he can, and draws his legs up so his feet are resting in front of him on the branch. He turns, swinging his legs to one side, so that if he wished, he could lean back in space and hang from the limb by his legs. Instead, he begins to stand, clinging to the trunk, his knees wobbling and watery, and just as he is nearly upright, the rope still knotted around his waist, he cries out, 'Help me,' before slipping and flying into the lake of fog.

When he comes up from the cellar, rifle over his arm, pushing aside the gates of camouflaging boughs and trees, Paul can see the man on the ground holding the rope, leaning backward towards the stream, pulling and losing his footing. At the other end of the rope, the child is in midair, struggling, reaching up, trying to pull himself along the line, whimpering in a strangled voice, 'Help! *Help* me!' It looks like the man is hanging his son, a noose tightening around the child's neck as his father tugs at the rope from the ground, grunting. A low gasping comes from the child, then the sound of his sleeves rubbing against rope, slippery and synthetic. From this angle through the fog, the boy looks more than ever like Carson.

Paul shifts the rifle from his shoulder and points it skyward, braces his legs and squeezes the trigger, watching as the man startles at the sound of the blast. He turns to face Paul and as he does, the man's fists open, letting go of the rope. The child floats through the fog, feather-light, and as Paul races to the tree, believing he can catch the boy

516

before he hits the ground, he sees those waxy, glassy eyes staring down at him, horrified, the child's face puzzled, his body contorting and scrambling through vapor, trying to find purchase in the mist, to grasp something, looking always down, staring at Paul, and at last crying out as his feet, his knees, his hips and chest and arms hit the ground, his head falling last, cracking against a stone rising up from the sea of fallen leaves, the rope tied tightly round his waist, his neck unmarked.

The man looks at Paul and does not even stop to attend to his son, but begins running in the direction of the stream. The rifle is still in Paul's hands and he raises it into position, finding the man in his sights, and pulls the trigger. The whole movement, the raising of the gun, the aiming, his finger pressing against the trigger, it all happens in a single instant. He does not think. Or rather, Paul looked at the man who was trying to kill the child who resembled Carson and saw a man endangering his own child, Paul's child. He has shot the man who was trying to kill his son.

In the fog he cannot see if the man is dead, but hears the body splash into the water. He runs down the hill and finds the man swimming away from him, thrashing in water up to his neck. Throwing the rifle down on the bank, Paul wades into the water, swims to the man, and catches him up in his arms. They stare at each other for a moment, treading water, the current pulling against their feet, drawing them westward. Paul blows out a stream of air, empties his lungs and then fills them again, closing his eyes and leaning forward, pushing both of their bodies down under the water, thick with silt and leaves and blood. He can feel the man struggling in his embrace, thrashing and crying out, the man's voice echoing through the clogged artery of stream, twisting and bouncing across its muddy bottom.

When the man's body is still Paul throws his head above the surface, breathes in dense wet air, and sinks below again, reaching for the man's body, pulling it up, swimming it to the bank, and feeding the dead arms through an exposed root.

When he turns the body over the child's eyes are open, staring at the sky. Paul leans close and holds his cheek just above the boy's mouth. He listens against the child's chest for a heartbeat, searches for a pulse in the thin neck, in the wrists. The rock is dark with blood, the boy's eyes crossed, glazed ceramic balls, blood marking his brow. As Paul looks into those dead eyes a convulsion shakes his gut. He has never seen human eyes so fixed, unresponsive, without light. Sprawling on the leaves, he is aware of how wet and cold he is. If he does not get back indoors he will slip into hypothermia.

With his dripping bandaged hands he touches the eyelashes, closes the lids, fingers the hair, looks closely at the scalp, the fingernails, the line of the jaw, taking apart the child in his arms. The boy is not Carson. There is no resemblance. His own sons are alive on the other side of the country. He wants to be anywhere but here, on this land, skulking through these woods. There is no reason to stay.

We were standing in the kitchen, both of us feeling, I think, as though we ought to go after them, both of us knowing that Nathaniel was not himself, or that, over the course of days, weeks, perhaps even months, he had become someone his wife no longer knew.

The sound was muffled but we both heard it. I looked at Julia and then, a moment or two later, moments dropping down between us, another sound arrived, and we knew. We flew out the back door, across the porch, down the steps, running over the mound in the middle of the lawn. Depress the gate's latch, pull it forward, but it would not budge.

'Keys?'

Julia shook her head and ran back to the house while I tried to pull myself up, throw my body over the fence, but it was too high and there was nothing to climb. Moments dropped all around me, accumulating in the fog, tying up my feet and knotting my tongue. I pulled my words to make a shout that exploded into stupid white noise.

Pushing me aside, Julia slipped the spare key into the lock, depressed the latch, and as the gate opened I could see the green-brown form of the man crouched in front of us, fifty paces away, at the foot of the tree. I knew Krovik without seeing his face, the body that strutted over this land, raping and routing. At his feet, in his hands, I could see the body of the boy, dishrag limp, hands whiter than fog. The rifle was on the ground, just behind the man. I could sense Julia about to scream but I turned to her, clapped a hand over her mouth, and picked my way through the fog. Leaning over within hitting distance, I pinched the gun between my fingers, whisked it from the ground to my shoulder, aiming at Krovik as he pivoted on all fours to look up at me, his face and whole body wet, running with blood and filth, nose draining over his upper lip, his chest heaving up the most horrible sobs I have ever heard. The rifle was weightless in my arms. I held it so he had no doubt of my abilities. My arms and back were steady. I directed him with the barrel: move now, to the side, get away from the child.

And then the mother must have seen her son, because she was screaming on the ground beside the man, pushing him over against the earth, raising up the small wet body, the head dripping as it lolled against the rock.

When the police arrived they told me to drop the gun. I curled my fingers free, placed it on the ground, and Julia explained who I was, that I was not the person they needed to arrest. As they put handcuffs on Krovik he turned to Julia and snarled: 'Your husband's in the water.'

The bodies were laid out together on the ground by the tree where we discovered Krovik and Copley. We followed the police to the stream, and Julia shook in silence, pushing away the hands that reached out to hold her steady. She sat on the ground a few feet distant from her dead son and husband, watching as I answered questions. Krovik was gone and the police were searching the area, picking through leaves and undergrowth as the fog condensed and daylight faded until one of them yelled, knowing his part so well, 'I've got something.' The others clustered round him and disappeared into the old storm cellar.

'As soon as I saw Krovik I knew,' I said to the officer taking my statement.

'Knew what?'

'That he'd been living somewhere on this land, hidden down below.'

'How's that?'

'The boy told me, he told everyone, but none of us could see it. Krovik was out of his mind. He loved this land as much as me. I just didn't want to believe it.'

When the police finished and the bodies were carried out of the woods, loaded into ambulances and taken away to the morgue, I led Julia back inside that house which always glowers, not least at twilight, its unblinking windows black and reflective as the streetlights shuddered in their hazy glow.

Neither of us wanted to speak or eat. We slow-danced around each other, drinking shots of bourbon, and then for a long time we just stood in the kitchen and I held her as she cried and shook, that fine-boned little body tight with energy and anger and the implausibility of grief.

Before we went to bed, three EKK vans pulled up outside. At first I thought they might be here to offer support but then I watched as the men in their riot gear broke down the door of the neighbors' house and dragged out the brown man who lived there, while the white man and child stood crying on the porch, held at bay by the men in their mirror-faced masks. Watching those two men, the brown and the white, I could not help thinking of the benefactor, Mr Wright, and of Great-Uncle George, still buried in their unburied way, unconsecrated, unmourned except by me, who sits meditating on the land and the times, the undulation and flow, the joining together and casting apart.

That night I heard Julia up and moving through the house. In the morning we looked into each other's faces, speaking only with eyes and expression: a muscle twitch, a narrowing of lids, lips cushioned over a trembling knob of chin. Language was dumb. Police came and went, examining the house, the basement, the pantry, the entrance they discovered, the burrow beneath the backyard, the hidden and the hiding.

The police were inept. Only the next morning did a man without a uniform suggest we go elsewhere for a day or two, while they dusted the house for prints, followed trails of invisible marks, pieced together a narrative of past action.

I drove us to a new hotel west of the old downtown.

'Would you mind staying with me, in the same room?' Julia asked. It was the first time she had spoken to me in thirty-six hours. If she had slept the previous night she did not look like it, eyes nestling deep in their sockets, cheeks sinking, hair clinging in oily ropes.

In the room on a high floor we sat on our respective beds with views of flooded land spilling around us to the west and south.

'It's time you had a bath.'

'A shower,' Julia says, 'I don't want to stew in my own filth.'

'A shower then.'

She looked at me, a sudden, furtive look.

'Would you sit in there?'

'Where?'

'Would you sit in the bathroom while I take a shower?'

I waited while Julia undressed and got into the

tub, drew the curtain and called for me to enter. I sat on the closed lid of the toilet.

'Are you there?' she asked.

'I'm here.'

'Will you do something else?'

'What?'

'Will you talk to me?'

'What would you like me to talk about?'

'Tell me a story.'

There was only one story that came to mind. It was neither happy nor even a story I know first-hand. It was the story I have cobbled together from rumor and historical document, from whis-perings I heard as a child, from the little I could pry from my mother when the old woman let the bolts on her tongue slip to speak the memories she contained. It is a story of land, of men on the land, of the way that men came to blows over land. It is a story, I know, without women. It is not my own story. I am merely its keeper, its guardian, its partial creator, since more than half of it is my own invention, my necessary speculation. I am the one who keeps it breathing, who brought it back to life in the first place, a resurrectionist. At first as I spoke I could hear Julia washing, moving under the water, shampooing her hair, sponging her limbs, but after the first minutes I knew she was just standing still, letting the water run down her back, scalding the white skin red, listening as I spoke above the murmur of hot rain.

'We know that others owned the land before the

benefactor, Morgan Priest Wright. Before him there was his father, Ambrose Balthazar Wright, who came west from Philadelphia, and before him a German immigrant called Carl Hauschildt from Hesse. Before Hauschildt there is no record of an individual owning the land, unless you count the president of the railroad company, or the president of the United States, or the distant kings of Spain and France. The railroad acquired the land from the United States Government and the government acquired it from France in 1803 as part of the Louisiana Purchase, and before that it had been controlled by Spain or France, depending on which one you asked, and explored and mapped in the early eighteenth century by a Frenchman who took a common-law Sioux wife while the land was under the shifting control of various indigenous nations that had been settled there for more years than I can say and did not recognize the claims of the European powers who sought to control it.

'Before the nations this land belonged to the animal world, was underwater for tens of millions of years, and before the animal world it belonged to nature herself, to the cosmos or whatever you wish to call what existed before life on this planet acquired complexity. Morgan Priest Wright inherited the hundred-and-sixty-acre parcel from his father Ambrose Balthazar Wright, who bought it from Hauschildt, who bought it from the railroad company for eight hundred dollars. Wright's father owned over twelve hundred acres at the time of his death, and left one hundred and sixty acres to each of his eight sons. Morgan, the eldest, who had learned the art of gardening at the knee of his mother, inherited the family home and was the only one to retain his plot, while his brothers sold off theirs with little regard for who was buying or what the future of that land and the people upon it might be. They had goodwill on their lips but self-interest in their hearts. Wright regarded himself as a benefactor from an early age – or if not a benefactor then a protector. His father had employed sharecroppers to farm most of the acres he owned, and when his brothers sold off the land, ignoring the fate of the families who farmed it, Morgan Wright tried to help those he could, turning the sharecroppers into tenants who paid him rent but could sell all they produced. And that's where the Freemans come into the picture.

'George Freeman's father and mother had worked the land for Ambrose, and George was born and grew up upon it with his brother John, my grandfather. When their parents died the brothers went on working the land for Morgan after his inheritance. John married Lottie Marshall from the neighboring county and she worked alongside the brothers. George did not marry, and as he reached full maturity there was a kind of recognition of interest between him and his landlord. My grandparents lived in the house where I

527

once lived, but George lived closer to Wright's own house in a small cottage whose ruined chimney is all that remains standing today in those woods. You will scoff at the possibility and euphemism of any "recognition of interest" and ask if there was not an element of exploitation, wonder at how the two men might have met, even when the land was still remote and rural from the burgeoning town, without being noticed by John and Lottie and the neighboring landowners and sharecroppers. The first encounter between George and Mr Wright was during a tornado in 1915, when George was twenty-one, in that storm cellar that still sits below the surface of the ground. As during a later fateful event, John and Lottie were away, visiting her relatives, and George and Mr Wright were ostensibly alone on the farm, sheltering from the green light of the tornado, from its freight-train thunder and the rainless pause before the cataclysm that did not come. Let us say that in those minutes, perhaps hours, spent alone underground on camp cots first employed by soldiers of the Union Army with a kerosene lamp to light them and nothing but the awkward silence of unequal power between them, they found their way across the social barricades towards the possibility of speech, and in speaking, not as landlord and tenant, but as two men removed for a moment from the world, two men exceptional in their difference, they discovered a common interest and a mutual understanding.

'Or perhaps, you will wish to say, Wright simply

528

forced himself on the younger man, took as he and his kind had taken in so many other ways. And in fact there is no way to be sure either way, so the story continues in a double vein, both possibilities evolving towards one perhaps inevitable conclusion. The men had congress, relations, in the half-lit dark, underground, in a storm cellar buried in the woods, between the big white house where Mr Wright lived and had grown up and the gray-timbered cottage where George Freeman spent his solitary nights, reading his Bible by lamplight and darning his own socks. Having discovered this possibility, an understanding was established: either an understanding of mutual desire, or one in which George relinquished yet another hard-won liberty in the interest of keeping his home and his livelihood on the land of his employer, doing what was necessary to secure the little security he had in the world.

'The house of Morgan Priest Wright was white, rectangular, and on the first two stories had twenty-four windows: eight on the front, eight on the back, and four on each side (there were an additional six dormer windows in the roof but these are of no consequence). Following his first encounter with George, Mr Wright used the twenty-four windows as a kind of signal clock, designating a specific hour to each window and informing George of the code. In order to arrange a meeting with his tenant, at eight o'clock in the evening Mr Wright would place a burning kerosene lamp in the window corresponding to the hour when he wished to see George on the following day. George, either desiring himself to see Mr Wright, or feeling he had no free choice in the matter, would contrive every night thenceforward to circumnavigate all the buildings of the farm, thereby checking for the signal. The meeting times were almost always in the evening, after dark, when the likelihood of the two men being seen disappearing into the storm cellar by John and Lottie or any passing stranger, poacher, or neighboring farmer was more remote.

'And so they began to meet regularly as time and the seasons permitted. Either these were meetings of genuine love, a free exchange of flesh and sentiment, or they were meetings of exploitation and submission. George left no text to tell us, and whatever text Wright might have written (outside of his last will and testament, which left everything he owned to George, and in the event of George's death to my grandfather John) was burned beyond recovery. Even if one had survived, we could hardly countenance it as objective or impartial or remotely true, given the age of its origins and the nature of the relationship that might, however impossibly, have been described. In other words, just because Morgan Priest Wright might have depicted the intimacy he enjoyed with my great-uncle as love or a reciprocity of equals removed from the forces of society does not mean it was, does not mean that he was even able to recognize the persuasive influence of his own position and power over a man who owned nothing but his clothes, his shoes, and the text of his God.

'Relations continued in this manner, undiscovered but perhaps half-understood by John and Lottie, understood in a way that remained unspeakable, until the fateful Indian summer of 1919, when a mob moving west from the city in search of Mr Wright, who by then had been elected mayor, and discovered the two men not in the storm cellar but in Mr Wright's house, sheltering together in Mr Wright's own bedroom. John and Lottie were away, and we can surmise that, believing themselves safe from discovery, and the mayor wounded from the chaos that had wracked the city in previous days, he and George did what they had never dared to do in the past: met and measured their relationship, whatever its nature, in a house instead of a hollowed-out cavern of stone and earth. The mob took them outside, dressed George in Lottie's clothes, tied the men together facing each other, and strung them up from a cottonwood tree, hanging them until they were dead. The mob torched Mr Wright's house but left untouched the house where my grandparents lived. When John and Lottie returned the next day, the tree and the men upon it sank into the ground and remain there to this day, hanging in the soft spot that throbs in your backyard.

'This is the history of the land you own. I used to say it was perfect land, redemptive land, but I no longer think this is true. There is no such thing as good land or bad land. There are merely cycles of goodness and badness upon it. For millions of years, monsters of the sea patrolled the space above the seafloor that would rise to be my family's farm, predatory monsters that battled and killed and fed on each other, filling the waters with blood, which filtered down, soaked through the deep, settled and held forth, growing rich and fertile, waiting for the seeds that would come and the monsters of men to walk the earth. Perhaps we are merely a future civilization's prehistory, terrible apes who soak the land with our own blood.'

Tonight I do not sleep: I lie in my hotel bed, thinking of great-Uncle George and the benefactor, of the white man and brown man next door, of Nathaniel and Copley, all the death and loss upon the land that used to be my farm. The only deaths on the land in my tenure were those of my parents and Donald, and those were natural, time taking what was owed, sometimes too early, but not with terror or anger. Lying between starched sheets, I stare out the window at the blinking lights of aircraft, the faster flash of satellites, the glowing blue letters of the corporate headquarters next door, letters that float in space at the top of a building that seems not to be there at all. In this hotel I can hear the same buzz I now hear everywhere: the engine of the building, the machinery of its hidden circuits, a buzz and a drone that can be escaped only by walking alone in the woods, where I can still settle down at the base of George Freeman's cold hearth, overgrown with ivy, filling up with dead leaves, and think again of lighting a spark.

# PRESENT

*. . . in our watching we have watched for a nation that could not save us*

Lamentations 4:17

At the house closest to the traffic circle, the one most exposed to the browning waste of undeveloped property and the hazards that go with such a position, a technician is installing a security system. His van is parked in the driveway with the radio blaring a country station while he affixes the hexagonal white plastic box above the front door. As she drives around the circle and back in the direction of Julia's house, Louise notices the van is from EKK. She pulls over and rolls down the window.

'You install many of these systems in Dolores Woods?' she shouts.

The man climbs down the ladder and trots over to the car, leaning an arm against the roof. He's little more than a kid, hair sticking out from beneath his EKK baseball cap, half-obscuring his eyes.

'This was the last house in Dolores Woods that didn't have a system. Folks had a break-in last week. We have total coverage here now.'

'Total coverage. What's that mean?'

'We have a contract on every house in this neighborhood. Dolores Woods is an EKK SafeZone.'

On Saturdays she has no responsibilities at the house. The day nurse will be there to help Julia attend to her father, Chilton, who shouts and cries, protesting when it's time for him to eat, to drink, to have a bath or go to the toilet. Every action other than sitting on the couch watching television or playing with his camera, taking pictures of Julia or Louise, of the new cleaning woman or the day nurse, is met with protest. The man is not interested in his survival or existence, only in watching. In fact, it is no longer clear to what extent he is aware of his body having needs: for food, for sleep, for excretion. There is more than one toddler in the house.

Stepping into the hallway she calls out, 'I'm back!' She does not and will never say that she 'is home', because as much as the house is the place where she now lives, she does not think of it as home. Home is where the turning lane and boulevard now bask. Home is covered in concrete and parkway and ornamental plantings. What remains of home lies in the old steamer trunk where Donald used to keep his sweaters, the inside of which retains a trace of his scent. Each year she opens it on his birthday and inhales briefly before closing it again for another twelve months.

There is no reply and Louise goes upstairs to find her employer and her charge, this thin old man who is beyond teaching, sitting in the room that used to be Nathaniel's study. After the murders, Julia told Louise she could stay for as long as she wished, guaranteeing employment of one kind or another until the day when she was ready to retire. 'And after that, who knows,' Julia said. 'But from my perspective I don't see any reason why you should ever leave unless you want to.'

'I don't want to take advantage,' Louise said.

'No, you couldn't. You help me remember.'

Chilton smiles when he sees Louise. He always smiles, for a reason none of them can tell since he no longer speaks in ways that make sense. The day nurses he dislikes, the cleaning woman he loathes, and, apart from Louise, only Julia gets a smile from her father. The camera is in his hands, and as Louise enters the room, he raises it and takes her picture. They have given up telling him it is rude to photograph people without asking permission since he never remembers the rule. In any case, the memory cards, which Julia puts aside once they are full, are not destined for wider circulation. Chilton looks at the pictures he has taken, but only for as long as he can remember having taken them. The balance of images sits in a box, and on one of Julia's computers, waiting for future analysis, for meaning to be drawn from so much abstract quotidian detail.

'How are you, Chilton?' Louise asks. The man smiles and Julia pats his shoulder.

'He ate a big lunch for a change,' Julia says. 'We walked up to the lot this morning. I think maybe a morning walk is better.'

'Where's Sandy?'

'He's taking a nap.'

This is their routine, the tenor of most of their engagements: talking about Chilton, about better ways to manage him, to make him more comfortable, to increase his appetite, and speaking of Sandy, the rough little being with long limbs and black-blond hair who now sleeps in the room that once belonged to his brother. They do not talk about the past. They do not talk about Nathaniel or Paul Krovik. Above all, they do not talk about Copley. The names of the dead are never spoken. It is the dead who must speak.

Louise goes down to the basement, passing Julia's workshop. The machine mounted on the counter wakes up as her movement activates its motion sensor. It has the face of a child but the skin is a hard, translucent white material, and the features cartoonish, except for the eyes, which are wet and mobile, blinking and staring.

'Can I help you?' it asks. Julia keeps saying she's going to put in a different recording but it still speaks in Copley's voice and the sound, so natural, makes Louise jump. She knows that the voice will remain because it is all that is left of Copley. Most nights, Julia retreats to the basement, locking the door behind her, spending hours talking to this simulacrum of her dead son under the guise of research: a machine has become her best and most intimate companion, the only solace and consolation she has.

'How can I help you?' the machine asks, turning its head to watch as Louise passes beyond its view into the pantry.

'What's the outside temperature?' she calls back.

'It's forty-two degrees Fahrenheit, with a wind from the northwest at five miles per hour,' the machine says. A prototype for a home-assistance unit, it is always and ever ready to help, to answer whatever questions it may.

The back wall of the pantry has been removed and the bank vault door to the fallout shelter is now always left open. When the police gave them leave to return to the house, Julia had the shelter emptied and redecorated, the red walls with outlines of half a dozen imaginary doors all obscured with heavy coats of white paint. There was a mess of boards and beams and broken glass right at the entrance, nailed together in a strange confusion, a madman's puzzle, surrounded by dirt and branches, leaves and rocks. Beyond the rubbish were the half-butchered carcasses of at least eight deer, rank and rotten, crawling with maggots, a stink Louise had never known in a lifetime on the farm. It took a month for professionals to clean it out, strip it, put it back together. She wonders now what to call it: a big basement with heavy doors, a hidden exit, a backup plan, a place to shelter in tornado season or the end of the world, which might be the same thing these days. The three rooms and the bathroom remain, the cupboards filled with a new stock of dried and canned goods. At the far end, Louise opens the lock on the rear containment door and steps into the old stone storm cellar, which is dark until she unlocks the wooden doors at the top of the stairs and pushes them open.

The woods are quiet, branches bare, and the sun is already going down. There's been no snow yet, not even a hard frost. Locking the doors behind her she presses into the trees, ignoring the paths, until she finds herself in front of the ruined stone chimney, more than a third of it in rubble among the leaves, a bare vine twining up through what remains, in and out of the stones, bringing the structure down by degrees.

Leading herself through half-darkness, she makes her way to the tree where it happened. The first branch, thirty feet or more off the ground, is connected to the trunk at a slight angle. She can see Paul sitting there, waiting for deer, watching the entrance to the storm cellar. And just as easily she can see the version Paul related at the trial: a father and son engaged in some strange struggle of rope and power, the child tied fast, the father, out of shape, pulling the boy's struggling body up to the branch, the way even a slight surprise, never mind the blast of a gun, would have been enough to make the overstressed father lose his unsteady grip, letting his son fly back into space and come to rest on the rock at the base of the tree, a rock that, even in this twilight, is marked by a stain. Although the autopsy was inconclusive she can also see Paul ambushing the father and son, tying up the child, beating him to death, and drowning the father. She can see it without any difficulty.

From the first day she met Nathaniel she recognized him as a man out of his proper territory, in a place where he did not belong or know how to behave. And he had a son who was also out of *his* territory, in a place where *he* did not belong. When you put a person in a place that is not natural to their being, there's no telling what they may do to try to fit in, to find a way of surviving. Louise knows Krovik's version of that day is possible, and knows as well that Julia will never accept it could be true. In the end, Krovik, who was poorly represented, was convicted of both crimes: the murder of the father and of the son. Louise suspects there might have been another crime as well, for which Krovik was never charged. Studying the new child each day, the boy who looks nothing like Nathaniel, with his long narrow nose, blank arctic blue eyes, and lion-fierce movements, Louise has little doubt that the man must be guilty. *And the women brought forth giants.* Everything has come asunder.

At his request, she goes back to see Paul one last time. Julia does not know about these visits and Louise sees no reason to tell her.

Either EKK security is getting lax, or their reliance on technology has increased, but this time she and Paul are left alone in the same interview room, no guard to watch over them. How long would it take for someone to reach them if Paul made a sudden move, wrapped his broad hands around her throat, pulled a shank from his sock and tried to stab her in the gut? But no, there could be no shank. She remembers he would have been strip-searched, that there is no chance of him carrying any weapon or contraband on his person, unless the prison guards are corruptible.

'Hi friend,' he says, sitting down across from her and encircling her chair with his legs.

'Hello, Paul.'

'We're still not friends?'

'No, I don't think we can be friends.'

'No, I guess not,' he says, sounding disappointed, in the same tone she once heard from so many boys just like Paul, resigning themselves to circumstances they had created but not chosen.

'Has anyone else come to see you?'

'My mom is all. She comes most days.'

'And your dad?'

'Once a week usually. I keep hoping my wife will come, or at least that she'll call. I've tried to call her parents, but they changed their number a long time ago. So I don't know where that leaves me. Or, I guess I do know where that leaves me. With you, and with my parents. And with the people who are looking forward to seeing me fry.'

'Except you're not going to fry.'

'You know what I mean. Some of the other guys say that's what it's like, if they get the mix wrong. Like your veins light on fire and burn until you pass out. And then—'

'And then?'

'I used to believe in something but I don't anymore. I don't believe I'm going anywhere. I just think everything stops, and maybe for a second I'll be alone, like outside the walls of this place, outside of the city, standing in a field, digging my bare feet into the ground, and then a fire rises up around me before it all goes dark.'

'Will you say anything before they do it?'

'Nah. I apologized at the trial for what happened. I had nothing against Nathaniel as a man, you know. He was just trying to do his best. I don't have anything else to say. I didn't kill the kid. And I'm not going to apologize for something I didn't do.'

She opens her mouth to suggest it might be the generous thing to do, the kind of gesture that would give someone else a sense of solace. 'It would be altruistic.'

'Yeah, I know that word. I know you think what *you're* doing is altruistic, coming out here and talking to me and watching me die. But it's not. It's . . . self-interested. You're trying to clear your own conscience.'

'My conscience is clear, Paul. I never did anything to you. And you have nothing to lose from saying a few good words.'

'I have nothing to gain, either. The governor won't be in the room.'

'The governor might not be in the room, but she might be watching.'

He looks at Louise and then up at the cameras in the ceiling, arches an eyebrow, shrugs. 'Maybe, maybe not. I bet she has better things to do than watch me.'

A long low animal sigh unknots itself from his mouth and he runs a hand through the stiff bristles on his head. She cannot imagine what is in his mind. No one else she knows has ever faced a scheduled end to life, recorded and announced, with the prospect of crowds outside, screaming jubilation at a death, while a smaller crowd pleads mercy, standing vigil with candles. Perhaps he really does want a friend; she knows he could use one. At this stage, a friend is about the only succor he's going to get, short of his ex-wife deciding, by some miracle of reconciliation, that she will allow him to see his sons before it is too late, before he is asked to strip to his underwear and is escorted into the room where curtains will be opened to a viewing gallery after he has been strapped to the table, his limbs secured with lengths of cushioned leather, the needle inserted into his vein, an opportunity afforded for him to make that final statement of repentance.

'What would you have me do here, Paul?' she asks. 'I want to do something for you.'

'You mean now?'

'There is no other time. This is the end of your time. This is the last time I will see you and the last time you will lay eyes on me. You notice I don't assume that you will *see* me, only that your eyes will rest on my body. I don't think you've ever really *seen* me, not in the way that I have seen you.'

The cockiness drains out, smoothed away, the smirks and quirks and eye-rolling stares exit left and right, all of them gone, until there is just the hardened dark face of a boy with lime-blue aquamarine eyes and the heaviness of loss about him, pulling him down now that the mask can no longer do the looking for him, propping him up in performance.

'No, I see you. I can see now,' he says, folding his hands on the table. 'That's enough. You don't have to do anything else. Just sit there. Just look at me.'


At ten to midnight, Louise tells Julia she is going out for the walk she has been planning since dawn, knowing she wants to be nowhere else but on the open fields of what was once her farm when one day turns over to the next, and another life, the fire and horror of that specific life, goes out of the world.

Although it is December the air is cool but not yet cold, the sky clear, the familiar winter constellations appearing where she expects them to be. The pavements are dry, the floodwaters of three years ago receding even as the unfinished houses remain in their hazardous state, eye-socket cavities rotting and dark, all the empty land untouched, weed-wild, pocked with utilities points and streetlights, waiting for houses that may never come. The grass is long and brown, wildflowers dried out rather than frozen and disintegrating into nourishing muck, everything tinder dry and aching, splitting, the soil seething with roots. Still good land, rich land, acres that could produce again, but it needs renewal, a new start. Taking the head of a tall prairie stalk in her fingers she scatters seeds on the wind, laughing at herself as if an invisible companion has seen through her intentions. Yes, *all* the time, every day, the fingers itch, the impulse flutters along the nerves, the hand reaches for what it should not touch, for what hangs in the pocket tonight, rattling light.

When she is out of sight of the houses, down an incline, past one of the old gullies where the cottonwoods still grow, a confusion of limbs in the moonlight, angling tree-beasts, she stops and finds a sheltered place in the open fields where the dead grass lies in bundles gathered together by the passage of wind and the movement of deer. According to her watch the first injection will occur in thirty seconds, the death following shortly thereafter. From the pocket of her coat she takes out the box, slides it open, removes two sticks, slides the box closed, and snaps the sulfurous heads against the friction panel on one side. Two yellow darts appear and merge as she drops the box back into her coat, cupping her hand round the flame, leaning close to the earth and waiting as the fire catches, draws oxygen to its heat, and takes hold.